THE OUD PLAYER OF CAIRO

THE
OUD PLAYER
OF CAIRO

a novel

JASMIN ATTIA

Schaffner Press

To my husband, Wael, without whom I'd know nothing of love.
To my children Sabrina & Phoenix who are my light.
My baby sister, Dahlia, my very first reader.
And to Mom & Dad: You believed before I did.

1

CAIRO, 1932

Kamal Abd El Malak loved Egypt the way a man loves a woman. He loved her from her blue Mediterranean north to her green lush south, where he'd once farmed sugar cane and pomegranates. He loved the way her rippling Nile stretched through her, how her plains flooded. He loved her deserts bare and foreboding, torrid by day and cool under velvet night. But most of all he loved her Cairo, its beating heart of music and dance and poetry and scholars and films and cars and buses and vendors. He loved the ma'asil tobacco that the coffeehouse waiters packed into the hagara and the percolating sound of the shisha. He loved the scent of coffee boiling in a kanaka every morning in his kitchen; the warm pita that when torn open let out a cloud of bready steam; and he loved his first daily bite of hot fava beans seasoned with lemon, oil, red pepper flakes, and cumin.

Kamal lived with his wife Selma and their four-year-old daughter Naima on the top floor of a five-story building. It had been built in the middle of Cairo on Gazirat Badran Street, in a time before the narrow road filled with fruit and vegetable vendors; before the cobblestones were laid in a westward path, intersecting with Nile Corniche Road; before the cabarets on the Nile became fancy red-carpeted sala theaters; and before the

Rod El Farag district came alive at night with oud music and belly dancers who shimmied their hips to the beat of the tabla. It was built even before the Suez Canal connected the Red Sea to the Mediterranean, and before the British sent their tall white-skinned soldiers to occupy Egypt's lands and her seas.

Wide zigzag cracks ran along the side of the building, exposing eroded tan bricks; and the painted wooden blinds were chipped and broken. The apartment had two bedrooms, a bathroom, and a dining room that was separated by a wall from the family room. In the first year of his marriage, he bought secondhand furniture with the meager pay he earned playing oud: a brown velvet banquette and a round copper-top coffee table etched in geometric Islamic designs, from the old man on the first floor, who was moving in with his children. At a bayaza shop, he found a used radio console and record player that he fixed with scraps of old wire. More recently, he bought a four-poster mahogany bed that Selma had seen at a furniture store in Ataba Square and had insisted they buy new for good luck. They'd chosen to put the bed beside the window so that the first rays of light would wake them every morning, and it was on the edge of this bed where, on a May evening, Kamal sat beside his birthing wife.

Om Hanafi, the midwife, dipped her hands in a bowl of sweet almond oil and slipped them under the sheet. "Don't stop pushing," she said, and spread Selma's legs apart with her elbows, until her young assistant came to help.

Selma reached for the white sheet that Om Hanafi had tied to the bed-post and twisted into a makeshift rope. She pulled herself up, bit into the sheet, and pushed. Sitting on a stool at the foot of the bed, Om Hanafi guided Selma toward her. "Stop pulling away."

Selma groaned, her cheeks flushed, and spittle gathered at the corners of her mouth. "I can't anymore. I'm dying. I'm going to die." She let go of the sheet and fell back onto the bed.

"You're only hurting yourself. Bear down until the end of the contraction," Om Hanafi said, like a mother scolding a child.

2

Selma drew in a deep breath. "'O Sovereign Lord Jesus Christ our God, the source of life and immortality'"— she shook with pain —"'bless this fruit of my body that was given to me by Thee; favor it and animate it by Thy Holy Spirit, and let it grow a healthy and pure body, with well-formed limbs.'" She took a handful of the sheet once more, barely able to finish the prayer, but the Prayer for Pregnant Mothers had to be uttered word for word. Faith through agony, devotion despite adversity were the most fruitful types of worship. "'Sanctify its body'"— she heaved herself up — "'mind, heart, and vitals, and grant this infant who is to be born an intelligent soul; establish him in the fear of Thee.'" Her scream cut through the room.

"Kamal." She turned to her husband. "If I die, take care of Naima. You're the only family she's got."

"You won't die." Kamal brushed away a few strands of hair that clung to her face, sticky with sweat. Despite the dark circles under her eyes and her puffy face, Selma was still beautiful. Her eyes carried the girlish innocence he'd fallen in love with one afternoon in Asyut when he'd caught a glimpse of her washing clothes with her mother in the tributary. He had asked for her hand in marriage only a month later, but his mother-in-law had refused the proposal because he was a Protestant, not a Coptic, and a musician at that, a career that wasn't in any man's favor, but Selma insisted that Kamal was destined for her. In those days, all his songs were for her.

"Every woman says she's going to die," Om Hanafi said. "You have a wide pelvis, and this is your second child." She fished a towel out of a bucket and spilled a capful of heady disinfectant between Selma's legs. "It will be a while longer, though," she said to Kamal. "The baby is stubborn and wants to come feet first. It's better if you go. If you are anxious, your wife will be anxious, and your baby will be born anxious. As they say, 'leave the bread to its baker.' I'll send for you when the baby comes, insha Allah." She wrung out the towel. "Everything will be fine."

Kamal kissed Selma on the forehead. "You are in good hands," he said.

Then he left the room closing the door behind him. Om Hanafi was right. Men were useless in times of birth.

The midwife was not a pleasant woman, but her white bun, the deep wrinkles on her forehead and around her lips, and her chaffed hands comforted him. And although nobody could be certain of a baby's sex, Om Hanafi had said that Selma's was a boy pregnancy. Her belly was high and round. Her morning sickness was fierce; and unlike during her pregnancy with Naima, her nose was puffy, her nostrils flared, and she had deep blue circles under her eyes.

A boy. A boy. He picked up his oud case from beside the front door and went down five flights of narrow stairs to the street. Having a boy would be a blessing. He'd teach him music, send him to the best school (if he could afford it), and show him how to be a man and protector of his mother and sister. Kamal pushed through the throng at the fruit and vegetable souk. The sticky, sweet smell of strawberries, bananas, and mangos mixed with the odor of onions and garlic. The market sprawled from Gazirat Badran Street to Nile Corniche Road, where every evening his favorite coffeehouse filled with patrons who came to watch the sunset, play backgammon, sip coffee, smoke shisha, complain about the British occupation, plan protests, and listen to Radio Cairo. But as he walked along the sidewalk his excitement waned, and he became more aware of his limp, the uneven sound of his shoes hitting the pavement. This impediment had faded into the background of his life, but now that his son was coming he thought about the shame of it; British soldiers beating him, a broken leg that never properly healed. And all of this for what? For mistakenly walking past a protest on his way back from music lessons? They were in his land and broke his leg for daring to want it back! But no, he'd let the anger go today.

The waiter had reserved Kamal's favorite table, under the awning with a view of the pedestrians and the Nile. Kamal took out his oud, his green leather-bound notebook, and a sharpened pencil. He ran his fingers along Al-Mutanabbi's words etched in gold on the back of his oud, a gift from his old music instructor. "Small deeds are great in the eyes of the small, and great deeds are small in the eyes of the great." It was his ritual, good luck before playing. Kamal used the edge of the backgammon board, with its mosaic inlay, to draw staffs and treble clefs, as his music teacher had taught him when he was growing up in Asyut. He crossed one leg over the other and rested the oud on his lap.

He strummed the strings with his beloved eagle quill risha, and his free fingers moved back and forth along the fretless oud's short neck, up and down, across the strings, sending sound vibrating through the hollow of the wood, until the soulful, low-pitched melodies became the sketches of a song. Kamal was proud of his skill. He had a large repertoire of melodic maqam scales, and unlike amateurs, he knew when to play regular and irregular motions with his risha.

Anyone who heard his music knew it was his just from its style, its improvised taqasim preludes which he usually began at the bottom of the scale and moved to the higher silvery notes. With his musical might he would compose for his son a song that taught him love without his having to utter the word, that showed him courage before he was introduced to fear, that painted a vision of green acacias, blue seas, and dusking saffron skies. His only regret was that his son would be born in a country that was still under British rule; a country in which there were clubs and restaurants prohibited to Egyptians. And for a moment he felt as though he'd already failed his unborn child, but what could unarmed men do against an army of colonizers?

When the sun set, the waiter brought Kamal extra candles, and patrons gathered around him. Since he'd moved to Cairo and become a professional oud player, he'd spent many evenings here, and people had come to frequent the coffeehouse just to catch an improvisation by Kamal, whether he was alone or practicing with his ensemble. They knew him as al awad Kamal—the oud player—and the owner didn't charge him for coffee or shisha.

A few hours later the breathless porter arrived at the coffeehouse with news of the birth. It was nearly two o'clock in the morning. Kamal packed up his oud, adjusted his tarbush, and ran home to see his boy. He ran over cobblestone streets past closed storefronts, mosques and the Coptic church he never attended, empty cigarette kiosks, sleeping beggars, and the Gazirat Badran post office. Then he ran up the five floors, resting at each landing only long enough to catch his breath.

He burst into the bedroom panting, threw off his tarbush, and dropped his oud case on the floor. The midwife was gone, and Selma was breastfeeding the baby. "Mabrook." He congratulated his wife and sat on the edge of the bed. "Mabrook." He kissed her forehead again. "We have a son?"

Selma said nothing, and Kamal ran his hand along the top of the baby's head. The thick black hair was still wet. He took Selma's hand and brought it to his lips. Her skin was dry, her nails chipped. It had been a long time since he'd felt this tenderness for his wife. The constant financial worries, her grueling days of sewing and taking care of Naima, his sleepless nights of song writing, his efforts to sell his compositions, to find work playing in coffeehouses and hotel lobbies and weddings, had dulled their love. Selma's eyes were swollen, and she had black and blue splotches all over her neck and chest. But now, as she held his second child, he felt a surge of awe and gratitude.

"How are you feeling now?" he asked.

"Tired," she said. The newborn had fallen asleep on her breast, wrapped in a blanket that Selma had knitted.

"Let me hold him."

The baby gurgled in Kamal's arms. "You have the shape of your mother's face," he whispered as he traced a finger along the baby's cheek and arm, then took one wrinkly finger between his. "And my fingers, and the color of her skin. What will we name you? How about Amin or Emad? Or Yousef?" He turned to Selma. "They'll call me Abu Yousef and you Om Yousef."

Selma said nothing.

"Or maybe Om Iskandar? It sounds nice, right?"

"Kamal." Selma put a hand on his shoulder.

"But Yousef is dignified. It sounds like a doctor's name, or maybe he'll be an engineer. But I'll teach him music."

"Kamal," Selma said, "how about we name her Nazli, after the queen? A girl is always a father's sweetheart."

She must have been saying that to ward off the hasad and keep the jealous spirits at bay. He'd heard of mothers doing that. Having a boy was a blessing to be protected. "Really, Selma," Kamal said, "we have to name him. I have to register the child. I say Yousef. What do you say, ya Om Yousef?" Om Yousef sounded good on Selma.

"It's God's will," Selma said. "I wouldn't say it if it weren't true." She took the baby from Kamal. "A girl is always habibet abouha."

But Naima hadn't been her father's best friend, not as much as he'd hoped. She'd always been closer to her mother. When she fell and scraped a knee, she cried for her mother. When Selma went into the kitchen, Naima followed her and hid under her galabeya. And worst of all, when he played his oud, she ran away and hid behind the old armoire.

"A girl?" The baby cried in Selma's arms.

"Don't be upset, Kamal." Selma's eyes welled with tears as the baby screamed. She put her on her breast once again, wincing, "I know you wanted a boy, but whatever God brings is a blessing."

"Another girl?" He stood up looking down at Selma, feeling sorry for her. Now she'd have no son to brag about. She wouldn't be the om of a boy. She'd just be plain Selma while her friends who'd had boys got their om titles and wore them like crowns. There was Om Ahmed from across the street, Om Hasan in the adjacent building, and that horrid Om Waleed. Poor Selma.

"Whatever God brings is good," said Selma, looking down at the girl.

"Om Hanafi is a fraud and a liar," Kamal said between gritted teeth before he left the room.

He sat on the balcony and watched the city's bustle wane. Apartment lights turned off one after the other. Drunks came staggering home, their laughter echoing down the alleyway.

Taxi doors slammed, and the man who lived on the floor below began his loud nightly snoring. Kamal fell into a grief he couldn't explain to himself. After all, they could try again for the boy, but he was already poor and was struggling to feed a family of three, now four.

He had longed for a boy to be a protector of Selma and Naima. Selma could rely on a son and Naima could turn to a brother when she needed a man to lean on. Now, Kamal's burden was heavier than it had ever been. Who would one day carry the Abdel-Malek name? Who would one day wash Kamal's body before burial? A woman couldn't do it. The thought of a stranger washing his dead body made him weep, and as the cool May winds blew in from the Western Desert, Kamal's head drooped against his chest, and he fell asleep with death on his mind.

At dawn the muezzin's soulful call to Fajr prayer woke Kamal. He rubbed his aching neck, squinted against the rising sun, and went into the apartment, closing the balcony door behind him. For a few minutes he paced around the small living room. He felt guilty for how he'd behaved, leaving the bedroom angrily and sleeping out on the balcony. What if Selma had needed something while he was asleep outside? Maybe it was his fault they hadn't had a boy. Maybe he wasn't strong enough to have a boy. He'd heard that men who ate a lot of meat had boys, but he could barely afford meat. Returning to the bedroom where Selma was feeding the baby again, he sat on the side of the bed. He took Selma's hand to kiss it and apologize, but she snatched it away.

"For a man who claims to be so worldly and so motafatah, you're very small-minded," she said.

"I'm sorry. I know it's not your fault. It might be my fault."

"Fault?" She scowled at him. The baby fell asleep on her breast, and she burped her against her shoulder. "Having a girl is not a fault, Kamal. God doesn't make mistakes. Who are you to question the wisdom of our creator? He made man and woman so that together they can fill the earth. You think women are weak, but we are strong. Look what God gave me the strength to do." She caressed the baby's head. Selma's long hair spilled against her shoulders, and this made him miss her. He longed for her old softness, the way she used to comfort him, her hand on his cheek, a lost glimmer of adventure in her eyes.

"I'm sorry. I know you're strong, but the world is an easier place for a man."

"Things are hard for women because men do not heed the word of God."

"You're right, but what can we do? We can't change the way things are. I'm sorry, hakik allaya," he said. He hated when Selma was upset with him. "I was selfish. I was only thinking of how alone I'd be. How you'd have your two girls and I'd be alone."

"Kamal, you're not alone. They're your daughters too." She gave the sleeping baby to him, but the girl woke up. She kicked hard and screamed. Her mouth stretched open.

"She hates me."

"She doesn't hate you. She's just like you, feisty and stubborn. Her first night on earth and she's fighting everything; sleep, food, her mother." Selma turned on her side. "I need to rest. Take the baby. In an hour, go down to Haaga Safeya to pick up Naima. I let her stay the night."

She instructed him to wake her up in two hours for the next feeding. "And name her," Selma said, yawning. "It's bad luck for a child to have no name." Selma had named Naima and she had promised that if they'd had a boy, he'd name the child.

"Don't you want to name her?"

"No," Selma said. "It's your turn."

Kamal sat in his chair in the family room rocking the baby, mourning her vulnerability and limitations. He felt sorry for her, for Naima, for himself, and for Selma. When Selma had been pregnant with Naima, Om Hanafi had predicted she'd have a girl, and he'd loved her with all his heart, but this time Kamal had hopes of having a son and he couldn't push away his disappointment. The baby made little fists and cried so hard she turned red. She was an exceptionally loud child. He tried walking around with her and taking her out onto the balcony in the fresh air. He rocked her again, standing up and then sitting down. Nothing worked.

"I know why you're crying," he said. "It's because you don't have a name, isn't it?" She kept screaming.

He looked at the old clock that sat on the side table. She'd been screaming for twenty minutes. It wasn't her feeding time and he didn't want to wake Selma. Kamal laid her on the chair and rubbed her belly, but she wouldn't stop. He picked up his oud, sat on the chair across from where she lay, and played his newly composed song, a song he'd written for the son, a song that sounded like galloping white horses and desert winds. He hummed the undulating melody as he strummed the strings. By the first measure, the screaming became crying; and as he played the first maqam, she quieted a little, still whimpering and opened her eyes.

Kamal played and sang improvised lyrics to his newborn girl as he searched his mind for a name. He tried to imagine the girl grown up. What would she look like? If she looked anything like Selma, she'd be gorgeous—olive skin, long brown hair, big brown eyes, long lashes, pink lips. What would she sound like? Would her voice be silvery or jagged and high-pitched like Naima's? Would she be brave or timid, strong or weak? Would this new girl survive the world, and if she did, would she triumph over it? The song he'd written was for victors, conquerors, defenders, and she would never be any of those things. She'd been cheated by fate. She was supposed to be a boy.

He closed his eyes and played his favorite hijaz maquam scale, improvising, defining pitches and patterns for his newborn child and as he strummed his oud he tried again to think of a name. The baby gurgled on the chair, but he imagined deserts and white horses, princes victorious in battle, powerful queens sitting on their thrones. He imagined a girl with long black hair and a smile that inspired poetry, almond-shaped eyes fierce and mesmerizing. And then he imagined the sound of the name Laila. He sang the melody along the hijaz scale, modulating between tones, "La, la, la, Laila."

And so, Kamal named the baby Laila after *Laila and Majnun*. The epic Arabian love story about a man who'd fallen so deeply in love he'd gone mad had always intrigued him. What kind of woman inspires love so over-whelming, it maddens? What kind of person has that power? Laila was love and poetry and strength. Laila was mystery and resilience. Laila was night and the distant brilliant stars in it. There was no better name than that.

Selma invited every family from the building to attend Laila's sebou, which would be held on the evening of her one-week birthday. Though she was still sore after the grueling birth, the day before the party she stood in the kitchen to prepare for the event. She'd managed to save enough from her sewing work to buy a leg of lamb, candied almonds, caramels, chocolates, and small cellophane bags to fill with goodies for each child who would come to bless her baby. Children cast the strongest blessings because they were pure of heart.

Selma seasoned the lamb with allspice, garlic, onions, turmeric, and ground cardamom. She added sliced potatoes and poured water and tomato puree over the top of the lamb before covering and baking it. She rolled grape leaves, stuffing them with a mixture of rice and ground beef, and cooked them with garlic and lemon. Then she sat down on the kitchen floor to control the pain that shot down her back, into her pelvis, and down the insides of her legs.

If her mother had still been alive, she would have helped her make the sebou meal, and would have calmed her when she was overwhelmed with a sense of loneliness and loss. As she sat on the kitchen floor, she took long deep breaths to keep from crying. Crying would be bad luck for her daughter. Still, Selma missed her home city of Asyut; its slow pace, its familiar faces, its scent of fresh silt and herbs in spring. She missed the way she used to speak Arabic, before Kamal had insisted she change her *g* sounds to *a* sounds, and her *j* sounds to *g* sounds.

"Cairene Arabic is the Arabic of refined businessmen, educated politicians, and glamorous movie stars," he'd said.

When she was able to stand up again, Selma reached for the two copper mortars and pestles she kept on the shelf above the stove. Setting them on the small kitchen table where she usually cut vegetables, she banged the pestles in the mortars to test the sound. They weren't noisy enough, so she sent Kamal to Khan El Khalili market for more tablas and then paid a visit to her fourth-floor neighbor, Aisha, to ask her to bring her mortars and pestles to the sebou and to pass the word to the other women in the building. This had to be the noisiest sebou in the history of sebous, and would ensure that any lingering evil spirits would flee their apartment, even their entire building. A girl had to endure enough jealousy from humans, and shouldn't have to deal with it from the spirit realm too, especially if she was beautiful. And Laila was going to be beautiful. A mother just knew these things.

An hour before the guests arrived, Selma sliced the lamb and arranged it on the platter she'd borrowed from Haaga Safeya, who lived on the first floor. Then she set the biggest pot she owned on the stovetop and dropped in a dollop of samna. When the clarified butter had melted, she added sesame seeds and sautéed them, then put in a mixture of moghat root, ginger, cardamom, cinnamon, sugar, milk, and water. As it thickened, it smelled just like the moghat her mother had made for each one of Selma's siblings' sebou celebrations. When the guests arrived, she burned incense and served the steaming drink in teacups. She handed each of the children a bag of chocolates and candies, and a long white tapered candle for the ceremony.

Selma placed her newborn girl in a large oval sieve she'd lined with a satin cloth and decorated with ribbon. She held the sieve away from her body and shook the baby just enough so that she rolled from side to side, and Haaga Safeya began the ceremony by banging her mortar and pestle. The loud noise made the baby cry, but most babies cried, and it was a good sign.

"Listen to your mother, not your father."

The ladies laughed, clapped, and trilled one zaghrouta after the other, just as they did at engagements and weddings and graduations. Selma closed her eyes and prayed to God that her life would be filled with these auspicious ululations.

Then Fatima from the third floor banged her mortar and pestle even louder and harder than Haaga Safeya. "Listen to your father and not your mother, but then you can ignore them both and listen to your auntie Fatima."

They went on, commanding the baby to be obedient, to listen to her parents, to do her chores, to sleep well, and to remain calm. Kamal led the men by beating on the tabla, and Selma carried Laila throughout the house to introduce her to the world, followed by a noisy parade.

"Laila," she said. "Here is Laila."

Kamal lit the candles for the children to carry as they followed Selma and baby Laila, and then directed them to sing and walk in a circle around the dining room table. "God protect her," they sang. "God nurture her to grow up and be big like us."

Naima didn't join the other children in song or eat the sweets. She just held onto her mother's dress, crying throughout the entire ceremony. But as much as Selma wanted to comfort her firstborn, this night was Laila's.

After the tour of the home, Selma placed the sieve on the floor and took seven steps, back and forth, over the baby. "In the name of God, the first step," the women said as Selma lifted her dress off her ankles to avoid tripping. "In the name of God, the second step."

Selma hadn't calculated how much money she had left in her purse, or even how much food might be left over for them from the party. It was one of the few times she'd allowed herself to indulge, to forget, to breathe. When the ceremony was over, she handed Laila to Haaga Safeya and ran into the kitchen to prepare the trays of lamb, potatoes, and stuffed grape leaves. She carried each tray to the dining room table and invited her guests to feast.

At the end of the evening, the neighbors left the apartment, carrying their sleeping children over their shoulders and leaving behind an unpleasant silence. While Laila slept in her basinet, Selma cleaned the kitchen and Kamal put their furniture back in place. There were no leftovers. Had she served too little? Did the neighbors think she was being cheap, after all her efforts? She swept the floors and then sat with Kamal on their small balcony to sip mint tea.

"Do you think it was a good sebou?" She wanted to reach for her husband's hand but was embarrassed to initiate a gesture of affection, even though she needed his touch, his kind words. Had the moghat been perhaps too thick? Had there been enough lamb? Maybe the grape leaves had been undercooked.

"It was perfect," he said, taking her hand in his. "The children were so happy with their chocolates, and the guests couldn't stop talking about how skilled you are in the kitchen, and how beautifully you'd made the dress, and how gorgeous Laila is."

"Stop. Don't say anymore," Selma said. She wanted to hear these compliments, but not at the risk of hasad. She flashed her palm at Kamal— "Khamsa to protect you"—and then at the inside of the house, where her girls were asleep, where she had prepared her meals, where she'd built a marriage and a family. "Khamsa to protect us all."

☙

The learned men said that the earth had a force called gravity which attracted the moon, keeping it in an orbit going round and round, creating the ebbs and flows of seas and rivers. The girl cheated by fate had the same force, Kamal thought. Except baby Laila was the amar keeping him in orbit. She was an alert child, and when he played his oud for her, she watched him with those big brown eyes and followed the movement of his fingers along the strings. He told Selma this, but Selma said that all babies were like that. Selma was wrong. She didn't see what he saw in their new child.

By the time Laila was four months old and laughed for the first time, Kamal found himself skipping nights out with his friends and rushing home just to tickle her belly, to hear that sound again, that gorgeous cackling that came from her little gut. As soon as Selma would let him, he took her with him for walks along the Nile. River air was good air. It had a scent of life in it; silt, greenery, fish. Life. He'd carry the girl on his shoulder and show her the world. "Asfoora," he'd point at the bird. "Al-Nil," he'd say pointing at the Nile. Once, at eight months he thought he'd heard her say "foora," baby speak for bird, but when he got home to show Selma, Laila didn't repeat it.

"Babies don't speak that early," Selma said.

"She's special," Kamal said. This, he kept to himself; she was special because she was supposed to be a boy, and because fate cheated her out of her manhood, it had given her something else, some compensation. If he'd said this to Selma, she'd have become angry with him. She'd tell him that God, not fate, determined these things, and God didn't make mistakes, she'd say. But then how did Selma explain that Laila's first word was Baba and not Mama. It must have meant something.

When Laila was about nine months old, she started trying to walk. She'd pull herself up on the side of the copper coffee table, take a few steps and fall. One time in her early days of walking Laila fell and hit her head on the foot of Kamal's chair. She wailed. Kamal went to pick her up but changed his mind. "So, you fell? Get up." He left her on the floor crying.

"Baba," she cried over and over again.

"Get up. Be strong. Be a man," he said; the last part about being a man just slipped out of him. She'd never be a man, he thought.

He knelt down to pick her up, but just then he heard the sounds of protesters rising from the street below. "Egypt for Egyptians!" the angry voices chanted. He backed away from his daughter, leaving her on the floor, and ran to the balcony to see the ruckus outside. The men held up their fists shouted, and waved their signs. "Egypt for Egyptians. Egypt for

Egyptians." He wanted to join the protestors, but what if he got hurt or killed? Who would care for Selma, Naima, and the baby girl? How could he die for his country and live for his family?

Laila screamed, still on the floor. Kamal ran to her. Her face had turned red, and she'd cried so much that the snot ran down her nose and onto her mouth. Still, Kamal decided not to pick her up. If he couldn't offer himself up to Egypt, then he'd raise a child who could, at the very least, survive her colonizers. "Laila, listen to Baba," he said. "Push yourself up. Up. Up. Up," he said waiting, watching. She cried for a long time and then finally she grew tired of crying. Then, as she whimpered, she used the chair to stand back up. "That's my boy," he said, and then looked around to make sure Selma hadn't heard it. He picked her up, put her on his shoulders, and took her for their daily walk going around the building to avoid the protests.

He thought a lot about things on that walk as he watched the sun plunge into the river. Fate had cheated her out of manhood, but maybe Kamal could fix that. He'd been contemplating independence lately, and what that might mean for Egypt, for his countrymen. But what was the shape of independence in a girl's life, and was it even possible?

Maybe he could raise her like a boy after all. Yes, he could raise her to be fearless, strong, free. Selma had raised Naima her way and Kamal had acquiesced because he'd been resigned to having a girl then, but what would stop him from raising this child his way? Nothing really. He was the father, the man of the house. He set the rules. It certainly wouldn't be easy. His society taught girls fear first, fear above all. But maybe he could do something different.

He remembered reading an article in *Al-Ahram* about women who'd shaped the last century. There were writers, scientists, activists, and even a pilot by the name of Amelia who'd flown across the Atlantic alone just a few years ago. He took Laila off of his shoulder and held her out so that he could look into her eyes, study her face. He'd raise this girl differently, he decided right there midway between his favorite acacia tree and the roasted corn pushcart. He'd keep her close. To hell with society. He put her back on his shoulders and resumed his walk, humming the song he'd written her. He'd raise a champion, a champion of everything.

2

CAIRO, 1939

The apartment seemed empty to Laila when Baba was not there, when he took his oud and disappeared behind the front door. Sometimes he spent the day at home and was gone all evening. Other times he was gone all day and only returned for a nap before leaving again. Mama spent her days in the kitchen or at the sewing machine, and Naima was in school. When she finally came home, she had too much homework to play with Laila. Every time Laila asked her mother when it would be her turn to go to school, and why other girls her age had already started school, Mama would say, "When a spot opens up."

Naima never played the games Laila liked to play with Baba. She wouldn't sword fight like Baba did with the long sticks he'd brought home one day (and Mama had thrown away) or let her punch her stomach to practice boxing. Naima wouldn't play soccer in the alley with the neighborhood boys like Baba had taught Laila; and when Baba was out, Mama never let Laila go outside. Nobody played tawla with her either. Besides, she couldn't play backgammon alone since Baba often took their only set with him.

When Baba wasn't home and Mama wasn't looking, Laila would climb onto the brown velvet banquette in the family room and pretend to be the

Arabian warrior princess Mawiyya, standing on the magical mountain of Qaf, pointing her sword—Baba's fountain pen—at an imaginary adversary. She pictured large armies charging at her, but she would not waver.

"Never flinch," Baba always told her. "Don't let the enemy see your fear." Sometimes Laila would run her fingers along the round copper-topped coffee table, searching its mysterious etchings for the secret map to the land of gold. She was the warrior soldier sent off by the king on a secret mission. The frayed, faded rug, once the color of berry jam, was Laila's flying carpet, which she'd use to get to the land of gold. And when she slipped between the two mahogany arabesque chairs, inlaid with mother of pearl, she became invisible and could hide from the monster in the kitchen brewing potions of fried onions and garlic.

Mama didn't let Laila play on the balcony alone, but when Laila heard the sounds of angry men coming from the street—at least twice a month—she would run to the balcony and lean on the railing to watch. They marched, holding signs and raising their fists and yelling things about Egypt and the king. Baba had explained that foreigners had come to Egypt long before Laila was born, and those foreigners had stolen things, precious things "from us." Those angry men, Baba said, were just trying to get "our things back for us." It was like "someone stealing Baba's oud," he once told her. "Wouldn't you be angry too if someone took my oud away?" When Laila watched these protests from the balcony, she clenched her hands and made up her own slogans. "Bad foreigners. Give us our stuff back," she'd say, never fully understanding what things had been stolen. Once when Laila was nearly six years old, Mama caught her on the balcony protesting by herself. She picked her up and carried her back into the apartment.

"You need to learn to stay out of men's business," she said as she closed the balcony door and locked it with a latch too high for Laila to reach.

But to Laila, the protests were always her business because if someone had stolen Baba's oud, she'd kick and bite until she got it back.

Each day before he left, Laila asked, "When will you be home, Baba?"

Sometimes he said, "After the Dhuhr prayer," or "Right before the Maghrib," or "I won't be home until after 'Isha." Even as a Coptic Christian, with the orthodox cross tattooed in blue on the inside of her wrist, Laila knew the timing of the Islamic prayers. She knew them as every Egyptian did, Christian, Jew, or Muslim, because they set the tempo of her days and the rhythm of the entire country. At those times, hundreds of muezzins ascended into minarets scattered throughout Cairo, calling their faithful to prayer. She would watch from the balcony as worshipers spread their prayer rugs, sometimes in the middle of the street, and knelt. When the prayers were over, she waited for Baba's silhouette to appear as he rounded the corner, approaching as he always did from the alleyway behind their building, the shortcut onto Gazirat Badran Street.

One day when she was seven years old, instead of waiting for Baba to play hide-and- seek with her and find her crouched beside the radio console, or hiding in the closet behind his shirts, or under the dining room table, she decided to greet him at the door. As soon as she saw him from the balcony, she sprinted back into the apartment, crouched down on the concrete floor, and pressed her ear against their front door. When she heard Baba's keys rattle, she sprang back up to her feet. Baba threw the door open and lifted her as high above his head as his arms could stretch. She relished those seconds of weightlessness, when her feet dangled in the air and she was certain her head would hit the ceiling. Then he brought her back down and pressed her to his chest. She took in his smell of sweat and the honeyed tobacco clinging to his black jacket, his mustache, and his red tarbush.

"Shatoorty." He didn't just call her shatoora, a skilled and capable girl; he added a *ty*— *his* smart and capable girl.

Laila brushed her hand against his stubbly cheek. "Play the oud for me, Baba." He often played a particular song for her, a song he'd composed and named "Laila" on the night she was born.

"Not tonight, habibty. Baba's been playing all night, and he's tired."

Naima came in from the kitchen and wrapped her arms around Baba's waist. Baba kissed her on the top of her head. Mama took his jacket to hang it in the bedroom. He turned on the radio to listen to the news and sat in his chair. A man said things on the radio about the Germans invading a place whose name Laila couldn't catch, and Baba said that a war of blitzkrieg had begun. He pronounced it slowly. "It means lightning," he said. "Hitler is going to sweep through Europe, they say. God help us if he invades Egypt."

Mama crossed herself, looked up at the ceiling, and whispered a prayer. Naima hid behind the settee, tears welling up in her eyes. "I'm afraid of lightning."

"Naima, come out, for God's sake," Baba said. "It's not real lightning the man is talking about. It's just war word."

With lightning no longer a threat, Naima came out from behind the settee and, as she always did, joined Mama in the kitchen.

Laila sat cross-legged at Baba's feet and tugged on the hem of his pants. "But, Baba," she said, "it's my song. I've waited all day to hear it. Please play it."

He ruffled her hair. "I promise that tomorrow morning, as soon as I have my coffee, I'll play for you."

When the newsman stopped talking on the radio, Baba went into the bedroom to change, and Laila sat by the front door and took his heavy oud out of its case. She tried to put it on her lap the way she'd seen Baba do, but it was bigger than she was, and she couldn't reach the strings. So she laid it on its rounded back and slipped her leg under the oud's neck to support it. Plucking a string, she took a deep breath and sang the note. She didn't mean for the sound to soar out of her, or to be so big and loud. It just happened. Baba burst out of the bedroom. The oud was Baba's most valued possession. It was handmade, one of a kind, with a star like design on its back made of alternating inlays of maple and walnut wood, and a special inscription she couldn't read. He'd told her never to touch it. "I'll play it for you," he always said, "but never touch it."

He stood over her and said nothing.

"I'm sorry, Baba." She let go of the oud and it slipped off her lap. "I won't do it again. I promise."

"Was that really your voice?" He picked the oud up off the floor. "So, you're a singer. You can sing?" Laila had sung before. She'd sung children's songs with Mama and Naima. She'd hummed to the radio, but all those times her voice was soft and quiet. This time when she opened her mouth and pushed the music out it was deep and clear, and it vibrated out of her in a way she didn't recognize.

She shook her head. "No, I don't think I can sing. But I can play the oud like you."

Baba picked her up and twirled her in the air. "You can sing," he said as her body rose up in the air and the room spun. "You can sing. You can sing."

When he put her down on the floor, he took her by the hand and led her to the family room, sat in his chair, and put the oud in his lap. She sat down at his feet again, her back to the copper coffee table, her toes grazing the carved foot of Baba's chair, her head turned up to watch and listen.

"I will play a note and I want you to copy it with your voice." He plucked a string with his risha, and Laila sang it.

He nodded. "This time, I want you to hold that sound longer." He plucked the next string.

She closed her eyes and took a deep breath, then sang.

"Good, now listen. When I'm done playing, I want you to copy it, just like you did with the single notes." His fingers moved up and down the strings, and when he was done, she sang the melody.

"Shatoorty, you see, this is how we talk in music. Like when you say, 'good morning' or 'I want milk,' except what I just played is called hijaz maquam. Can you say that?"

Laila nodded. "Hijaz maquam."

"Good. Since we broke up the sounds, we are ready to use all these pieces of sound to make any song we want, but we can't make it without timing. Let me ask you a question. When do you eat breakfast?"

"In the morning."

"So, can you eat breakfast at dinnertime?"

She shook her head.

"That's right. That's why we musicians break up the length of time we hold each note, like when I slice your bread. Sometimes we only want two slices, sometimes four, sometimes eight, or even sixteen. If you sing the note in the wrong time, then the song will sour. Go like this." He clapped his hands once, palm to palm, and then once again, back of the hand to palm. "Doom, teck, teck. Doom teck. Repeat."

Laila clapped the beat. "Baba, I know this. I want to sing a whole song."

"You might know it, ya binty, but you haven't practiced it." He clapped the same pattern again. "Pay attention. Doom, teck, teck. Doom, teck. We will sing a whole song when you understand the foundation."

They continued this way. Baba played a melody. They sang it and then broke it up into segments, clapping to the maquam rhythm.

When the 'Isha prayer blared through the city, Baba put his oud down and patted Laila's head. "That's enough for today. Time for sleep." In the room she shared with Naima, he tucked her under her soft cotton quilt. "You have a gift, Laila. I've known it since the day you were born. But you have a lot to learn still. If you love your gift with all your heart and you practice every day with me, you'll be singing for big audiences someday. You'll be a star."

"Hader, ya Baba. I will practice," she said, and as she drifted into sleep she imagined herself singing on a stage in front of a sea of people.

❧

For nearly two years, until Laila was almost nine, Baba gave her lessons every evening while Mama and Naima sewed. In those years, they played less soccer, did less pretend sword fighting, and the tawla playing became a rare event. Once Mama had called Laila into the kitchen to teach her how to make eggs, but Baba held onto to Laila's arm. "You have no time for eggs, Laila." Then he told Selma that Laila couldn't go into the kitchen because she was learning to be a singer. This didn't bother Laila because singing was the most fun of all. Baba invited Naima to join and learn music too, but she refused, preferring to sew instead. Mama told Baba that teaching Laila to sing would serve no purpose, and at bedtime Naima bragged that her skills would someday be put to use while Laila would have learned nothing of value. At first when Naima said those things, Laila got angry. She yelled at her sister, and one time got in trouble for punching her in the shoulder. Naima never stopped taunting Laila, making fun of her voice, her music, but over time Laila learned to ignore her sister. She learned to turn on her side and fall asleep because Baba's was the only opinion that mattered.

Laila learned different maquam scales, how each was composed of sets of pitches, how the notes in them were separated by half tones, whole tones, three-quarter, and five-quarter tones. She learned how to sing taquasim, modulating between one maquam and chaining it to the next, and then returning to her starting point, her home maquam. She learned all the scales; rāst, sabā, nahāwand, hijāz, hijāz-kar, ʿajam, and sīkā. When she practiced singing, Baba reminded her to prepare her voice by inhaling before a refrain, to raise her chest and open her mouth as she sang so that her strong voice reached the far ends of whatever space she was in. He borrowed Om Kalsoum and Mounira El Mahdeya records from friends, and they'd listen to them over and over until they'd memorized the song and lyrics. Then he'd play on his oud and she'd sing.

"When you're older," Baba said, "I'll teach you poetry, and you'll sing to it."

What Baba wanted for Laila and what Laila wanted for herself were the same, and the harder he worked to teach her the more freely Laila dreamed of becoming a real singer, one whose name was known, whose songs were broadcasted on radios and sung in homes.

෴

In the fall of 1941 just after Laila's ninth birthday, Mama received word that a spot had opened up in Notre Dame de la Delivirande Catholic School for Girls, that Naima had been attending. Mama sewed Laila uniforms from fabric remnants and bought her new shoes from Al Moski market. They shopped at Haag Ahmed's stationery store at the bottom of their street, across from the linen factory, which always smelt of burning coal and rotten eggs. Mama had an account at Haag Ahmed's store, and he was lenient about her installments. There wasn't enough money to buy a leather bookbag, but Mama made her a satchel out of old canvas and buttons she'd found at the bottom of her sewing box.

On the first day of school, Mama braided Laila's hair, gave her a warm glass of milk, and packed her feta cheese and olive sandwiches. Before Laila left the apartment with her sister, Mama cried. "Take care of your sister and say a prayer on your way," she said to Naima. Then she waved at them from the balcony when they reached the street.

La Deliverande School sat at the edge of a vast colonnaded courtyard. Acacias and date palms provided shade over a row of stone benches, and a staircase led up to the main entrance. It was a three-story building, adorned with arched windows and green shutters, and a church steeple rose from behind the school.

Laila ran up the stairs ahead of Naima.

"Wait." Naima tugged on Laila's bag. "That's not where we attend." She pointed at a small building that sat on the school grounds beside the church. "That's where we go."

"Why there?"

Naima took Laila's hand.

"I don't understand." Laila looked behind her at the beguiling courtyard, the girls in their patent leather shoes, gleaming white socks, and leather bookbags.

"The big building is for the rich girls whose parents are paying for them, and this small building is for us poor girls. The church lets us go here for free. That's why you had to wait for your spot. Kids who pay start school much younger."

"Why doesn't Baba pay them?" Poor people lived on the streets. Laila wasn't poor.

"Because he can't afford to. Our baba is an awad. Awads don't make money, you silly girl."

"Well, can we play on the big playground during recess?"

"No." Naima shook her head. "That's for them. This is for us." She pointed at the small patch of grass inside the fenced area that surrounded their flat-roofed brick school building. "We play here and we eat here. Listen," Naima whispered as they walked across the school grounds, "the nuns are not easy. They'll want to catch you up because you are starting late. Don't cry when they yell at you. They don't like that. They'll speak to you in French even if you don't understand. When Sister Marie says 'bonjour', you have to say 'bonjour' back. Don't chew with your mouth open at lunch, and most of all, don't talk during the lesson."

Inside the building were three small classrooms, and Sister Marie, the Headmistress, put Laila in the beginners' class with the younger girls. "If you pay attention and you do well, then we will move you up. For now, you have to go la bas." She pointed to a classroom down a dark corridor. Laila's desk was in the middle of the front row. After the morning bell rang, the teacher put a tattered booklet on her desk. "Do you know your alphabet?"

Laila shook her head. She had spent all her time on music, and Baba hadn't talked to her about the alphabet. He'd made her memorize lyrics, but he'd never shown her how to read them. "I know music language," she said.

"If you're not singing for God"—the nun pointed up—"then you shouldn't sing at all." She handed Laila a pencil and a stack of tracing paper. "By the end of the day, you should have copied the whole alphabet."

Laila flipped through the book. "That's not the real alphabet."

"Of course it is."

"But Baba's newspaper is in Arabic. This is …"

"French. French. You're in a French school. This alphabet"—the nun tapped firmly on the book—"will set you free. Arabic is of no use to you." Then she walked away.

Laila couldn't understand how the language she spoke and heard every day was of no use to her. When would she ever speak French? To whom?

Laila traced the letters just as the teacher had told her to, while she listened to the class of younger children learn arithmetic and reading. They spoke Arabic words and translated them to French. As Laila traced, she memorized the sounds of the words and the rhythm of the syllables when the students pronounced them, just as she had been trained to learn music.

౭ౢ

Since Laila and Naima were both in school, Mama took a cooking job for an Italian lady named Signora Morpurgo who lived in the wealthy district of Zamalek, an island in the middle of the Nile. Each day after school, Laila walked there to help Mama. Because Naima was older, she went directly home after school to do the chores, to prepare for dinner, and complete any unfinished sewing. When the dismissal bell rang, Naima hugged Laila, made sure the younger girl's books and homework were in her bag, and then checked that the button on Laila's satchel hadn't come loose. Naima helped her cross Habib Shalaby Street and then pointed her west, toward Kasr Al Nil Bridge, which connected the island of Zamalek to the rest of Cairo. Naima always warned Laila not to talk to anyone.

If Laila had a half piaster, she stopped at the riverbank before crossing the bridge to buy an ear of roasted corn or roasted chestnuts or sugarcane juice. Then she'd stare at the bronze lion statues that flanked the bridge at each endpoint. Baba had told her that a French sculptor had built them. As she crossed the bridge, she never looked down, afraid of the dark rippling waters beneath her; and when she reached Zamalek, she found serenity in rows of trees and the pink, yellow, and purple flowers that decorated private gardens. There, mansions had separate doors for servants.

Gardeners tended to the outdoors, butlers to the indoors, maids mopped the floors and shined the silver, and washerwomen did the laundry.

Signora Morpurgo taught Mama how to make spaghetti Bolognese and béchamel sauce the Italian way. One day Laila overheard her bragging about Mama's cooking to Madame Caron, her neighbor, whom she'd invited over for tea. Madame Caron peeled off her white gloves, revealing bright red polish on her fingernails, before she sat on the banquette. The ladies talked over steaming tea and the sweet flaky mille-feuille that Madame Caron had baked.

"If Paris wasn't under the Nazi devils, I'd have gone home and brought you some mille- feuille from the best bakery in the world. I tried with this, but the ingredients here, well, they're not the same. You must have some, though," said Madame Caron. "C'est delicieux."

"Merci." Signora Morpurgo took a bite of the pastry and then set it down on the small floral-patterned plate. "You know how I feel about politics. No good can come from the discussion." Then she began talking about the greatest new addition to her staff, Selma. Laila didn't like the way she spoke Mama's name so carelessly. Signora Morpurgo said that Selma's béchamel never lumped because she had a strong arm, as a worker should. The women spoke to each other in broken Arabic since Signora Morpurgo didn't speak French and Madame Caron knew no Italian. Their accents sounded so funny that Laila had to muffle her laugh so they wouldn't hear her.

"Then I simply must have her too, especially if she's sharp." Madame Caron shook her head. "You can't imagine how many of these Egyptian dimwits I've hired and fired because of their inability to understand any-thing." Was that what all the foreigners thought; that Egyptians were dim-wits? It upset Laila. She felt as though she'd shrunk in her own skin, the way a grape shrivels into a raisin. Baba and Mama were not dimwits! They were smart, productive, respectable people. Why had Madame Caron said that?

Signora Morpurgo shifted in her chair. "But Selma works for me. I doubt she has any more time."

"Money has a way of making time," Madame Caron said. "First, I'll taste her food, and then we'll see if I even want her in my kitchen."

After tasting Mama's food at a ladies' luncheon later that month, Madam Caron offered Mama fifty piasters a week to cook for her in the evenings, after her shift at Signora Morpurgo's. Mama bargained for seventy-five piasters.

"I cook Italian food," she said, "and I will learn any recipe you give me. I never forget an ingredient, and I'm evenhanded with salt. That's a rare skill."

"But you can't cook any French food yet," Madame Caron said as they haggled in Signora Morpurgo's kitchen. "Italian cuisine does me no good, and I will need to spend time teaching you."

They settled on sixty piasters. "Not one piaster more," Madame Caron said, wagging her finger at Mama. Mama sighed and said, "All right, but my daughter comes with me."

Madame Caron's swimming pool extended the length of the house with tennis courts behind it. Marble steps led up to the main door, but Mama and Laila used the servants' entrance in the back.

After Laila had done her homework at the small kitchen table, and after she and Mama had washed, peeled, chopped, spiced, and fried, Laila would venture out of the kitchen to the grand foyer where two curved staircases rose to the second floor. She often stared up at the crystal chandelier hanging on a silver chain between the staircases. Sometimes she ran her fingers along the tapestries hanging all along the corridor that led from the living room to the kitchen. She would sneak into the salon where there were burgundy velvet settees and a shiny black piano. And she would peruse the den where bookcases lined the walls. How could one person read so many books?

One day, while on one of her secret tours of the mansion, Laila stepped into the salon to look at the piano. She'd never touched one before. Though nobody had told her she wasn't allowed to play it she knew someone would get angry if she did. She stood in front of it for a long time, afraid to sit.

But after a while she couldn't resist and pressed the keys one by one to ascertain the notes. Then she put together a melody, a part of a song Baba had played on the oud.

"Who are you?"

The small voice startled her, and when she turned around, she recognized Madame Caron's daughter, whom Laila had watched many times from the kitchen window as she took swimming and tennis lessons. She was wearing a sky-blue lace dress with a white sash at the waist that tied in a bow, shiny white shoes, and white socks. Laila had never seen a dress as beautiful, even in the windows of Omar Effendi department store. But how did the girl's legs not get cold in a dress so short?

"I'm Catherine," Madame Caron's daughter said as she held out her hand. "Do you want to play upstairs?" Her Arabic was much better than her mother's. Her skin was whiter than Laila's, her hair a shade of honey, and she smelled of roses.

They climbed one of the staircases and went into Catherine's room. She had a wrought iron canopy bed with lace ruffles at the bottom and a pink satin comforter. A big stuffed brown bear sat between two pillows. Catherine knelt by a toy chest, painted with scenes of children playing in an orchard, and pulled out two dolls.

"Do you want this one or this one?" Her voice had a clear ring to it. Maybe she was a singer too.

Laila chose the blonde one with blue eyes because light skin and light eyes were the best kinds of skin and eyes. She'd had a doll once. It wasn't as beautiful as this one, but it had been a gift from a relative who'd come to visit. Laila no longer remembered the man, but she still recalled the bright pink-bowed box in which the doll had been nestled, and the joy of sniffing the doll's soft silky hair, which smelled of powder. She still had that doll, but now her hair was matted and her face was dirty. One of her arms had broken off. Baba had glued it back on, but it no longer moved like the other arm. Catherine's doll was new and beautiful.

"Do you want to change her clothes?" Catherine pulled out a box of doll dresses and tiny shoes.

Madame Caron burst into the room and spoke French words to Catherine. Laila recognized the language, but she hadn't yet learned to understand it. Catherine left the room, looking down at her shoes. Laila put her doll on the bed and followed, but Madame Caron stopped her. "Wait, Laila. Come with me."

She led Laila into another room. The bed was bigger than Catherine's and had a gold headboard that went halfway up the wall. Madame Caron opened a mahogany armoire with a key she'd taken out of her pocket. "You like chocolate?"

Laila had only eaten chocolate at Christmas and Easter, and even then, only when visiting relatives brought some. Madame Caron opened a porcelain box with rows of balls wrapped in red cellophane. "Take one."

Laila took a piece, sniffed it, unwrapped it, and popped it into her mouth. She didn't bite into it, though. She just let the chocolate dissolve in her mouth slowly.

"Take another. They're from Paris, from my home. I've kept them here for a long, long time." Madam Caron ruffled Laila's hair.

Laila took one and put it in the pocket of her long school skirt, to bring to Baba. "You're a sweet girl." Madame Caron put the box back into the armoire and locked it. "But you know, Catherine doesn't have a lot of time to play. From now on you should stay with your mother in the kitchen. It's better this way. Do we understand each other?"

The kitchen was hot and smelly, and there was no place to sit except on the floor on a mat where she and Mama ate lunch. She would much rather play dolls with Catherine. "Can't we play during her breaks?"

"No," said Madame Caron as they left her bedroom. "Now go along and help your mother in the kitchen."

Over the weeks and months that followed, Laila worked hard at school and kept out of trouble, but Sister Marie didn't move her up a level as Laila had hoped. One day, she called Laila into her musty office and leaned over her large wooden desk. "You lack too much foundation still. Your reading is atrocious. You need to practice your reading and handwriting before I can think about advancing you."

"But the words jumble when I look at them," Laila said.

"Pray about it." Sister Marie leaned back in her chair and dismissed her, but Laila didn't need to pray about it. She didn't believe she needed to learn French. She was going to be a singer and Baba's music was in Arabic.

Her teacher taught her a French alphabet song to help her remember. Laila hated that song. The rhythm of it was like chewing stale bread. One day when she was in recess, she sang the alphabet to one of Baba's compositions instead, and in between each grouping of letters, she inserted ya habibey, the way she'd often improvised with Baba using maquam.

"I knew we'd have a problem with the awad's daughter," said her teacher. "It seems we got lucky with your sister." She dragged Laila by the collar of her blouse to the corner of the room and put a dunce cap on her, chastising her in front of the class of laughing girls. "You sing the way I taught you, and none of this 'my love, my love' business. Where do you think you are, a cabaret?"

That same afternoon, before the dismissal bell rang, Sister Marie called Laila to her office. "Give this to your father." She handed Laila a sealed envelope. "And tell him that if he wants you back in school, he needs to come here himself."

Baba laughed when he read the letter on the balcony. "You sang *ya habiby* with your alphabet?"

"I'm sorry, Baba, I couldn't help it. I was so bored with the alphabet song. Please don't tell Mama."

"Sit down, Laila." Baba pointed at the frayed wicker chair. She sat. "Sometimes," he said, "you have to hide your singing from people who don't deserve to hear you. When you're in school, just do everything their way because they'll never understand our way."

"But why do I have to learn this stuff if I'm going to be a singer?"

"Because." Baba leaned in closer to Laila. "Everything you learn along the way will help you be a better singer. Trust me."

The next day, Baba walked Laila to school. She went into her classroom with the rest of the girls and Baba stepped into Sister Marie's office, closing the door behind him. When Laila got home that night, Baba said, "You won't have any more problems with Sister Marie."

"What did you say to her, Baba?"

"I taught her about Jesus."

3

CAIRO, 1942

Every night, by the time Laila and Mama returned from Madame Caron's, Naima would have cored zucchini and washed the fruits. She'd have sifted through rice and would have completed the sewing work. Laila's chores when she got home were to collect the dried laundry from the clotheslines, set the table with bowls and spoons, and wash the dishes. After dinner, she returned to the foot of Baba's chair for their nightly lesson. By then Laila had learned several Om Kalsoum songs and a new piece that Baba had composed. She'd also become skilled at memorizing poetry and pronouncing classical Arabic, even though she couldn't yet read Arabic and continued to fall behind her peers in French at school.

One day after Laila had turned ten, Baba said he was taking her with him to the coffeehouse. "She's ready," he said to Mama. "It's time."

"A coffeehouse is no place for a girl," Mama said. "I let this go because I thought you'd come to your senses, that you'd realize you can't take a girl there. What will people say if you take a little girl to a man's place with smoking and belly dancers and who knows what else? Singing at home is one thing, but to do it in public?"

"They'll say whatever they'll say. Useless words from useless people." He took Laila's hand and closed the door behind them.

They descended the narrow stairs, their footsteps echoing in the dark stairwell. They walked along Gazirat Badran Street heading west, toward the Nile, past the Church of the Great Martyr Saint George, where Laila attended mass on Sundays with her mother and sister and without Baba, past the post office and the neighborhood mosque. He took her hand in his again, and she felt the calluses on Baba's fingertips against the back of her hand. They pushed through a crowded fruit and vegetable market, with vendors' carts lined up on either side of the narrow street. Horse-drawn buggies and automobiles rolled by, leaving clouds of dust and the odor of manure. The clucking of chickens mixed with the drone of voices touting ripened raspberries and roasted chestnuts and freshly squeezed guava juice.

Then they turned north onto Nile Corniche Road and into the Rod El Farag district of coffeehouses and cabarets. As the sun set, vendors waved strings of jasmine necklaces looped along their arms. In each coffeehouse musicians warmed their instruments: the piping of the nay, the deep daf drum and the shallower tabla, the violins and ouds and the qanuns. Men's fingers danced along the thin goatskin membrane of the riqq, creating the beat that forced a belly dancer to move her hips from side to side so fast, her whole body vibrated.

Inside Baba's coffeehouse, a wall of windows overlooked the Nile. The windows were left open so that the breezes from the river flowed in as city lights reflected off the water. Patrons, mostly men in galabeyas, arrived in groups and filled the small round tables in front of the stage. There were a few women at the coffee house, but Baba told Laila not to talk to them, that they were entertainers, and not artists like she was. Baba tuned his oud as his musician friends arrived, and he introduced Laila as "the next Om Kalsoum. You don't believe it now, but wait until you hear her. One day she started to sing, without direction, without instruction, just natu- rally, rabany kidda. I've been working with her ever since."

"Enough talk then," Ahmed, the qanun player, said. "Let's see what Kamal's offspring can do."

"Yalla," Baba said. "Laila, habibty, just like I taught you." He adjusted the oud on his lap. "Don't rush, okay?"

Laila stood up. She was nervous. She'd never performed for anyone but Baba. She focused on the strings and the position of Baba's fingers, took a deep breath, and let her voice go. It came out deep and low and reverberated from her so clearly and loud that she felt it move the chairs and tables and the coffee cups on top of them. Her voice sounded to her like someone else's. It had a slight rasp around the edges of the notes, but smooth inside them. At that moment it sounded bigger to her and for a second she lost track of where she was. How was this sound coming from her? How had she remembered the words? Baba's bandmates were staring at her, and she wasn't scared. But why? Nobody other than Baba had ever paid her any attention. When she talked, adults spoke over her or told her to be quiet. Now, the adult men were quiet. All eyes were on her. When she'd finished the patrons gathered around, clapped and whistled, and that response made Laila feel a new kind of elation, a euphoria that she sensed with her skin as if warm golden droplets of rain were falling upon her. She even felt a little taller, as if the floor itself had risen beneath her and pushed her up. From that moment on singing at home alone felt like half a dream, incomplete. She needed an audience.

"Masha Allah," Ahmed said. "God protect her. She's mawhooba. I thought you were crazy for bringing this little girl here, but now I understand. She must be where music is."

After that day, Baba took Laila with him to practices at the coffeehouse, and to weddings where he played with an ensemble. Sometimes he played on the terrace at the Shepheard's Hotel or Hotel Continental, where men wore suits with cuffed pants, ties, trench coats, and fedoras; and women wore dresses with thin straps or halter tops, revealing their shoulders and chests, and smoked cigarettes. Some of the women danced with men in the ballroom, and others tilted their heads back when they laughed with the British officers at the bar. How were they able to dress that way, dance that way? Nobody said anything to them. Baba told Laila that everywhere she saw British officers, there would always be at least one German spy. "Impossible to detect. But they're there," he said one day as they were walking home. Ever since then, Laila looked for spies everywhere.

By the time Laila turned eleven her singing had matured so much that Baba's bandmates invited her to perform with the ensemble, not just during practices but on stage when they played songs that Baba had written. They'd had a singer who occasionally sang with them, but even Laila knew she wasn't that good. The band promoted Laila locally as a child prodigy, and when she sang, audiences quieted, and she often heard their sighs of awe as her voice caught them by surprise.

Sometimes at the coffeehouse, Baba wrote new music and lyrics with his friends. When they took breaks, they smoked shisha and discussed poetry and, always, politics: His Majesty Farouk I, the Germans who'd just been defeated at El-Alamein, the French who were still occupied by people called Nazis, and of course, the British who still controlled the Suez canal. They had heated arguments that Laila didn't understand. She kept quiet and listened, accumulating questions.

Often they walked along the banks of the Nile before they settled in the coffeehouse for the evening. Together they watched the sun sink into the river, spreading hues of citron and violet before the sky dissolved into the black velvet night. Baba had once explained that the ancients believed that Ra, the sun god, traveled to the underworld every night in his boat, and that light would reappear only upon his return from his perilous journey. He said that the ancient Egyptians believed that everyone took that same journey after death, and that was why they buried the pharaohs with all their belongings.

"How much gold was in the boy king's tomb?" Laila asked. Baba had answered that question before, but she asked it again because she loved the way Baba replied.

He smiled and spread his arms wide. "More gold than a hundred horses could carry away. So much gold that it would make your eyes hurt just to look at it."

37

During these sunset walks, Laila asked Baba as many questions as she could. Why were the British in Egypt? Why did that man Hitler want to take over so many countries? How did some people own land while others did not? One day, the same year she was called a prodigy, (though she never felt like one) she asked Baba why they were poor.

At first he didn't reply. He remained quiet, and Laila threaded through the acacia trees, walking a few steps ahead of him. He caught up with her and put his hand her shoulder, turning her toward him, and knelt down so that he was at her eye level. "Do you really believe we are poor?" he asked.

She shrugged. "That's what people say."

"What people?"

"Mama, Naima, the nuns, the neighbors," she said.

He took a deep breath. "It is true, we don't have a lot of money, and sometimes we can't buy what we want, but poverty doesn't always have to do with money, Laila. Some people have poor souls. Their hearts don't feel." He tapped his chest. "Their ears listen but can't hear. Their eyes don't catch the colors in the sky. They buy things, but they don't feel happiness. They have many people around them, but not one true friend."

"So, we're not poor?"

"We are poor because we don't have a lot of money, but we're rich in other ways. And right here, right now, as I look at you, I feel like the richest man in the world."

"Well, if you're rich, then I'm rich too." She picked up a river stone and put it in her pocket, then climbed onto a large rock and jumped off, while Baba held onto her hand so that she wouldn't fall.

"Listen, Laila, don't believe everything people tell you. You must always question things. Answers to complicated questions are never simple. I know that may be hard to understand right now, but someday you'll comprehend what I mean."

One winter evening that same year, as Laila and Baba were about to leave for the coffeehouse, Mama tried to stop them. "You shouldn't take Laila there anymore," she said. "She's a young lady now,"

"And someday soon she'll be a woman. "

"What does that have to do with anything?" Baba reached for his tarbush.

"People gossip. Her reputation is at stake. Someday it'll be time to marry her. What suitor will accept a wife who's spent her days in cabarets singing with an awad?"

"My daughter's reputation is impeccable. Besides, do you want to sacrifice her gift for stupid gossip? Selma, Laila can be something big, something special. Then those people won't matter. There's always somebody saying something. Can't we focus on what's important?"

"What people say will always matter. It will always be important. There are eyes everywhere, Kamal, and word spreads throughout this city like the Khamsin windstorms. Look at her long hair and her changing body. She's not a girl anymore. Nargis and her devil-tongued daughters have begun talking about Laila's outings, her singing, her late nights seated among strange men. Haaga Safeya told me so. And she also said that she heard Mutwali talking in his shop to customers, telling them that he'd seen Laila coming up the stairs past midnight and that he'd never want that kind of a wife for his son. Naima is getting older now, Kamal. Soon suitors will be asking about her, and whatever Laila does will reflect on her sister."

"Baba?" Laila's throat tightened. Not going with him to the coffeehouse anymore was unthinkable, but she didn't want to hurt Naima either.

"Enough with this nonsense." Baba opened the front door, and a draft of cold air rushed into the foyer.

"I'm talking nonsense now?" Mama yelled. "You act as if she's a boy. She's not a boy."

"My daughter is smarter and stronger than any boy I've met. I'll put her up against any of them."

"You've gone mad," Selma said. "It doesn't matter how strong she is or if she can play soccer or box or sword fight or whatever is in your head." Selma tapped her temple. "Can't you see? She's a girl. She's vulnerable no matter how hard she hits. She's going to get married someday, have children. We'll have to answer to suitors and their parents."

Laila let go of Baba's hand and ran into her room. Naima was sitting cross-legged on the bed braiding her hair.

"Where are the scissors?" Laila said.

Naima pointed at the drawer in the nightstand. "What are they fighting about?"

"Me. Mama doesn't want me to go to the coffeehouse anymore."

"She's right, you know."

"Mind your own business," Laila said. She opened the nightstand drawer and took out the scissors. Then, standing in front of the mirror and before Naima could stop her, she pulled her long, thick black hair up into a tight ponytail. Then she cut into it with the scissors. Her hair fell to the floor in a semicircle around her. Naima gasped; Laila's hair was short and uneven.

"There," she said, and put the scissors back in the drawer. "Now there's no long hair to worry about."

"Are you magnoona? What insane girl cuts all her hair off? Mama is going to kill you."

"I'll die anyway if I can't sing," Laila said, and walked out of the room to present herself to her bickering parents.

They were still fighting. Mama was saying something about the impracticality of art, and Baba was telling her that she had lost whatever refined senses she once had. But when they saw Laila's hair, the arguing stopped.

Mama brought her hands to her face and screamed. Then both Mama and Baba pointed at one another and said, "Look what you've done."

Mama took off her wooden clogged slippers and lunged toward Laila, slapping her thigh with the hard wood. Baba got in between them and shielded Laila. He took the slipper from Selma and yelled, "Kifaya."

"No, *not* enough. No punishment is enough for her defiance. Today it's hair. Tomorrow it's everything else."

"It's an act of self-determination, of freeing herself. She'd rather cut her hair than be in your prison. Can't you see? Birds can't live in cages. Don't you want better for your daughter?"

"Don't *you* want better for your daughter?" Then she stepped away from Baba. "Take her," Mama said, her voice quivering. "Take her and go."

Laila felt guilty. She didn't mean to make Mama cry, but she had to go back to the coffeehouse. She had to keep singing in front of people.

Baba took her hand. They stepped out of the apartment onto the landing, and he shouted down the stairwell, his voice booming through the building. "Go tell Mutwali we don't want his sons for our daughters. And tell Nargis if anyone wants to say something, let them say it to my face if he dares."

They left for the evening. Baba was quiet until they got to the corner of Nile Corniche Road. "You shouldn't have cut your hair," he said as they turned onto Rod El Farag. "Your mother isn't entirely wrong. I've known this day would come, but I ..." Baba paused. "I suppose I put it off, hoping you'd always stay young, that people wouldn't notice you were getting older." He shook his head. "Stupid."

"But—"

Baba shushed her and pointed at her hair. "We have to fix this mess you've made. And from now on, there will be new rules, rules I should have put in place a while ago. Your mother is right. You're growing now, and I wasn't paying enough attention. You're better than any boy, but you still are a girl. First, you must remain seated next to me at all times. Don't speak to anyone if I'm not there, and never talk to the belly dancers. And your hair ..." He paused and looked at her, shaking his head. "When it grows back, it should be braided tightly before leaving the house. Next time you should wear a looser galabeya. This is for your own good. You come with me to learn the craft of music, nothing more. Nothing less. Remember that."

"Hader, ya Baba," she said.

Baba took her to his barber. "I don't know where else to take you," he said. "Besides, it's too short to style." When they got inside, Baba whispered something to the barber. The barber nodded and sat her at a chair in the corner, away from the front door. He tugged at and snipped the uneven chunks of hair on the back of her head. When he was done with the back, he told Baba that it was as even as he could get it.

41

"Can you make it look a little feminine?" Baba said.

"There's nothing feminine about what she's done," the barber said, turning Laila's chair to face him. He knelt down to cut whatever bangs she had. They were face to face, and the cold scissors pressed along her forehead. "Next time," he said to her, "don't cut your hair short. Girls are girls and boys are boys." He looked at her with disgust. "Is this the one who plays soccer in the alley?" he asked Baba. "I heard about her. She kicks everyone."

"Just cut the hair," Baba said.

When he was finished, Laila ran her fingers through her hair. Her head felt lighter, but when she looked in the mirror, she fought to hold back her tears. She didn't want the barber to see her cry. What did he mean anyway about girls being girls and boys being boys? She was as tough as any boy, but she didn't intend to look like one. She'd loved her long hair, which had grown to her low back. Baba had always told her never to let a boy see her cry, especially when she played soccer with them. No matter how hard she got kicked in the shin or how much the scraped knee stung, she'd learned to keep herself from crying. She'd bite the inside of her mouth or pinch her forearm or tug at her hair until it hurt and distracted her from the thickening in her throat.

"I love it," she lied. Her hair was uneven in the back, one piece near the crown of her head stuck up in the air, and her bangs were too short.

The barber shook his head. "Perversion," he muttered.

Baba paid him and headed toward the coffeehouse.

Baba's friends made jokes about her hair as soon as they saw her, but to Laila they were like family, and she laughed with them at her impulsiveness. In a way, she was proud of the courage she got to cut her own hair. Nobody did that, and that made her unique. After the novelty of her hair had worn off and Baba had relayed the story of the fight with Mama to his bandmates, they patted Laila on the back and invited her to play backgammon with them for the first time. "Let's see what you can do with that short hair," Ahmed said.

Later they played music, Laila sang, and the belly dancer, who was the final act, shook her hips to the tabla drum. After that, Baba walked Laila home, tucked her into bed next to Naima, kissed her on the forehead, and left the apartment again, locking the door behind him. She knew he and his friends would go to an evening spot they referred to as "the place," a mysterious location Laila dared not ask about, and from which Baba returned at dawn.

ভ৹

At school, the girls pointed at Laila's hair despite the pink headband Mama insisted she wear to school. They laughed at her, called her the bald boy, and one girl suggested her new name be Aly instead of Laila. For weeks Laila sat alone at lunch and played by herself at recess.

It didn't bother her much. She was already accustomed to doing things alone. The more she ignored the girls, the more they teased her, until one day the girl who'd suggested everyone call her Aly flicked Laila in the back of the head while Laila was sitting at the playground bench.

When she felt the annoying flick, Laila didn't stop to think. She turned around and grabbed the girl by the arm as she was trying to run off. Laila pushed her down on the ground, straddled her, and punched her in the face.

"My name is Laila, and I'm a girl."

The girl's nose bled, and she screamed so loud the nuns ran toward the scene.

"What's my name? Answer me?" Laila punched the girl again.

"Laila," the mean girl whimpered. "It's Laila."

Then Laila felt a pair of hands pulling her off the girl. They sent for Baba to pick her up that day. Sister Marie wanted to expel Laila, but Baba begged for a second chance. It was his fault, he said. He'd raised her to be a little rough, thinking it would be good for her. "I didn't think ahead. I didn't realize what it would mean to raise her this way," he said.

Laila didn't believe him. He didn't really regret it, did he? She couldn't imagine her life having been any different, of her days being spent with Mama in the kitchen instead of with Baba playing soccer, boxing, or learning oud.

Sister Maria didn't respond to Baba. Instead she opened the Bible and read scriptures to them. "For your sake, I read in Arabic," she said with a French accent. She read from the book of Proverbs about a good woman, which consisted of a long list of what good women do, how they sew, work hard, save money. "Nowhere in here does it say a good woman can hit hard." Sister Marie pointed at the open Bible. "Heed the word of God and you shall never fail," she said, and closed the Bible, setting it gently on the shelf behind her desk below the gold-trimmed French Bible. "I'll give you one more chance, but any other offenses and I have no choice. Je vais l'expulser de l'ecole." Sister Marie stressed the *p* of expulser.

Baba thanked her, took Laila's hand, and they left the school.

"You know how I told you to punch anyone who bothers you?" Baba said. Laila nodded. "We need to change that rule. Only punch if someone hits you first, and I don't mean a flick or tug at your hair. I mean punch you. Please, Laila, don't make me see that woman again."

"Yes, Baba," Laila said, secretly happy she'd punched the girl. Now she'd never bother Laila again.

That day when Mama got home, Naima told her about the fight, news of which had reached even the rich girl part of the school.

Mama and Baba fought so hard and so long, Mama had no energy to make dinner. "You feed the kids for once," she said, and went straight to bed.

Baba fumbled in the kitchen. He boiled a few eggs and toasted a piece of bread. The three of them sat at the table and quietly ate.

4

ALEXANDRIA, JUNE, 1943

Early that summer, Mr. Metzger, the owner of Cecil Hotel in Alexandria, offered Baba a job playing oud in his hotel after he attended a wedding where Baba played. He'd pay him two pounds and fifty piasters a week and give him an apartment to stay in for the summer.

"It's much more than I'd make here in Cairo, and it's a steady income for once," Baba said to Mama over dinner. "Besides, Signora Morpurgo and Madame Caron are leaving for the summer, so you have no reason to stay in Cairo."

"Why don't you go work at the British camps right here in Kasr Al Nil? I hear they pay well. Om Waleed's two brothers work there, and each of them was able to buy new furniture and jewelry for their wives. And Aisha's brother works in Ras Gharib. I don't know doing what, but he makes good money too."

"Selma." Baba wagged his finger at Mama. "This is the last time I ever want to hear you mention working for those invaders, those parasites. Have you forgotten what they've done to me?" Baba tapped his leg under the table. "I'd rather starve than work for the British. You know what Aisha's brother is doing in Ras Gharib? He's working for British Petroleum, who is stealing our oil." Baba circled his hand around the table, as if the oil had been taken from Naima and Mama too. "They take it. They sell it, and the money goes straight into the British government's coffers. They pay Egyptians nothing to slave in the desert, and to top it all off, as if those thieves weren't bad enough, they require a passport for anyone entering the city. A passport," Baba yelled. "A passport to enter a city in my own country!" He slammed the table. It shook, and the cups and bowls quivered.

For a few minutes everyone sat at the table in silence. Mama looked down at her plate. "I didn't know these things, Kamal," Mama said in a softened voice. "But still, people like us don't go to Alexandria. People like the Carons and the Morpurgos go to Alexandria."

"What do you mean people like us? Aren't we flesh and blood like everyone else?" Baba took a bite of the koshari. "Didn't God make the sea for everyone?"

"Yes, but we don't dress like them, talk like them, eat like them." Mama shook her head. "We should stay here in Cairo with dignity."

"Dignity? That's nonsense. You carry your dignity wherever you go. Listen, I'll get you cloth. My friend, the one whose son I taught oud, owns that store in the Daher district. He'll give me a discount, and you can sew the latest fashions for yourself and for the girls. Is that what you're worried about?"

"Really, Baba?" Naima's eyes widened. "We'll have new clothes like those girls in the movies?"

"Yes," he said. "And I'm going to take you to the beach, and you'll see the fish swimming in the clearest bluest water."

"Is it scary?" Laila had never seen the sea.

"Nothing is scary. Warriors like you don't get scared. Show me your muscles," he said to Laila and she flexed her biceps like the spinach-eating cartoon character she'd seen in the movie trailers.

"Stop with the muscles, Kamal. She's a girl," Mama said, but Baba just took another bite of his rice and lentils.

In the weeks leading up to their summer in Alexandria, Mama sewed two sundresses each for herself, Laila, and Naima. She copied the styles from a fashion magazine she'd seen at a kiosk on their way back from Madame Caron's. She'd stopped and studied the design, and then stayed up that evening to cut the patterns. "Why should I pay for the magazine if the picture is fixed in my mind?" she said. From Al Moski, she got them matching sandals with pink plastic flowers on the straps, which the shopkeeper had left over from the previous summer's inventory, and for which Mama bargained so much, the shopkeeper eventually told her to take them and never come back. As she was leaving, he said, "Next week I get a shipment of new sandals from Port Said. Come and see what I have."

ের

Mama packed sunflower seeds, dried coriander, and a homemade jar of clarified butter in her overstuffed canvas tote, which she carried over her shoulder and then held on her lap for nearly three hours, as the train took them from Cairo to Alexandria.

Never having been on a train, even in third class, Laila and Naima fought over the seat next to the window. After too much shoving and pushing, Baba settled it. "Naima, you sit next to the window until we get to Tanta, and then trade seats with Laila. If you two fight, I won't take you to the beach. Is that what you want?"

About thirty minutes into the trip, Mama vomited from the window while clutching her tote, cursing the train, the tracks, and travel altogether.

They arrived at Alexandria's Ramla Train Station in the early afternoon. Baba carried the oud case on his shoulder, held the suitcase in one hand and the map Mr. Metzger had given him in the other. "He said the Italian consulate was on the left." Baba spoke to no one as he oriented himself. "We need to head this way." He pointed the map down a long sidewalk. Mama took the girls' hands and pushed through the crowds of travelers, following Baba out under a cloudless blue sky, and into a salty breeze that rustled the palm trees lining the perimeter of the station.

"Look." Naima pointed across the street at the harbor.

Laila hadn't imagined just how blue the sea would be, almost aqua, like a silk dress Mama had once sewn for a customer. "The sea has a sound, maybe even a rhythm." She tugged on Mama's hand, but she didn't respond.

"Like a huge breathing giant," Naima said, distorting her face, "that will take you from your bed while you're sleeping."

"Stop that." Mama nudged Naima. "Pay attention to where you're going instead of this nonsense."

The Cecil Hotel was less than a five-minute walk from the train station. "It looks like a castle." Laila squinted as she looked up at the four towers.

The hotel's arched doorway was flanked by two large arabesque sconces, and a gloved doorman greeted them. Inside, a shiny marble floor led to a grand curved staircase, on either side of which were two wrought iron elevator cages operated by uniformed men. The gilded furniture was upholstered in red velvet. A red carpet ran the length of the lobby and ended at the reception desk, where Mr. Metzger had told Baba a key would be waiting for him.

"Kamal Abd El Malek," he said. "Mr. Metzger has something for me."

The hotel clerk nodded and gave Baba an envelope. "We've been expecting you, sir." He pointed toward the hotel's main doors. "The building where you'll be staying is out these doors and across the street, on the north side of Ismail Square. The address is right here." He tapped the front of the envelope. "Oh, one more thing." He handed Baba a suit bag. "These are two uniforms, one to wear while we are laundering the other for you. See you tomorrow? Mr. Metzger is serious about punctuality."

Baba nodded, smiled, and slung the bag over his shoulder. As they walked out, Laila tugged on his arm. "Can we ride in the elevator before we go, please?" She had never ridden in an elevator.

Mama shook her head and took Laila's hand. "You know better than to bother your father for such silly things."

The apartment was at least three times larger than the one they had in Cairo. It had a living room, family room, dining room, three bedrooms, two bathrooms, and a kitchen almost as big as Signora Morpurgo's. The kitchen had a big white refrigerator, an oven with a four-burner stovetop, and a built-in counterspace for cooking. At home they had two burners and a small table for cutting vegetables. Each bedroom had a four-poster bed, lace coverlet, an armoire on one side and a vanity with an oval mirror on the other. And on each nightstand there were fresh flowers.

After touring the apartment, Mama stood at the kitchen door and cried, "How is this possible with the war and the scarcity? We can't get used to this. The girls can't get used to this."

Baba wiped the tears from her face. "Selma, enjoy it for now. Let us leave tomorrow to God."

Laila and Naima threw the doors open to the balcony, which ran the width of the apartment and wrapped around the corner, giving them a full view of the beach. Girls and boys wearing swimsuits played ball in the sand. A few people were flying kites, and ladies sat under colorful umbrellas.

Mama leaned over the rail and squinted. Then she gasped, bringing her palm to her chest. "Dear God, is that a two-piece swimsuit she's wearing? Is that bare skin I see? What shame. What indignity."

"Can we go now?" Laila took Baba's hand.

"Me too? I want to go," Naima said.

"A promise is a promise," Baba said, "but first we have to get you swimsuits. You can't swim with a dress."

"No." Mama wagged her finger. "Good girls don't bare skin like that. I won't allow it, especially Naima. She is a woman now. I don't understand these mothers sitting there on the sand without a care while their own daughters run around like that showing their skin. If you want to take them in the water, they can wear their galabeyas. I packed one for each of them." Mama returned to the apartment to open the suitcase. "If my mother were alive, she'd die all over again."

"I'm teaching them to swim, Selma, not to drown." Baba followed her into the apartment. "The galabeya weighs down like an anchor in the water. Besides, we're in Alexandria now. Nobody knows us here. And as the saying goes, 'eat what you wish and dress as people wish.'"

"Then they don't have to swim at all. What purpose does swimming serve?" She stood up, leaving the suitcase unopened.

"Not everything you do in life has to be done for a reason, Selma. Some things we do are just for enjoyment, just for pleasure. Do you even remember what it's like to do something for no reason? Now, who's coming with Baba to the beach?" He turned to the girls, opening his arms wide as if readying to carry one in each arm.

Mama refused to go. She stayed in the apartment to dust the windowsills, take inventory of the kitchen utensils, unpack the suitcase, and make dinner.

Baba bought Laila and Naima matching yellow floral swimsuits from the shop on the corner of their new street, near Ismail Square. He also bought them two bottles of Coca-Cola, the least expensive umbrella in the store, two towels, and a beach tote. They changed in a bathroom by the beach cabanas, and Baba chose a dry spot close to the shore to set up the umbrella.

"Who's going to catch me?" Baba ran toward the sea and disappeared into the clear water.

Laila held Naima's hand. They took small timid steps in the sand toward the daunting shore. "The sand feels like a million ants around my feet," Naima said.

"It's hard to walk in." Laila took a bigger step. "I keep sinking in it."

"Come in." Baba surfaced from the water, his voice muffled by the sound of the waves and squealing children.

"Come back, Baba. Walk in with us." Naima's voice dissipated in the breeze.

He shook his head. "No, you must come to me." He waved them over. "Be brave, you will be able to reach, and when you get here, I'm going to teach you how to swim better than a fish."

"I can't," Naima cried. Tears ran down her cheeks, and she squeezed Laila's hand. "I'm scared. I know I shouldn't be, but I am."

"You can do it." Baba came closer to the shore. "Here, it's not that far now. You trust Baba, don't you?"

"Yes." Naima shivered.

"Me too," Laila shouted to the sea. "I trust you too, Baba."

"Then come."

Laila tugged on her arm, but Naima refused to budge. She dug her feet into the wet sand at the shore and screamed with each foaming wave. But Laila reveled in the tingly feel of the waves washing up against her feet, and each one seemed to sing her name.

"Then I'm going without you." Laila released her sister's hand and ran toward Baba. She slipped down the slope and sank under the water. It was the first time she'd ever been submerged. She held her breath. Baba picked her up out of the water and held her against his chest.

"Shatoorty," he said. Laila coughed, blew sea water out of her nose, and blinked the sting from her eyes. She didn't cry, though she wanted to.

"It burns my nose."

He patted her back. "You'll get used to it."

Every morning they had breakfast, put on their swimsuits, packed their beach tote, and headed for the beach. Eventually Mama joined them wearing her new sundress and a pair of sunglasses Baba bought her from the shop below their building. Naima finally got into the water too, but she never swam. She just waded in waist deep and ran back out onto the shore. By the second week, Laila was swimming with Baba far out where neither of them could touch the bottom. He taught her how to float, ride a wave with her body, and swim to and from the shore. Swimming was the most glorious freedom Laila had ever felt, the buoyance a euphoria she couldn't put into words, even when she tried to explain it to her sister. "It's the closest thing to flying, I think," she said. Naima seemed uninterested as she sat next to Mama, chatting about the dresses they'd seen in the vitrines on the way to the beach, planning how they'd copy and cut their patterns before they forgot the details.

At night Laila went with Baba to watch him perform at the Cecil Hotel. Baba had gotten permission to bring her along, and Mr. Metzger agreed on account that she was a music student and that he liked Baba.

But Laila had to be "out of sight" at all times, so she often sat on the floor in a corner of the bar beside a large potted plant. Nobody ever noticed her. There was a female singer who sang as Baba and the ensemble played. She wasn't famous, but Laila was mesmerized by her. She was tall, thin, and had long golden-brown hair. Most of all she had a sweet soulful voice, but it wasn't as powerful as hers. This Laila was certain of, and she thought about what it might be like to be singing every night, wearing red lipstick in a shimmering strapless dress, before a new audience.

On weekdays, Baba played in the lounge bar where British officers celebrated successful returns from the fighting in the desert by drinking out of silver mugs engraved with LRDG, which Baba explained was the unit crest. Laila memorized the letters, and later learned they stood for Long Range Desert Group. The men didn't pay much attention to Baba's oud, and Laila couldn't sing as she had at the cafes where Baba and his friends had more control over the entertainment. But when the belly dancer came, they perked up and whistled. They clapped and shoved bills in the openings of her costume. Laila loved the red and gold costumes the belly dancer wore and the beaded tassels that hung off her hips.

On Saturdays, Baba played in the grand ballroom, where he was part of a number the hotel named the Oriental Segment, which followed a jazz band that played as foreign couples danced slow, touching each other, looking into each other's eyes. When Laila told Naima about this, she giggled and told Laila that foreigners were strange, but Laila didn't agree. She thought the foreigners were elegant and refined, and she wished she could dress like them and one day dance to a jazz band just like that. This, though, she kept to herself, afraid it would get to Mama and cause more problems.

One morning Baba woke up earlier than usual. Mama and Naima were still asleep, and Laila heard him heading out the door. She ran out into the foyer. "Baba, where are you going?"

"To the beach for a swim. I didn't think you were awake. Want to come?"

Laila squealed with delight, ran to her room, put on her swimsuit, a knit swim cover, and flip-flops. They walked to the beach, passing early risers sitting at cafés, sipping coffee and eating pastries. It was too early to need an umbrella, so they only brought towels; and when they got to the beach, they spread them on the sand and then jumped into the sea. The water was calm and the waves small. Laila watched red, blue, and orange fish swimming around her feet. Baba picked her up and threw her as far as he could, and she swam back to him. They splashed each other, and Baba taught Laila how to swim under the water without holding her nose, counting how long she could hold her breath.

On one of her trips under the water, Baba pulled her up from the water long before she'd run out of breath. "Laila," he said, his expression suddenly serious. "There's a strong current pulling us in. Don't be scared."

He dug his foot in the shifting sand of the sea floor. "Listen to me," he said. "I'm going to throw you this way, away from the current." He pointed beyond a pathway forming in the water. "You will swim straight to the shore. Don't stop until you get to the shore. Wait for me there. I'll be back."

She screamed, "Baba, no!" but he didn't pause. He didn't look her in the eyes before he threw her. It was the hardest and farthest she'd even been thrown, and though she wanted to cry, she swam to shore just as Baba had instructed. When she got out, she jumped up and down, screaming for Baba as she watched him being pulled out farther and farther into the sea. At first, she saw his head, shoulders, and arms, then just his head and shoulders, and finally just his head. After a few minutes, she couldn't see him at all. She wailed running up and down the shore looking for anyone to help until she found a young fisherman. She couldn't say anything to him except, "My baba is drowning. I need your help. I need your help."

The fisherman told her to calm down, he had a boat they could go looking for him in. "Baba," she wept, stepping into a small rowboat, which was sitting on the shore. "We have to find him. We have to find Baba."

Laila pointed and tried to stop crying so that she could see better. "He went that way." She got into the boat, and the fisherman pushed it into the water and then climbed in. He rowed over the waves and in the direction that Laila had pointed.

"Insha Allah, we'll find him. Insha Allah." The man said a prayer under his breath, and she heard bits of the prayer over the waves lapping on the sides of the boat. He said something about God the merciful and good. She held on to the sides of the boat, an empty fishnet behind her. There was no sign of Baba. Laila squinted against the sun, searching for a head, a hand, a foot kicking the water. But nothing. The man paddled deeper in the sea, farther and farther from the shore, until off in the distance they both saw something.

"Is that him?" The man pointed at a dot in the sea, not deeper in but closer to shore, parallel to where they were rowing fiercely over the waves and against the wind that blew against them.

Laila squinted once again against the sun. "I can't tell if it's him. I can't see."

"There's another set of oars behind the net. Can you row?"

Laila had never rowed before. "Yes," she lied. They got closer. "Over there. He's swimming to shore."

Laila was afraid to believe it was Baba and afraid not to believe it. She rowed as hard as she could, her arms and shoulders aching. As they got closer, the man in the water began to look more like Baba, his dark hair, the movement of his arms, the determined stroke of his swim.

"I think it's him," she said.

The fisherman rowed toward the man in the water, but the man had gotten to the shore by the time the boat got close enough to rescue him. Laila jumped out of the boat to swim to Baba, but the fisherman plucked her out of the water and put her back into the boat. "Izborey," he said, demanding her patience. "I'll take you to shore." And together they rowed back toward land. She thanked him and jumped off the boat. Then she ran to Baba, who had fallen on the sand to catch his breath. Laila threw herself into his arms and sobbed.

"Don't leave me, Baba. Don't ever leave me again."

"I told you I'd be back. Why didn't you believe me?" He panted.

"I couldn't see you anymore." She wiped her tears and gasped for air, her chest tired of crying.

He dried her tears and said, "Let's go home now. We'll come back tomorrow."

"No," she said, taking his hand as they walked off the beach. "I'm never swimming again."

"You're swimming tomorrow, after tomorrow, and for the rest of your long life," he said. Then Baba waited for the fisherman to bring his boat back to shore. He shook his hand, thanked him, and prepaid him for some fish. "I'll take whatever the sea gives you," Baba said.

Baba and Laila walked back to the apartment in silence, and neither of them ever spoke of the incident again, but Laila never forgot how Baba looked when the sea almost took him.

5

CAIRO, 1946

One cold morning in late January as they walked to church, Mama told Laila and Naima the story of Saint George, the martyr for whom their church had been named. "He refused to recant his Christianity." Mama pointed to the sky. "Diocletian, the evil emperor, became so angry that he tortured Saint George. He put him on a wheel and rolled him over boards pierced with sharp pieces of iron." Now she made a rotating motion with her finger. "But the torture had no effect on him. Not even a wound marked his body. Do you know why?"

"Because God sent his angels?" Naima said. Cars zoomed past as they crossed Gazirat Badran Street, leaving clouds of noxious fumes.

"That's right, but Diocletian didn't give up easily. He kept trying different methods of torture, but still, God was on Saint George's side. Finally, Saint George was taken to the Roman temple to worship idols. The stone idols began to talk. They admitted that they were the instruments of Satan and that God was the only true God. After seeing this, many Romans began to believe in God and Jesus and became Christians dedicated to the church. Then Diocletian had Saint George beheaded, and that's why he's a martyr and why our church is named the Church of the Great Martyr Saint George."

"But Mama," Laila said. They were nearing the church, its dome and steeple coming into view. "Why did God let Saint George die in the end? Why didn't God protect him like he had been?"

"Maybe it was because God wanted Saint George in heaven with him," Naima said.

As they arrived at the church steps, Laila looked up at her mother. "But why allow him to be beheaded at the hands of a pagan? It doesn't make any sense."

Mama slapped her across the face.

Laila brought her hand to her stinging cheek. Her throat thickened, but she swallowed past the tears. Once they were inside, she followed Mama to the women's side of the aisle and sat next to Naima.

"You shouldn't have said that," Naima whispered in her sister's ear. "When will you learn to keep your mouth shut and stay out of trouble?"

"When you learn to speak up," Laila whispered. "Why didn't you defend me? Don't you ever have questions?"

"I never question God."

Laila and Naima crossed themselves from left to right with the priest. The smell of incense, with undercurrents of cedar and frankincense, permeated the church. The priest began the hymns and chants while the deacons clanked cymbals and played triangles; to Laila, the holy percussion sounded discordant. She gazed at the relief of Jesus nailed to the cross. Who was she to doubt God's judgment when Jesus had suffered to pay for the sins of humanity?

The priest spoke: "Glory and honor, honor and glory to the all holy trinity, the Father, the Son, and the Holy Spirit."

But God's presence didn't fill her body and mind and soul as the priest said it would. When she prayed, her thoughts drifted to the lyrics of Baba's new song, or the vast distance between the earth and the stars, or the new American movie playing at Cinema Metro. When the congregation prayed, she didn't even close her eyes. She watched the parishioners—a mother holding her baby, a man teaching his son to bow his head, a grandmother who'd fallen asleep on her daughter's shoulder.

She caught Botros glancing in her direction. When she looked at him, he looked away.

Botros was the most eligible young man in their church. He'd just graduated from the Jesuit School for Boys and had a job at Telecom Egypt as a switchboard operator. His name was spoken over tea and cookies at every women's gathering in the neighborhood. To parents, Botros was desirable because he was the son of a church deacon and had a stable job. But the daughters saw the tall, muscular young man with long dark eyelashes and dimples. Was Botros interested in her? And if so, for how long?

"Glory be to the Father and to the Son, and to the Holy Spirit, now and forever and to the age of all ages. Amen, alleluia."

Laila chanted with the rest of the congregation, trying to focus on holy words, but questions kept arising, questions she dared not ask out loud again, but that, as far back as she could remember, she'd always asked herself. Why did God punish all of mankind because one woman ate an apple? Why did God allow Satan to pose as a serpent? Why was Lot's wife turned into a pillar of salt for looking back at her burning city? Laila would have looked back at *her* building had it been on fire. And did Adam and Eve's children marry one another? Of the hundreds of people sitting in the church, hadn't any of them thought about this?

She thought about what it meant to be a Christian, and why or how it was different than being a Muslim? Nobody spoke about those things. People just knew who was Muslim and who was Christian whether it was by their name or by a cross pendant worn on a necklace or a cross tattoo on the inside of the wrist inked by the priest on wailing babies, a Koran pendant also worn on a necklace. People just knew that Christians were a minority, and nobody discussed it. Holidays were celebrated together. Laila's Muslim neighbors came over for Christmas and Mama cooked meals for Ramadan and took them to her Muslim fasting friends. Mama had always said that religion was a personal matter. So, why then was it so important for Laila to believe in Saint George or Jesus? Why couldn't Mama let it be personal for Laila too? Laila remembered what Mama had told her and Naima about someday marrying a good Christian boy, some-one who'd shared their belief in Jesus. What faith? Laila didn't know if she believed in faith itself. Church was the place she felt the most lost, the most out of place.

After the liturgy, Laila rushed outside and waited for Mama and Naima on the crowded steps. The church was stuffy and dim, but the midday sun beat down on villas, mosques, churches, and people on the crowded streets. Across the throng she noticed Botros waving. "Come here," he mouthed. Laila shook her head and looked in the opposite direction. It was improper to be seen talking to a boy, and she had already been in trouble once today.

But Botros worked his way toward her through the crowd. He stood a discreet distance from her, angling his body so that it seemed he wasn't speaking to her but to a nearby group of boys. She could have moved away, but she was too curious.

"Can you give something to your sister?" he said.

"My sister?" Laila felt foolish. She was only thirteen and Naima was almost seventeen. Why would nineteen-year-old Botros be interested in Laila? Besides, Naima was the taller and thinner. Her eyes were the color of honey, her hair had golden streaks, her skin was fair. "I don't think she wants anything from you."

"Just give it to her." He handed her a bar of chocolate wrapped in crin-kly gold foil. She dropped it into the pocket of her prickly plaid skirt. "The chocolate is for you," he said, "because now you're officially the keeper of a big secret, but the note is for your sister. Please give it to her in private. I trust you." He winked, then slipped through the crowd.

That night in their cramped bedroom, Laila sat on the bed next to Naima, who was unbraiding her hair, running her fingers through it. Laila unwrapped the chocolate bar, peeling off the layer of gold foil. Taped to the back of the bar was a small folded piece of paper with "to Naima" in blue ink.

"Your admirer sent you this." She gave her sister the square of paper. "Clever and sneaky."

Naima held the note under the dim light of the only lamp. She read and reread it, smiling and blushing.

"If you read your homework that carefully, you'd be a star student." Laila inched closer. "Let me see. What did he write you?"

"No." Naima pushed her away. "It's private. Besides, you can't even read."

"Of course, I can read," Laila lied, and tried to peek at the letter.

"Move." Naima pushed her to the side.

"All right. Then I'll tell Mama first thing in the morning. She'll slap you harder than she slapped me on the church steps." Laila bit into the chocolate bar. It wasn't nearly as rich or creamy as the chocolates from Madame Caron's tin.

"Go ahead," Naima said. "But then you'll have to tell her how I got the letter, won't you? And she'll know you talked to a boy in front of the church."

"I have my ways. I'll find out one way or another what's making you blush like that." The next day after school, Naima made Laila stand with her in a long, noisy line at Om Ahmed's fruit stand. "We don't even have money for fruits," Laila said.

"Just listen to me and be quiet."

The stand was one of dozens in the Rod El Farag fruit market, but Om Ahmed, a stout, thin-haired woman with rotting teeth, had a reputation for selling the freshest strawberries and the sweetest guavas.

Botros arrived minutes after Laila and Naima. He cut into the line behind them and handed the man who was behind him two piasters to quell his protest.

"So, this is why you said three o'clock?" Naima said, still facing forward in line, careful not to look back, as if neither of them knew the other. Laila stood next to her sister, listening to the exchange between Naima and Botros.

"You're as smart as I thought you were," Botros said. "By midafternoon the line is like this, every single day. Did you read my poem?"

Naima blushed.

"I noticed you at church," he went on, "but you probably didn't notice me. Did you?"

"I knew who you were," she said.

"I thought we could talk here." He kept his hands in his pockets and bobbed his head, pretending to be an impatient customer.

"About what?" The line moved, and Naima took a small step forward.

"Everything. What do you like to do? What do you dream about? Do you enjoy school? How many children do you want? Things like that."

"I don't like school because the teachers are harsh. I love to sew. I want three children, but if God wills, I'll have more. I want my own fancy atelier, like the ones in Zamalek, but I never learned how to sew the complicated things that rich women wear. I sew for women from our neighborhood. So, I said to myself, 'Naima, don't be silly,' and now I just want to get married and be a mother."

Laila had never known that her sister wanted her own shop. In all the years they'd shared a room, Naima had never mentioned it, and Laila had never asked.

"Maybe someday you can learn to sew those fancier clothes," Botros said.

"Maybe."

Each day for the next two weeks they met at Om Ahmed's fruit stand at three o'clock, Laila standing next to her sister to protect her from suspicious eyes. Sometimes Botros brought them both cotton candy or Coca-Cola and buttered popcorn, or paper cones of roasted chestnuts. He told Naima about his trips to Alexandria, its white powdery sands and the endless blue of the Mediterranean Sea. "I'll take you there someday," he said. She never told Botros that Baba had already taken them to Alexandria. She just told him that she cooked, and about the time she'd seen Faten Hamama on the big screen when Baba had taken them to Cinema Metro. Botros explained how a switchboard operator's job was done; there were only a limited number of lines and sometimes he had to cut people off when they'd talked too long. When the three of them got near Om Ahmed's stand, they would separate without buying anything.

One day Botros asked to be alone with Naima. "Please. There's an alleyway behind the post office where nobody walks. I need to speak to you."

Naima shook her head. "If my parents ever found out, they'd kill me. If you have something to say, just say it with my sister here. She won't tell." She took Laila's hand and squeezed it.

He lowered his voice to a near whisper. "There are things a man must tell a woman only when they're alone."

"No. I can't," Naima said.

Laila nudged her arm. "Just go. I'll stand at the end of the alleyway and pretend I'm lost. If someone walks by, I'll whistle."

Naima and Laila walked around the post office from one side and Botros from the other; then Naima joined him in the alleyway. Laila watched as they ducked behind an abandoned building. She paced back and forth, listening to the voices of boys playing soccer a few streets away, the distant sputter of automobiles, and the clip-clop of horse-drawn carriages.

Naima came out of the alley alone. A few strands of hair had pulled out of her braids, and her cheeks were flushed.

"Are you all right? What took you so long?"

"He asked me to marry him," Naima said. "I said yes, and then he kissed me."

"He kissed you?" Laila had only seen men and women kiss in foreign movies. She'd never seen Baba kiss Mama, not even on her forehead. "What did it feel like?"

"It was wrong. I couldn't resist—his eyes." She smiled. "He says he's going to come to the house with his parents to propose."

Laila had never thought of Naima getting married. Marriage was a strange thing Mama talked about, a distant event that never took shape in Laila's mind. Now she would have to sleep in her room every night without Naima, walk to and from school alone, and have no sister to argue with. "Mabrook," Laila said. Congratulations.

"Tomorrow we're taking a different route home," Naima said. "We must avoid the fruit stand. I won't meet him again until I have an official proposal. I can't."

At first, all Naima talked about was Botros: his voice, his elegant manners, his brilliance. Then, after a few days, she became anxious and suspicious. "If this was a trick just to kiss me, I hate him. God forgive me." She crossed herself.

"Naima," Laila said, "you know how long these things take. Be patient."

But a week passed, and the proposal still hadn't come. The next Sunday before church, Naima told Mama that she had a stomachache and asked to stay home with Baba.

"You're making me go to church alone?" Laila said. "You know how much I hate going."

"I can't bear to see him. I'm so embarrassed." Naima threw open the armoire and took out the letter he'd written her. She tore it up into tiny squares and dropped the pieces of paper in Laila's skirt pocket. "Find him and give him the torn-up letter, every little bit of it. Throw it at him if you have to. Tell him I never want to see him again. Tell him he's a liar and a pig."

"And I'm supposed to do all of this without making a scene?"

"I don't care. Just make sure he knows I'm finished with him."

After the final prayer, Laila went outside the church and found Botros talking to a group of friends. She tapped him on the shoulder, and when he turned around, she reached into her pocket for the handful of her sister's torn letter. "Here," she said, throwing the shreds at him.

The tiny squares floated to the pavement, and he knelt down to pick up the pieces. "What was that for?" he asked.

"Naima says she doesn't ever want to see you again. She says you're a liar and a pig."

"Wait." He stuffed the paper in his pocket. "I know what she's thinking. Please tell her it's not like that. I love your sister and I still want to marry her. It's my parents. I need a few weeks to convince them."

"What's wrong with my sister? Why do you need to convince them?"

"Your sister's not the problem. You are." He pointed at her.

Laila bit the inside of her lip, "What do I have to do with this?"

"It's about your singing with your father at coffeehouses. When I told my parents about Naima, they asked around about your family, you know, how parents usually do. That's when they found out that your father isn't even a Coptic. He's Protestant. That's not even a religion. Not only that, he's an awad, and to make matters even worse, he's training you to be a singer." He shook his head as if she were something to pity.

"My father is a gifted oud player and there's nothing wrong with being a singer. And he's a good man, Protestant or Coptic. It doesn't matter."

"I know, but my parents are old-fashioned. Listen, tell Naima I love her. Tell her I wrote my uncle in France, and he's going to talk sense into my parents. I'm sure of it, but I need time. Tell her I think of her day and night. Tell her to wait for me."

"You're a coward. If you were a real man, you'd come propose to the woman you love no matter what." Then Laila kicked Botros in the shin the way Baba had taught her too, ran down the church steps, and decided that if she ever got married, it would be to a man who'd sail seas and cross mountains for her.

When Laila got back from church, Naima was sitting in their bed and wanted to know everything. "Did you tell him? What did he say? What was his reaction?"

Laila told her how she threw the paper at him and called him a liar and a pig as instructed. Then she told her about Botros's parents, what they'd found out about her and Baba, and how they opposed the marriage. "But I kicked him really hard in the shin," Laila said, proud of herself.

Naima stood up and because she was taller, she looked down at Laila. "You." She pointed at her, just like Botros had. "It's your fault. Mama said this would happen. Your singing and the business with the coffeehouses and Baba's oud playing. I swear, if I lose Botros because of you, I'll never forgive you." Then Naima threw herself on the bed and wept into her pillow.

"You're even stupider than I thought," Laila said, and joined Baba on the balcony.

For three weeks, Naima didn't speak to Laila. She stopped talking to her at night before they both fell asleep. As soon as she got into bed, she gave Laila her back. "It's not my fault," Laila whispered one night on the second week of Naima's silence.

"It will always be your fault," Naima said with her back to Laila. "You're stubborn and selfish. You don't need to sing, but you do it anyway even though you know it will hurt me and Mama."

"I didn't know it would hurt you, and besides, how do I choose? If I stop singing, it'll break Baba's heart. Are you more important than Baba?"

Naima never responded to Laila. She cried into her pillow instead and said, "I wish I'd never ripped up his poem."

"I wish I kicked him in both shins," Laila said before they both fell asleep.

A month later, after Naima had almost given up on ever marrying Botros, Mama made an announcement at dinner, once she'd served the rice and stew. "A proposal came for Naima."

Naima looked surprised.

"Who is it?" Baba ripped a piece of pita bread and dipped it into his bowl of fasoolya stew. Mama had used more green beans than meat and Baba was fishing for the scarce meat in his bowl.

"It's Gergis's boy, Botros. His mother asked me after church if they might call on us."

"And what do you think of him, Naima?" Baba's tenderness made Laila jealous, and she felt guilty for it.

"He has a good reputation, Baba. And a good job."

"He's a clown," Laila said.

"You keep your childish opinions to yourself." Mama wagged her spoon at Laila.

Baba ignored Laila and continued his conversation with Naima. "But have you spoken to him? Do you know him? A lifetime together is not built on jobs or reputations."

"But good reputations are the basis," Mama said.

Laila mouthed the word clown to her sister across the table.

"I spoke with him a few times—at church. In a group of friends," Naima answered her father. "He seems like a good and decent man. I can be comfortable with him." She looked down at her bowl and pushed the rice and green beans around.

Baba nodded and dipped another piece of bread into his bowl. "Then we will host him and his parents here next Sunday for coffee. Your mother will make sweets, and we will leave the rest to God."

The family spent the week getting ready. Baba borrowed extra chairs from a friend's shop, since they owned only a settee and two chairs. Mama bought dates, butter, sugar, and flour to make the cookies. Naima used the money she'd made from sewing to buy cloth remnants from Khan El Khalili market to make herself a new dress, and Laila took her measurements: eighty-seven centimeters at her bust and hips, and sixty-one centimeters at the waist. Mama said she was too thin and lacked feminine appeal, but Laila thought her sister was stunning, just like Ava Gardner.

Mama sent Laila around the building to borrow a silver tray from Aisha and a white embroidered tablecloth from Fatima to cover the scratches and dents on their dining room table. Every woman in the building had borrowed it at one time or another. It appeared at Christmases and Easters, at Ramadan nights when families gathered to break the fast, at sebou birth celebrations, and at henna parties. Mama took out the gold-rimmed demitasse set she'd inherited from her mother.

On the following Sunday after church, Botros and his parents finally arrived. Like his father, Botros wore a suit and tie and a red tarbush. He fidgeted before he gave Naima a bouquet of jasmines and lilies wrapped in green tissue paper and tied with a red bow; its heady scent filled their small entryway. His mother, Samia, wore a navy dress with pearl buttons, a simple pearl necklace and earrings, and carried two boxes of chocolates. Baba had also put on a suit and tie, and Mama wore the embroidered galabeya she kept for formal occasions. (Although Naima had let it out for her, it was still tight on her hips.) Naima's pale-blue dress had an A-line skirt, a demure V-neck, and cap sleeves, and she'd tied a white sash around her waist. The dress was too light for winter, but she had wanted to wear something airy and beautiful. She'd added kohl around her eyes and a deep brown mascara the local hairdresser had concocted out of goose fat and soot. She had reddened her lips with sweet almond oil mixed with dried beet root powder. Mama had said red lipstick was too brazen.

Mama motioned for Samia and Gergis to sit on the settee and for Botros to take one of the arabesque chairs, while Mama and Baba sat on the borrowed ones. As they'd rehearsed, Laila and Naima retreated into the kitchen to prepare the sweets and the coffee while the parents made small talk.

Naima filled the copper kanaka with water and added sugar without stirring so that the sugar would caramelize as the water boiled, and then slowly disperse. "He looks handsome, doesn't he?" she said.

"Yes." Laila was arranging Mama's date-filled sugar cookies onto the silver tray.

Naima added powdered coffee into the water and stirred the coffee only after it began to steam. "What are they saying? Can you hear?"

Laila shook her head. "No, but Mama and Samia are probably complimenting each other, as usual." The protocol irritated her, and she tugged at the lace dress Mama made her wear which had once belonged to Naima.

Naima waited for the first foam to form at the top of the coffee, then she removed the kanaka from the burner, spooned the first foam into each cup, and returned the kanaka to the burner. When the second foam appeared, she poured the coffee into each demitasse and set the cups on a tray. Laila followed her out of the kitchen with the silver tray of cookies and offered them to the guests.

Samia took the first sip. "Your coffee is exquisite, dear."

When Naima sat in the chair across from Botros, Gergis began to talk.

"As you know, we are here to ask for your daughter Naima's hand for our son Botros. I've watched her grow up and blossom before my eyes. She's a good pious girl, and you should be proud of her. We are also proud of Botros. He's graduated from the Jesuit School, and he now has a job at Egypt Telecom, and can become a good provider for a wife and children."

"It is our honor to accept your proposal," Baba said. "Of course, Naima must agree first." He turned to Naima. "Do you agree, ya binty?" His eyes glistened as he called her my daughter.

"Yes." Naima blushed.

Mama and Samia began trilling their best zaghrouta, and the screeching echoed in the stairwell, five floors down to the streets of Cairo. This alerted everyone—the beggars, bakers, butchers, the lady who sold guavas—that Naima had received and accepted a marriage proposal. Then the mothers hugged each other, kissed on both cheeks, and took turns hugging and kissing Botros and Naima. The men hugged and kissed too, then sat down again and sipped their coffees.

Botros reached in his breast pocket and pulled out two jewelry boxes. He opened the first one, took out a gold chain necklace with a delicate heart pendant, and fastened it around Naima's neck. Then he opened the second box which had two gold bands in it. Botros took Naima's hand and put the engagement dibla on her right hand. Naima put the larger band on his right hand. The rings would be moved from the right hand to the left on their wedding day. Mama and Samia trilled more zaghroutas. Then Samia took three gold bangles off her wrist, put them on Naima, and kissed her on both cheeks. "Mabrook," she said.

"Now that it's official and Botros has given Naima the shabka jewelry, we shouldn't wait too long," Samia said to Mama when she sat back down. "The devil is crafty, and the young are his prey. We aren't rich, as you know, but we are comfortable. Gergis's salary at the post office is sufficient, and I can plan for a wedding after we break the Easter fast. We can host the reception in our apartment. I'll take care of the flowers, the entertainment, the food, and drinks. I have a beautiful rooftop garden where we can set up the kosha for the newlyweds to sit. What do you say, Naima?"

"Whatever you see fit, Auntie." This was the proper address to older women.

"I'll leave the engagement party to your discretion," Samia said to Mama. "Though it must be held before the fast. It's the only way. And we must have duck and lamb, and at least two types of desserts. And sharbat to drink. I have a large family, you know."

"Samia," Gergis said. "The engagement is hers to plan."

"Of course. I'm sorry." Samia took another sip of her coffee. "Our family apartment has five bedrooms, and we have but one son. My girls are already married and living with their husbands, so Naima and Botros will live with us, as will their children someday."

"God willing," Mama said. She opened one of the boxes of chocolates and offered everyone a piece.

"As the bride's parents," Gergis said, "you're responsible for furnishing the newlyweds' apartment." Baba shifted in his chair. "But don't worry. Since they'll be living with us, we only ask that you buy the bedroom set. A man and his wife should start their lives on a new bed. Don't you think?"

"Of course." Baba bit into his cookie, and a few crumbs fell onto his new shirt.

Baba stayed quiet the rest of the visit, leaving the women to discuss the details of the engagement party and wedding. But as Botros and his parents were leaving, he stood up to shake hands with Gergis and in a near whisper said, "I know that the mothers want to have the wedding as soon as possible, but I think it would be wise for us to give the children time to get to know one another."

"We'll see." Gergis nodded.

Over the next few weeks, Naima and Mama visited the Khan El Khalili market daily, either before Mama's shift at Signora Morpurgo's or after her grueling evening at Madame Caron's. They searched for lace remnants, trimmings, and beads. Sometimes after school Laila took over for Mama at Madame Caron's so that she could go home and work on the extra sewing she and Naima had taken on to make extra money. Many times, Naima worked late into the night, and within a week of her engagement, she stopped going to school altogether. "What difference does it make now? I'm getting married." Laila began walking to school alone.

The wedding was set for April 18, the first Friday after Orthodox Easter. Friday was the Muslim day of prayer, and so the rest of the country always had the day off. This gave Mama two weeks to plan for the engagement party, which had to take place before the beginning of the fifty-five-day Easter fast, during which no animal products could be eaten.

The cost of the preparations was more than they'd anticipated. Mama started an account at the butcher's so she could afford food for the engagement party. She bought three ducks and a leg of lamb; it was the only time Laila had ever seen the butcher send a helper to carry the meat up to their apartment. Mama spent days stuffing grape leaves with minced meat and rice, the way rich people made them. She baked kobeba with bulgur wheat and made kofta patties. She made Om Ali for dessert, soaking the puff pastry in milk and coconut. She baked thin, dense basbousa cake made with semolina flour and drenched in honey syrup.

At first Selma was going to host the engagement party in their apartment and in her neighbor's apartment across the way. Their neighbor had volunteered the space, and Selma had accepted. That way guests could also make use of the landing in between the two apartments. But Botros's mother invited more people at the last minute, and Selma had to move the party to the rooftop, and make two more ducks and four more cups of rice. Naima paid little attention to the arrangements. She spent her days bathing, brushing her hair, and choosing outfits to wear on her dates with Botros. Since they were officially engaged, they were given some liberties.

Though they weren't allowed to go to the movies because Mama said it was too dark at the theater, they had Baba's permission to take walks along the Nile Corniche. They had an hour and a half time limit each day.

On the day of the engagement party, the women of the building helped Mama take the food to the rooftop. The porter swept the front entrance of the building and put up lights that he'd purchased as a gift. Mama tried to pay him, but he refused. "Naima is one of our own. The least I can do is give her lights for her engagement." The building was a family, and Naima's guests became everyone's guest. Someone lent them chairs, another person brought up a record player, and Haaga Saafeya collected portable kerosene burners to keep the food hot on the rooftop. The porter carried up cases of Coca-Cola, and the porter's wife greeted the guests as they entered the building, directing them up the stairs to the rooftop. At the party Baba played his oud, and he had recruited his friend to play the tabla, but Naima had asked Laila not to sing so she didn't. The women danced and pushed Naima onto the floor with Botros. They tied a scarf around her hips, and Botros clapped to the beat as she danced.

Within a half hour of the buffet's opening, all the food Mama had made ran out. There was nothing left except for a plate of pickles. Mama's food was so good that the guests, especially the men, put mounds of it on their plates and returned to the buffet for seconds and thirds, and the food line kept forming even after the buffet was empty.

Samia took Mama aside. "Selma, what happened? Didn't I tell you there would be a lot of people? I thought you'd have prepared. I thought you knew what you were doing?"

"I cooked for three times the number of guests. They just ate like beasts in famine," Mama said.

"Well, do something before people start talking," Samia said, and sat back down at her table.

Mama gathered the building's women. They stood talking in a circle in the darkest corner of the rooftop. "What are we going to do?" Mama began to cry. "This is shameful. What will they say about us? That we're cheap? I can't bear to hear it. I can't."

Nargis from the fourth floor, who'd been talking badly about Laila, said, "One of our own cheap? I'll cut their tongues before they say that."

Then Fatima from the third floor came up with a plan. "What does everyone have in their ice boxes?" she said.

One of the women had just bought cold cuts and cheese from the grocer. Another had half a pan of leftover baked negresko chicken pasta, and Haaga Saafeya had kabab hala stew left from when her grandchildren were over. "They hardly ate any of it," she said.

Fatima cleared the serving platers off the buffet and told the guests that this was only the first round of food and that the second round was being heated and was on its way up. Laila's job was to refresh everyone's Coca-Cola to keep the guests distracted and satisfied until they could replenish the buffet. Then each of the women went to her apartment to prepare a plate of fresh leftovers. Within twenty minutes, each of the Selma's neighbors had returned with a platter, and the buffet was full again. There was a cold cut platter, bowls of olives and pickles, a steaming platter of rice with seasoned onions that Haaga Saffeya had improvised at the last minute, a pot of spiced beef stew, squares of freshly baked (or so thought the guests) negresko, sliced chicken with potatoes in tomato sauce, and roast beef with gravy. When the porter's wife heard about Mama's painful dilemma, she brought up a batch of balady bread she'd baked that morning.

"I make it from cracked wheat bran the way my mother used to bake it in the village," she said proudly as she set a stack of the hot bread on the buffet.

The women decided to stand behind the buffet table this time and serve the food so that they could control the portions each guest took. When Samia turned around and saw the buffet had been restocked, she gave Mama a wink and waved at her from her table. Fatima, who was standing next to Mama, said, "God help Naima."

"Yes, God help Naima," Mama said.

After the engagement party, Mama tried to pay everyone back, but the ladies refused. Each of them said the same thing. "You're family." And every time Mama heard those words, she cried. She cried from the first floor to the fifth. To repay them, Mama and Naima sewed each of them a new galabeya using the best fabrics they had, and wrapped them in pretty cellophane paper that she'd bought from the bookstore at the bottom of the street. Laila delivered each package with Mama.

Once that was done, Mama began working on Naima's trousseau. She was out of money, so she started a gamea, calling on the neighborhood women to pool their money together and create a borrowing circle. A gamea was the only way poor families like Laila's were ever able to buy anything expensive, such as fabric, needles, thread, and ribbons to sew Naima's entire trousseau. Even Laila was recruited for simple tasks— arranging the thread, picking up after Mama and Naima had cut a new pattern. When the work was complete, Naima had two nightgowns with matching robes, three skirts, four blouses—one for each season—one pair of pants, a simple dress, a beaded party gown, a cloche hat, and a fitted red wool coat with big white buttons down the front. It was Laila's favorite.

Still, there was the matter of the bedroom set. Baba had assured Mama and Naima that he'd be able to save the money, but by the middle of March, he had only been able to save two pounds from playing oud at weddings and the bedroom set cost five.

"Madame Caron needs a new gardener," Mama said over dinner. "I told her you might be interested in the job. It would only be a few days a week, and she said if you wanted the extra work, she'd give you priority."

Baba looked up. He was different since Botros's proposal, sadder, more tired. He didn't go out on Thursday nights as much as he had before, didn't ask Laila to sing or even practice with him, and sometimes he lifted the needle off a record before the song had finished. He often skipped tea in the balcony and retreated to bed early. "But I don't know anything about gardening," he said.

"It's nothing," Mama said. "The old gardener used to trim the hedges and water the flowers. She has special flowers from her country that need to be watered every other day. That's all, really. I watched him a few times from the kitchen window."

"Please, no, Baba," Laila said. "I don't want you to work for Madame Caron."

She and Mama were accustomed to working in someone's house, going in through the back entrance, staying hidden from sight. But not Baba. She wouldn't let him belong to Madame Caron, not even temporarily. Baba was for music.

Mama pointed her spoon at Laila. "Be quiet. When your father and I speak, you keep your mouth shut."

"I'll take on more sewing," Naima said.

Mama shook her head. "You're already working day and night."

"Then I'll quit school and work mornings." Laila began to cry.

"You won't quit school," Baba said. "I'll take the job. It's all right, Laila. We need the money. Nobody is paying for oud lessons now, and I want your sister to hold her head up high. And I'll be putting money aside for you too, when you get married."

"I don't want to get married," Laila said, "if it's going to make you work for that witch."

"What do you have against Madame Caron?" Mama said.

"Can't you see we're the dirt on the street to her?" Laila could hear herself beginning to yell. She wanted to tell Mama that she'd heard Madame Caron call all Egyptians dimwits. But she couldn't. It would hurt too much to say it, and even more for anyone to hear it. "I work there every day. I slice and chop and clean with you. I sift through the rice and I go once or twice a day to the market for her, and yet she isn't paying us for two cooks. Is she? She feeds us crumbs, and we accept it like fools. But I won't let her do that with Baba too."

Baba slammed down his palm, shaking the table. "Enough. Since when do you raise your voice like that? Kiss your mother's hand at once and go to your room until I excuse you."

Laila got on one knee and kissed Mama's hand. "Forgive me, Mama." Then she went to her room and wept into her pillow.

6

CAIRO, 1946

Baba negotiated a payment of thirty-five piasters per day with Madame Caron and convinced her that to maintain a beautiful garden, she needed at least three visits a week from him. Laila watched and listened to them from the small kitchen window of the Caron villa. She calculated that if Baba worked for the next month and didn't miss a day, he'd be able to pay for Naima's bedroom set and have one pound and twenty piasters left over.

"You're asking for a lot." Madame Caron looked Baba up and down. "Well then, I expect everything to be perfect. I know your wife must have told you that I'm a little picky, but that's how I'm able to keep my home tidy and clean. You understand?"

He nodded. Madame Caron was taller than Baba, so she looked down at him as she spoke. She took Baba around the grounds. He trailed behind her, and they stopped at the far end of the enormous backyard, too far from Laila to hear their voices. Madame Caron pointed at plants in the gardens around the swimming pool, at the trees and a ladder near the tennis courts. Her hands rose and fell as she kept talking and Baba kept nodding.

"The last gardener didn't trim the trees," Mama said as she peeled potatoes for the baked chicken. "Someone else did that."

"She'll take all she can get," Laila said. "That cheap—"

"Hush. Someone will hear and we'll all be fired. You'll ruin everything."

As Baba and Madame Caron walked back toward the villa, Laila could hear them again. "And these are just my most favorite things in the whole world," Madame Caron was saying. "I brought the seeds from France myself." She bent down and touched a sunflower. "In my country, they grow wild in the fields as far as the eye can see. I used to run in fields like that when I was a child. Here, I had to plant them in the early spring two years ago. They're the kind that grow all year, you see, and I had to plant just then because sunflowers don't blossom unless they're planted in cool soil. But after that they do very well in the heat. To an extent. After all, they're not native to the desert."

Baba bent down and ran a finger along the petals. "They're a work of art."

"I'll need them watered every other day. That's all really." She took a cigarette out of a silver box she kept in her pocket, lit it, and blew out a plume of smoke that just missed Baba's face. "Oh, and I'm sure Selma has explained where the back door is. And I'll pay you at the end of the month. If you're late, you'll be docked." She pointed at Baba with her cigarette. "And if you miss a day, I won't pay you for it. I'm sorry, but that's how I run things."

Three days a week Baba trimmed the hedges, fertilized the grass, pruned the trees by the tennis courts, and even cleaned the swimming pool. Most importantly, he watered Madame Caron's sunflowers from France.

And during the month before the wedding, he took every oud engagement in any ensemble he could find. He played at engagement parties, weddings, and coffeehouses, and spread the word among his friends and acquaintances that he would substitute for any oud player anywhere.

Sometimes, Laila joined Baba and sang while he played. Sometimes she brought water or snacks for the weary musicians; other times she sat cross-legged on the floor in a corner and watched Baba play—by far her favorite thing to do. He worked late into the night and then woke up early in the mornings on the days he had to go to work for Madame Caron.

One afternoon after Baba had returned from working at Madame Caron's, one of his bandmates, Ahmed the qanun player, came over with news. He frantically knocked, and Baba looked worried when he opened the door. "Ahmed? What's wrong?" Baba said. His friends never came to the apartment. They always met at the café, so it was unusual for him to arrive unannounced in the afternoon.

"He asked for you by name," Ahmed said breathlessly as he walked in. "He came to the café and asked for Kamal Abdel Malek. That's what he said in his afrangi accent. He told me to give you this." Ahmed gave Baba a small piece of paper. "I just ran over here to tell you. He wants you to play tomorrow."

Baba motioned for Ahmed to sit. "What are you talking about?" Then, before Ahmed could reply, he told Laila to go into the kitchen and ask Mama to bring out tea and cookies. Laila worried that they might not have cookies. Mama and Baba would be embarrassed. After all, everyone tried to hide being poor. It wasn't something they spoke about, but just a truth she understood. People would always know they weren't rich, but no one should ever learn just how poor they were. Laila didn't want Ahmed eating her last cookies. Still, she did as her father said, hurrying back to the family room to hear the rest of Ahmed's news.

"Apparently, there's a big event and the khawaga likes our music. He has a good ear. And it's at The Suez Canal Club. I've yet to meet a musician who's played there." A smile spread on Ahmed's face.

Baba shook his head. "You know they don't allow Egyptians in there, unless they are serving or cleaning."

"Who cares?" Ahmed uncrossed his legs and leaned in toward Baba from across the coffee table. "This is good money, and they're sending you--" he pointed at Baba, as though accusing him of something– "a private car to take you to Ismalia and back. What more do you want?"

Just then Mama put a tray of tea, sugar, milk, and cookies on the coffee table, inviting them to drink and eat. Then she looked sternly at Baba and returned to the kitchen.

"I want dignity. I want..." Baba took a breath. "I want something I can't explain." Baba said this looking down at the table, or at his hands, or maybe at the few cookies in the small plate.

"Kamal, don't be stupid," Ahmed said. "When a connected khawaga asks for you by name to play at an elite club, you go! You don't get idealistic. This is the best exposure you'll ever get. All it takes is for one person to mention your name to the right people and just like that you are making records. Political problems were here before we were born, and they'll be here after we die. First the Ottomans controlled us, then the French, now the British." Ahmed leaned in closer to Baba across the coffee table. "You think not going will save Egypt, bring her one step closer to independence?" Ahmed mocked a protestor's fisted hand. "You need to think of yourself now, your family, and your daughter who is about to marry."

Baba didn't look up at Ahmed. He stared at his teacup. "I know you're right, but I..."

"I nothing." Ahmed took his last sip of tea and bite of Mama's cookie. Then he got up to leave. "I gave you the message. I did my part. The rest is up to you." He pointed at Baba and shook his head. Laila was angry with Ahmed and didn't understand why.

That night Mama and Baba argued in their bedroom. Laila sat in bed and Naima pressed her ear against the wall that separated the two bedrooms. She delivered the news in whispers. "Mama's mad at Baba and says he should go, but he says he won't cow down to the British." When the fighting ended Laila and Naima sat in bed arguing about whether Baba would actually go to Ismalia or not. Laila said Baba would not go and Naima said he definitely would because Mama would make him.

The next day Baba paced the apartment back and forth, and Mama didn't speak a word to him all morning. Then after the dhuhur prayer Baba got dressed quietly, and just before he picked up his oud and left the apartment, he knelt down, kissed Laila on the forehead, and whispered, "Forgive me for doing this." His eyes reddened and filled with tears.

Naima hugged Baba, and Mama smiled and kissed him on the cheek, wishing him a safe journey.

This realization caused a burning in Laila's chest and her hands began to tremble as she started to cry. Baba was going to bow down to the British after all, but only because he had to, because he needed to.

One day in late March, when Mama, Baba, and Laila were at Madame Caron's, a violent Khamsin sandstorm flew in from the desert. It was midday, yet the sky became dark within seconds. Baba was in the garden on a ladder, trimming a tree. Laila screamed from the kitchen window for him to get into the house. As he scampered down the ladder, debris flew everywhere—branches, leaves, even bricks from the roofs of other villas. Baba covered his head. Mama began to pray and tried to pull Laila away from the open window.

Madame Caron ran out into the garden, a bundle of linen sheets in one hand and in the other a bag full of what looked like short spears. She was obviously screaming at Baba, but the wind was so violent, Laila couldn't hear her. Her skirt flew over her head, but she didn't bother to pull it down. Baba ran toward the house as Madame Caron dropped what she was holding and waved him over.

"Get in the house," Laila shouted.

Baba began to cough. Laila knelt on the floor by the kitchen sink but bobbed up to peer out the window every few seconds. She watched as Madame Caron pointed at her sunflowers, screeching as she tried to shield them with the sheets from the wind-driven sand. Baba drove the spears into the dirt to pin the sheets over the flowerbeds. He pointed at the villa; Madame Caron shook her head. Baba pushed Madame Caron toward the house, cupping his hand over his mouth, then covered the rest of the sunflowers from France before staggering into the house through the back entrance and collapsing on the kitchen floor in a coughing fit.

Madame Caron, in tears, thanked Baba as if he had saved her child. She ordered the butler to set a cot up in the kitchen. Then she brewed Baba a concoction of lemon and ginger tea and dropped in a white tablet that Laila didn't recognize. Laila sat on the floor next to Baba as he lay on the cot, and she rubbed his chest as he coughed.

"Where is Naima?" he asked when he was able to take in a breath.

"God willing, she's home." Mama drew the cross across her chest.

Madame Caron gave Baba the tea. "I put a medicine in your tea. An antihistamine."

As the storm died down, Laila and Mama continued to prepare dinner. Baba's cough subsided, but never disappeared.

Two days before the wedding, Mama hired a ballana to remove every hair from Naima's body with hallawa sugar wax. Laila heard her sister's screams from behind their closed bedroom door. And that night, Mama asked Laila to wait outside the bedroom. She had things to discuss with Naima in private.

While Naima and Mama talked, Laila made a pot of anise and chamomile tea for Baba's cough.

She gave him the cup of tea, wishing him a speedy recovery.

"Ya Laila." Baba's voice was hoarse. "Now that Naima's wedding is almost here, you and I can keep practicing the new song."

A crisp April breeze blew in from the Western Desert. "When you're better, Baba." She reached for his hand, feeling for the calluses on his fingertips as she used to when she was a child.

"There's an audition at Radio Cairo in less than two months," he said. "They're looking for a new act, something fresh. That's us, Laila. Together, we can be something much bigger."

Laila wanted more than anything to sing for people and hoped that soon her life might bend further toward music. "But Mama. You know how she feels about all this."

"Leave your mother to me. I just need you to concentrate on singing, only singing. Your mind has to be clear and focused."

When Mama left the bedroom, Laila slipped under the covers beside Naima. "What did you talk about?"

"Just wedding things." Naima stared at the ceiling, her face drained of its color.

"What kinds of things?"

"You'll find out soon enough." Naima turned on her side, giving her back to Laila.

The next morning Laila went with Baba to the furniture store on Soliman Pasha Street to pay for the bedroom set, which would be delivered when the newlyweds returned from their honeymoon in Alexandria. The store was owned by a short, bald Syrian man named Habib, who offered them tea. "They will never need to buy another bedroom set," he said. "This set will last a hundred years. You made a good choice. Insha Allah, your daughter will live in hana and bliss with her new husband."

Baba nodded. "For what I'm paying, I will send it back if there is even a scratch on it." He took Laila's hand, and they left the store. "When I married your mother, I took her with the clothes on her back, and we slept on rags on the floor until we found jobs. Now, they want furniture and dresses and ducks." He led her across the street. "Come. Let's see an American movie. I have a little money saved. Life is more than work and sleep."

For the first time in his life, Baba purchased first class tickets. An usher took them up a grand staircase and seated them close to the screen. The picture was *The Best Years of Our Lives*. Laila couldn't read the Arabic subtitles. She didn't need them: she watched the soldier come home from war, his wife embrace him, kiss him, the streets in America, and the vast houses. Were there men and women who loved that way? Even Naima didn't seem as in love with Botros, but Laila thought about how she wanted to be loved that way, not just liked, but loved. On their walk home, Baba said, "Someday, I'm going to see America."

That night Baba went to the coffeehouse, and the neighborhood women gathered for Naima's henna night. They filled the small family room and spilled out onto the landing outside their apartment. They took turns trilling their best zaghrouta as a Sudanese artist drew scrolling floral designs on Naima's hands and feet. They drank sharbat that Mama had made that morning from strawberry juice, rose water, and sugar. They played records, and the women clapped to the beat of the tabla while Laila and Naima danced, an old scarf tightly wrapped around Naima's hips to accentuate her swaying. When the party was over, Mama rolled Naima's hair in curlers and made her a cup of warm milk to ease her nerves.

At the church, bride and groom sat on red velvet chairs. The priest blessed their rings and anointed them with olive oil. Hundreds of guests attended the reception on the roof of Botros's apartment building. Belly dancers balanced candelabras on their heads, and a wedding singer sang love ballads while the women danced until morning light. Baba, weary and feverish, had played a song on his oud that he'd secretly written for Naima. It was the only time Laila wanted to get married.

When all the guests had left, Mama held Naima in her arms, wept, and whispered something in her ear. Then Laila threw herself into her sister's arms and held on tight until Baba gently pried her away to hug his Naima. The newlyweds left to board a train to Alexandria, where they would spend a month in a rented apartment overlooking the Mediterranean.

ॐ

The day after the wedding, Baba couldn't get out of bed. He convulsed with chills and fever. Laila and Mama took turns putting cold compresses of water and vinegar on his head, legs, and hands. His face had turned yellow, and he coughed up green phlegm. He was in and out of sleep; and when he was awake, he wasn't coherent, talking about birds and songs and people Laila had never heard of.

"We need a doctor." Laila put on her galabeya and pulled her hair into a ponytail.

"We don't have money for a doctor," Mama cried. "I don't know what to do."

"I'll get money."

Laila ran out their front door, down five floors, and out into the street. It was two o'clock in the morning, and she didn't have a piaster for a taxi or bus or even a horse-drawn carriage.

She ran west on Gazirat Badran to Nile Corniche road, then ran south past coffeehouses where men smoked shishas and watched belly dancers' final numbers, and fancier cabarets still full of patrons. She passed pairs of drunk men walking unsteadily down the street and beggars asleep on newspapers. She stopped to catch her breath, then crossed Kasr El Nil Bridge to the island of Zamalek. It took nearly an hour to reach Madame Caron's villa. Only when she pounded on the door did she notice that her sandals had torn and her feet were bleeding. At first nobody answered the door. Then a light turned on, and through the glass panels flanking the door she saw a man in green silk pajamas coming down the curved staircase.

"Who the hell are you?" he asked when he opened the door.

"I'm Laila. I work for you with my mother as cook. May I speak to Madame Caron?"

"Brigette!" He left Laila on the doorstep and headed back up the stairs as Madame Caron hurried down, her floral silk robe billowing behind her, her hair in curlers, and her face coated with a white layer of night cream.

"Laila?" She pulled Laila into the foyer and closed the front door. "What in God's name are you doing here at this hour? Why are your feet bleeding?"

Laila began to weep. "Baba. He's sick. We don't have money for a doctor or medicine, and you're the only person I know who can help."

Madame Caron said nothing, and Laila collapsed at her feet. "Please. I'll do anything. Anything for my baba. I'll sweep for you. I'll garden. I'll cook. I'll shovel. Whatever you need. Just please help me."

"Of course. Laila. Of course. Get up. Please." She guided Laila to the settee in the parlor, then woke up the butler and handed him a stack of bills. He was to take Laila with him, pick up the doctor who lived across the street, and take them both in a taxi to where Laila lived. But when Laila arrived with the doctor, Baba was unconscious. Mama lay weeping on his chest.

The doctor moved Mama off Baba and checked his heart with his stethoscope. Then he took his pulse. "Help me prop him up," he said. Mama, Laila, and the doctor propped Baba up. The doctor asked them for cold compresses. "We need him conscious to give him the medicine."

"Baba, wake up." Laila tapped his face. He moved his head but he didn't open his eyes. "Baba, open your eyes," she said. Still, he was in a state of delirium.

Laila threw off her partly torn sandals, slipped in the bed next to Baba, the blood still fresh on her feet, and sang the song they'd been practicing. "Baba, how's the pitch?" She stopped in the middle of a song to ask. She knew she was on pitch. So, she decided to sing off pitch, to mess up the lyrics, to change the arrangement. Those were the things that irked him the most, the things that made him flinch as though a fly were buzzing around him. Maybe then he'd wake up. She sang badly, making all of the mistakes he hated. Finally, after a few minutes of cold compresses and Laila's annoying performance, he opened his eyes and said groggily, "What's wrong with you, Laila? We have a contest in a month."

As soon as he finished that sentence, the doctor put a pill on Baba's tongue, and Mama brought a glass of water to his lips. "Drink, habeeby. Drink, bil shifa," she said, wishing him a quick recovery. It was the first time Laila had ever heard Mama call Baba habeeby, the first time she'd seen affection in her mother.

The doctor gave them strict instructions. Baba had to finish the full pack of medicine, stay hydrated, and sleep propped up. That night Laila stayed up all night with Mama, and the two of them took turns putting cold compresses on Baba until his fever finally came down.

7

Baba lost weight in the two weeks he was sick. His face was sallow. He had a dry cough that got worse at night, and he didn't have the energy he once had. He wasn't yet strong enough to resume his gardening job at Madame Caron's, but because he'd rescued her sunflowers, she gave him an extended paid vacation. She'd never given Mama a paid vacation.

Mama made Baba beef bone broth soup every day. Haaga Saffeya brought him a concoction of herbs to boil and drink, saying it was the best thing for body aches. Baba's friends came by to visit. They missed him down at the café, they said, and urged him to join them the following Thursday night, play his oud a little. "It will do you good," Ahmed, the qanun player, said.

But Baba shook his head. "Not yet, but soon, Insha Allah."

Baba did only one thing after he was able to get out of bed and walk around the apartment without feeling dizzy, and that was to practice for the Radio Cairo competition with Laila. He had a calendar tacked to the wall above his nightstand, and he'd drawn a red star on the date of Friday, May 31.

For three weeks before the competition, when Laila wasn't at school or helping Mama at Madame Caron's she was practicing with Baba. He'd composed and written his own song, and Laila's job, he told her, was to breathe life into it. He was tough during those practices, chiding her for forgetting a maqam or mispronouncing a lyric. If she sang too fast, he made her stop, take a deep breath, and start the song over.

"You're not singing a Western song, Laila," he said during one of their practices when she rushed through a measure, though she didn't know it. "If you really want to sing, you have to remember what I always tell you; our music doesn't speak the language of the West. It follows other rules, rules formed in the mountains, and on the shores of the Mediterranean, and in the harvesting of grapes and olives, and right here in our Cairo. Arabic music doesn't rush. It takes all the time it needs to weave itself through you." He moved his hand through the air, undulating, bending, and curving it along invisible lines. "We have a good chance of winning this, Laila. All you need is to feel the meaning of the song."

She imagined what life might be like if they'd won the contest. Maybe she'd quit school and sing full time. Maybe she'd become famous and make enough money so that Mama could buy all the meat she wanted, and Baba would never have to work for Madame Caron again. She'd wear pretty dresses on stages and maybe buy those pink shoes she'd seen in the window display of Cicurel's department store. She wanted it so badly that she was afraid to want it at all.

Baba explained to her that his was a song about unrequited love. "Can you imagine wanting something so badly that it hurts, and never being able to have it?"

"Yes," Laila said.

"Now imagine the pain of it. A broken heart feels like a fire burning inside you, gowakey, and there's nothing you can do to put it out. Sing like you're on fire, Laila."

"Have you ever felt that way, Baba?"

"Yes," he said, and adjusted the oud on his lap, then tuned it.

Her throat thickened, and she bit the inside of her lip. "Were you ever really that sad?"

"Yes."

"Who was she, Baba?"

"That doesn't matter. What matters is that you feel it, that ache in the soul, in your roh." He tapped on his chest as if the soul lurked just there under his skin, or maybe deep inside his chest cavity.

"Does it still hurt?"

"When I think about it," he said.

This moved Laila and she didn't understand why, but she bit the inside of her lip again to keep from crying.

Baba must have noticed that her eyes glazed, or perhaps they were red. "Take every emotion you feel now and sing with it. Sing with it until it cleanses your soul."

She closed her eyes and sang, her voice deep, broad, filling the small apartment with Baba's big pain. And the words she'd never lived brought her a new hurt she'd begun to imagine. When she finished the song, Baba put down his oud and pushed himself out of his chair. Taking Laila's face in his hands, he kissed her forehead and said, "Don't feel too sorry for me. Your mother finally married me."

He sat back down in his chair and said, "Now, let's talk about your eyes."

Laila was used to closing her eyes as she sang. She imagined the music moving up and down with her voice as if it were a thin silver string. This was something Baba had told her to do when she'd first started learning, but now he wanted her to pay attention and open her eyes more than she closed them. He put a full-length mirror in the family room and told her to watch herself practicing.

"Move your hands, express yourself. Look at your audience," he said at the beginning of every practice, positioning her in front of the mirror.

She hated looking at herself while she sang. Singing was her chance to leave her body and travel into the ether of a song, and having a mirror in front of her forced her to not to fly, to stay inside her flawed body, contend with the curves of her face, the part of her hair, and her awkward, thirteen year old, budding breasts which were neither like a child's or like a woman's. But she forced herself to get used to it.

The night before the competition, Baba gave her a teaspoon of honey and made her go to bed early. That morning, he kept her home from school so that so she could rest and practice one last time before the contest that evening. Even Mama, who still disapproved of Laila's singing, kissed her on both cheeks, said a prayer for her, and walked Laila and Baba to the taxi. "In the name of the holy cross," she said as Baba pulled the car door closed.

The contest was held in the Radio Cairo building in the downtown. The waiting room was full of contestants. There were male and female vocalists. Some were accompanied by their pianists. Others bragged about singing without accompaniment. But nobody had an oud player.

"They're going with European-style music," Baba whispered to Laila. "They think the oud is old-fashioned. Well, wait until they hear us." Just then a woman came out crying and cursing at the contest director. This made Laila nervous, and she began to shake her legs and fidget. Baba told her to stop. "You're not her," he said.

They waited for two more hours for their turn, and when a man came into the waiting room calling out the names of Kamal and Laila Abd El Malek, only three people were behind them.

"I'm Waleed, the manager of this competition," he said as he ushered them past the window overlooking the broadcast room, where a man was talking into a microphone as he read from a stack of papers. "If you win," Waleed said, "you'll be a regular in that room." He pointed, smiling. "If you win." He stressed the if.

There were five judges in the small competition room. Each smoked a cigarette, and their ashtrays were full. They didn't introduce themselves. Waleed was the only one who talked. He pointed at a spot marked on the floor with blue tape. "You'll stand there," he said to Laila. Then he pushed a wooden stool next to her for Baba to sit on. He adjusted the stool and nodded at Baba. "You'll sit here."

Before Baba sat down, he addressed the silent judges, who looked tired, and said that they'd be performing his original piece.

Baba tuned his oud, and Laila made eye contact with each of the judges just as she'd practiced at home. Still, nobody smiled at her or even gave her a nod of approval. It seemed as though they were already disappointed. Had they made up their minds before they performed? Baba closed his eyes, strummed his oud, and played his song's intro. At first the song was soft and slow. He plucked with his risha and made music with the lilt of a bird gliding the air currents up and down. The judges perked up in their seats like Baba had fed them a delectable bite and they wanted to taste more of it. And then the music got louder, faster, as though the gliding bird had soared into the sky, far up above the clouds.

Laila took a deep breath and, as she'd practiced, pushed the song out of her chest. Her voice came out deep and broad, huskier than it had been when she'd started years ago, before she understood that music could carry pain with it; and though she didn't fully understand it, she felt it. "My heart." She lifted her hands in the air and stretched the lyrics over Baba's maquam. Her voice and his oud became one to her, and as she performed, she couldn't distinguish between them. "My heart, I'm dying of love." Which sound was her voice and which was the oud? The judges had stood up by the first refrain, and her nervousness left her. She felt nothing but the music. It was the first time she'd ever known that kind of freedom, and it possessed her. Baba didn't notice the judges. His eyes were still closed, his head moving with the music as though he were in a trance. After they'd finished their song, Laila and Baba received a standing ovation. She'd done everything right; every rest, every note, every lyric.

When they left the Radio Cairo building, Baba said that it was her best performance. "You were like an angel," he said. She relaxed, happy not to have to think about the competition, but anxious about the results. The stressful process had taken the fun out of singing, and out of Baba too. She asked him if they could get an ice cream, and he agreed. "Anything you want," he said.

Before they crossed the street, Waleed from the radio station caught up to them. He was panting. "Wait. Mr. Kamal, wait," he said, trying to catch his breath. "I need to speak to you."

"Is there a problem?" Baba said.

"No. Not a problem at all. Actually, I came to tell you that I can make you the winner. I can make all your competition disappear," he said, waving his hand as if shooing a fly.

Baba furrowed his brows. "What do you mean?"

"For fifty pounds," Waleed said.

Laila took Baba's hand. "Are we going to win?"

"Of course." The man tried to pinch Laila's cheek, but Baba pushed his hand aside.

"Address me. Not my daughter."

"All right," Waleed said. "I'm addressing you that you can change the course of your and your daughter's lives if you pay me fifty pounds."

"What are you talking about?" Baba said.

"Let's call it a tip for my efforts. Oh, I know fifty pounds is a lot to come up with. I'll give you a few days. There are plenty of ways to delay competition results. What do you say?"

Fifty pounds was at least a third of what Mama and Baba made together in one year.

There was a long pause, then Waleed said, "What? You don't believe me? Don't worry, Waleed delivers on every promise." He patted Baba's arm.

Baba put his hand on the man's shoulder. "Kamal Abd El Malek doesn't cheat." Then Baba gave Waleed a shove, and he stumbled backward.

"You're going to regret this," Waleed said, shouting as Baba and Laila turned to cross the street. "You were the best, but best doesn't pay my bills."

"That dog," Baba said when they'd gotten to the other side.

He bought Laila an ice cream cone from a pushcart vendor in the downtown. "I'm sorry," he said. "I'm sorry I put you through all of this for nothing. For a crook like Waleed to ask for a bribe ... Forgive me, ya binty." His eyes glazed with fresh sorrow, and the streetlights cast a shadow on his gaunt face.

"Why didn't you pay it, Baba?"

"Because we don't cheat. Because buying something that isn't for sale mars you forever."

"So, we're not getting the spot on the radio?" Laila said, licking her ice cream unable to taste its sweetness as she tried to hold back her tears.

"I doubt it," Baba said.

He stared at the Radio Cairo building across the street. "A bunch of corrupt thieves," he muttered, his mouth pursed as if he had tasted something sour.

When they got home, Mama wasn't there. She'd left word with the porter's wife that Naima had just returned from her extended honeymoon in Alexandria and Mama had gone to visit. Baba sat in his chair and turned on the radio. Laila went into her room, which still felt empty without Naima in it, and lay on her bed.

⁊⁊

About a month after the competition, Baba answered a knock at the door. Laila went to see who it was, thinking it might be one of the neighbors dropping by for a cup of tea. A young man stood at the door. He wore a suit, but his tie was loosened. "My name is Kareem. I was one of the judges at the Radio Cairo contest," he said.

"And you want a bribe too?" Baba started to close the door, but Kareem held it open.

"Please. Wait. I don't want a bribe," the man said. "I'm here on behalf of Mohamed Abdel Wahab."

Baba let go of the doorknob. He took a step back. "Is this some kind of joke?"

Mohamed Abdel Wahab was one of the biggest actors, singers, composers, and movie producers in Egypt. He'd just starred in *Forbidden Love* with Ragaa Abdou.

"Abdel Wahab doesn't joke," Kareem said. He took a card out of his pocket and gave it to Baba. "See, my name and title are right here. Kareem Al Asyuty, casting director."

Baba held the card in his hand, looking at it for about a minute. Then he looked back up at the man and said, "Come in."

Kareem obliged and entered..

"How do you take your tea?" Baba said.

Mama made a pot of tea, and Baba invited Kareem to sit out on the balcony. The four of them sat in the summer evening breeze, and Baba coughed too often and too hard, cupping his hand in front of his mouth. As he sipped Mama's tea, Kareem explained that he'd been impressed with their performance at the contest. "I thought you'd win," he said. "I'd forgotten all about it, but I thought of you again when we got the script for a new movie that Abdel Wahab is producing. He's starring in the film, of course, and is looking for a girl to play the younger female character. But because it's a musical, he's looking for someone who can sing. Naturally, Laila came to mind, so I got your whereabouts from the contest files."

"Is it a chaste character?" Mama said.

"Yes, ya madam," Kareem said. "The character is young and innocent. In fact, she'll be in traditional Upper Egypt garb. That's where the character is from."

Mama took a sip of her tea and leaned back in her chair.

"The music?" Baba said.

"Abdel Wahab writes and composes all his music. He's just looking for a voice. We'll teach her the music."

"Of course," Baba said.

"What about Baba's song?" Laila asked.

Kareem looked at Baba and then back at Laila. "Maybe Baba's song will make it into the next movie," he said, smiling. "It's a beautiful song, after all. But Abdel Wahab likes to infuse European style into his music."

"Like what?" Baba said, annoyed.

"Like tangoes, sambas, rumbas, that kind of stuff." Then Kareem explained that the audition would be in one month at Studio Masr. "Do the same thing you did for the contest. Don't change a thing," he said, and put down his teacup.

When Kareem left, Baba put his hand on Laila's cheek. "This is the chance we've been waiting for, ya binty. This is what we've been preparing for. And a face like yours was made for film." Baba looked tired, and he lowered himself into his chair. He took Kareem's card out of his pocket. "Laila, go put this inside my music notebook in my armoire." She did as her father said.

In the weeks leading up to the movie audition, Baba's cough worsened. He didn't have the strength to play his oud and slept most of the day and Naima came to visit every other day. Still, Laila practiced singing in the mirror. A few days before the audition, Baba spiked a fever again, and Mama sent for the doctor. He listened to Baba's chest with his stethoscope and, without saying much, gave them two medications to give Baba, one in the morning and one at night.

"It will make him sleepy, but it will help with the chest pain," he said.

Just as they had before, Laila and Mama took turns putting cold compresses on his body throughout the night, but by the morning of the audition, Baba was unresponsive. Laila shook him.

"Wake up, Baba." She put her head on his chest and heard his heart beating and his labored breathing. "Baba, wake up. Baba, please wake up."

"Go get a doctor, any doctor." Mama pulled some money from her bra and put it in Laila's galabeya pocket. "Give it all to him. But go quickly."

Mama kept trying to wake Baba, tapping his face hard, and Laila ran out of the apartment. She ran as fast as she could. The only thing she could think of was to go to the nearest pharmacy and ask for a doctor. At least the pharmacist would know someone.

There was a long line at the pharmacy, and Laila pushed and shoved her way to the front of the line. "I'm sorry," she said. "It's an emergency." A man yelled at her, and the woman who she'd cut in line spat at her, but Laila didn't care. Finally able to talk to the pharmacist, she said, "I need a doctor, any doctor. My father is very sick."

The pharmacist said, "Next building over, first floor. Knock hard. He's usually sleeping at this hour." Laila ran.

It took a few minutes for the doctor to get dressed, and Laila waited outside his apartment door. Then he asked for payment before they even left his building. She gave him all the money she had. "Follow me," she said.

When Laila and the doctor arrived at the building, Haaga Saffeya and Nargis were waiting at the front steps. They told her not to go upstairs, that Mama couldn't wait for Laila and had found another doctor who was already up there with Baba. When Laila refused to wait, the porter tried to hold her back.

"I want to see Baba," she said, and pulled herself out of his grip, running up the stairs, her heart beating frantically.

Nargis tried to catch Laila, but she tripped on the hem of her galabeya by the time Laila passed the first floor. She should have helped Nargis up after her fall, but Laila thought only of getting to Baba. When she reached the third-floor landing, she heard Mama's tortured screams and wails. It was a sound she'd never heard before and would never forget. She looked behind her. The doctor she'd found was gone. She screamed, expelling all the air out of her lungs until her legs collapsed beneath her and she fell to the ground.

8

Haaga Saffeya and Nargis carried Laila up the stairs, and when Laila saw Baba lying on the bed with a sheet over him, she screamed and fainted again. The neighborhood women called for Naima and told her about Baba's passing as gently as they could. Botros was the closest to being Baba's male next of kin, so he and his father washed Baba's body in preparation for burial. That same scorching afternoon, they buried Baba at the Protestant cemetery in accordance with Islamic laws, in which the dead had to be buried the same day they died.

For Laila, faces blurred, days melted into one another, voices faded. The only clear sound that played and replayed, like one of Baba's records, was the sound of her screams when she'd realized Baba had died. After that, sorrow filled her with such heaviness, her legs barely carried her from the bed to the chair, where she sat as visitors came to offer condolences.

In her dreams Baba was still alive. He sang to her, played his oud, took her to the movie theater, patted her head, called her shatoorty. But when the sun rose, he was gone. Sometimes, in the morning, she visited Mama's bedroom to look at Baba's things. She stood in front of the oud case, which sat in the corner. She never dared to open it. Music had died with Baba. She didn't want to hear anyone else play the oud, nor did she want to sing another song.

As the months passed, she got the courage to open the mahogany armoire. Inside, it smelled like musty old wood. Empty hangers swung and clanked against one another where Baba's brown tweed blazer and shirts once hung, a hollow space of his vacated life. The only thing still there was the navy-blue blazer he'd performed in, and on the shelf underneath lay his green leather-bound songbook. She didn't touch any of it.

Madame Caron sent her butler with a meal every day for the first two weeks. But at the end of the two weeks, the butler had a message for Mama. She was to report back to work in Madame Caron's kitchen or she wouldn't have her job any longer. It would be good for her to get back to work, he added before descending the narrow stairs. Naima spit at the threshold when he left. "Tell that to your rotten employer." But Laila had no energy to say or do anything, not even to cry.

"That horrible man is right," Mama said, pushing herself up from the chair where she'd wept for two weeks. "We have to get back to living. Your baba wouldn't have wanted us to succumb this way. He loved life. And he wouldn't have wanted you to spend your first months of marriage here dressed in black, Naima."

"But this is my fault. If it weren't for my wedding, then Baba would still be alive today." Naima sobbed.

"Stop it," Mama said. "Life and death are in the hands of God. You know this, ya binty, so dry your eyes before you go home." Mama tugged on Naima's arm, pulling her up from the settee where she'd been sitting. "Get up. It's time. And you." She approached Laila's chair and smoothed the girl's messy hair. "You have to eat something. It's been days since I've seen you eat." She wore her graying hair in a tight bun, her skin had a yellow tint to it, and her eyes were puffy and swollen. She went into the kitchen, returned with a bowl of rice cooked in sweetened milk, and gave it to Laila. "One bite at a time," Mama said. Then she opened the front door and said to Naima, "Yalla, ya binty, your place is with your husband now."

Naima leaned down and kissed the top of Laila's head. "Take care of yourself and of Mama. I'll visit soon." She wrapped her black shawl around her shoulders and left.

The next morning, on their way to Madame Caron's house, Laila and Mama made a stop at La Delivirande School. "Don't be sad." Mama nudged Laila as they neared the small building. "What you've learned, you won't forget, and what I will teach you next will serve you best. You'll see."

Laila walked on to the building as Mama stood outside the small fenced-in playground where Laila used to eat her lunch as she watched the rich girls play in the big field behind the school, or memorized the French alphabet, or secretly hummed Baba's newest composition. The melodies came to Laila as she entered the school, but she blocked them out by counting her footsteps.

It took thirty-two footsteps to get to Sister Marie's office. The door was open. Her face softened when she saw Laila. "Come in, my girl." She pointed at the chair across from her chipped wooden desk. "Sit down." Laila sat, ashamed of what she had to do. "May he rest in peace, my dear." Sister Marie's voice wavered. "God had other plans for your baba."

In the past year, Laila had improved in school, staying out of trouble, memorizing French vocabulary for homework (though reading was still hard for her and she'd thought she'd never need it), getting high grades in arithmetic. Most of all she learned to keep her voice low, just like the sisters wanted.

"Why does God take people from the ones who love them?" Laila wanted so badly for the sister to give her an answer, something to keep her heart from feeling as though it would stop at any moment.

"Who are we to question God? We are but his servants."

Laila looked down at her black galabeya, fearing her eyes would betray her and reveal her lack of belief. What kind of God inflicts this kind of pain? Her only ally had been Baba, and now there was nobody left to doubt with.

Sister Marie reached across the desk for her hand, and Laila let her hold it. The sister's palms were as weathered as Mama's, and this gave Laila comfort. Comfort she hadn't expected from Sister Marie. After all, she had always been the source of punishment and embarrassment for Laila. Sister Marie had been harsh and unwavering, and Laila had believed her to be incapable of kindness. Yet as Laila held her hand, she longed to throw herself into the depth of the nun's embrace and weep.

"These things are hard for us to understand, Laila. You must have faith. Faith comes from the heart, not the mind. Can you really comprehend eternity?"

Laila looked up at Sister Marie, at her covered hair, the gold cross that hung around her neck. She shook her head. She really didn't understand eternity. The only thing she could think of was the sky and how it never ended, and yet when she tried to imagine it, her thinking seemed to collapse.

"Of course not," Sister Marie said. "See? There is so much we cannot and should not know. Pray, my child. Pray every day and every night. God is love, and he will guide you and grant you peace. Shun the devil when he lingers."

Laila withdrew her hand from Sister Marie's. "I have to work with Mama. There won't be time for school anymore. It must be part of God's plan." She waited for a reaction from Sister Marie.

"Take your books and papers from the classroom. You're a smart girl, Laila. When you're not working, read at night. Review your grammar and mathematics. Don't forget the mathematics. God bless you, my child."

"I love mathematics, Sister Marie. I can calculate in my head, you know."

"Everything is the work of God," Sister Marie said as Laila got up to leave.

From the corridor, Laila heard the teacher giving a grammar lesson. She explained that every noun was either feminine or masculine and took either *la* or *le* before it. When Laila entered the classroom, the teacher stopped her lesson and directed everyone to pray for Laila's baba in heaven. A gasp came from the girls who would never again be her classmates.

When they said amen, Laila took her workbooks and papers out of her front row desk. She drew the bundle to her chest and stepped out before she wept.

Madame Caron kissed Laila and Mama on their foreheads when they arrived at the servants' entrance. "May he rest in peace," she said. Laila hated Madame Caron, and she hated that phrase. Death didn't belong with the words rest and peace. Death was cruel and ugly, and Baba's death was all Madame Caron's fault. Mama didn't dwell on Baba's passing or the bitterness of widowhood. In the kitchen, she held back her tears, though her eyes glistened, and began negotiations.

"There must be a new agreement, Madame. What you ask of me is not one person's job. Because of our new unfortunate circumstances, I can't afford for Laila not to work. I withdrew her from school today." Mama took Laila's hand. "If you can't pay her, tell me now, and I'll look for new employment." Mama looked up at Madame Caron, whose tall and thin body seemed to bend toward Mama, like a tree in a fierce wind, but Mama, short and stout, clad in black, was sturdy and immovable.

Madame Caron reached in the pocket of her long gray skirt, pulled out a cigarette and gold lighter, lit the cigarette, and inhaled. As she drew in her breath, she stood up straight. "Very well," she said, blowing the smoke out of her nose, "but only half. I'll pay her half of what I pay you. After all, she's only fourteen."

Mama shook her head. "She's almost fifteen, and I can't accept half. I will teach her to cook like the best of them in a month. Nothing less than three-quarters of my pay. Otherwise, I leave, and you will need heaven's intervention to find as talented or as honest a person to manage your kitchen day in and day out."

Madame Caron glared at Mama, and Mama glared back. Did Mama blame Madame Caron for Baba's death too? Laila was afraid to say anything to Mama. Madame Caron raised an eyebrow and took another long drag on her cigarette. "I agree, but under one condition. You must leave Signora Morpurgo and be mine full-time. What do you say?"

"Very well. We have a deal." Mama took off her black shawl and laid it in a bundle on the kitchen table. "Now, tell me, what would you like me to prepare this week?"

"My husband has been craving duck confit. And now that I know you're mine alone, I'll teach you food the real French way. I grow the herbs in my garden, you know." Madame Caron took off her rings and placed them in a bowl on the windowsill above the sink. "I learned everything from my mother. How I miss her and our chateau."

Madame Caron spent months in the kitchen with Laila and Selma. Each day she taught them how to make a new dish. First, she taught them the sauces, but she skipped béchamel sauce. Mama had already mastered it at Signora Morpurgo's, and even though it was the Italian way, Madame Caron said it would do for now. So, she taught them velouté, espagnole, hollandaise, and sauce tomat. When she spoke the name of a sauce or a dish, she insisted that Mama and Laila repeat after her. She instructed them on how to shape their lips to produce the correct sound. Laila pronounced well on account of her short stint at a French school, but Madame Caron said Mama's pronunciation was hopeless. "Mafeesh faydah," she said in her broken Arabic. After that she insisted that only Laila learn the name of the foods. "Say cassoulet," she'd say, opening her mouth and narrowing it. Or "Say, coq au vin."

It took six months for Madame Caron to trust Mama and Laila to cook food her way. Mama made small changes to the recipes when Madame Caron wasn't around. She added more salt and crushed extra garlic. She ground up the thyme with a mortar and pestle instead of cutting it with a knife. She put a sprinkle of ground red pepper in the espagnole sauce to give it a flair.

Madame Caron never noticed. She just complimented Mama for following instructions and took credit for being both a talented cook and teacher. Mama and Laila laughed in the kitchen. The first time they laughed after Baba's death, they looked at each other, stopped immediately, and continued chopping, peeling, and boiling in silence.

When Baba was alive, the music always separated Laila from her mother. Now, the kitchen had brought them together, and for the first time Mama told Laila stories. She told her about the small village she'd come from and about her parents, who'd died one after the other. She told her how village people's accents sounded, and how strict her own mother had been. "I was so terrified of my baba, I sometimes peed in my pants when he yelled." She told Laila about Baba in his younger days when he'd courted her, when he'd come round to the small farmhouse and play his oud, luring Mama into a web of love. "I was young then. Young and naive, but your father, Allah yerhamoo, he was a good man with a big heart."

During these times Laila felt as though she'd just met Mama, that the woman cutting and cooking next to her wasn't her mother at all but a neighbor who'd maybe just moved in, a new friend. The work they did together was tedious and mundane. It couldn't and wouldn't transport Laila as music had. She wouldn't love it as she had loved music, but there was comfort in repetition, in routine, and in a practical skill. She understood this now in a way she never could have if Baba were still alive. This made her want to love her mother more.

At home, Mama taught Laila to sew the way she'd taught Naima. Though Laila didn't like sewing she didn't resist learning because it distracted her, and it was the only way she and Mama would survive. Baba had left them with nothing. First, Laila learned to mend. Then Mama taught her to follow patterns, to embroider, and to design simple dresses. Sometimes they didn't have sewing work, and those were the times when Mama prayed under her breath, cried in her bed. Laila heard her, for Mama's whimpers seeped through the thin wall separating their rooms. What Madame Caron paid them both barely covered the rent, utilities, and food.

Laila learned how to buy the cheaper things with Mama. She'd never shopped before Baba had died because she'd been too busy singing. At the market they bought broken rice, bones for soup, trimmings of leftover fat to flavor the okra stew, brown bananas, and day-old bread. Sometimes

Mama put the bread in the soup. Its stale, resistant grit against the teeth was more tolerable that way. The broken rice required longer hours of sifting because dirt and pieces of tiny pebbles nestled in poor people's rice. When there was sewing work, Mama saved the little money they earned in a jar that she kept on the shelf above the stove, next to the pickled beets.

Until the day of Baba's arbeyeen, the forty days post-mortem memorial, Naima came to visit every day. Afterwards, she only came on Fridays. Mama said that for forty days after his death Baba's soul would wander, visiting places he'd known like their small apartment, the coffee shop, and his fresh grave, but that after the fortieth day, after the priest had said his holy prayers, that God would escort Baba to heaven and that his soul would wander no more. But Laila knew this wasn't true.

Baba had once explained it all to her on one of their many visits to the pyramids. He'd loved to compose music on the Giza plateau and observe the pyramids against the rising sun. He'd often taken Laila with him. Once he told her that the arbeyeen wasn't a Christian tradition at all, but the result of the brilliant ancient Egyptian mummification process in which the Pharaoh's body would be soaked in salt for forty days to prepare the body for eternal life.

When the body was removed from the salt in preparation for the next phase of mummification, ancient priests preformed special incantations. "This is the origin of our music," he'd once said before filling a fresh page with notes. Laila had known then when to be quiet so that the music would come to Baba and stay long enough to be written.

One October day around the sixth month after her wedding, Naima arrived for her weekly visit later than usual. Mama and Laila were sitting on the balcony sifting through their weekly rice. Naima took a seat beside them and helped. Her hands were dry, her nails cracked and uneven.

"I'm pregnant," she said as she sifted rice.

Mama hugged her and kissed her on both cheeks. "How I want to let out a zaghrouta, ya binty, but it hasn't been a year yet, and ..."

"I know, Mama. It's all right."

Laila kissed her sister too. "How do you feel? Are you happy?"

"I feel awful. I can't stand the smell of food. I vomit all day. I can't keep my eyes open no matter how many hours I sleep. My mother-in-law thinks I'm making it up so I don't have to work, but I really feel sick, Mama. I don't know what to do."

"I never liked that woman," Laila said, and Mama kicked her foot.

"I'll send the porter to tell her that I'm keeping you here for a few days, just until you feel better."

"What about Botros?"

"He can come too. You two can sleep in your old room and Laila can sleep next to me." Laila couldn't bear the thought of sleeping in Baba's old spot.

Naima shook her head. "No, I have to go home."

"Then have dinner with us tonight, and you can go back home."

Mama made Naima a light soup of chicken broth and rice, then she boiled ginger to make a tea for her. "The first few months are hard, but after that, you'll be just fine. You'll see."

As Naima sipped the soup, Laila saw that her face was drawn and pale. Marriage was supposed to be hana, not this misery.

As she was leaving that night, Naima threw herself into Mama's arms. "I'm scared," she said.

Mama took Naima's face in her hands. "Don't be silly, ya binty. Every woman you see has given birth to four, five, or ten children. Once you have the baby in your arms, you'll forget the world and you will feel the sort of happy only a mother can understand."

After Naima left that night, Mama sat in Baba's old chair and said, "I pray your sister has a boy. Otherwise that old crow of a mother-in-law will never let her live it down."

For nearly three years, Laila kept to her place in Madame Caron's kitchen where she mourned her father, there she experienced fullness of loss as she chopped, peeled, fried, sauteed and baked. Baba's death was the death of their shared dream. She grieved that part of herself that could never again dream of a stage and an audience. She'd never know how that audition might have gone. These chances come once in a lifetime and then opportunity's door shuts and locks forever. But it didn't matter. Without Baba it was all tasteless.

She never wandered around the house like she used to as a child. When she entered the den or the music room, she did so in her capacity as the cook or the occasional helper.

Sometimes Catherine greeted Laila if she saw her in the kitchen. "Bonjour, Laila," she'd sing in a carefree voice. Twice a year when Catherine cleaned her closet, she stopped in the kitchen to give Laila a bag of gently used dresses, most of which Mama altered, lengthening or loosening to make them decent enough for church. From the kitchen window, Laila would watch Catherine take her daily swim or play tennis on the clay courts beyond the pool. Once a week, she heard her practice piano with a Russian teacher. Catherine didn't have an ear for music, and when she played the wrong keys, Laila cringed and grit her teeth.

Almost two years after Baba died, Egypt went to war against a new country called Israel. Laila had heard Madame Caron talking about it to her husband over dinner. Israel, he'd said, was the fulfillment of a promise the British had made to the Jews. It would be a short war, Mr. Caron had said, but Laila didn't understand why, and now that Baba was gone, she'd had nobody to ask.

Mama didn't understand it either. She only told Laila that the porter had said that Egypt wasn't at war alone, that Syria and Jordan were fighting too. "It's got something to do with the British mucking up our borders and dividing us as they wish," Mama had explained to Laila as they cored zucchini, the green of it coating their hands. Then she stopped only for a second to look at Laila. "Your father was right, Allah yerhamoo. The British have brought us nothing but heartache and calamity. What can we do? It's all in God's hands. He will do what he sees fit." Then she returned to coring Madame Caron's zucchinis. It was the last conversation Laila had of the war which lasted less than a year.

Though Laila had tried to block any longing for a time when she used to sing with Baba, when Catherine had her lessons Laila felt a fresh stabbing pain of loss. It wasn't just in her mind or heart. She felt loss in her body, a stinging, falling sensation that rushed from her head down her spine to her toes. To cope with it she made other noises. She turned on the faucet to wash lettuce or crushed extra batches of garlic with the mortar and pestle, and she focused only on the action she was doing, training her eyes and ears on the repetitive, hypnotic motion of her hands.

One spring morning a few months after the war had ended, Madame Caron came into the kitchen and gave Selma a bag. "This is for you to wear."

Mama peeked inside the bag and then looked at Madame Caron. "What in the name of God is this?"

"One is for you and the other is for Laila. You see, I'm having a birthday party for Catherine in two weeks." She smiled. "She'll be seventeen, a young woman."

Mama reached in and took out a black maid's uniform with white lace trim, a white collar, and an apron that tied around the waist.

"You want us to wear these scandalous dresses? What for? Why?" Mama held them out in disgust as if they smelled bad.

"Please. Just for the birthday party. You're the only people I trust. Oh, don't worry. I'll hire people to wash the dishes and do whatever else you need, but I want you to make the food and serve the appetizers. You must understand there will be important people here, and I can't have you be seen wearing a galabeya. It simply won't do. Not for this party."

Mama put the uniforms back in the bag. "I'll try it on, but if it's too revealing, I will add length to it and loosen it from the haunch."

"All right, Selma, do what you wish with it, but please, just for the party, wear it, for God's sake."

Selma and Laila cooked for a week before Catherine's party. Madame Caron said that fifty people were invited. "I want a long table with only French cuisine, just the way I taught you." She listed the menu, counting the items on one hand. "I want boeuf bourguignon, coq au vin, cassoulet, au gratin, and duck confit." She shifted her glance from Laila to Selma, as if searching for tacit agreement. "Yes, and we should have salade niçoise to start. For the hors d'oeuvres, which you'll be passing around, Laila, we absolutely must have gougère, saumon fumé, and of course foie gras en croûte." She stopped and surveyed the kitchen. "We'll need another refrigerator, won't we?"

"Another refrigerator?" Mama said. "You'll need another kitchen. Fifty people?"

"Very well, I'll have all the ingredients delivered and I'll see about the extra refrigerator." She smiled; her eyes filled with glee.

Madame Caron assembled an army to prepare for Catherine's birthday. Several gardeners tended to the herb garden, the mango trees, the flower beds, and her beloved sunflowers from France, which had flourished over the years. The maids polished every piece of mahogany furniture, and Madame Caron insisted they polish the dining room table and console twice. The extra but temporary servants were tasked with washing every rug in the villa, taking down every curtain, and polishing the silver serving bowls. The baseboards and chair rails were repainted, and the marble floors polished.

Madame Caron rented round tables, white chairs, and white table-cloths, and the butler set them up around the swimming pool. Inside the villa, part of the parlor was emptied, and long buffet tables were set up against two walls. A space was made for a dance floor for les jeunes, and a large round brass table was set in the corner for Catherine's birthday cake, which Madame Caron had ordered from Café Groppi, the famous bakery in downtown Cairo. When she arranged the silver platters along the hot buffet and the cold buffet tables as a trial setup, she realized that the table for cold foods would look empty, so she added more items to the menu.

"Selma, I want to add salade des tomates, salade des carottes, and salade des pommes de terre."

Immediately Mama and Laila went to the market, stood in line at the vegetable stands, and walked to Madame Caron's in the heat carrying heavy bags of tomatoes, carrots, and potatoes. In the kitchen they washed and peeled the vegetables. Mama sliced the potatoes and soaked them in water to keep them from browning. That night they returned home so tired that Mama fell asleep in Baba's chair, skipping dinner; and Laila slept in her work clothes on top of her cotton bedspread so she wouldn't get the sheets dirty.

The day before the party, Madame Caron pulled Laila aside and showed her the proper way to serve hors d'oeuvres. "When you serve, you must smile, just slightly, a polite smile. Don't look anyone in the eyes. Look at their shoulders. But that won't be hard for you since you're short. You'll hold the tray like this." She demonstrated with one hand. "And when they ask what it is, you must know each food. You remember what I taught you?" Laila nodded. "And never touch the food. Let the guest select. Each soft hors d'oeuvres will have one of these in it." She pointed at a box filled with ivory toothpicks that sat on the mahogany table. "But the items on crackers will be picked up by hand, so you will need to hand them a small silk napkin."

On the day of the party, Laila stood in the grand foyer holding a silver tray of hors d'oeuvres that she was to offer to each guest. The uniform skirt fell to her knees, and though she wore white stockings, her legs felt bare. The guests arrived promptly. Women wore long beaded dresses in navy or black and made of silk, taffeta, and lace. As they reached for an hors d'oeuvre, Laila observed the impeccable embroidery on the décolleté or bodice of their gowns, their diamond necklaces, and large gem rings. They smelled of rich oils, maybe sweet almond, rose, jasmine, and other scents similar to incense. Each family brought a birthday gift for Catherine. All the gifts came in large boxes wrapped in silver, red, or gold paper.

The younger girls, Catherine's friends, wore bright colors like yellow, pink, and baby blue. Catherine descended the staircase in a lace-trimmed lavender gown. It was strapless, cinched at the waist, and flared out in a long tulle skirt. Her blond hair was pulled up in an elegant chignon. It was the first time Laila had ever seen anyone in a strapless gown, and every young man there—all of them dressed in suits and ties, with silk handkerchiefs in the jackets' breast pockets—turned to look at her. All except for one, who tilted his head, made eye contact with Laila, and said "Merci" as he reached for a foie gras en croûte. He was taller than the rest, had light brown hair slicked back with pomade, and big hazel eyes with long lashes. She didn't know how to respond. Madame Caron didn't say anything about conversing with the guests, and she was afraid.

Then she remembered her first few lessons at La Delivirande. "De rien," she replied.

"A maid who speaks French?" He seemed surprised, as if he hadn't expected a reply at all.

"I'm not a maid. I'm a cook," she said, focusing on his shoulders, just as Madame Caron had instructed her to when speaking to guests.

But he leaned down, forcing her to look at him. He wore a gold chain with a gold cross pendant hanging from it. "Where are you from?"

She shook her head. She wanted to tell him to stop talking to her. He smiled. "You're from the city of No?"

"Rod El Farag," she said softly.

A girl in a yellow off-the-shoulder gown tapped on his shoulder. "Allons-y, Amir, it's time for the dances."

"Pardon," he said to Laila, and then he took the girl's arm and led her to the dance floor.

When he left, Laila struggled to steady her hand, angry with him for noticing her, for talking to her.

Madame Caron had hired a man to entertain the guests. He had brought with him several record players and changed records after each song. The adults took their seats outside by the swimming pool, but Catherine's friends continued dancing. The girls giggled and blushed as the boys took them by the hand and led them to the dance floor. They danced to songs Laila had never heard before. If Mama had caught a glimpse of this scene, she'd have called it the devil's work. Laila had never been touched by a boy, nor would she be until her wedding night. Though marriage had never been on her mind like other girls. The notion of marriage and motherhood had gotten lost between her old singing, aspirations of stardom, and now poverty. Still, good girls didn't behave like Catherine and her friends.

She had observed this kind of life when she went with Baba to see him play in hotel lobbies, when she saw movies at the theater, but it was the first time she'd watched someone she actually knew have this kind of freedom. Seeing these girls dancing with different partners, their mothers and fathers sitting around them drinking champagne as if this were all normal, reminded her just how different she was from these rich foreigners. Before Baba had died Laila had never compared herself to the Carons, never longed for their wealth. She'd had her own treasure with Baba and it had consumed her. But on this day Laila imagined Mama resting on Madame Caron's chair for once in her life, sipping on something sweet, and she imagined herself in a beautiful silk dress with her hair up in a fancy do and her nails painted in red. Still, she had her pride and wouldn't let herself cross into envy. So, she stopped imagining. Baba had always taught that the only difference between the rich and the poor was money, and money came and went.

When it was time to set up the buffet, Laila took the silver platters into the kitchen for Mama to fill and then returned to place each one on the tables. There were twenty-two platters in total, and Laila came and went twenty-two times. Mama had looked tired all day, and she sat on the kitchen chair a moment at a time to take the weight off her swelling feet. Under the harsh kitchen light, her graying hair looked thin and wiry, and the blue under her eyes looked almost black. The wrinkles around her mouth seemed deeper. Though she was younger than Madame Caron, Mama looked a decade older.

As she was rushing in and out of the kitchen, Laila saw the boy named Amir dancing with Catherine. He held her close to him, and Catherine's hand was on his shoulder. She looked like a flower in her lavender dress, and the studded hairpins in her chignon sparkled like stars in the night sky. For a moment, Laila stopped to watch, imagining herself in Catherine's place, just for that one dance. But the butler tapped her on the shoulder, pointed at his watch, and gave her a disapproving glare.

Later in the evening, after dinner, when Laila was carrying a platter back to the kitchen, she felt someone's hand on her waist. "I saw you watching us dance." She recognized his voice.

She jerked away, and some sauce au poivre spattered on her uniform. How dare he touch her?

"I have work to do. Excuse me." She continued toward the kitchen.

"Wait," he said. She stopped, her back to him.

"I know you saw us dancing. Would you like to dance like that?"

"No," she lied, and hurried to the kitchen.

9

CAIRO, 1949

When people referred to Amir's father, they always uttered his first name, middle name, and official title together. Spoken, those three words became one entity, like a holy trinity. Makram Youseff Pasha. The title of pasha evoked in Egyptians a vision of a man dressed in a military uniform decorated with medals, wearing a red sash across his broad chest and a felt tarbush upon his head; in his grip a long standard given to him by the late King Fuad at an official ceremony in Giza Palace.

Makram Youseff Pasha owned a textile factory in Cairo and two-thousand feddans of land in Aswan along the Nile. There, cotton fields stretched until ground met sky, and the eye became confused between the fluff of cotton and the clouds of heaven. The fellaheen, eternally poor, labored the lands on the backs of donkeys, planting, watering, harvesting; their thin, sun-soaked faces and hands browned and cracked. The cotton that grew in those fields was the long- staple variety, the best kind; and when it was made into cloth, it was strong, silky, lustrous, and soft. But most Egyptians never felt the softness of their own cotton because it was sold to well-paying foreigners. The cotton was harvested, delivered to the factory in Cairo, spun into textile, and loaded on ships headed for Europe and America. And so, the family's land was the womb from which all their wealth was born, and Amir was the only heir to it.

When Amir was a boy and his father took him to visit the cotton farms, he would often stand by the riverbank and imagine himself floating up the Nile, carried by its dark fertile waters. He'd close his eyes and see himself journeying along the water like a leaf, from the cotton fields in Aswan to their house in Cairo, meandering for days through the tens of villages in between.

The villagers would wave at him and he would wave back. When he took this imaginary journey, he never got wet, never sleepy, never cold, never hungry. Eventually, when he'd gotten his fill of citron sunsets and starlit skies, the Nile would magically deposit him in Zamelek, on the eastern shore of Gezira Island, in front of his mansion. He'd open the wrought iron gates and walk past the swimming pool and the gardens of bougainvillea and jasmine. Then, unaffected by gravity, he'd scale the sides of the gold-plated marble edifice and climb onto the second-floor balcony that led to his bedroom. Inside his princely room there was a large gold-framed bed above which hung a crystal chandelier. When he was a child, he imagined that by night the chandelier transformed into a large spider, and that as soon as he was alone it would climb out of the ceiling to devour him. Amir cried every night for his mother, but no matter how many times he screamed, "Mama Hoda!" she never came. Instead, she sent in one of the nannies to assuage his fears. Nobody conquered the crystal spider until Hakima came to live with them. She was from southern Egypt, just like all the servants. She was his favorite nanny, the only one who, in private, called him my son; and although it was just a term of endearment, he'd never heard those tender words from either of his parents.

Hakima used to pull him close to her warm chest when he shivered with terror, kiss the top of his head, and say, "Ya ibny, don't be afraid. Hakima is here. I will crush anything that dares to hurt you." She always smelled like sweetened milk and honey, and when she put her weathered hand on his cheek, he reveled in its safety. Anyone with hands that rough must know how to fight off spiders. All the nannies who'd come before Hakima had fled the mansion on account of Amir's unmanageable behavior, his disrespect, his complete disregard for rules. He snuck into one nanny's room at night, rustled the curtains, and pulled on the sheets until she was convinced the house was haunted and fled in terror. His next nanny suffered a bad fall and broke her leg after Amir irritably dropped oil in the hallway. His parents had to send that one back home. With the nanny just before Hakima, Amir refused to take baths and ran from her every night until she breathlessly gave up and left. But Hakima stayed. She endured Amir's shenanigans, somehow inducing feelings of guilt and remorse in him so that from the time he was eight years old, one look from her could make him abandon any mischief.

One day when Amir was ten, his father burst into his bedroom waving his report card. As usual, Amir had been sitting in front of an easel, painting.

"So, this is what you do with your time, you donkey?" Makram Youseff Pasha crumpled the report card and threw it across the room. "Who gave you permission to paint?"

Throughout his short life, Amir didn't spend much time with his father, and when he did, the pasha's formidable presence rendered Amir speechless. He just looked at his father and then at the floor where the crumpled paper had landed.

"Average?" his father yelled. "My son average? I got you tutors, didn't I? You should have improved by now." He lunged toward the easel, pulled the small canvas down, and stepped on it. It cracked and tore. Then he flipped over the palette of paints Amir had been using. Red, blue, green, and yellow splashes of paint splattered across the parquet floor. Amir wished his father had beaten him instead of destroying the painting. As he left the room, his father said, "Don't you understand that you're the only heir to all of this?" He fanned his hand around the room. "Don't you see that I need you to be serious, to be a man, to take over the empire when

I'm gone? I don't want to die knowing that all I've built will end up in the hands of a damn painter." Then he slammed the door, his heavy footsteps fading as he descended the stairs.

Hakima helped him clean the paint off the floor. "Ya ibny," she said, "don't be sad. Your father means well. You're his only son, al waheed. He's right to be worried." As she picked up the broken painting, she stopped for a moment and gazed at the torn canvas. "What were you painting?"

"The lands in Aswan, the Nile, and the sky, but I don't want to look at it anymore." He turned his head so that all the shades, shapes, and outlines were out of his sight. "I don't want to paint ever again."

She left the painting on the floor, took his hand, and both of them sat on the edge of his bed. "You can always paint in your mind. You can look at anything you want in your mind. You can create pictures, stories, songs, or poems. In my village, people don't know how to read or write, but they make poetry in their head and then they recite it. You can lock whatever you want in here"—she tapped a finger on his temple—"and nobody can take that away from you."

When she said that to him, Amir felt a new freedom. Even though he was imprisoned in the cage of his father's iron will, his thoughts were his. He didn't paint again, but when he noticed beauty, he captured it in his mind, cataloguing images, hues, contours, reflection. Beauty was everywhere. It was pleasure. It was in nature, in objects, and eventually he realized that the ultimate beauty was in women.

After the day Makram Youseff Pasha found his son painting, he started taking Amir hunting on the last Friday of every month. They hunted quail in autumn and desert animals like hyenas. Once Amir almost shot a desert gazelle, but he couldn't pull the trigger. The gazelle was a beauty, and unlike the birds he'd shot in the past, he was close enough to the gazelle to see its eyes. His father took the rifle from him.

"To be a good hunter, you must be fearless and merciful." He leaned in, closed one eye. "And kill quickly." He pulled the trigger, and the gazelle fell over, leaving a cloud of sand in its wake. Then Makram Yousef Pasha waved at the gofer who waited in the car. "Go pick it up," he shouted, and his voice echoed against the desert cliffs. Then he patted Amir on the back. "Have you ever had gazelle stew?"

That night when the servant put the large clay pot of gazelle and potato stew on the table, Amir saw only the gazelle's eyes; and when she ladled the stew in his bowl, he pushed the food around without taking a single bite.

"You're not eating," Makram Youseff Pasha said.

Amir scooped only the rice on his fork and swallowed it quickly.

After dinner, he vomited the little he had eaten. Hakima helped him change into fresh pajamas and brought him rose water to drink. "Bil shifa, Insha Allah," she said, wishing him a speedy recovery, and ran her fingers through his hair as he drifted to sleep.

In school, Amir tried to apply himself, and though his grades improved, he was never at the top of his class. He never cared enough about book knowledge, not like his classmates who talked about Hafez, democracy, and the theory of relativity, who shared books with one another and passed them around. Amir didn't care for books. They were cumbersome and impractical. He liked things he could touch and see, things he could collect and store. He collected rocks, stamps, coins, ties, and silk handkerchiefs. If he saw something and he liked it, he wanted more of it and started a collection. When he felt uneasy, he'd open his albums and flip through the coins, running his fingers along them. Or he'd open his closet and look at his possessions; knowing they were still there was pleasure in and of itself. For Amir, owning something, anything, gave him the same fleeting satiation of having a large hot meal. Soon it was forgotten, and he was hungry again. Whenever his father returned from a business trip, he'd hand Amir a coin from a faraway place. "For your collection," he'd say, and nod approvingly.

When he was sixteen, Amir heard his mother's shriek come from her bedroom. "It's gone. It's gone and I know who took it." Her voice reverberated off the mansion's domed ceilings. Hakima was with Amir in his room, making his bed and tidying his books and papers for school, when his mother burst into the room. She pushed the door open with such force that the papers rustled. "My diamond." Hoda pointed at Hakima. "Where is my diamond? Answer me."

"My lady, please stay calm. I don't know what you're talking about."

"Well, then, let me remind you." Hoda lunged, her long silk robe billowing behind her, and grabbed Hakima by the arm.

Amir, half a foot taller than his mother, stepped in front of Hakima and tore his mother's hand off her arm. "You," he said to his mother as she heaved in anger, "are not allowed to touch her. She has no use for your stupid diamonds, and you know that."

"She stole my diamond. Don't defend her." Hoda's voice shook.

"Get out of my room." Amir pointed at the door.

Hoda stepped back, studied Amir's face, and left the room.

Hakima stood still where Hoda had attacked her, her shaking hands on her cheeks, her face flushed. "She's your mother," she cried, tears streaming down her face. "You shouldn't have talked to her like that."

Amir took Hakima in his arms, patted the top of her head, and said, "I'm your son and you're my mother, and that's all."

After that, Hakima carried the sadness on her face, atop her shoulders that hunched, in her eyes that lost their brightness. She ate less, drank less, lost weight. Amir worried about her. He even got her a doctor, but the doctor said there was nothing wrong with her. All she needed, he explained, was some rest. One night she went to sleep and didn't wake up. Even now, seven years later, Amir still cried over Hakima, still missed her. Every year on the date of her death, he cut a single red rose from his garden and put it on her grave. A few months after Hakima died, Hoda found her diamond in a small crevice in the floor behind her dressing table.

ৎৎ

Amir stepped onto his bedroom balcony thinking of Laila and keenly felt the weight of his father's factories and the bales of cotton that supplied them, the executive position he held in the prosperous company, and the endless, repetitive meetings with buyers. He unbuttoned his shirt collar to stop the suffocation he was feeling. There was nothing about the family business that he liked except for the money. He cast his gaze beyond the estate gates to the sycamore trees that lined the wide bustling street and longed to escape into the dusking saffron sky. Branches blew in the twilight's breeze, and men trickled out onto the street for another splendid Cairene evening.

Where would he go that night? *All About Eve* was playing at Cinema Metro. He'd talked to his friends about going to see it, but Om Kalsoum was singing in Azbakeya Gardens. Or he could just listen to the live broadcast of her on Radio Cairo. Maybe later, he'd spend time in the bar at Shepheards Hotel, flirting with a French blonde or Italian brunette, drinking himself into exquisite inebriation. If things went well, and they usually did, he could take one of the women back to his apartment in Heliopolis, the one he'd rented solely so he could make love to any woman he fancied.

But everything bored him these days. In the last several weeks, since that servant girl had snubbed him at the Caron party, even the sweetest diversions had become monotonous and tasteless. He'd nearly worn out his *Songs by Sinatra* album, and Billie Holiday had lost her effect on him. Even Edith Piaf couldn't pull him out of his dark abyss; and reading poetry, though salvation for other fools, was too much effort for his restless soul. His friends were of no use now. They were all occupied with their futile politics. Of late the topics on everyone's tongue were Egypt's failure to protect Palestine and the formation of the state of Israel. It was King Farouk's fault, they said, his shame. It was his ineptness that led to an abysmal Egyptian military with its poorly trained soldiers and dilapidated equipment. The king was only concerned with his art collection, his car collection, his women. All of this at the expense of the Egyptian people.

Amir never cared for these types of discussions. Besides, he happened to like King Farouk. After all, the royal family had been an ally to his family, and facilitated much of their business. What did it matter if the king liked to have things, and who cared about Palestine?

That girl, though. That girl holding a silver platter. She was the kind of natural rabany beauty that couldn't be found in elegant salons or bars or hotels. What was it about her, the few words she'd spoken, her eyes she'd tried to avert from his? Was it her pink lips, petite frame, shiny ebony hair? Or maybe he'd just liked the way she said no, unafraid, even a little daring. But she couldn't have been that daring. After all, she was just a servant. What kinds of experience could she have possibly had? Even as she'd held the tray, her hands had trembled, not noticeably, but enough for Amir to sense her newness to a way of life that for him was so familiar. In some ways, she reminded him of Aisha, one of the many family servants he'd had when he was growing up.

Aisha had been responsible for the laundry and the cleaning, the grocery shopping, and the scrubbing of the floors. She cut vegetables and watered the roses, lavender, and dahlias around their mansion. Perhaps he was twelve or thirteen, he didn't remember, and maybe she was fifteen or sixteen. He used to watch her when she scrubbed the bathroom floors on her hands and knees, making white suds all over the slippery tiles.

He would study the curves of her body beneath her dress, which often got wet and clung to the most beautiful places. In those days, he hadn't seen a naked woman. He had only imagined what lay underneath Aisha's galabeya, though at times it gaped in the front to reveal a peek of her nipples. She was the first girl he'd truly craved. He had resigned himself to just musing about her, until one night she visited his dark room. She didn't ask anything or explain her presence.

She just crawled under the sheets and put her hands on him while he got hard. Then she guided his hands under her galabeya, allowing them to wander all the parts of her body, exposing to his touch what was secret by day.

For months they did this every night after his parents and Hakima had fallen asleep, fondling and climaxing together. And during those months he thought only of her, lived only for the darkness of his midnight room, the fleshy scent of the two of them together. Then one day he came home from school to find Aisha was gone. His mother had ordered her back to her family in Upper Egypt, back to the crops of sugarcane and cotton and beans, back where the Nile drifted downward and northward toward the Mediterranean.

When Amir asked his mother why he'd sent Aisha away, she said, "You know why, and never ask me about her again."

Amir always regretted not being able to fight his mother for Aisha. There had been too many social barriers for him to overcome, and he had no way of bringing Aisha back even if he'd wanted to because he didn't know exactly where she lived. For years after she left, Amir dreamed of Aisha, longing to once again feel her warm breath on his neck and to taste her confection kisses. He still recalled the feel of her long silky hair between his fingertips and her golden body against his skin. Now he was feeling that same maddening gravitational pull from the servant girl, and he was in a position to do something about it.

Gathering information about her was the easiest part of his quest. As soon as he'd learned that her name was Laila, he repeated it to himself, letting the l's fall off his tongue in the privacy of his room, as if saying her name might summon her body to his. The only things he'd been able to coax out of her at the party was that she was from Rod El Farag, so that's where he started.

First, he sent their driver's son, Basyouni, on a mission to Laila's neighborhood, armed with a stack of bills to buy information. Then Amir waited. A day later, Basyouni returned with Laila's entire history.

"You're better than government intelligence." Amir patted Basyouni's back and gave him a twenty-five piastre note.

Basyouni folded the bill and stuffed it into his pocket. Then he told Amir about Laila's beautiful voice, her sister, Naima, and her mother-in-law, the St. George church they all went to on Sundays, the old conflicts between Laila's father and mother over Laila's singing at cafes, and how she and her mother cooked and sewed to survive.

"You got all of this from the fruit saleslady?"

"No, I got this from the bread vendor who works Naima's neighborhood. His sister knows the tenant on the first floor of her building?"

"Does Laila have any prospects? Has she ever been engaged or ..."

"No. She has an impeccable reputation. She's never been seen as much as talking to a man. And since her father died, nobody has proposed to her. Poverty can be a deterrent." Basyouni had a thin tan face and big teeth that protruded from his top lip when he spoke. When he made the slightest effort, beads of sweat dripped down his face and trickled along his neck onto his shirt collar.

As Basyouni recounted what he'd learned, Amir painted Laila for himself on an empty canvas. With every new stroke of color, her picture became clearer, and he folded her into his life. "Good work," he said. "Now, I want you to observe every step she makes. I want to know what time she leaves her apartment, what streets she takes, where she goes on her days off. I want to know everything. And if you deliver, I will put more notes into your pocket. If the information turns out to be inaccurate, you'll never work for me again."

A week later, Basyouni told Amir that Laila went to the market every morning and then headed to Zamalek with her mother, each of them carrying a tote of groceries. At night, she and her mother walked home over Kasr Al Nil Bridge. Fridays, their day off, they stayed home, and Sundays they went to church. "She's never alone," Basyouni said.

"Keep watching her." Amir gave him a one-pound note. Basyouni put it in his pocket, then pulled it out to glance at it before he pushed it back down deep in his pocket. "Everybody does something alone." Amir shoved Basyouni by the shoulder. "Now go. I'm losing my patience." Basyouni left.

Not being able to talk to Laila, even to see her, frustrated Amir, and the longer he waited, the deeper his desire for her became. He dreamed of her. When friends talked to him, he only caught parts of what they said. How would he get Laila? What would her skin feel like? How would she taste when he kissed her? What would her pleasure sound like?

It wasn't until a full month after the birthday party that Basyouni returned to Amir with a new detail. Some Sundays after church, when Laila and her mother didn't have work at the Caron house and Laila's sister didn't go to church, Laila walked alone from the Saint George church to her sister's apartment, while her mother returned home. "But it's not every Sunday. And there's no way to know when her sister won't go to church."

"It's all right. I'll manage from here, Basyouni. You've done good work."

Basyouni bowed his head in his deferential manner as Amir gave him another one-pound note.

Every Sunday for three weeks, Amir drove his Cadillac convertible over Kasr Al Nil Bridge and out of Zamalek. He parked across from the church and watched for Laila to exit through the heavy wooden doors. Most of the time her sister attended with her husband and son, and Laila walked home with them. He hated the waiting, hated this godforsaken part of Cairo; void of gardens, overcrowded and dusty, sidewalks broken, buildings old and cracked. But Amir was hunting. Patience and accuracy were the keys to success.

On the third week, Naima didn't leave the church with Laila. Amir watched Laila kiss her mother on the cheek. As soon as mother and daughter parted, Amir got out of his car and began following Laila; down Shubra Street, onto Bolaq Road, and over Al Laymoun Bridge, where lime vendors sold their fruit, and under which trains rumbled in and out of the railway station.

Laila walked fast, and she weaved in and out of crowds with skill. Each time Amir considered approaching her, she was already crossing a street or ensconced in a large crowd of pedestrians.

Finally, when they got over the bridge, she stopped at an ice cream vendor on the corner. She reached in her bag, pulled out a few coins, looked at them for a moment, and then put them back into her bag. She kept walking, but luckily Ramses Street, the last crossing before her sister's building, was crowded and difficult to cross. Amir quickly devised a plan. He stopped at the ice cream vendor, cutting in front of the line and giving the man behind him a pound to quell his outrage, ordered two ice creams, and rushed to the corner. He tapped Laila on the shoulder. It was the first time he'd seen her face that close since she'd said no to him.

He held the two cones out to her, as if this conversation were a continuation of many before it. "I wasn't sure if you liked strawberry or vanilla, so I bought one of each." The ice cream had already begun to melt. She didn't say anything, a vacuous look on her face. Did she remember him at all? She didn't reach for a cone. "Yalla, take one before it melts. Didn't you want ice cream? I saw you looking at it."

She reached for the vanilla, still silent, but as the crowd began to cross the street, she didn't. She stepped to the side, letting the impatient mass pass her by.

"Most people would say merci." He licked his strawberry ice cream from the side so that it didn't drip on his suit jacket. "Look, you better eat it or it's going to get all over you." He bit into the side of his cone.

She started on her ice cream. She looked at him, then at the ice cream vendor, and then at the crowded street. He wished he could kiss her despite that awful galabeya she was wearing, her worn-out sandals, and her chipped fingernails. He wanted to undo her tight braid that was coiled up into an awkward bun and run his fingers through her long black hair, watch it spill over his satin pillows. "You remember me, don't you?"

She nodded and took a small bite of her melting ice cream, dabbed her full pinkish lips with her fingers, and said, "You really liked the foie gras en croûte."

"No, I liked you. The foie gras was just an excuse." Another throng of pedestrians began to accumulate, and the pair stepped farther away from the crossing.

She took another bite of her ice cream, and it dripped down her hands. "And what's your excuse today?"

He handed her a silk handkerchief from his pocket. "I have no excuses today. I've been tracking you down for the last two months just to talk to you. But we better start walking to Naima's so you're not too late."

He'd expected surprise from her, even a little awe at his ability to collect information, at least a gasp of some kind. But she didn't react at all. She took the last bite of ice cream, wiped her hands, thanked him, and then handed him back his handkerchief, sticky with ice cream. Then she looked at him in a way that bordered on defiance.

"Amir," she said, and now he was surprised that she knew his name. "You may have time on your hands for excuses and months-long spy games. But I don't. I know what your life is like—parties, alcohol, dances with pretty girls, suits, and shiny shoes." She pointed at his feet. "My life is spent in Madame Caron's kitchen and hunched over my sewing machine. If I have time, I make myself a galabeya." She tugged at the waist of her worn frock.

"All of that doesn't matter," he said as a motorcycle took a shortcut over the sidewalk, zooming past them.

"Sure, it matters. If you care at all for me, you'll stay away. The worst thing a girl can have in these parts"—she fanned her hand out as if to display the crumbling buildings, broken sidewalks, and rickety shops—"is a bad reputation."

"How do you know my name?"

"I heard the girl in the yellow dress say it before you two danced." She adjusted the slipping straps of a satchel that hung off her shoulders.

He hadn't expected any of the things she'd said to him. He'd thought she'd be flattered and maybe coy. Everything he had prepared to say to her, the entire conversation he'd imagined, fled from his head on a tide of anxiety. It was the same type of anxiety he'd felt when he was a schoolboy taking an oral exam in front his teacher and the weeks of study dissipated from memory.

"I have to go before anyone sees us. Thank you for the ice cream." She turned and joined the throng once again, ready to cross the street. If he didn't say something soon, he'd lose his chance.

"I want to hear you sing."

She turned around and walked back to him, looking straight at him. Was it curiosity in her eyes or anger? "I stopped singing when my father died, but you probably already know that too."

"But the music didn't die."

"Why are you doing this?"

"Because I just want to talk to you. I'll wait for you right here next Sunday and the one after that. Promise me you'll come see me."

"You don't understand anything," she said, and crossed the street. He watched her until he lost her silhouette in a sea of people.

10

The following Sunday Laila wore one of Catherine's discarded dresses, a polka dotted A-line she'd altered before Mama could ruin it with sleeves made from material that didn't match and extra hemming that hid the knees. She covered her shoulders and chest with a long black shawl, pulled her hair up into a bun, and walked to church with Mama. Before leaving the apartment, Mama had crouched down and tugged at the hem of Laila's dress, which fell right above her knee. "Remind me to lengthen it later," she said. But Laila wanted more than anything for Amir to see her in that dress at that length, a length she'd measured in front of her oval bedroom mirror. She wanted him to see her in something other than the maid's uniform she wore at the Caron party, or the galabeya she'd worn a week earlier. This way she might claim some measure of dignity.

At church they sat in the third pew from the front; Laila next to Naima, and Mama next to Samia, Botros's mother. Naima bounced the baby on her knee, and every time he squealed in excitement, she covered his mouth so his voice wouldn't rise above the monotonous liturgy of St. Basil. "Look at you!" she whispered in Laila's ear. "Who are you trying to impress?" Naima shifted in the pew and tugged on her galabeya where it tightened around her pregnant belly. The once beautiful galabeya had been part of

Naima's trousseau. Mama had chosen the material for its bright red and blue floral print. Now, its colors were faded from frequent washing and drying in the harsh sun. Its hem was frayed, and there was a small tear at the shoulder seam.

"Nobody. Be quiet." Laila pretended to listen to the priest, but as had happened all week, she could think of nothing other than her short encounter with Amir the previous Sunday. Why had he followed her? What did he want? Why her?

"It's Meena Morcos, isn't it? He's good looking and almost done with the police academy, a good catch."

"No," Laila said, nudging her sister with her elbow.

"Don't tell me you have your eyes on Naguib. He's broken off three engagements, you know."

"No," Laila said.

"If you tell me …" She stopped bouncing the baby and leaned in even closer to Laila. "I can make the introduction. You're not getting any younger, you know." The baby cried, and Mama reached past Samia and poked Naima's shoulder. For the rest of the liturgy, Naima stayed quiet.

After church Laila kissed Mama good-bye at the top of the stone steps and started the walk to Naima's apartment. Botros carried the sleeping boy and took his mother by the hand so she didn't trip over the large cracks in the sidewalk. Then he crossed the street ahead of Laila and Naima, who walked more slowly with each passing week.

"Well? Are you going to tell me?" Naima said as soon as they turned off Gazirat Badran Street and onto Al Zananeeri.

"He's not from church. I met him at the Caron party." Laila took off the shawl, rolled it up, and put it in her tote.

She told her sister about the tight uniform Madame Caron had made her wear at the party; about the girl in the yellow dress, Amir's suit, the way he smiled at her, the way he followed her into the kitchen, how she'd watched him dance with Catherine. "He seemed interested in me then, but I know what these rich boys want from us poor girls. Mama warned me about that. You know what he asked me? He asked me if I wanted to dance with him. As if I could dance with him right there in my uniform with food on my apron."

They started up Al Laymoun Bridge. "Rich people can be very stupid," Naima said. "It's a wonder how they make all that money."

"He stopped me on my way to your place last week, right at the ice cream stand at the bottom of the bridge. He said he's had me followed. He knows everything about us. He knows about Mama, Baba, my singing, you and Botros, that I see you on Sundays. Everything."

"I'm not surprised." Naima rubbed her belly and stopped to take a break at the top of the bridge. "People like him are connected. They have personal spies. Did anyone see you two together?" A train pulled out of the station, rumbling the bridge. Naima leaned over the rails, pointing at the train. "I wonder where that one is going."

"Can you believe his audacity, though?" Laila said as they began the descent. "As I was leaving, he said he'd wait for me, and he yelled this out in the middle of the street. Naima, someone could have heard him, and then what? He's dreaming if he thinks I'm going to meet him again."

"But you are going to see him," Naima said. "And you're all dressed up for it too. No shawl, nothing."

"No, he's going to see me right before the crossing to your building. Just watch."

"Point him out to me."

"I won't need to," Laila said, and took Naima's arm, slowing their pace as they approached the ice cream stand. As they got closer to the stand, Laila sped up and swerved around the ice cream stand.

Amir was there, wearing a light pistachio-colored linen suit and a pair of shiny shoes, different from the ones he'd worn the week before. He had one handkerchief in the front pocket of his jacket and another in his hand. When Laila and Naima passed, he used it to wipe the sweat from above his brow.

"In the name of the holy cross," Naima said after they'd passed him.

128

"He's royalty. He's pure royalty. Did you see how he was dressed? Even his socks matched his suit."

"Nobody is royalty, Naima." But Amir looked different from the common men who wore suit jackets over their galabeyas.

"He was staring at you. I saw him."

"It can never be. He's from one level and we're from another. He said he'd wait, but then what?"

The two of them walked in silence until they reached Naima's building. Then Naima asked the question Laila knew she would. "Is he Christian?"

Laila nodded. "He was wearing a gold cross pendant on his chain. I noticed it at the party."

"Because if he were a Muslim." Naima shook her head.

"I know. It would break Mama," Laila said. "But religion aside, look at him and look at me."

"So?" Naima said. "Look at you. You're perfect. Listen, let him wait. Let him wait in the sun week after week, and then we'll see how long that morafah rich boy lasts outside the comforts of his shaded Zamalek. As they say, al maya tikateb al ghattas, water tests the best diver."

For five weeks Amir waited in the that same spot, wearing a different suit and shiny shoes, wiping the sweat off his brow, his white face reddening in the Cairene sun. Laila alternated between the polka-dotted dress and her old galabeyas. One day after the fifth week, while she was helping Naima bathe the baby, Naima said, "It's time you talk to him. He's serious, Laila. No man in his social class is going to wait that long to talk to a girl who he knows won't give in to him. He can have any girl he wants, but he chooses you. Why else would he wait there? He must have good intentions."

Laila leaned over the tub, filled a pitcher with warm water, and spilled it on the baby, rinsing him off. He screamed and Naima wiped the water off of his face. "There's no point. Even if he entertained the idea of choosing someone like me to marry, his family would never allow it. Never." The baby kicked splashing water onto her as she lifted him out of the water.

Naima took the boy and wrapped him up in a towel, then brought him to her chest. "What God wants will be, and nobody stands in the way of God. I'm in my seventh month now. My back hurts and my feet are always swollen. I can't keep going up and down the bridge and the stairs or walking to church. Botros is too cheap to get a taxi. So, I can't go to church much longer, and if I don't go, nobody here goes. Botros is too lazy and Samia, the old crow, won't leave her son for a minute. She's afraid to fall off the sidewalk." They both laughed.

"I don't even know what to say to him." Laila followed Naima down the corridor and into the bedroom.

Naima closed the door behind them. "See what he wants. Maybe he's tired of the rich girls. It'll kill you if you don't just find out. It'll kill me too." She laid the baby on the bed and Laila dried him off. Then Naima pinned a fresh diaper on him and dressed him in a blue pajama. He gurgled and gnawed on his fist. "Don't so much as hold his hand. You understand? He needs to know he's dealing with a clean girl from a respectable family. Only talk to him in public, but don't be conspicuous. Stay in crowds. They're the best place to hide. After you meet with him, come straight here. I'll cover for you if anyone asks. But don't be too late."

Each day leading up to the Sunday meeting, after she'd returned from cooking at Madame Caron's, Laila busied herself with sewing work. She took extra pieces from her mother's pile and hemmed and mended until her fingers hurt and her eyes blurred. They rarely sewed new clothes for anyone. People who could afford unused fabrics didn't come to Selma to have clothes made. Their clients wanted merely to maintain the shabby clothes they already had. Over the years the clients had become like family, brothers and sisters in poverty, and handing over their dilapidated clothes to Selma and Laila was like sharing a secret, revealing a shameful part of their existence that could be hidden with Laila's thread and needle.

She let out little girls' school dresses so their families didn't have to buy new material. She sewed the seams with care, making the alteration unnoticeable. If she found a stain, she washed it out with water and vinegar.

Then she ironed the dresses, arranging the pleats neatly on the ironing board before she pressed them. She fixed frayed pant hems by opening the old seams and adding backing material to create a new hem. This way men could go to work with some measure of self-respect. At times, even if a client didn't ask for it, she removed an old collar from a shirt and sewed on a new one from cloth remnants Mama kept in a hat box in her closet. But the one task that pained Laila the most was taking in the waist on slacks or a dress that she'd taken in before.

That Sunday, as she had promised, Naima didn't go to church, and Laila took the route to her sister's apartment just as she did every week. But this time she weaved faster through the pedestrians on Shubra Street. She skirted fruit-filled pushcarts and the vendors whose kabobs filled the air with the scent of roasted lamb. She expertly crossed the street between cars, trams, and buses onto Bolaq Road. There was no time to waste, and she didn't want to be late to Naima's. When she got to Al Laymoun Bridge, she slowed, adjusted the belt on the dress, and smoothed her ponytail.

"I've been waiting," he said as she approached.

The tips of his shiny shoes were barely scuffed, as though he'd never walked more than a block in them. His light brown hair was slicked back, and he wore a gray suit made of lustrous sturdy linen, the kind of cloth store owners kept in reams behind the counter, away from common hands.

"I know," she said. "I'm sorry for that, but I came to tell you that you shouldn't wait any longer. Please don't do this to me or to yourself. Six weeks is long enough. Forget about me now." But she didn't want him to forget about her, and she was tired of being on guard, worried about what people might say. Why couldn't she just talk to him for a while without having to plan the next decade of her life?

"You came here just to tell me to forget about you?" He was even more handsome than she'd remembered. He had green eyes, long lashes, and light skin. When he spoke, there was no hesitation in his voice, and nothing seemed to burden him. No wonder Catherine had wanted to dance with him.

131

"Yes," she said just as a bus stopped at the street corner where they were standing. She turned her back to it, hiding herself from any passersby.

Amir squinted against the midday sun, shielding his forehead with his hand. "Well, since we're never going to see each other again, can I at least buy you a kazooza?"

She agreed. He bought her a cold bottle of Coca-Cola from Abu Adel's grocery shop adjacent to the ice cream stand. As he gave it to her, he said, "Do you still sing?"

Nobody besides Baba had ever asked her about her singing. She couldn't talk about singing without talking about Baba, and it was the first time since he died that she'd talked about him at length to anyone. She told Amir about her singing lessons, how she'd surprised Baba with her voice, and how he'd taught her maqam. She told him about the contest and the contract she'd almost signed. When she ended one story, he asked her to elaborate. For the next hour they stood talking and sipping under the awning of Abu Adel's. She told him about the times she'd sung in the cafes in Rod El Farag, and how Baba had come to name her Laila. "He named me after the night sky and the Laila from *Laila and Majnoon*." She told Amir about the walks along the Nile and the trips to the pyramids at Giza, when Baba would take her just to sit quietly and compose. "I stopped singing when he died," she said, holding back tears. "Not a single note."

She didn't talk about the grueling days at Madame Caron's or her sunflowers from France that killed Baba. She didn't tell him about the scant amount of food in her kitchen or the nights she'd hear Mama cry because she didn't know where the money would come from.

Amir told her about the tenderness of his nanny Hakima, her wise advice, her endless supply of love, and how he often felt undeserving of that love. "I was naughty, you know, but she was always patient with me." Then he told Laila that he had once begun to paint but didn't pursue it. "My father didn't like the idea of his son becoming a painter." He took the last sip from his Coke bottle. "I wasn't that good anyway. But I collect things, you know." He told her how he had collected coins and stamps and other beautiful things, that he prided himself on finding something of value, not because he wanted to make money from it but because he wanted to possess it. And he explained the great lengths he went about to acquire something, sending letters to tens of international sellers, or sometimes paying more than something was worth just to have it.

"Why buy something you don't need? You won't use the stamps, will you?" Why was she prolonging the conversation? They would never speak again, no matter how badly she wanted to.

"When you want something, you want something."

"Sometimes you want something but you can't have it."

"What do you want?" he asked.

What did she want? In the years after Baba's death, she'd concerned herself only with surviving. Wanting something was a luxury she considered out of her reach. "Before Baba died," she said, "I wanted to be a famous singer. I also wanted to know how to read and write like other girls, but now I don't think about what I want anymore." Was that the truth, though? Didn't she also want respite from her poverty? And if that were the case, would she be willing to admit it to Amir?

"Do you want to meet with me again?" he asked.

She shook her head. "No."

"You didn't enjoy yourself?"

"Of course, I enjoyed myself." She gave him the empty bottle of Coca-Cola so that he could return it to the grocer. "But I still don't want to see you again."

"What if I said I want to see you?"

"Like I said. Sometimes we don't get what we want. I'm sorry. I have to leave. My sister will be upset."

"I'll never stop waiting," he said as she crossed the street. "I'll be right here next week."

❧

Laila rang the doorbell three times before Naima opened the front door carrying her son on her hip. She held a ladle coated with thick lentil soup, and when she handed Laila the toddler, a droplet of soup fell on Laila's shoulder. "Take him," Naima said. "He won't stop crying." Laila ran her fingers through his soft brown curls. "Where have you been? The old crow asked about you."

Laila followed her sister into the kitchen and closed the door behind them. Naima leaned over the stove and dipped a spoon in the pot, tasted the liquid and cringed. "Too much cumin." Steam rose above the pot from the boiling soup. "Well, tell me what happened." She mashed potatoes in a bowl and stirred the mash into the soup.

If this misery was marriage, Laila wanted none of it. Naima did all the work while her mother in law and husband sat on the balcony all day. At least when Laila toiled, she toiled for her own mother, not for a stranger. "He's not at all as I'd thought." Laila rubbed her nephew's back to comfort him. "He's sentimental. Can you believe he puts a single red rose from his garden on his late nanny's grave every year on the anniversary of her death?" Neither of them had gone to visit Baba's grave. "He looks like Errol Flynn, doesn't he? I wish you could have seen him today. In the sun, his eyes are the color of those green jewels you see rich ladies wearing. And he wants to see me again, but I said no."

Naima tasted the soup again, lowered the heat, and placed a lid on the pot. She pulled a chair out across from Laila and slowly lowered herself into it. "So that's it? No more Errol Flynn?"

"It can't lead to anything. I'm just an awad's daughter, and his father is a pasha. Besides, Madame Caron has her eye on him for Catherine, and she'll get what she wants. She always gets what she wants."

"Forget about Catherine. Forget about what you think is possible or impossible. If he's there next week, then you should talk to him again. But don't get carried away. You have to be taeela. He can't sense that you like him too much."

"Alright. I'll see what he wants, but I'm only going to meet with him once," Laila said.

Naima laughed. "We'll see about that."

For three weeks Laila and Amir met under the same awning, drinking Coca-Cola or eating ice cream. In those weeks Laila told Amir about the summer in Alexandria, Mama's cooking, and Naima's marriage. Amir told her about his travels to Paris, Vienna, and Rome. He told her about the opera and the *Mona Lisa* at the Louvre and Michelangelo's *David* in Florence. "Someday, I'll take you to see the world, Laila," he said, and she loved believing him.

Each week she put on her cleanest galabeya or her polka-dotted dress. Sometimes she braided her hair. Other times she put it in a bun, but she never let it down. Mama wouldn't allow it. As she hurried from church to meet him, she pinched her cheeks to give them a rosiness.

One Sunday, almost a month after their first date, Amir said, "Aren't you tired of meeting here? No place to sit, no place to talk, people bumping into us."

"This is the only place where I can meet you without getting in trouble. At least if someone sees me here, I have an excuse. I can say that I'm on my way to my sister's and that I stopped for a kazooza."

"Azbakeya Gardens is only a short walk from here. There are benches to sit on and trees to give us shade."

"I can't," Laila said.

"Why not? What's the difference between talking to me here or talking to me in a beautiful garden? Don't you trust me? Come on. Aren't we friends?"

"Yes, but there's no time."

"We'll walk fast."

Laila wanted to go, and so they walked to Azbakeya Gardens through back streets Laila didn't know until they got to Emad El Din Street. From there they walked south to Al Ataba Square where Baba had bought Naima's bedroom set. Then they passed the Hotel Continental on the south side and the Shepheard's Hotel on the north. A wide flagstone walkway led up to Azbakeya Gardens. Towering sweet-scented date palms lined the perimeter of the park, with acacias and sycamores scattered throughout. The meandering grassy walkways were dotted with shrubs of yellow flowered samwa, purple sweet alyssum, and jasmine.

"Come. I'll show you my favorite spot." Amir reached for Laila's hand, but she didn't take it. They walked side by side to the north end of the park where a stream cut through the lush greenery and ran under a wooden bridge that led to a small waterfall. They stopped on the backside of the waterfalls. "I need to make a confession. I didn't bring you here to talk."

Would he try to kiss her now, and if he tried would she let him? Naima kissed Botros and they got married, but this was different.

"I brought you here to hear you sing."

She hadn't imagined he'd ever make such a request. She couldn't sing now. She wasn't prepared, hadn't practiced, and they were in a quiet garden.

"I don't sing anymore," Laila said, edging a few steps farther into the shade of the rock wall of the waterfalls.

"But you have to. It's all I can think of."

Why was he thinking of her singing? "I don't know what to sing, and I haven't practiced in years."

"Sing Om Kalsoum, just one line for me. I beg you. Please." Nobody had ever pleaded with her this way, and she felt some power within her. Maybe she had something to give?

But what if she forgot the melody or what if her voice cracked at the height of a maquam? And yet she felt like singing now. She cleared her throat, took a deep breath, closed her eyes, and sang. "Min katar shouqi sabqat amri. Washfat bokra walwaqt badri." She knew she'd missed the sound of her voice but hadn't realized just how much until the singing came out of her again. She'd missed how it resonated, the way she sang Baba's songs ranging from throaty lows to clear highs, the vibrating strum of Baba's oud. But when she got to the end of that line, she sang another line, and another, until she'd sung the whole song, every word flowing out of her just the way Baba had taught her when he'd sat in his chair playing the oud.

136

And she heard the oud so clearly although it wasn't there. It didn't matter that Amir was watching her. In that moment it didn't matter that anyone might hear her. The only thing that mattered was that she sing that song.

"No wonder your father saw you as a star," Amir said when she'd finished. "I've never heard a more beautiful voice in my life. And it comes so naturally. You really haven't practiced in years? How am I going to get through a whole week now without seeing you and hearing you sing again?" Then he reached for her hand, and she took it. Their time in the garden had ended.

They walked hand in hand through Azbakeya Gardens, and he told her that long ago there once was a lake under their feet, but that it was drained when Ismail Khedive instructed Barillet Deschamps to design the park like Parc Monceau in Paris. "That's why it's in an octagonal shape."

The next Sunday as soon as they met at the ice cream stand, they started toward Azbakeya Gardens, and this time Amir held a bag filled with white tissue paper and a red ribbon wrapped around the handle. When they got to the waterfall, he gave her the bag. "I have a small gift for you. I know you can't actually take it home, but I wanted you to see it." She had nothing for him, and this made her feel inadequate.

Inside the bag was a paper rolled up with a red bow around. When she unrolled it, she realized it was a small painting of her wearing a pink dress, silver shoes, and a diamond necklace. Her hair was down. The paint colors were vivid. The background was cloudy, and it seemed she wasn't standing on the ground. Was it her? It looked like it could be her, but maybe it was somebody else?

"It's a watercolor."

"It's beautiful," she said.

"Of course, it's beautiful because it's of you. But you're more stunning than anything I can paint."

"My hair." She ran her finger along the long brown locks in the painting. "It's down." How had he known her hair had a slight wave to it, or that it parted on the right? And the dress in the painting was cut low so that her cleavage showed. She was embarrassed that Amir had seen her breast this way even if it were in his own imagination. Had he pictured her naked? What had he seen? Would her breasts really look like that if she'd worn the imagined dress? Laila had never thought of her body like that, as something to be painted, seen, admired. She felt shame, but also a new warm exciting emotion that was everywhere within her drowning the shame out.

"I've spent nights dreaming of you like this with your hair down, trying to imagine how it might look in the sunlight. Will you take it down for me? Just for a minute?"

She could have said no, but she didn't want to because now she was curious about herself too. She pulled the pins out of her bun, one by one, collecting them in her palm, loosening her thick hair until it fell around her shoulders and along her back. She'd forgotten what a relief it could be to release the bun after it had been so tightly wound.

"Just how I'd imagined it." He ran his fingers through her hair. Then he took her face in his big warm hands and kissed her.

That day, before they left the garden, he helped her pin her bun up, and each time his hands grazed her neck or shoulders she got that same feeling the moment he'd kissed her. Then he walked her back to the ice cream stand where they'd been meeting for nearly two months. On their way she said, "What about Catherine?"

"Catherine who?" he said.

When she got to Naima's she didn't tell her about the kiss, the painting, or the singing in Azbakeya Gardens. But she had to tell her something because Naima expected a detailed report when they went into the kitchen and closed the door.

"Tell me everything," Naima said.

"Nothing new happened," Laila lied. "We just talked as usual in front of the grocery stand."

"But he didn't say anything about maybe proposing? By now he should be telling you his intentions."

"Not yet, Naima. He's from a different level. These people drink wine, wear fancy clothes, and dance cheek to cheek at parties. They don't talk about intentions of marriage like we do. If you were at the Caron party, you'd understand." Maybe he'd never ask to marry her. Maybe this was just a small escape from the drudgery of her life, and perhaps she could be happy with that.

"The only reason I told you to talk to him," Naima said, "is because I thought he was serious. But if nothing comes of this and soon, then you should stop seeing him."

If Laila told Naima about the kiss, her sister would tell her not to see him again until he came to the house and asked for her hand in marriage, just as Botros had finally done for Naima. She spent the day helping Naima cook, clean the house, and feed the baby. She thought about everything. What did she want? Were these fluttery feelings inside of her love? And if they were, did she have any control over them? She had no answers.

That night when she went home and Mama had gone to sleep, Laila locked her bedroom door, took off her clothes, let her hair down, and stood in front of the oval mirror. She turned it so that the lamplight from her nightstand shone into it. She studied her naked body; the different shades and textures of her skin, the curves of her breasts, the faint stretch marks on her thighs.

She'd seen herself in the mirror every day of her life but had never looked at herself as a woman, a woman who could be attractive, who could be kissed, not until she'd seen herself painted into a dress, cleavage showing, hair down.

She knew how to behave like a boy. Baba had taught her that. She could play soccer, push herself through crowded streets unafraid, argue fiercely with a vendor who gave her back too little change, punch someone if she had to. When she was young, she'd cut her hair (an unthinkable act for a girl) and worn loose galabeyas, hiding her body just so she could sing at cafes with Baba. Her father had spent all his energy teaching her to survive "better than any man," he'd said, but she was a woman after all, and Amir had seen her that way. She looked at her reflection for a long time, and as she thought of Amir, ran her hands along her body. She touched herself and imagined that it was him. She felt pride, then shame, then pleasure.

Laila kept meeting Amir, and she kept kissing him behind the waterfalls in the north end of Azbakeya Garden week after week, without ever answering the questions she'd asked herself and without asking him what might happen next.

Six weeks after the first kiss, Laila came home from after a long day at Naima's and found Mama waiting by the door. As soon as Laila closed the door, Mama slapped her on the face. Laila screamed and pressed her hand to her cheek.

"Not a sound!" Mama said, gritting her teeth. "Wala kilma. If the neighbors hear this then they'll be sure it's true."

"What's true?"

"That my daughter, the daughter of the late awad, had been ruining our good name all over the city, dating a pasha's son. What do you think a pasha's son wants with you?"

Laila wanted to say something but couldn't. She was ashamed of having lied, of having gone against her better judgment. But most of all, she was ashamed of doing it all with the pasha's son while she knew it could never end well.

"Samia just left," Mama went on. "She figured it out when you showed up time after time late to your sister's, and then she started digging around. People saw you with him. And to think that your sister knew. Wait until I get my hands on her."

"Leave Naima out of this."

"Out of what?" Mama lunged at her again, wrapping Laila's long braids around her hand. "Out of what?" Laila stumbled backward, feeling the painful tug against her scalp. "Do you realize what happens to girls with bad reputations? They end up as old spinsters. You want to be a spinster?"

"I don't want to get married like that, like Naima. I'm not a piece of meat," Laila said.

"Then it's as I suspected. You're ruined." With one hand still wrapped in Laila's hair, Selma slapped her daughter once more. Laila screamed. Then Selma pushed her away, and Laila stumbled back into Baba's chair.

Mama slapped her own face with both of her hands. "The shame of it, the shame of it," she repeated over and over until she sank to the ground weeping, her head in her hands.

Laila crouched next to her mother, putting her hand on her back, "Mama, it's true I've been seeing him, but nothing shameful happened between us. We rahmet Baba." She swore upon her father's soul. "I'm the girl you raised. Nothing has changed."

Selma dried her cheeks with the back of her hand. "You deceived me," she said, and pushed herself off the ground, her cracked and chafed hands shaking. "Next Sunday I'm coming with you. I have something to say to the pasha's son, and if you dare warn him, you're no longer my daughter." Then she went into her bedroom and slammed the door behind her.

11

Selma had intended to go to church that morning. It was the day she planned to confront Amir and she needed God's blessings. But she couldn't bear the condescending glares, the whispers, or the looks of pity. In her bedroom she prayed to the painting of the Virgin Mary, the undefiled, incorruptible, chaste Virgin Mary. She closed her eyes, bowed her head, and knelt, despite the excruciating pain in her knees. Maybe the pain gave the prayer more weight. Whatever happened today, she asked for wisdom and strength.

She put on her navy galabeya, though she wanted to wear black. Then she washed her face and used a cold washcloth to compress the swelling around her eyes. She put on her sandals, went to Laila's room, said "Yalla," and waved her toward the door.

They descended the stairs, and Selma was careful not to let her footsteps be heard, to avoid the torrent of sickening comments. They used the building's back door, escaping the porter's eyes. Still, as they'd passed each floor, she'd heard the women talk—"That's what happens when you raise a girl in a cabaret"; or "Even the awad wouldn't have approved"; or "I'm glad I married off my daughter young. Now she's mastoora, and what better protection than that of a husband?"

Once on Gazirat Badran Street, Laila walked slowly. "Don't try to stall," Selma reprimanded her daughter, who'd been silent for a whole week. Silent on the way to Madame Caron's, silent in the kitchen, silent on the way back at night, silent while they sewed. The day she'd confronted her, Laila swore she was still a virgin. Selma considered taking her to Om Hanafi, the midwife, to certify Laila's virginity, but that would be a tacit admission of inappropriate behavior. No matter how secretive a trip to Om Hanafi would be, somebody, somehow, would find out. Selma had to stand firm in the face of the rumors. But how? "Walk faster," she said through gritted teeth. She wanted Laila to respond, to say anything, but Laila said nothing all the way from Gazirat Badran Street to Al Laymoun Bridge.

Before they got to the ice cream stand, Laila finally spoke. "I know I can't stop you from doing whatever you're planning on doing, but please, Mama, please don't make a scene. You have to know that I did nothing wrong."

"That's what you have to say to me? After all of this, that's what you have to say?" Rumbles and whistles of arriving and departing trains from the nearby station made it hard for Selma to be heard. "You're worried about my embarrassing you, but you never had qualms about embarrassing me or your sister?"

Selma took Laila's hand. The sound of thousands of tapping soles tore her nerves as she pushed through crowds, dragging her daughter behind her.

"Is that him?" Selma pointed ahead.

Laila looked down at the ground.

It was the first time Selma had sensed her daughter's shame, and that shame scared her. "Go ahead of me then. I don't want him to see me yet." She shoved Laila two steps ahead of her, and her daughter almost stumbled. Selma stayed back a few meters, and then before Amir could say a word, Selma stepped forward and joined them, pushing Laila to the side. Now face to face with the pasha's son, she could tell him what she'd wanted to say all week. "So, this is how society gentlemen behave? Secretly dating girls like a coward." Selma raised her voice. "Have you no dignity? No pride?"

The boy stuttered at first, but he collected himself quicker than Selma imagined he could or should. "I'm sorry. I don't know who you are."

"Let me introduce myself then. I'm Laila's mother, the woman you haven't respected for months." She reached for his tie, and its silky feel angered her even more. He was so tall that he arched over her as she tugged, but he didn't resist, though she thought she saw a flash of anger cross his face. He could have pushed her away, she was certain of that. Was it remorse, or was he trying to look as though he were a gentleman, a man who'd never mistreat an older woman.

"Mama. Please stop," Laila said. "You're acting crazy."

Selma ignored her daughter and addressed the pasha's son. "You think we're all pawns, don't you? You think because we're poor that we can be bought and sold like a painting or a piece of furniture. Isn't that right?" She pulled at the tie even harder, until he came close enough for her to see the beads of sweat on his face and to see that he was no boy. He was a man. "My daughter is not for sale." She yelled this so loud, people began to gather around. She hadn't planned on making a scene, but her anger was so fierce that she lost control over herself.

"Please," Amir said, adjusting his tie after she finally let go. "You're wrong. Laila is everything to me. We can talk somewhere quietly about this. It's too loud here. I can explain. My car is parked across the street."

Selma spat at him and at the country that made her a servant and him near royalty. "I won't get in your car, and neither will my daughter. You've done enough damage to our family. Now leave us alone. If I ever see your face in our neighborhood, I'll have every baltagi in Rod El Farag beat you to a pulp." The words came from deep within Selma's chest and scraped her throat so that her throat burned. She took Laila's hand once more and pulled her away from the curb, back toward the bridge.

What had she said to him? Selma didn't know any baltagis. She'd never associated with hoodlums. Had she really spat at him? She'd planned on saying so much more, but in the moment, she lost her words in a flood of rage. Then she felt a hand on her shoulder, and when she turned around, that rotten man stood there staring at her.

"Amir?" Laila said, and Selma kicked her foot.

"Ikhrassi," Selma said, and Laila shut up as told.

The boy didn't even lower his eyes in deference. What audacity! "I haven't been disrespectful to your daughter in any way," he said. "All I wanted was to speak to her, to get to know her, and we've done so in the light of day with people around us. I don't see any shame in that."

This was his apology? If Kamal were alive, he'd have punched him. He'd have recruited half of Cairo to bring this boy to his knees right there in the middle of the street.

"You may be able to fool an innocent child," she said, speaking over the sound of cars zooming past, "but you can't fool an old lady. I've earned my streaks of white hair." Selma patted her tight white bun. "If you have any decency, then you'll leave her alone and let us live our lives in peace. That is, if there is any peace left for us."

"I can't live without her," the pasha's son said. "I can barely survive the days of the week until I see her again."

"Poor boy!" Selma brought a hand to her cheek in mock sympathy. "Well, in that case I'm just going to have to let you two carry on for the sake of your well-being. To hell with her reputation and customs and common courtesy."

"I love your daughter."

Laila gasped. Selma squeezed her hand. "Don't talk about things you don't understand, boy." Then she dragged Laila toward the street crossing.

But Amir ran after them again, and this time he ran around them and stood in front of them, as if he wouldn't let them pass until he had said what he wanted to say. Selma was ready to slap him, come what may. What would he do, jail an old lady?

"I want to marry her."

Selma didn't expect these words. Pashas' sons didn't marry poor uneducated, illiterate girls, but he didn't falter.

"I want to marry your daughter," he said again. "And I'm asking for her hand in marriage, right here, right now."

If this was true, it would be the sweetest redemption for Laila, and yet a proposal done improperly was an insult.

"If you want to marry her and you want to ask for her hand in marriage, you know what to do."

Selma looked fiercely at Laila staring at the boy, and wondered how it was that she'd forgotten to teach Laila the art of coyness? How stupid, she thought, the two of them looked. "Let's go, Laila." She grabbed a fistful of fabric from the back of Laila's galabeya and yanked her out of her stupor. As she hurried her daughter away, Selma could only think that she'd been so busy surviving, she'd neglected to teach Laila how unfair life really was, but that was no excuse, and now look what it had come to. Laila would be so crushed when she realized that no proposal would come, that there could never be a marriage between her and a pasha's son. Why hadn't she stuck to her own kind? Why hadn't Laila shown interest in a boy from Rod El Farag, from their church? Still, Selma could see how someone like Amir could easily dazzle a girl like Laila. He was handsome, rich, elegant, and it was clear he'd had a lot of experience. Had Laila really had a choice in the matter? After all, Selma had fallen in love at the song Kamal had played for her, sitting outside her bedroom window. How she missed him now.

When Laila and Selma got home that day, Laila went straight into her room. She didn't say anything to her mother, not on the street, not up the stairs, not in the morning when they woke up and had their coffee before heading to Madam Caron's. They didn't chat as they cut, chopped, and sliced. The silence between them gave Selma the time to doubt her daughter, to imagine all the sins that might have happened for six long weeks, but she didn't feel anger like before. She felt grief. She felt as though a stranger had come into her house and torn a suckling baby from her breast, and now that baby was gone, perhaps even dead. "You'll forget, you know." Selma said to her daughter as they were walking out of the gate of Madam Caron's house. They hadn't spoken for nearly two days.

"I know," Laila said.

It was another three days before a knock came at the door. Selma looked through the peep door. There stood a funny-looking short man, dressed in a white long-tailed coat and red tarbush carrying three white boxes tied with red ribbon. When she opened the door, he announced himself as the official butler to Makram Youseff Pasha, that he was carrying "a message and gifts," and asked for permission to enter so that he could put the heavy boxes down. Selma heard him, but she pointed at her ear as though she were hard of hearing. She wanted this announcement to echo down the stairwell. She wanted it to be heard by all the gossiping building tenants. He spoke louder. "I'm Makram Youseff Pasha's butler. I bring gifts with me, and a request from the Makram Youseff Pasha and his wife Hoda to pay a visit."

"What does the Makram Youseff Pasha want?" Selma almost yelled, ensuring that her voice traveled down at least to the fourth floor. That's all she needed really. The fourth floor would tell the third, who'd tell the second, who'd tell the first, and the porter would then tell the kiosk vendors across the street, who'd spread the news throughout the fruit and vegetable market.

The butler blocked one ear and cringed. Selma contained her laughter, and when Laila came out of the kitchen to see who it was, Selma waved her back in. "Are you Madame Selma?" the butler asked, nearly shouting.

Selma nodded, trying not to be too hopeful about the visit. The gifts could be a token of apology and nothing more.

The man continued. "I'm here to deliver a message from Makram Youseff Pasha. His son Amir Makram Youseff Pasha would like to pay a visit to make an official proposal to your daughter ..." He pulled a notepaper from his pocket and read, "Laila Kamal Abd El Malek." He folded the note and put it back in his pocket. "They'd like to come tomorrow at sunset."

147

"Ahlan wasahlan," Selma said, agreeing to the next day's visit as she moved to the side, letting in the butler. After he'd placed the boxes on the small coffee table, refused a cup of tea, and left, Selma stepped out onto the landing and trilled the loudest zaghrouta she could muster. As the butler descended the stairwell, doors opened throughout the building and neighbors rushed up to the fifth floor, swarming around Selma. When all the women had gathered at the landing, Selma made a full-throated announcement.

"Laila, my daughter, caught the eye of a pasha's son, and because of her chastity, he's coming here to ask for her hand tomorrow. Because of her chastity," she repeated.

The women trilled one zaghrouta after the other, and soon the entire building seemed to vibrate in unified ululation.

When she went back into the apartment and closed the door behind her, Selma took Laila in her arms, held her close to her chest, and both of them wept in joy. "Mabrook ya binty. God has blessed you."

"I told you, Mama. I told you I didn't do anything wrong. He's a good man, isn't he? You thought he'd never come. I know you thought it would never happen, but it did. It did."

"It's turned out all right, Laila, but you played a very risky game. From now on you have to be very careful with everything you do and say. It's not done until the priest marries you two. Until then anything can happen."

"Hader Mama." Laila said, and Selma was relieved to have her obedient daughter once again. Her daughter had not been ruined. She was still a virgin. Otherwise, Amir would have never sent the butler. She was proud again.

They sat on the settee and opened the boxes together.

Laila told her that the box on top was from a place in Soliman Pasha Square called Groppi. She said she recognized the shape of the name. "It's owned by a Swiss family, Mama." Inside the box were rows of chocolates and pastries the likes of which Selma had only seen at

Madame Caron's, but even Madame Caron hadn't bought assortments of such variety and quantity. The chocolates were stacked in layers one on top of the other.

"Take one, Mama." Laila picked up a round chocolate and fed it to Selma. It was the first time since Kamal had died that Selma had seen such glee in her daughter's eyes. The chocolate tasted like nothing Selma had ever known. In all the years she'd worked for Madame Caron, she'd never offered her one piece of candy. And when Kamal had bought chocolates, Selma had left every last piece for the girls. This piece tasted sublime, and she chewed slowly. But the box was filled to the brim. She and Laila couldn't eat all of that, and she didn't know how long it would keep. Madame Caron sometimes left chocolates in crystal bowls throughout the villa, but for how long? Selma couldn't let any of this go to waste.

"Mama, look," Laila said as she pulled out a thin-strapped fuchsia-colored silk dress from the second box. It had a fitted bodice and an A-line skirt with an underskirt of tulle. "I think it's from Cicurel or Benzion. I think I've seen something like it in the vitrine."

"This is imported. It must be." Selma wanted to examine the material, but Laila held the dress up against her body. "Isn't it beautiful, Mama? Isn't it something?" She twirled around the family room, and the dress's skirt rose up into the air like the dervish dancers in the street. It reminded Selma of the days when Laila was a little girl and would jump from the settee to the chairs, pretending she was an ancient warrior.

The box on the bottom contained a dress too, but it was a larger size, and it was the most elegant shade of burgundy she'd ever seen. Was it really for her? She put her hand inside the box and took the material between her fingers. "Taffeta," she said. Then she pulled it out and realized the boy had properly estimated her size. How did he know such things? Even as her daughter twirled with joy, and with the rich taffeta between her fingers, Selma nonetheless felt a dizzying apprehension.

The next morning Selma and Laila walked to El Attaba Square to buy flowers. "Rich people like flowers," Selma said as she leaned in at the flower kiosk to smell the arrangements. "We should put a bouquet on the side table beside the big chair."

The saleslady made them a bouquet of white flowers whose names Selma didn't know.

The only important thing was that the flowers be an auspicious white. They stopped at the grocer to buy tea and sugar and flour. Then they walked to Naima's apartment to share the amazing news and to invite Naima and Botros to be present for the proposal. Botros's mother invited Selma to stay for tea, but Selma declined.

"I can't," she said. "Makram Youseff Pasha and his wife are paying us a visit tonight to ask for Laila's hand. I have a list of chores to do."

"Mabrook, your Laila is beautiful, after all," Samia said, but Selma saw jealousy in those small conniving eyes, so she flashed her palm twice at the old crow, muttering, "Khamsa. Khamsa."

"You think I'm jealous?" Samia said.

"One can never be too careful." Selma smiled, and then she left with her head held high.

On their way up to their apartment on Gazirat Badran, Selma stopped at Haaga Saffeya's to enlist her in making date-filled cookies and baklava. She wanted to show the pasha that she was a skilled cook who had taught her daughter well. Just as she had done for Naima's proposal visit, Selma borrowed tablecloths and extra cups and saucers from her neighbors, who upon seeing Selma swore that they were not part of the rumor mill. Selma didn't believe them, but she forgave them anyway.

Most of that morning, Selma and Haaga Safeya rolled cookie dough in the kitchen, filling it with date paste. Then they ground up the nuts and made syrup for the baklava. When they realized time was running out, Selma ran to the third floor to fetch Aida, and soon there were six hands in the bowl, and Selma felt blessed, for where God had taken family, he had given friends.

Naima arrived by early afternoon to help her sister bathe, arrange her hair in an updo like those rich ladies, and put makeup on, which Selma had warned had to be tasteful and natural.

Just before sunset, everything was ready. The bouquet of white flowers was in a borrowed vase on the side table next to the big chair. The baklava and date-filled cookies were baked and arranged in alternating rows on a large borrowed silver platter. The coffee, tea, sugar, milk, and honey were placed on the small kitchen table so that Laila wouldn't have to fumble for them in cupboards. The floors were swept, the windows washed, and the small rugs dusted. Laila and Selma wore their new dresses, and even Naima wore an empire waist dress she'd borrowed from a neighbor.

"We should play some music," Botros suggested as the four of them waited in the family room.

Naima turned on the radio behind the settee. She fiddled with the stations. "Play something afrangi. Rich people like afrangi music," Botros said. Naima settled on a station. It sounded like some of the strange music they played in Madame Caron's house. To Selma, Western music had no character, no undulations, no pause to feel the pain of it, no repetition to let the words soak into the soul. It was like drinking tea without sugar. But she agreed to leave it on.

As the clock ticked and the sun set, Selma began to worry. What if all of this was a dirty game? What if they didn't come? Where would she hide from the shame? Laila fidgeted in her chair, Botros hummed to the awful music, and Naima rubbed her belly.

An hour passed, and each of them became visibly tense. Did the butler mean at sunset or after sunset? Why didn't she ask him for a time? Now, Selma sat in her chair, wondering whether she should start cleaning up and send everyone home. What a disaster that would be. She prayed for patience, for wisdom.

Finally, a knock at the door. "You get the door, Botros," Selma said, convinced that God had intervened.

Laila and Naima followed Botros, and Selma stood to greet the visitors.

"Ahlan Wasahlan," Selma said as Makram Youseff Pasha, his son Amir, and his wife Hoda came in. "Please sit. We are honored with your visit."

They were dressed as Selma had expected. The father and his son wore suits, ties, shiny shoes, and tarbushes. The father was even taller than his son, but the mother was short and plump. She wore a champagne-colored suit, but the jacket seemed tight, buttoned around her nonexistent waist. She didn't smile like the father and his son. And after the introductions were made, when she leaned in to give Selma the two customary kisses, one on each cheek, her lips made a kiss in the air, as though she was disgusted. Selma sat in Kamal's old chair and seated Madame Hoda and Makram Youseff Pasha on the settee across from her. Botros, Naima, Laila, and Amir sat on borrowed chairs along the wall. As soon as they had sat, though, Laila popped up again. Excusing herself, she and Naima went into the kitchen to prepare the tea, coffee, and pastries.

Makram Youseff Pasha spoke first. "Thank you for welcoming us into your home."

"It's our honor, ya Pasha." Selma had always believed that money never made a person, that people were all the same in the eyes of God, but when the pasha spoke, he was intimidating. It was the way he sat upright before he spoke, and how slowly and deliberately he uttered his words.

"Let me get to the point," he said. "My wife and I have been trying to get Amir to settle down for years. But, as you know, he's our only child, and well, we've spoiled him a bit. He has refused every girl we introduced him to. Nobody was good enough. Nobody made him happy. He couldn't imagine himself with anyone. Then, to my surprise, just days ago he told us the news of his courtship with Laila."

"The courtship was not with my approval," Selma said.

"I know and I apologize for that. My son has always been impetuous."

"So, your daughter snuck around behind your back?" Hoda said.

Selma ignored the comment, and the pasha glanced disapprovingly at his wife. He continued.

"But I trust my son's judgment, and if he finds your daughter Laila suitable and loves her, then I'd rather he marry someone he loves than someone we choose for him."

Hoda let out a sigh.

"And so, we've come to ask for your daughter's hand in marriage."

Just then Laila and Naima arrived with trays of pastries, coffee, tea, cups, and saucers. They set them on the coffee table and quickly passed out the plates and forks, poured the teas and coffees, and sat back down. Laila sat in the chair next to Amir and looked at him. Her cheeks flushed as he smiled at her. Then she crossed her legs and folded her hands in her lap, keeping her gaze lowered. Selma remembered the trepidation she'd felt when Kamal had proposed to her, and when her mother began to prepare her for wifedom.

She had accepted womanhood as a gift from God. She'd never questioned the inequity of the bedroom (only the man deciding when, how, how often) or the pangs of childbirth or the sheer exhaustion thereafter. But now that one of her daughters was unhappily but tolerably married, and the other was about to venture on an unknown journey Selma understood why Kamal had wanted Laila to be a boy. God is the only one who makes these decisions, and to God she must submit.

"What do you say, Laila?" Selma turned to her daughter. "The pasha is requesting your hand for his son. Do you accept?"

Laila nodded. She blushed, and Amir took a blue velvet box out of his jacket pocket.

"Of course, she accepts," Hoda said. "Amir is a golden catch." This time, her husband nudged her.

Selma didn't respond. Hoda was obviously baiting her, counting on an altercation to end a marriage she clearly didn't approve of. But who was Hoda compared to the women of Rod El Farag or the village in Asyut? Selma had been trained under much harsher conditions, where tongues doled out lashes like whips.

"This is just an engagement period," Hoda continued. "They can use this time to get to know one another, and then decide if marriage is the next move."

"No." Selma shook her head, and everyone in the room went silent. Even the sound of cup to saucer halted. Amir sat still with the box in hand.

Botros and Naima turned to each other, and Laila said something under her breath that Selma didn't catch.

"Let's leave then." Hoda put her teacup down and stood. "You heard her. She refuses the proposal."

"Wait," Botros said. "I'm sure there's an explanation. Isn't there, Mama Selma?"

Selma didn't get up after Hoda. She stayed in her chair. "I'm not refusing the marriage. I'm refusing the engagement. I'm honored by the proposal, but things aren't as Western in Rod El Farag as they are in Zamalek, and there is already talk of Amir and Laila having been seen together. An engagement would have been fine had Amir proposed properly from the beginning, but now, it's either a wedding or good-bye."

"Good-bye," Hoda said, and turned to the door.

"Wedding," Amir said, leaning close to Laila.

"Sit down, Hoda," the pasha said.

She sat down.

"I'll marry her right now. Send for a priest." Amir opened the box and took out a diamond ring that twinkled in the soft light of the family room.

"Let's not be rash," Selma said.

"Let's not." Hoda turned to her son, giving him a chastising look. But Amir took Laila's hand, placed the ring on it, and kissed it.

"I know what I want and I'm not changing my mind. I'll marry Laila right now. I'll marry her next week. I'll wait ten years if I have to." He pulled another box from his jacket pocket. This time it was a bracelet. It had so many gems on it, Selma couldn't count the colors and varieties. He clasped the bracelet on Laila's wrist. When Botros proposed Naima had gotten two gold bangles. Nobody in the family had ever owned anything gemmed.

"It's beautiful," Laila said, her glances shifting between the ring and Amir as if there were no one else in the room. And now, she didn't look as shy as Selma hoped she would. Once again she regretted not preparing Laila. Selma had assumed that Laila knew not to look directly into Amir's eyes or smile so unabashedly or, worst of all, look so comfortable with him. There was honor in the awkward unfamiliarity of an unmarried couple.

"Well, if we're going to do this, let's do it right," the pasha said.

"Take all the time you need," Selma said. "But unless Laila and Amir are married by a priest in a church, I won't allow any interaction whatsoever between the two. You understand, of course." For the first time since Kamal had died, she felt his presence, as if he were there guiding her, and she swallowed past a lump in her throat.

The pasha shook his head. "Of course, I don't understand. It's customary for an engaged couple to meet, to talk, to get to know one another."

"That's the problem," Selma said. "They met. They talked. They got to know one another. So, until they are legally married, I won't allow any further interaction."

"How backward," Hoda said. Then she turned to her son, "Do you see what you're getting into?"

Laila started to say something, but then Selma cut her off. "You're right Hoda. We are backward, but this is the kind of backward that we take pride in."

"I'm going to leave this up to my son. He's a man and he can decide," the pasha said and then sat back in the chair.

"It will take no less than a year to prepare for a wedding. You want my son not to see his bride for a year? How cold," Hoda said.

Selma worried. After all, one year was long enough for Amir to forget Laila. Selma hadn't thought the wedding would take a year to plan when she'd made her stipulations. Now, she couldn't back out of it. Laila glared at her from across the room.

"One month," Amir said. "I'll have everything ready in a month. I know the owners of every hotel in the city. I know the best caterers in town personally, and I have a connection at House of Worth in Paris. One telegram and I'll have a gown here for Laila in weeks."

"You see? One month. What's one month in a lifetime?" Selma tried to mask her relief.

"But the people. We have to accommodate our guests." Hoda's voice rose, an annoying whine to it.

"Everyone will come even if the wedding is tomorrow," Amir said, publicly rebutting his mother in a way Selma had never seen. In one way it could be good for Laila to have a strong man by her side, uninfluenced by his mother the way Botros was. On the other hand, here was a young man who lacked respect.

"What about the priest?" Hoda said. "And what about the church?"

"Leave it to me," Amir said.

"Then that's it. We have an official engagement," said Makram Youseff Pasha as he stood and hugged his son. He leaned in to kiss Laila on the cheek. "Mabrook, ya binty." He congratulated her, calling Laila his daughter. There was a calm relieved smile on his face, and this gave Selma a sense of peace and sorrow all at once. She wished Kamal had lived to see his baby girl betrothed to a pasha's son. Maybe all of this was the work of God after all. Then Selma trilled a long zaghroota. Naima's zaghroota followed. Soon the neighborhood women trilled from their balconies. Finally, she and her daughter were redeemed.

12

Madame Caron stood in the doorway of the service entrance, smoking her morning cigarette. She wore a light blue dress, and the desert winds blew its skirt against her long, skinny legs. "Good of you to show up," she said as Mama and Laila arrived, lowering their heavy grocery totes to the ground outside the door.

"Is there a problem, Madame?" Mama asked. "We're not late, are we?"

Madame Caron took a drag of her cigarette and then let out a cloud of smoke. "You thieves." She said, her voice deep and gravelly.

"We're not thieves," Laila said.

"What's that then?" She pointed her cigarette at Laila's ring. "Isn't that stolen?"

"This is mine. It's my engagement ring," Laila said.

"God is good." Mama's voice was steady, but she stumbled on her words. "The proposal came just last night. We could hardly wait to tell you the good news. And the ring is part of her shabka."

"I already know. I know that your daughter stole my daughter Catherine's suitor!"

For a second Mama didn't respond, and then she said, "That's nonsense. No such thing happened."

"You weren't there, Selma. You were working in the kitchen, but I saw it. I just dismissed it." She threw the cigarette on the ground and stepped on it with her patent leather high heel. "I thought to myself, it can't be. But it's true. Laila was flirting with Amir at the party just before he danced with Catherine. I couldn't hear what she was saying, but I now know she was stealing him. She knew Catherine had her eyes on him, and she got to him, bending his ear with God knows what."

"That's not true," Laila said, fighting the thickening feeling in her throat. "I never spoke to him. He approached me. He's the one who followed me for months. And there was nothing between him and Catherine in the first place."

"You mean to tell me he'd prefer you." Madame Caron jabbed her bony finger at Laila's head. The finger scraped through the air, down her body. "Over my Catherine? You probably promised him things and did things good high-class girls don't do, and because he's a decent man, he felt sorry for you and decided to marry you to save you from a lifetime of shame."

"Madame," Mama said sternly, "Laila wouldn't do that. I raised her to know better. You've known her since she was a child. You know better too."

"All I know is that she's always envied Catherine. Always." Madame Caron raised her voice. "After all my generosity." Her face was red. Her nostrils flared, and her blond silky hair blew in the strengthening wind.

"We never covet," Mama said. Her hand shook as she shielded her eyes from the sun. "Jealousy is a sin against God. Nothing you're saying is true. This is a big misunderstanding, but we can sort all of this inside. It's vegetable day. There's a lot of work to do, and the sun is in my eyes." Mama picked up the grocery tote and tried to step in, but Madame Caron put one foot outside the door, blocking her from entering.

"You don't work here anymore. It's out of my hands. Your fiancé's butler came by this morning. He announced the engagement and resigned on your behalf."

"That can't be true. He didn't say anything like that to me," Mama said, her voice quivering.

"Leave now," Madame Caron said. Laila followed her gaze from Mama's face to the street. "Barra, I said. Barra, you and your slut daughter." She pointed with her foot in the direction of the road.

Mama dropped the tote on the ground. A few artichokes and zucchinis fell out and rolled onto the flagstone pavement. She covered her ears with her hands. "No." She shook her head, sobbing. "This is all wrong. Stop saying those awful things."

"Maalish, Mama," Laila said, and patted Mama's back to comfort her. "Let's go. She's a heartless woman."

Mama turned her back to Madame Caron, still covering her ears. Before Laila followed, she took a step closer to Madame Caron, close enough so that Laila could smell the cigarette stench on her clothes and the faint scent of stale perfume. She remembered the way she felt that day Madame Caron had banished her from Catherine's playroom, how small and helpless she'd felt being when she'd given her a piece of chocolate and sent her back to the small, hot kitchen.

"You've never cared about anyone but yourself. We were nothing but your property, and you're just upset that the pasha's son found you and your daughter bland and tasteless."

Madame Caron opened her mouth to speak, but no words came out. Then she stepped inside the house, slamming the door.

As they walked around the house and off Madame Caron's property, Mama calmed down, wiping her tears with the cuffs of her galabeya. "What are we going to do now? We don't have a job, Laila. We have no money. With your wedding coming up …"

"Mama, do you think the pasha is going to let us pay anything for this wedding? If he resigned on your behalf, then he's doing you a favor. Imagine not having to slave in that woman's kitchen, buy her groceries, make her awful food, cater to that spoiled brat. Just imagine. Besides, we have our sewing."

"You think depending on the pasha's son's money is any better? We'll be indebted to him, his father, and his stuck-up mother."

159

"It won't be a debt. I'm going to be his wife."

"Did you know about Catherine?" Mama said as they walked past the wrought iron front gates.

Laila didn't respond.

"You better answer me, girl. Did you know that Catherine liked him?"

"I heard her talking to her friends at the party. I saw her dancing with him, but that's it. Besides, Mama, he never felt the same way about her."

"Still, it was wrong of you."

"Wrong? That woman and her daughter have taken everything from us. They took our dignity, our strength, and they even owe us back wages. Baba died for her stupid flowers, and you're telling me that I was wrong?"

"Baba didn't die for her flowers," Mama said. "Baba died because God decided it was his time."

"No, Baba died because God is cruel."

They hadn't even crossed the street when Mama slapped Laila's face, just like she had that day at the church steps, just as she had when she discovered Laila had been seeing Amir. But this time Laila didn't bring her hand to her cheek, or gasp, or even tear up. So, Mama raised her hand to slap her again.

"Hit me, Mama. Hit me all you want, but it won't change reality. It never can."

Mama let her hand fall to her side. They crossed the street and walked in silence the rest of the way home, over the Kasr El Nil bridge and all the way to their neighborhood on Gazirat Badran. As they started up the stairs of their building, Mama said, "That kalba Caron never even paid us for today's groceries."

"She is worse than a dog," Laila said. "Dogs are loyal."

Amir's butler was waiting at the front door of their apartment. He wore the same long-tailed jacket and white gloves he'd worn the day he delivered the news of the proposal. His face was sweaty. When Mama saw he'd been waiting, she quickly unlocked the front door and invited him in.

"Thank you, but not today. I'm here to give you something, and to tell you that you can stop working for that Madame Caron. I tried to get here first, but I couldn't make it in time."

"We just got back from there. She fired us," Laila said.

"I'm sorry about that. Please don't tell Amir Pasha that I was late. Please." From the front pocket of his jacket, he pulled out a red and blue bordered envelope and gave it to Mama.

"You'll receive the same amount the first of every month. Amir Makram Youseff Pasha would like you to consider it as a perpetual wedding gift. And he says that once the wedding details are finalized, he'll send word, but that it won't be long."

Mama didn't smile, and her face reddened. "Why didn't they tell me they were going to resign on my behalf?"

"There's money in there." He pointed to the envelope in Mama's hand.

"Why didn't anyone tell me about this plan?" She raised her voice. "Answer me or I'll tell them you were late, and that I was put in an unbearably embarrassing situation."

"I'm not privy to these conversations. I don't know anything except for what I'm told." The butler's voice wavered. He looked pleadingly at Mama.

When the man left, Mama lowered herself into Baba's chair. She put the envelope in her lap.

"Why are you so upset? Open it." Laila sat on the floor at her feet just as she used to sit at Baba's feet when he played the oud.

"I don't know anything anymore. But none of this feels right." She stared at the sealed envelope.

"That's because you're not used to good things happening," Laila said. "Just open it."

Mama tore the envelope with her thumbnail and took out the bills, giving them one by one to Laila, who flattened each bill on the coffee table until they'd counted out two months' salary.

"It would be nice to rest," Mama said, "to sit out on the balcony, to eat real beef stew once a week. It would be nice to help Naima and her children. I'm just not used to taking money for nothing."

"What if this money is payment for everything you've already done? What if you're meant to rest a bit?"

"The world doesn't work that way, Laila. Nobody ever pays you for nothing. Now, let's clean this place in case another one of his people pop up again like a gin." Mama took the money and stuffed it in her bra. Then she and Laila made the beds, swept the floor, washed the balcony, and dusted the furniture.

Later that day an ecstatic Naima came to visit, knocking wildly at the door. She rushed in and dropped down on the settee, rubbing her belly, barely able to catch her breath before she explained. The butler had paid her a visit, had given her an envelope filled with cash. "He said it was gift to help prepare for the wedding. The old crow tried to take it, but the butler wouldn't give her the envelope. He kept saying that the envelope was from Amir Makram Youseff Pasha and addressed to Naima Kamal Abd El Malek. You should have seen her face. Thank you, God. Thank you, God." Naima put her hands together in prayer, looking up at the ceiling.

"Don't leave your money at home," Mama said.

"Of course not. I'm not the naïve girl that used to live in this house." She reached under her galabeya and pulled a stack of cash from her bra, waving it in the air. "My money goes where I go." Then she stuffed it back in her bra and slammed her palms on the coffee table, startling Mama and Laila. "You know what we're going to do today? We're going to eat meat, and none of us is going to cook it." Naima had a wild look in her eyes, a look of adventure Laila had never seen on her sister. Standing up, her pregnant belly protruding, Naima wrapped the shawl around her shoulder and said, "I'm treating us to the best kabab and kofta money can buy." Then before Laila could offer to go with her, and before Mama could convince her not to spend her money, she bolted out the door.

Naima returned in a half hour carrying a bag brimming with kabab and kofta. She set it on the dining room table and unwrapped the spiced roasted lamb kabab and beef kofta patties. The meats sat on layers of piping hot pita bread and beds of chopped parsley so that the bread had soaked in all the meat juices. She kept reaching in the bag for the sides; hummus, baba ghanouj, mint and cucumber yogurt. The three of them sat at the small table saying little until they'd eaten it all.

Mama leaned backed in the dining room chair. "The last time I had kabab and kofta was the day after my wedding. My mother brought it over for my sabaheya. Your grandmother, ala yerhamha, could make the best kabab in the village. People used to buy meat and take it to her kitchen so she could spice it for them."

"I tasted it once with Baba after performing at the café," Laila said. "The people had all left and the owner was so happy with our music, he bought us all kabab and kofta. I only got a few bites."

"I can't remember ever having anything like it, but I knew how it tasted," Naima said, "because I've been smelling it all my life. Every time we walked past the kabab kiosk, I breathed in the taste. It's a whole world apart from fava beans and falafels."

That evening, the three of them sat on the balcony and watched the sun set over their city. They sipped tea and laughed about Baba's old eccentricities; how he wore his slippers in the house but took them off before going out onto the balcony; or how he drank his tea black but wouldn't eat watermelon without a layer of sugar; or how he slept covering his face with a pillow. They talked about Botros's mother too, how nasty she was and how she clung to her son. And then they started on the wedding, the dress that hadn't come, the church that hadn't been reserved, and the flower girls that hadn't been chosen. They guessed at the number of guests who'd be invited and what kind of food might be served.

"Stop talking about it." Mama flashed her palm at the girls. "Someone could hear you and strike you with hasad."

Later, when the number of pedestrians in the street had dwindled, Mama and Laila walked Naima down to the street and waited with her until she hailed a taxi and got into it safely.

On their first day of freedom, Mama and Laila had planned to sleep in.

But neither of them could sleep past dawn. In the kitchen Laila filled the kanaka with water, boiled it, and stirred in a heaping spoonful of powdered coffee. She served it black in a demitasse just the way Mama liked it. The two of them sat on the balcony to watch the sunrise.

"You know something," Mama said. "I've never watched the sun rise. Even on my days off I busied myself with chores, and your father stayed up so late that sometimes he fell asleep as the sun rose. It's more peaceful than I'd imagined."

At dawn the sky was the color of pomegranate. The building rooftops, busy by day, were still in their quiet slumber. Even the stray dogs and cats seemed too tired to announce themselves this early in the morning.

"What are we doing today?" Laila said.

"What are we doing tomorrow and the day after that, and the day after that?" Mama fixed her gaze on the horizon.

"I don't know," Laila said. What would they do? How would they live like the rich women who didn't work? Rich women like Madame Caron had outings, tea parties, nights at the opera to keep them busy. But Mama and Laila didn't do those things.

That day they decided to make molokheya soup. They went to the souk and bought fresh green molokheya leaves, garlic cloves, coriander seeds, chicken, and rice. But because they'd always been so efficient at picking through the rice, chopping the molokheya, and cleaning the chicken, lunch was ready early, and they sat on the balcony again after finishing it, waiting for two o'clock to come. At Madame Caron's, they usually ate lunch sitting on floor mats in the kitchen, eating whatever they'd brought from home or sometimes Madame Caron's leftovers. That night they finished all the sewing work they had left, and the six days of freedom that followed each passed more slowly than the last.

On the one-week anniversary of the proposal, Laila began to worry about why the butler hadn't returned with the wedding details. She thought about these things as they sipped on their morning tea on the balcony. Maybe Amir was just finalizing the wedding plans, she told herself. He probably needed more time to arrange things. What if Amir's mother was sabotaging the whole thing and Laila never saw him again?

"Mama?" Laila said.

"Don't say it. There are gins everywhere. Don't say anything. It's only been a week," Mama said, and bit her nails.

"Then I won't sit around and wait, Mama. Let's go out tonight. Let's go see a movie at Diana Palace. There's a new movie. I saw the advertisement when we were walking back from Madame Caron's. Laila Murad is in it."

"Are you magnoona? I've never been out of my house after sundown except for work, and now, at this age, you want me to go alla hal sharey around the city like a ..."

"It's only a movie, Mama, not a cabaret. And you're not that old. Yalla, it's just silly of us to sit here and wait." Laila nudged her mother. "We can take Naima too. It'll be fun."

"No, Naima should be home with her husband. It'll upset Botros if we just pop in and take her, and the old crow is probably bending his ear about the money. It'll only be trouble for your sister."

"So, you'll go? You'll go to the movies?"

"Amry lil la," Mama said, throwing her arms up in the air.

Laila hugged her mother. "You'll see. You'll love it."

Mama refused to take a taxi to the downtown area. It was a waste of money. "As long as we have legs, we can walk," she said.

They walked from Gazirat Badran Street through Shubra, over Al Laymoon Bridge, passing the kiosk where Laila had met Amir, past her sister's building, and onto Soliman Pasha Street. They walked past Cicurel's, Benzion's and Omar Effandi's department stores, which towered above the small boutiques where women dressed in high heels and silk dresses shopped for shoes, purses, and jewelry. Then they passed Groppi's crowded ice cream parlor, the Egyptian Diplomatic Club, and Café Riche, where Laila had sung once with Baba, and turned on Al Alfi Street, finally arriving at Diana Palace. It was one of tens of cinemas in the downtown, but every time Laila had passed by Diana Palace with its sleek curved-corner front and its large movie billboards, she'd wanted to go in. But it was a high-class cinema, and after Baba died, she could never afford it. The movie *Ghazal Al Banat* was playing, and the beloved actress and singer Laila Murad was starring.

Mama didn't like the name of the movie. "It's obscene. *Flirtation of Girls*? What kind of film are you taking me to?"

Laila pleaded with her mother at the front of the box office line, until finally one of the moviegoers who was standing in line behind them assured Mama that she'd already seen the film once and that it was just fine. Mama reluctantly agreed to see it but refused to buy first class tickets, which cost five piasters more than the second class.

"How much is a third class ticket?" Mama asked the lady at the box office. "There are no third class tickets," the lady said.

Mama took the money out of her bra and paid. Past the box office they entered a grand foyer and took one of the wrought iron double staircases to a landing. Nonchalant women in long gowns and men in suits and ties passed them on the staircase, but Mama and Laila held onto the railing dressed in their galabeyas and took each step with care. When they got to the landing Mama stood in front of an enormous carved mirror that reflected the sparkling lights glittering from a massive crystal chandelier. "In the name of the holy cross," she said.

At the top of the stairs a uniformed man wearing white gloves escorted them to their seats. "In the name of the holy cross," Mama said again, looking up at the enormous domed ceiling and velvet tufting on the upper part of the walls. But as the lights dimmed and the film reel rolled, it became clear the movie wasn't just fine like the lady had said. The film raised more questions than either Mama or Laila could answer, and those uncertainties made the chances of Amir going through with the wedding slimmer than ever.

The movie was about a spoiled pasha's daughter named Laila who'd failed her Arabic exams in college. When her father hires a poor Arabic tutor, the tutor arrives at the palace so overwhelmed by the opulence, he mistakes the dog's caretaker for the pasha.

"Does Amir have a dog nanny? Is that how they live?" Mama asked at the opening scene, her voice so loud a man from the row behind her hushed her.

"I don't know," Laila whispered, vested in the fate of the poor teacher, who reminded her so much of her own baba. Laila hadn't thought to ask Amir these things. She'd never been to his palace, though she knew he lived in Zamalek and that his life was even more luxurious than the Carons'. In the movie, as the lessons began, the teacher fell in love with his spoiled student and even believed she might love him back. That was when the movie paused and the lights came back on.

"That's it?" Mama yelled. "That's what I paid for?"

"No, Mama." Again, Laila whispered. "It's the entre'acte. We take a break now. We buy a kazooza and some chips. Then the movie resumes."

"Do we have to pay more for it?" A few girls sitting in second class with them laughed at Mama as they walked down the aisle. Although they weren't wearing glittering gowns the girls wore pretty floral skirts and silky blouses.

Laila took Mama by the hand, and they went back into the foyer where men smoked their cigars and their wives sipped concoctions in fancy glasses. Laila and Mama were underdressed even when compared to the second-class moviegoers who wore skirts and blouses or pretty dresses and had their hair styled.

Laila ordered two kazoozas and one bag of chips to share. But the soda was too bubbly for Mama and she gave the rest of her share to Laila. "What do you think is going to happen to the poor teacher?"

"I don't know," Laila said.

They watched the rest of the film without any interruptions from Mama. The teacher's hopes were dashed when he learned the student wasn't in love with him, and that because of his station in life he was never a consideration in the first place. Throughout the movie Laila thought about her life and the events in the film. They were eerily similar. Why? Surely the movie wasn't based on her life, but it had to be based on her society. And if the message was that her mismatch with Amir couldn't and wouldn't work, then had she been too optimistic? When the lights went back on, Laila got up quickly from her chair, took Mama's hand, and they pushed their way out of Diana Palace.

They walked home in silence, and when they got to the apartment Laila took off her engagement ring and gave it to Mama. Mama clasped it in her palm, said nothing, and they both went to their bedrooms.

It took another three agonizing days for their fears to be quelled. During those days, Mama and Laila stayed home. They didn't spend any more of the money, which would run out at the pace they'd been going. Mama bought just what they needed from the vegetable market and didn't visit the butcher. Laila had no appetite anyway. A bite of fava beans for breakfast and a sip of tea was all she could eat. What if she was like the poor teacher and Amir was the spoiled daughter, and what if he'd come to his senses and realized he was far too wealthy, far too sophisticated to ever marry her? Laila might be able to withstand the blow, but Mama might die from the shame of a broken engagement.

At sundown, ten days after the proposal, a knock came at the door and Laila opened it, hopeful, but it wasn't the butler. Outside the door stood a tall, thin man with a trimmed white beard who wore a suit and tie and the same kind of shiny shoes Amir wore on their dates. He carried a white bag and a hard metal case that had "U.S." printed in black. He introduced himself as Pierre Michelle and said that Amir Makram Youseff Pasha had sent him.

"Itfadal," Mama said, inviting him in, and he wiped his foot at the doorstep before coming into the apartment. He sat on the settee in the small family room and set the white bag and case on the floor beside him. Mama sat across from him in Baba's old chair. Laila hurried into the kitchen to make tea. After she served it, she sat in the chair across from Pierre Michelle. He took a sip of his tea and then took a small pad of paper and a shiny silver pen from the breast pocket of his suit jacket.

Clearing his throat, he took a moment to review what was written on the front of his pad. He said he had been temporarily hired by Amir Pasha to help him prepare Laila and her family for the wedding, which would be held in a month. The ceremony, he explained, would be at the Botroseya Church in Zamalek. Laila and Mama could invite whomever they chose to attend.

Pierre gave Laila the white bag, which was filled to the top with wedding bonbonnieres made of candied almonds. Each was in a miniature silver basket wrapped in white lacy cloth and tied with a ribbon on which was printed "Laila and Amir 6-23-49."

"You can pass these out as invitations. The reception, though, will be for your immediate family only, and that's why I'm here. You all must be trained."

"Trained for what?" Laila said.

"So many things," Pierre said, consulting his pad again. "There's the wedding waltz you have to learn, of course, and what to say in the greeting line, proper etiquette during the dinner."

Laila had never seen anyone waltz in real life, only in the movies

"No." Mama shook her head. "They can dance in private all they want after the wedding, but not in public like that for the whole world to see. Who does that?"

"My lady," Pierre said, "the entire civilized world does that."

"Mama," Laila said.

"This wedding is in four weeks." He put the metal case on the coffee table, unfastened the latches, and opened it. Inside the case there was a turntable, arm, and crank. "It's portable," Pierre said. "It's American, a leftover from the war." He pointed at the "U.S." on the side. But Laila didn't know how U.S. meant America and she was too embarrassed to ask. "It's not the newest model but it's sturdy." He patted the side of the case. There was already a record on the turntable, but Laila couldn't read it.

"Have either of you heard of the Swan Lake Waltz by Tchaikovsky?"

"Afrangi music?" Mama said with disgust.

"Yes," Pierre said, "a Russian afrangi. Swan Lake is a ballet. It's a tragic love story, but the opening waltz is just …" He kissed his fingers and threw the imaginary kiss into the air.

"Isn't there a love song that isn't tragic?" Mama said.

"I'm afraid not. At least, nothing as beautiful as the Swan Lake Waltz." Pierre stood up and put out his hand to Laila. "Mademoiselle, would you do me the honor of this dance?"

Laila hesitated and turned to Mama, who shook her head in disapproval but said nothing else. Laila had only held Baba's hand and Amir's. It felt wrong to hold another man's hand, but Pierre looked even older than Baba would have been. And he was here because Amir had asked him to come. There was no time for hesitation. The wedding was in four weeks, and like the man said, there was so much to do.

Laila stood up and took the old man's hand.

13

Selma sat on Kamal's chair watching Laila dance with the stranger whose name Selma couldn't pronounce. She'd tried to say Pierre, but her P's had always come out as B's. She heard the difference in sound but could never correct it. Laila, who'd learned the sound at school, had even tried to teach her. She'd held a tissue in front of Selma's lips and told her that when she'd made the P sound, the air would burst out of her mouth and rustle the tissue. The tissue never moved, and Selma stopped trying to say the foreign P.

The afrangi music was beautiful, and Selma hated that she liked it. The song started softly like the pitter patter of a toddler's steps, and then it soared like those birds that perched on her balcony railing before flying off into the blue sky. Pierre talked to Laila about the order of her steps, about where she'd put her hand on Amir's shoulder, where Amir would put his hand on her back, box shapes she would make on the floor with her feet. They counted from one to three over and over again, wahed, itneyn, talata. Pierre explained how vast Amir's dance floor was at the palace, how when she danced, they'd travel together around a spacious marble floor with guests sitting at big round tables, their eyes on the newlyweds.

When Selma was a young bride, her wedding had been planned in a week. Her mother and mother-in-law got together and cooked duck stuffed with rice. Her mother sewed her a wedding galabeya and hand embroidered it with sequins. They dipped her hands and feet with henna, and melted sugar into wax to pull the hair off her body. The invitation was by word of mouth. Her father had gone around the village announcing the date. Their dances had no steps to practice, no counts, no hands placements. They just moved to the beat of the tabla. The women swayed their hips, the men of her village danced with a stick, twirling it around and around. Laila's wedding and all its preparations were as foreign to Selma as the elusive P.

Laila and Pierre rose and fell together with the music. They took their steps at the same time, Pierre stepping forward and Laila stepping back. As they twirled around the tight space of the meager family room, Selma sank deeper into her fears. Her daughter was about to exit the only life she'd ever known and enter into a realm Selma knew nothing about. How would she guide her daughter if the rules were unknowable, if the guardrails she'd always depended on were gone? If a couple had a marital problem, their two families rallied around them and helped them solve it. A man raised in her baladi way respected his mother, showed deference to his mother-in-law, understood certain obligations toward his wife and children. What had the pasha taught his son? He didn't respect his mother, that was clear from the start, and he didn't give much regard to old society's rules. Did he know how to love, and did he truly love her daughter the way Kamal had once loved her? Laila smiled as she twirled to the music with Pierre. She really was a beauty. Her lips were pink and full, and her eyelashes curled up so naturally she didn't even need mascara, and her skin never had a blemish. Even during the years when young girls got blemishes, Laila never did. But what did her daughter know about the afrangi life? How would Selma prepare her?

The music stopped. "Brava, Laila," said Pierre, "but you need to practice. Tomorrow, I expect you to do better." Then he closed up his case, thanked Selma for her hospitality, promised to return in the morning, and left.

As soon as the door closed, Laila squealed in excitement, jumping up and down like a child, not like a woman who was about to bear the responsibility of marriage. "Did you see me, ya Mama? And did you hear that music? It was like cotton candy, and sunshine, and maybe a blooming flower, but one that smells good like a rose or a jasmine."

"Laila, we should talk."

"Hader, ya Mama," said her obedient daughter, but Laila didn't sit to talk. Humming the afrangi music, she rested her hand on an imaginary shoulder and danced around the family room, into the kitchen, and the two small bedrooms.

It was Kamal's fault, allah yerhamoo, raising her like a boy with less restrictions, less inhibitions, and most importantly, less fear. He'd always told Laila, "Don't let anything scare you. Never fear anything." But that was all wrong for a girl. A man needed to be fearless, but a woman had to fear. Fear kept girls out of danger. And now it was too late.

"Laila, we have things to do," Selma said. "You need to take a break from the dancing, ya binty. We have to get serious."

"Is it about Amir? Will you let me see him now?"

"No," Selma said. She wished her daughter didn't long so much for the pasha's son.

"But why, Mama? Every bride sees her fiancé. Naima went out with Botros, didn't she? Why can't I have the same freedoms?"

"Because you desire him too much. That's why." She shouldn't have used the word desire. It meant things Laila shouldn't know yet. And what would she ever do with desire anyway? Desire was a shameful burden a woman must carry, and the more of it she had, the heavier the weight. Better if she never desired. "You have to understand that the only power you have as a woman is control over yourself. I'm not a stupid woman, Laila. I know what happens when young couples court for months. Now that you're engaged, your guard is down, and anything can happen. I don't trust you not to be impetuous."

"But Mama …"

Selma held up her hand. "The answer is no. Now, please focus. We have things to do." Laila shook her head. Her face reddened with anger like it had when she was a child and Selma didn't let her play soccer in the alleyway until her father came home.

Selma put her hand on her daughter's soft cheek. "Have patience, ya binty. The wedding is a few weeks away. Once you're married, you'll see him as much as you want."

Then she took her by the hand into the kitchen. They made tea, sat on the balcony, and discussed their plans. First, they had to pass out the bonbonnieres and invite all the neighbors to the wedding ceremony. Mama had to make sharbat to pass out to drink before the wedding, send for the ballana to come over the house and wax Laila's body and put henna on her, just as they had for Naima. "Then there is the wedding night," Selma said as she sipped on her tea.

"Mama, Naima told me everything. You don't need to …"

"It's my job to tell you myself."

Laila lowered her gaze. This duty of motherhood was Selma's least favorite, but she couldn't let her daughter go into marriage without proper instruction. She would tell her exactly what Selma's mother had told her. "At first it's awkward. It may even hurt, but don't push away or kick your husband, and don't cry. Be strong. Endure it. Do whatever he wants. Some men are gentle. Some are more aggressive. God made them that way. There's nothing to do about it. Remember that when you become his wife, he has hak alleyky. And that means you're his by God's will. Whatever you do, don't talk to him about these matters and never initiate even if you want to, but you shouldn't want to. These things are on the man to start, to stop, to do, or not to do. Do you understand?"

Laila nodded; her gaze still lowered.

"Most importantly," Selma continued. "Keep the sheet for me. Your blood is your honor. I will come by on your sabaheya to get it. I don't know how they do things in the palace, but in our neighborhood the sheet is just as important as the priest's blessing. You hear me?"

The smile that had been on Laila's face while dancing was gone, and now she had a sullen, serious look about her. Had Naima not mentioned the blood to her? Was Laila afraid of the pain? She'd sobered her daughter and Selma regretted it, but what choice did she have? Life would happen no matter what. Better to be prepared than caught by surprise.

"Don't worry." Selma reached for Laila's hand, and Laila grabbed it. "It will be all right."

"I'm not thinking about that, Mama. I'm worried about you. What are you going to do here all by yourself? Why don't you come live with me and Amir? I'm sure he won't mind. I'm sure they have a great big palace with plenty of rooms."

Selma pulled her hand from her daughter's. "No, ya binty, it's time you start your own life with your husband. There is no place in that palace for me no matter how big it is. I'll be fine. I have my neighbors and my sewing to keep me busy. Besides, you'll have babies soon, and I'll come help you every day. And you can come visit me too. But this little place your father found for us will always be my home." Selma missed Kamal. Why hadn't she been more tender? Now, none of it made sense, yet here she was setting her daughter on the same inexplicable path. Maybe she should give her different advice. But what if she told her to be more open with her husband and he took advantage of her? That outcome would be unacceptable. Selma concluded that losing self-worth was much worse than having been a little too cold.

ೞ

Pierre came every morning. He taught Laila how to speak in a low modulated voice, how to address people by their proper titles. There was a difference between a bey, an effendi, and a pasha, and they were never to be confused. There was even a special way to drink tea. It was improper to blow on it to cool it down, to click the spoon against the teacup when stirring in sugar, to set the spoon on the table, to eat a cookie with the mouth open.

Each time he came they practiced the dance, and Selma had come to love that hour of instruction. She loved the grace with which her daughter moved her dainty feet, the way her ponytail bounced with the notes up and down, how she swayed as though a gentle wind moved her from side to side. And although the afrangi song was about a tragic love story, Selma believed it was auspicious music. By the end of the second week Laila had learned the dance; and to make sure she'd be prepared for the wedding reception, Pierre brought with him high-heeled shoes and a heavy makeshift wedding dress skirt for Laila to practice in. It wasn't easy for Laila in the shoes. She slipped and stepped on his toes. The skirt made her trip a few times, but the man with the white beard and cool blue eyes was patient and calm.

At the beginning of the third week Pierre brought with him a bag full of dinnerware wrapped in white cloth. He asked for permission to use the dining room table, and then set the table for four. He put down so many plates and glasses of different sizes that Selma lost count. He set multiple forks and knives on either side of the plates, and explained that afrangis ate their food in order and used different utensils for each course.

"One plate comes with food. You eat the food, and the plate is picked up. Then you get a new plate. Truly, this is the hardest part and requires a lot of concentration. Make sure you tell Naima and Botros to be here for dinner tomorrow. I'll bring the food and we will practice one course at a time."

Botros and Naima arrived just before sunset the next day, and Pierre arrived shortly after them. But this time the butler came with him, and together they carried a large metal box with a lid to the kitchen. Pierre shook hands with Botros and kissed Naima's hand. Naima giggled and Botros rubbed his chin. They sat at the dinner table, and Selma invited Pierre to sit with them, but he'd only set the table for four people. "Merci, Madame Selma, but my job is to be the teacher today. I'm certain we will have other occasions to eat together. Today, I will serve you, and all you have to do is follow my instructions."

"Where's the food?" Botros asked. "What are these knives for? Are we eating or doing surgery?"

Naima kicked him under the table.

Pierre held his hands behind his back and continued, ignoring Botros. "As soon as you sit down, remove the napkin from the plate and unfold it onto your lap." The four of them followed the instructions. "When everyone is served, then you can begin eating. Never start before everyone at your table has been served." He snapped his fingers, and the butler came into the dining room, picked up the plates that were still set from the night before, and returned with four plates on which was food that none of them recognized. "What you see here is one of the most famous French hors d'oeuvres. It's called foie gras paté en croûte."

"What is it?" Selma said, trying to guess what it might be. She'd seen patés at Madame Caron's, but never in a square that way.

"It's goose liver made into a paté, and what you see on the outside is a pastry. Think of it as the French version of kibda."

"This isn't kibda," Botros said.

Pierre turned to Botros, stared at him for a second, said nothing, and continued. "I want you to pick up your fork with your left hand and your knife with the right. I will demonstrate on Laila's plate. As you're doing this, it is important not to make noise with the utensils."

Laila stood up, and Pierre sat down in her chair. He demonstrated cutting one small piece off the paté, holding the fork and knife at complicated angles. Naima got it right on the first try. Botros got the motion right, but the mushed liver fell onto his lap before he could taste. Selma laughed but lost her piece too, and it rolled off the table and onto the floor. Pierre ran his hands through his thinning white hair and took a deep breath. It took a while before any of them could properly eat the first course, but they managed to get through it. The French kibda was delicious, even though Selma thought it needed more garlic and a hint of allspice.

They ate four other courses this way. They fumbled and lost utensils. Food fell onto the table, their laps, the floor, and one time something slipped off Laila's plate and skidded across the table until it hit the edge of

Naima's plate. This all happened before they even got to the part of how to use the napkins to wipe their mouths. Pierre had to remind them to chew with their mouths closed and not to talk while chewing. But it was hard not to talk because Selma wanted to comment on the food, ask how it was prepared, understand what spices were used. There was a fish plate that didn't look like fish, and beef that was sliced and undercooked to the point that it was still pink in the center. Selma tried to take her piece to the kitchen to finish cooking it in a pan, but Pierre said that this cut of meat had to be eaten pink in the center. Why didn't afrangis like to cook their food? Selma let her stews simmer for hours.

"I can't remember the names of any of these things," Laila said when they'd gotten to the dessert. "I've prepared similar things at Madame Caron's, but nothing like this."

"Don't worry, mademoiselle. It's more important to know how to eat it than to remember its name. That will come in due time."

Next, Pierre taught them how to pick up their glasses and how to drink something without a sound.

"I don't see why it matters," Botros said.

Pierre cleared his throat. "It matters because you are going to be sitting among high society, and the last thing you want is for anyone to think of you as ..."

"As what?" Botros stood and threw his napkin on the floor. He'd gained some weight since he'd married Naima, and his shirt was taut around his belly. "I'm a good man. I work hard. I take care of my wife and children. Who cares if I make sounds when I sip or if I don't like cold duck liver? Who do you want me to pretend to be?"

"Monsieur Botros, please," Pierre said. "Just calm down."

"Botros, what are you doing?" Laila said, her voice quivering.

Botros didn't respond to Laila.

"Come on, Naima, we're leaving. And unless I can eat my meal with pita bread without worrying about all these forks and knives or the damn sound they make on the plate, Naima and I are not coming to the wedding."

"I don't want to leave," Naima said. "Monsieur Pierre is right. He's teaching us good things."

"He's teaching us to be fake."

"I'm not leaving and I'm going to my sister's wedding."

Botros picked up a plate and smashed it on the floor. "I'm your husband. You'll do as I say."

Naima started to cry, and Laila cried with her sister. "Don't break my plates, you savage," Pierre said.

"I'm not a savage, but you're a pimp." Botros loosened his tie.

"I might as well have been teaching a donkey." Pierre raised his voice and beads of sweat formed on his forehead. "Look what you've done. The women are crying."

The butler came running in from the kitchen, asking what was wrong.

Selma stood and pointed at Botros. "Shut your mouth and sit down. We made a lot of sacrifices for your wedding too, and you're going to do this for us. Laila, dry your eyes and pick up the broken pieces so no one gets hurt. Naima, stop crying, it's not good for the baby."

Everyone quieted. Botros sat down. Selma took her seat and looked at Pierre. She didn't want to address him because she couldn't pronounce his name and she didn't know how to say monsieur either, so she cleared her throat and nodded to him. "Please continue with the training."

Pierre whispered something in the butler's ear, and he quickly served the dessert. It was the easiest to eat and it was the most delicious, a light, creamy chocolate concoction that lingered in the mouth just long enough to taste it fully. After everyone had eaten the dessert, Pierre quickly packed all the dinnerware back into the empty metal container, and both he and the butler left. Botros and Naima followed soon after.

Before Naima left, Selma told her to calm her husband down when she got home and not to argue with him in front of the old crow.

౿ఎ

The next morning the butler delivered the wedding dress.

"It arrived this morning from Paris," he said loud enough for Selma to hear.

The dress came in a cream-colored box with gold lettering. Laila carried the box to her room and laid it on the bed. Selma removed the lid, setting it on the chipped wooden nightstand. The dress was wrapped in white tissue paper, and after carefully removing each layer of paper, they picked up the heavy gown together. It took the entire length of the room. "In the name of the holy cross," Selma said as she spread out the gown's train, running her hand along the elaborate embroidery of pearls and crystal. Also, in the box was a lace veil, a tiara, a blush- colored gown for Selma, and two pairs of high-heeled shoes, a white satin pair for Laila and a silver one for Selma.

"I'm glad it has sleeves," Selma said as Laila held the gown against her body.

"What kind of beads are these, Mama? They're like jewels."

"I don't know," Selma said, "but there's definitely nothing like it in the stores where I've been. Yalla, ya aroosa, try it on."

It was the first time Selma had called her daughter a bride. She'd always been afraid of hasad and the gin who were listening, but now that she'd uttered those words, she couldn't swallow past her thickening throat and the tears that she'd held back for so long, and which now came all at once.

Laila stepped into the wedding gown in front of the oval mirror. Then Selma pulled the heavy beaded dress up, holding each sleeve so that Laila could slip her arm into it. She held the dress closed from the back and saw that the buttons had been left unsewn so that final adjustments could be made. A bag full of satin buttons was attached to the inside of the dress.

"You look like an angel," Selma said, holding the dress on Laila, unable to wipe the tears that welled in her eyes. She temporarily pinned the dress marking where she'd sew each button. Then she put the tiara on her daughter's head and fastened the long lace veil to it. "No, you look like a princess. No, not a princess, a queen." She pinched the waist. "We'll still have to take it in about two centimeters on each side." Then she noted that the bust was tight. "I can move the top few buttons to make room."

Selma spent the next day altering Laila's gown. Together she and Laila sewed on all the buttons and then tried their dresses on again. Selma's was a little too long, so Laila hemmed it while Selma carefully inspected the embroidery making sure the beads weren't loosening.

The closet wasn't big enough for Laila's wedding gown, so they laid the dress on her bed and decided that for the next few days, Laila would sleep next to Selma and keep her room as a dressing room.

"Mama, this is all a dream. I'm afraid to wake up," Laila said to her mother that night before they fell asleep in the same bed. It was the first time since Laila was a little girl that she'd slept next to Selma.

"It's not a dream." Selma ran her hands through Laila's long silky hair, the way she used to when Laila was a child and couldn't fall asleep. "If only your baba was alive to see all of this. He'd be so proud of you."

Laila sat up in the bed. "Mama, I've been singing again. You might have heard me in my room. I know you don't approve, but I can't help it. The music comes out of me, and lately I've been hearing it play in my head. Baba comes to me in my dreams almost every night."

"It's expected, ya binty, with your wedding and everything."

"Amir loves music and he said when we get married, he wants me to sing to him."

"When you're married, you do what your husband wants. Now let's go to sleep."

"I want Baba's oud. I want to take it to the palace with me."

"No." Selma sat up in her bed. She'd dreaded this moment for years. "Let the oud stay here. Please." She pointed at the corner where the oud case had stood since the day Kamal had died.

"Mama, let me have it. I think Baba would have wanted me to have it."

"No," Selma said. "It's bad luck."

"My father's oud can never be bad luck."

Laila pushed the covers off, slipped from the bed, and went to the corner of the room.

"Don't touch it," Selma said.

But Laila didn't listen, or maybe didn't even hear.

Selma pushed herself out of bed, the pain in her knees throbbing, and stood between Laila and the oud case. "Please go back to bed, Laila. Leave the oud to tomorrow."

"Mama, you're acting strange." Laila reached behind her and tugged at the case, pulling it out of the corner.

"Please don't." Selma grabbed the case. "If you love me, you will put that case back where it belongs." Guilty and desperate, she pointed at the corner where the case had been for years.

"Mama, what's wrong with you?" Laila hugged Kamal's case. Stubborn. Laila was stubborn since the day she was born. "It's my wedding gift from Baba. At least let me believe that."

Selma stepped back. There was nothing more to do. What would she tell Laila? How would she explain?

Laila laid the case flat on the floor, squatted beside it, and ran her hand along the dusty leather. Then she unlatched and opened the empty case.

Why didn't she scream or cry? Selma had hoped she wouldn't make a scene, but her silence was worse. Now she wanted her to cry, to mourn, so that Selma could take her baby girl in her arms and comfort her.

After a few seconds, Laila closed the case, latched it, and propped it again in the corner.

Without shedding a tear, she asked, "Who'd you sell it to?"

"You remember Ahmed?"

Laila sat on the corner of the bed, her head in her hands. "I had to, ya binty, we had to eat. I had run out of money."

Laila got up. "Ahmed doesn't even play the oud. He plays the qanun." She put on one of Selma's galabeyas, wrapped a scarf around her shoulders, twisted her hair up in a bun, and slipped on a pair of old sandals.

"I don't know," Mama said. "Maybe he wanted to start playing. I didn't ask."

"Don't wait for me. This may take some time." Laila said.

"Magnoona, where are you going at this time of the night?" Selma raised her voice, but it had lost its motherly edge, its command. It sounded like a question, carried the rhythm of an apology, and so no matter how much she wanted to stop Laila from leaving, she couldn't do it.

"I'm going to find my baba's oud," Laila said, and left the apartment.

14

Laila ran west on Gazirat Badran Street, lifting the hem of her galabeya so she wouldn't trip on the uneven sidewalk. The sound of isha prayer blasted through the city. "Allahu Akbar, Allahu Akbar." Muezzins from every mosque called the faithful to prayer, their words slightly out of sync so that the prayer seemed to echo through the tight alleyways of the empty vegetable market. Laila ran. She ran past the post office, busy cigarette kiosks, and shopkeepers closing up for the night, stopping only once to give a crippled beggar two piastres.

She turned north onto Nile Corniche Road and entered the entertainment district of Rod El Farag. A cool summer breeze blowing in from the river billowed her shawl, so she trapped the fabric underneath her elbows. She scanned the Nile-front cafés and slowed down. The awnings looked different from the way she'd remembered them. Some buildings seemed bigger than before. Café patios were more crowded with men smoking shishas, and the street vendors had changed where they parked their carts. The roasted corn vendor she'd known wasn't there, and young boys sold jasmine necklaces on every corner. She was lost, until she saw the old ship-building yard in the distance where the railway bridge crossed the river into Zamalek. Baba had often taken her there to watch the ships being built, telling her stories of Aladdin and Sinbad the Sailor. "That one," he'd say, pointing at a half-built ship. "Sinbad's looked just like that one." She ran once again, toward the shipyard and the café she'd known.

The front entrance of the café was blocked with men who crowded the doorway, unable to find a seat inside. Laila went around the back to the old performers' door, which was left unlocked. She waited backstage, listening to the ensemble play Baba's songs, songs he'd never had the chance to sell, songs that had become so popular, the café barely had room to stand. She peeked from behind the curtain and watched the men play on stage just as she had when Baba was alive. The belly dancer shook her hips to the percussive rhythms of the riqq and tabla and undulated to the oud, the sad, flutelike nay, and the soulful strings of the qanun. But Ahmed wasn't the one playing the qanun or the oud. There was a new player, a young man Laila didn't recognize. The only person she recognized was Hussein, a man she used to call uncle. When the curtains closed, and the audience applauded and whistled, Laila backed away from the curtain, giving the men room to exit backstage.

"Laila," Hussein said as he wiped the sweat from his forehead with the back of his hand. "Is that you? Masha Allah, how you've grown."

"Amu Hussein?" It was the first time she'd seen him since Baba died.

"Ya binty, what are you doing here alone at this time of the night?"

Just as she was about to answer, the rest of the ensemble crowded around Hussein. "Ya gamaa, "he addressed the group. "This is Laila, Kamal Abd El Malek's daughter. She sang with us since she was this tall." She was now taller than the man who'd once carried her on his shoulders.

The musicians sighed in reverence. "Allah Yerhamoo," said the new oud player. "I'm still trying to learn his music. He had a rabany talent."

"Why are you here at this hour, Laila?" Hussein said, this time more in the tone of a reprimanding father than an old acquaintance.

"I'm looking for Amu Ahmed," she said. "I just found out that Mama sold him Baba's oud, and I'm not sleeping tonight until I get it back."

"I haven't seen Ahmed in years," he said. Hussein told Laila that six months after Baba had died, the ensemble broke up, and Ahmed made a pilgrimage to Mecca. "When he came back as a haag, he swore off music, alcohol, belly dancers, and even shisha."

"Then tell me where he lives, and I'll go there myself." Laila pulled the shawl halfway over her head. "I'll pay whatever he wants for it."

"You're not going anywhere except for home."

"Tell me where he lives, Amu Hussein. Please. There's not time. I'm getting married in a few days. I want to take the oud with me to my new home."

"I don't know where he lives. He used to live on Gazirat Badran, not far from you. They say he got rich selling religious trinkets. He moved to the fancy side of Shubra. But where in Shubra? Allahoo yelam." He lifted his hands into the air, palms toward the ceiling as if to say that the whole endeavor was hopeless.

Laila closed her eyes, trying not to cry in front of the musicians, but it was futile. She wept and used the edge of her scarf to hide and wipe the tears.

"Don't cry, ya binty. Please don't cry." Hussein put his hand on her shoulder. "You can't change what Allah has written. Everything that happens, happens because Allah wills it."

Laila didn't believe that. The world had no reason, no fairness, no heart, and she refused to be its victim any longer. She would find that oud, and tonight. "Help me find him, please, Amu Hussein. Please. The oud is the only thing I have left of Baba. If I'm here begging you, then Allah willed that too."

"It's impossible. I don't know where Ahmed lives. Besides, you need to get home. I'm sure your mother is looking for you, and if your fiancé finds out you're out, what will he think? A girl alone and out at this time of the night?" Hussain shook his head.

"When I was a little girl"—Laila dried her tears with the shawl—"I used to sit at Baba's feet and watch him play. He wasn't with us when he played, you know? When he strummed that oud, Baba and I would travel to another world together. It was like some magical land only the two of us knew."

"I remember," Hussein said. "I remember the first time he brought you here. We thought he had gone mad, but then you sang."

"Amu Hussein, Baba's death is cruel enough. If there's a small chance we can find his oud, please don't kill it tonight. Help me try to find it."

After a long pause Hussein threw his hands up in the air in acquiescence. "Amry lil la. I suppose I can try. You know what they say, 'He who asks never loses his way.'"

"We're coming with you," said the young oud player. And the rest of the ensemble followed.

Laila walked north on Nile Corniche Road, surrounded by the musicians, all of whom promised to help her find the Haag Ahmed, who'd gotten rich and moved to the fancy side of Shubra. They led her through back roads she'd never seen, past a pharmacy, a barber shop that was still open, a small confectioner, and a cheap open-air movie theater that played last year's movies. As they walked, she told Amu Hussein about her upcoming wedding, Amir, Mama, and the life she'd led since Baba had died.

They turned on Shubra Street and passed Pasha Muhammad Ali's palace where the king's extended family lived. The colonnaded palace had a park extending down to the Nile with rolling gardens of roses, lavenders, and dahlias. She'd always fantasized about picking flowers from the gardens to make a bouquet for Mama. Just past the palace, the well-lit taller buildings looked new, their elaborate stone facades clean, and greenery separated the buildings instead of the muddy alleyways of her neighborhood. In front of the buildings sat hefty porters who were awake, unlike the porters in the poor neighborhoods who slept hunched over in their rickety wooden chairs. The moment felt surreal to her. She'd acted on pure impulse after realizing that Baba's oud case had been empty, that his beloved instrument had been sold years ago. Had she really believed she'd find it? Or was this caper just a way to deal with her grief, to mourn Baba fully?

"This is where we start." Hussein pointed at the third building in. "We ask the porters. They all know each other and the intimate details of every resident."

As soon as they approached, the porter stood up. He was a tall, broad, rotund man. "Masa El Kheyr," Hussein said to him.

"Masa El Noor," the porter said. But he didn't smile, and his gaze shifted from one musician to the other.

"We're looking for Haag Ahmed," Hussein said. "He's the owner of the religious stores. We're old friends."

"If you're really friends, you'd know where he lived." The porter pointed at Laila. "What kind of a girl roams the street with strange men at this time?" he said in his deep raspy voice, his white galabeya tight around his belly.

Hussein reached in his pocket and gave the porter money. "This girl is like a daughter to me, and she needs to see Haag Ahmed. It's urgent. You don't have to tell us where he is. Just tell him where we are. Tell him it's Hussein and Laila, Kamal Abd El Malek's daughter."

The porter looked down at the money in his palm, unimpressed, and then stared at Hussein, saying nothing.

Hussein reached in his pocket again, and again gave the porter more money.

The porter put the money in his galabeya pocket and called for his son. The boy, who looked to be nine or ten, came running from a small room on the ground floor of the building. He rubbed his sleepy eyes. The porter told him to go to Amu Yasser's building. "You know where that is?" The boy nodded. "Tell Amu Yasser to tell Haag Ahmed that he has visitors, Hussein and Kamal Abd El Malek's daughter. Ask him if I should send them up."

The boy stood still, looking up at his father for a few seconds. The porter slapped the boy on the backside of his head and said, "Pay attention, ya walad. What are the names of the visitors?"

The boy repeated their names. "Mazboot," said the porter, and the boy ran.

A few minutes later the boy returned out of breath. "Haag Ahmed says Itfadaloo. I'll show you the way." The porter sat down, and his son led Laila, Hussein, and the five other musicians four blocks farther down Shubra Street to a building that must have been new because it had an elevator. Laila had been on an elevator only once, in Alexandria when Baba took her with him to the Cecil Hotel and the owner, Mr. Metzger, let her ride it to the top.

The building's porter, Yasser, called the elevator for them and secured the wrought door shut. When they made it up to the top floor, Haag Ahmed was standing at the doorway wearing a royal-blue silk galabeya and holding a sibha of aqua and gold prayer beads. He'd grown a beard, which was graying, but had shaved his mustache in the way of conservative clerics. Was this really Amu Ahmed, the mischievous drinker who flirted with belly dancers?

"Ahlan, ahlan, ahlan," Ahmed said, taking Hussein into a long embrace, patting his back hard. "Just because I don't go to cafés doesn't mean you can't come see your old friend." Ahmed invited everyone into his apartment, where a crystal chandelier hung from the high ceiling of the spacious foyer. They sat on the gilded furniture of his living room, and Ahmed called for the maid to serve them tea, apologizing because his wife was out visiting her sick mother. Otherwise, he explained, he'd have insisted they try her delicious cooking.

"Laila, you've grown. Masha Allah. How are you, ya binty?" He leaned forward in his chair, cycling through the beads of the sibha.

Laila opened her mouth to speak, but Hussein interrupted.

"You see, ya Haag Ahmed, Laila is getting married, and today she found out that you bought Kamal's old oud, Allah yerhamoo, from Selma. And she'd like to buy it back from you. You know how important it was to Kamal."

Laila took all the money she had out of her bra and put it on the coffee table. "I'll pay whatever you want."

"Ya binty," Ahmed said, "please take your money back. Your father was my brother"— he patted his chest—"and I am your amu Ahmed. I would never let you pay for your father's oud. We all know the preciousness of a musician's instrument."

The maid returned to the living room with a tray of tea, milk, sugar, and cookies. She made everyone's tea to their liking, stirring with silver spoons. During those few long minutes, Ahmed didn't say anything further about the oud. Laila looked around the room for it, but it wasn't on display. Of course, a religious man like him might have hidden the oud. She hated the situation she was in, the vulnerability of it felt beggarly. If Baba had been alive, he'd rather have starved than sell his oud, and yet could she blame Mama for what she'd done?

Laila sipped her tea. She couldn't broach the subject again. It would be rude to hasten the man who'd so graciously opened up his home at nearly midnight.

After the tea had been served, Ahmed asked Hussein about all the people they once had known, and then Hussein introduced Ahmed to the new players. All the while Ahmed fingered through his ninety-nine beads, each bead representing one of the ninety-nine names for Allah. They talked about the old days when they'd practiced Baba's songs until dawn. Then Ahmed turned to Laila.

"And you, ya binty, how are you? How is your mother, and how is your sister?"

"Thank God, ya Haag Ahmed, we are all doing well. Naima is married now. She has one boy and a baby on the way."

"Masha Allah," he said.

"And Laila is getting married," Hussein said. "And guess who she's marrying. You won't believe it. Makram Youseff Pasha's son." He beamed.

"Masha Allah," Ahmed said. "Whatever Allah wills happens. No man can stand in his way. Mabrook," he congratulated her. Then Ahmed ran his fingers through his beard. "I'm afraid I don't have what you're looking for." His eyes became red and glistened. He cleared his throat and let his gaze fall down to his lap. "When I bought your father's oud, Allah Yerhamoo"—he lifted his hands to the ceiling, and the blue beads clanked as they hung from his fingers—"I wanted to keep it, but when I came back from the pilgrimage to Mecca, I had no money and I needed something to start a new business." He took a deep breath and shook his head. "I'm sorry, but I sold the oud a few years ago."

Laila took a sip of tea. Her throat constricted, but she resolved not to cry in Amu Ahmed's living room. Trying to keep her voice from quivering, she said, "Do you remember who you sold it to?"

"I don't remember. The buyer had come through a friend. All I know is that he was a Jewish man, a musician or a collector, but that's all."

"Wait here," Ahmed said. Then he left his visitors in the living room as he stepped into what looked to be a bedroom at the end of a long corridor.

"I'm so sorry," whispered the young oud player.

"I really thought Ahmed would still have it," said Amu Hussein.

"I have to find that oud," Laila said, but chances of finding the oud were slim. There were tens of Jewish neighborhoods. Besides, she didn't even have the buyer's name. What was she going to do, knock on doors looking for a Jewish man who played the oud? But Baba would have never given up. He'd have looked for it in every corner of the city, and she resolved to keep looking for the oud until the day she died.

When Ahmed returned, he gave Laila a red velvet box and said, "Please accept this as a gift from your amu Ahmed."

She opened the box, and inside it was a gold necklace. Ahmed shrugged. "It's a small gift, but …"

"Don't say that. It's beautiful and very generous of you," Laila said. "Thank you."

Ahmed walked them down to the street, hailed two taxis for the group, and paid for both of them. Hussein accompanied Laila home while the rest of the musicians took the other taxi. It was almost two o'clock in the morning when Laila returned. As soon as she walked through the door, Mama took her into her arms.

"Thank God. Thank God," she said, and still holding Laila in her arms said the first part of the Agpeya Prayer in her ear. "'O Master, Lord, God the Almighty—the Father of our Lord, God, and Savior Jesus Christ—we thank you for every condition, concerning every condition, and in every condition, for you have covered us, helped us, guarded us, accepted us unto you, spared us, supported us, and brought us to this hour.'"

Then she finally let go of Laila. "I was dying of worry. What did you do? Did you find Ahmed? Is he well?"

Laila nodded. "I found him, but not the oud. He's a Haag now. He sold Baba's oud a long time ago." She gave Mama the red velvet box. "He sends his love and congratulations."

Mama opened the box, gazed at the gold necklace, and then put the box in her pocket and took Laila by the hand. "I have something to show you."

"I feel broken and I'm tired, Mama. Please just let me sleep."

"Trust me." Mama tugged on Laila's hand, insisting that she come with her into the bedroom they temporarily shared.

Mama opened the squeaky doors of her mahogany armoire, and as always, there was a musty scent of old wood. Empty hangers swung and clanked against one another where Baba's brown tweed blazer and his single performance suit once hung. Mama reached for the top shelf. "I kept it here for you. I didn't know if you'd ever want it, but I kept it." She pulled out a dusty green leather-bound notebook and gave it to Laila.

Laila thumbed through the yellowing, crackly pages of Baba's notebook. "I remember this. He took it everywhere and wrote in it at night."

"He wrote your song on the very first page on the day you were born. Remember that song you used to beg him to play? Maybe someday these songs will be played again. I know it was the oud you were looking for, but this notebook was one of your father's most prized possessions."

Laila turned to the first page and ran her finger along the fading penciled notes. "You're right Mama. These songs will be played again, but they'll be played again on Baba's oud. I'm going to find it," Laila said. "Even if takes me a lifetime, I'm going to find it!"

That night she dreamed of the oud. It was nowhere, in nobody's hands, and yet it played all of Baba's songs.

15

The next morning, Mama called for a ballana named Aida, whose job was to remove every hair on Laila's body. She arrived carrying a blue mesh tote and wore a faded floral galabeya. Aida was a thin woman whose face was as weathered as her hands. Mama put a clean sheet over the bed so that the hallawa sugar wax wouldn't ruin the old cotton coverlet, and left Laila alone in the room with Aida.

Aida took a tin out of her tote, opened the lid, took out a wad of hallawa, and began to knead it, pulling it apart and folding the gummy ball onto itself until it was soft and malleable. "It's fresh. I cooked it this morning," she said.

Laila sat down on the edge of the bed, and Aida started on her arms, spreading the warm hallawa along her forearm in the direction of the hair growth, pulling it back in quick, successive, painful motions.

"When I'm done with you, you'll be as smooth and shiny as a candle. Besides, you're not too hairy, so it won't hurt as much. You should see some of the hairy beasts I've cleaned up in my days." She lifted Laila's arm and spread the hallawa in her armpit. "Some girls use up to four tins." She pulled, and Laila screamed from the pain. Aida didn't react. "You're two tins, at most." Then she squinted, examining Laila's legs. "Not even."

When it was time for Laila to lie on her back and spread her legs open, Aida gave her a pillow. "Scream into this if you need to. I'll be as quick as I can." Laila screamed into the pillow with every swift pull of Aida's deft hand. Laila had known that married women kept their bodies hairless, soft to their husbands' touch, but now as the electric pain traveled down her legs she questioned and cursed the custom. Why did a woman have to suffer? Why didn't men have to pull their hairs out instead?

When she was finished, Mama brought Laila a fresh lemonade and paid Aida. Before Aida left, she turned to Laila and said, "Listen, I'm going to tell you what I tell all my clients. There's nothing more repulsive than a hairy woman. Once your hairs get to be the length of a fingernail, send for me. I'll pull them right out."

"No," Laila said, wagging her finger at Aida. "I'm never doing that again. That was awful."

Aida laughed and said, "Of course you will. You'll see."

&

Over the past month Mama had sewn and embroidered Laila's henna night galabeya. It was a deep red with gold and silver beading, and it would be the last dress she'd wear before putting on her wedding dress the next day. Along with Naima, she invited every woman from their building and the two neighboring buildings to the event. Just as she had for Naima's engagement party, she borrowed serving platters, tablecloths, chairs, two extra tea sets, and glass cups for the wedding sharbat, which she'd spent two days making with rose syrup, strawberries, and hibiscus.

The women arrived dressed in galabeyas of orange, red, blue, and yellow. They wore lipstick, eyeshadow, and mascara. Little girls had bows in their hair and wore either little galabeyas or big puffy dresses. Mama cooked. She made lamb and rice, stuffed pigeon, stuffed duck, kobeba, and somehow managed to get shrimp from Alexandria, which she baked with cumin and served on a tomato sayadeya rice.

195

After dinner the women drank the sharbat and began their ululations when the henna lady arrived. She mixed the red henna paste in a small basin Mama brought out, instructing Laila to put her hands in it so that the henna colored her palms, and then the soles of her feet. The women made one zaghrouta after the other, and when one woman stopped to take her breath, a few others started, moving their tongues from side to side until the entire building rang with the sound of chaotic celebration. Some of the women sat on the floor around the coffee table and used it as a tabla drum while others clapped and sang wedding songs. They put a jingling scarf on Laila's hips and chanted, "Dance, dance, dance," until Laila swayed her hips to the rhythm like a bride was supposed to. Throughout the dancing, Laila couldn't stop thinking of Baba, his death, and his lost oud. She believed that maybe he had sent her out to get his oud and she'd failed him. At the same time, she felt guilty for not being as happy as a bride should be. After all, she was marrying the man of every girl's dreams.

The women pushed Mama onto the makeshift dance floor and then Naima, whose belly made it hard for her to move although she tried. Soon they made a circle around the bride, her mother, and her sister, each taking a turn dancing with them.

Haaga Saffeya from the first floor made a special request, but not before asking for Mama's permission. "Would it be all right," she said, "if Laila could sing us the henna song?"

Mama agreed, and Laila stood in the middle of her family room as the women sat on the floor, gathering to listen. She closed her eyes and sang, wishing Baba were there to accompany her with his oud. She imagined the rise and fall of the music on a thin, wavy silver line, the way he'd taught her to. "El henna, ya henna. Ya shiback habibey, ya eiyney." She swayed with the lyrics, about a woman so in love she'd do anything for her man. Laila had missed Amir and knowing that she was a day away from being his wife was bliss.

It was the first time in a long while that happiness had intruded. For years Baba's death had been an unbearable wound. As she sang the henna song, she missed Baba with a part of her that was coming alive again, but for the first time Laila began to accept that Baba was gone.

She sang the refrain again. "El henna, ya henna. Ya shiback habibey, ya eiyney." She listened to the sound her voice made as though it weren't hers and she liked it. Though she hadn't practiced, her voice had matured over the years. It had deepened, become more powerful. It carried and commanded attention, and she thought about what might have happened had she made it to the movie audition.

୧୨

The morning of the wedding Pierre came over to practice the waltz with Laila one last time. She wore her new wedding shoes and the makeshift wedding dress skirt she'd been practicing in for a month. But when he reached for her hand, Pierre stopped the record. "Mon Dieu. What's this?" He held her hand in his, palm up like a palm reader from the souk.

"Wedding henna," she said.

He let go of her hand and ran his fingers through his hair. "Amir Pasha will kill me. This has to come off."

Pierre took a handkerchief from his front jacket pocket and dabbed the sweat off his forehead. "Madame Selma." He turned to Mama, who'd come running out of the kitchen with an apron over her galabeya. "We absolutely must take off this henna. Please tell me you know how to remove it."

Mama put her hands on her waist and said, "Henna is good luck for a bride."

"It won't be good luck tonight if your daughter doesn't take it off right now."

"Why?" She raised her voice.

Pierre looked up at the ceiling. "It's my fault. I forgot. I just forgot." He took a deep breath. "In Amir Pasha's society, brides don't put henna on their hands. It's just not á la mode these days."

"I don't care," Selma said. "This is our tradition."

"Maybe he's right, Mama," Laila said. "Maybe we have to take it off."

"No, he's not right," Mama said. "Even Cleopatra used henna."

"Cleopatra didn't marry Amir Youseff Makram Pasha," Pierre said, staring at Mama.

Mama and Pierre stood quietly for a minute, each looking at the other from across the coffee table.

"A paste of baking soda and lime," Mama said, and went to the kitchen.

Pierre sat down on the settee and exhaled. Laila sat in Baba's chair, staring at her red palms. "Monsieur Pierre," she said, "if the upper classes don't put henna on their hands, what do they do on henna night?"

"How should I know?" he said. "Maybe they sing and dance, but they don't color their hands." He fiddled with the crank of the record player, muttering something Laila couldn't hear.

"A henna night without henna? That's like a feast without lamb," she said.

Mama returned with a small bowl and spilled the paste onto Laila's palms, spreading it with the back of the spoon. Tears rolled down her cheeks.

"Madame Selma, I'm so sorry for this. Please, Madame, don't cry. This is all my fault." Pierre got up and paced around the room.

Mama didn't respond, wiping the tears with the back of her hand. When she was done spreading the paste, she said, "Five minutes," and went back into the kitchen.

A few minutes later she returned with a wet kitchen rag, knelt next to Laila, and wiped off the paste. All of the red good luck henna came off onto the rag. She whispered in Laila's ear, "Don't tell anyone you still have it on the soles of your feet."

With Laila's hands clean of henna, Pierre started the record player, and they practiced the waltz one last time. "Remember, look at him when you're dancing, not your shoes, not your dress, not the people around you. And never look surprised. Whatever you see tonight, no matter how marvelous it looks to you, you must pretend that it's mundane." As they danced around the coffee table and in between the chairs, Pierre added, "From this night on, you're the star, my dear girl."

When the waltz had finished, Pierre closed the record player case and said, "Thank you for this dance." He kissed Laila's hand and reminded her that the hairdresser and makeup artist were on their way. At the door, about to leave, Pierre tapped the front pocket of his suit jacket. "I almost forgot this." He took out a small box wrapped in silver paper and tied with a red ribbon. "It's a little gift from me to you."

Laila unwrapped the gift. It was small beige box with black print.

"It's Chanel No. 5," he said. "A most elegant perfume for a most elegant young woman."

Mama came out of the kitchen to thank Pierre and to say good-bye. Her eyes were still swollen from crying. He took her hand and kissed it too. "Please forgive me for all the inconvenience, Madame Selma. I meant no harm." Laila had never seen a man kiss Mama's hand, not even Baba. "I have something for you too." From his jacket pocket, he took out a gold necklace, a khamsa hand pendant hanging from it. "May I?" he said, and Mama nodded. He fastened the necklace around her neck. "So that the hasad can never find you or your daughter."

"Will we see you at the wedding?" Laila asked as he stepped out onto the landing.

"You can count on it," Pierre said.

16

Naima arrived before the makeup lady and hairdresser. She helped Laila pack a small suitcase she'd lent her. Naima neatly folded a few dresses Laila and Mama had sewn, copying the patterns from magazines and billboards, and Baba's green leather-bound songbook. After that, Naima was too tired to do much else and sat on the edge of the bed holding her heavy belly.

Laila's closet was empty. How was it that this was her last night here? She looked around the room, at her old bed, the chipped nightstand, the tattered cotton blanket she and her sister had fought over as little girls.

The hairdresser curled Laila's hair into long ringlets that fell along her back, and the makeup artist put a blue shadow on her lids, dark eyeliner and mascara to enhance her almond-shaped eyes, and red lipstick on her lips with a dab of Vaseline for shine. Mama, Naima, and the hairdresser worked together to pin the tiara to Laila's hair and then fasten the veil to it so that neither slid during the ceremony and reception. "You look like a queen," Naima said, holding up a mirror to Laila.

Laila put on the new lace lingerie from Benzion department store that she'd bought with Mama, white lace panties and a matching bra. Then she took her new perfume out of its box, pulled out the thick glass stopper, and dabbed the perfume behind her ears, on her décolleté, and on her wrists.

Naima and Mama held the dress open as she stepped into it. Together they pulled it up, and Laila slid her arms into the sleeves. Mama buttoned the back, repeating "In the name of the holy cross" until she'd buttoned the dress all the way up. When she was done, she let out one long zaghroota that set off a chain reaction outside the apartment door, where Haaga Saffeya and some neighbors had gathered to watch the bride descend the stairs in her wedding gown. As Laila went down each flight of stairs, the neighbors clustered at the landings, trilling zaghrootas, clapping, throwing rice, singing songs. All the while, Mama and Naima held her long train above the ground so that it wouldn't get dirty. Laila was most afraid of tripping, so she held on tightly to the wrought iron railing. A shiny black sedan was parked outside her building, and the driver, who wore a suit, bow tie, and white gloves, stood beside the car with the rear door open.

At the El-Botroseya church, Makram Youseff Pasha walked Laila down the aisle wearing his military uniform decorated with medals, a red sash across his broad chest, and a felt tarbush upon his head. Laila imagined Baba's presence too, not by her side, but hovering over her, guiding her into a new life, blessing it, forgiving her for not finding the oud. "I miss you, Baba," she said in a whisper and swallowed back her tears. At the altar the pasha put her hand in Amir's and sat down. She hadn't seen Amir since the day he'd given her the engagement ring, and now with her hand in his again it was as thrilling as the first time he held her hand at the park and kissed her behind the waterfall. Amir wore a long-tailed tuxedo and pinned on his right lapel was a round medal of his family crest. He smiled at Laila and whispered, "You are stunning." His voice, his warm hand holding hers, the churchy scent of incense converged into a sense of full legitimacy. She'd never had that feeling before. It was as though she were finally in the right place, doing the right thing.

Mama and Naima sat in the first pew next to Hoda on the women's side of the church. Mama cried as soon as Amir took Laila by the hand,

and she kept crying through the matrimonial hymns, the exchange of the rings, the anointing of holy oil, the wearing of royal capes, and the blessing of the marital crowns. At the end, when the priest gave his admonitions and advised Laila to submit to her husband and call him lord, Mama stopped crying and began her zaghrootas, which she elongated so that the zaghrootas lasted for the newlyweds' entire walk up the aisle. The rest of the women at the church followed Mama's ululations, but none were as loud or as piercing as hers.

In the car Amir kissed Laila and took off one of his white gloves to fix the red lipstick that had smudged on her lips. "I can't believe we're here," he said, as the driver pulled out of the Abbaseya district. "Eight Sundays," he said. "We spent eight Sundays apart. Do you know that I used to park below your building just to watch you have tea in the balcony? Did you see me?"

"No," she said, "and it's a good thing Mama didn't see you either. She'd have killed us both."

"What do you think of the Rolls Royce?" Amir said. "It's on loan from the king's royal fleet."

"It's beautiful." She didn't know what a Rolls Royce was. All fancy cars looked the same to her.

The driver took a longer route back to the palace in Zamalek to give the guests time to arrive ahead of the bride and groom. During the drive, Laila and Amir talked about the two months that had passed. Laila told him about Madame Caron, the night of kabab, the empty oud case, and the day Pierre and Botros got into a fight. Amir told her that he'd used every connection he had to get the dresses from Paris's House of Worth, book the Botrosseya church— which was popular since it was the seat of the pope—and reserve the caterers. "And I called Mr. Metzger at the Cecil to talk to him personally about the honeymoon suite. I can see us now sitting on the beach all day and going to parties all night."

Laila remembered how Baba had talked about Mr. Metzger. To Baba, he'd been an important and powerful man, someone who'd been generous with him, hired him for the summer, and given him a seafront apartment to enjoy. But Mr. Metzger hadn't been someone Baba could just talk to; he had to wait in line to speak with him. When Baba wanted to bring Laila to watch him play, he'd deferentially asked Mr. Metzger for permission.

The driver stopped in front of the palace. Amir got out of the car first, opened the backseat door for Laila, and took her hand, helping her with the long train and veil. Laila didn't know exactly how many feddans of land Amir's sprawling family palace occupied, just that the palace dwarfed Madame Caron's villa, with its tall columns flanked by statues, large wrap-around verandas, and Mediterranean-style arched windows.

Hundreds of guests gathered outside the palace gates to be part of the couple's zaffa. As Laila and Amir stood outside the gate arm in arm, Mama and Naima rushed to drape Laila's train on the marble steps. Just below at street level, four white horses danced to the beat of the tabla. Beside the horses, three men dressed in white Bedouin garb played the mizmar, their lips pressed up on the tip, their cheeks puffed with air.

Two uniformed men wearing white gloves opened the front gates, and the line of performers and singers that had been waiting outside filed through the entrance first. Laila and Amir followed the parade while family and guests trailed behind them singing wedding songs. The zaffa continued down a long red-carpeted pathway, led by a troupe of belly dancers balancing candelabras on their heads while shimmying their hips, followed by a wedding singer and tambourine boys who shook their instruments in time to the music. The newlyweds walked slowly through the arabesque courtyard, past the Moorish fountain, and into the marble foyer, which had two winding staircases and a grand crystal chandelier that hung from three floors up.

Pierre met them at the foot of the stairs, which made the Diana Palace look mediocre. Beyond it was a vast round ballroom where the marble floor had circular patterns just as Pierre had described, and wall sconces cast a dim light on endless tables. Amir and Laila stood back with Pierre as the guests entered the ballroom dressed in beaded silks and fine tuxedos. Then Pierre said, "It's time."

Amir took Laila's hand. "May I have this dance?"

"Avec plaisir," she said, just the way Pierre had taught her, and from the corner of her eye she caught him smiling. They walked into the ballroom to loud applause, and then the waltz from Swan Lake played, but the music didn't come from a crackly old record. It was played by a live orchestra that took up a large stage at the back of the ballroom. Laila positioned her hand on Amir's shoulder just as she'd practiced with Pierre, but Amir was taller and bigger than Pierre. His feet stood farther apart than Pierre's, and his movements seemed heavier. Although Pierre had prepared her for their difference in stature, Laila got nervous. She tried to follow Amir, but she lost count and lost the rhythm. Within the first minute she'd already stepped on his foot once and stumbled twice. Amir squeezed her hand. He looked disappointed or maybe embarrassed. But he kept smiling. When the dance ended, he took her hand and kissed it as the guests gave them another round of applause. Then he led her to their kosha, two red velvet chairs with ornate gold arms that had been set side by side under a canopy of water orchids and chrysanthemums.

"I thought Pierre practiced with you for a month," he said as they sat and the photographer took snapshots from behind his tripod.

"We practiced. We practiced every day."

"Smile for the camera," he said, and she feigned a smiled.

"I don't know what happened," she said.

"Just do me a favor and please stay focused tonight." He kissed her hand again for the photographer. "People are watching."

Just then, Hoda, Amir's mother, joined them at the kosha. She had brought a friend, a portly woman in a sky-blue gown. "Laila, dear. May I introduce you to my dear friend, Madame Violet."

Madame Violet kissed Laila's cheeks and turned to Hoda. "Mon dieu, Hoda, she is très belle. Why haven't I seen her in social circles? Had I laid my eyes on her first, I'd have snatched her up for my son before Amir had a chance to say bonjour." She laughed, her hand on her plump chest.

"That's because our darling Laila was abroad for many years with her father who, God rest his soul, was a very important diplomat." Hoda gazed down at Laila and touched her cheek. "Now, let's leave these two alone. The dinner is about to be served."

Laila had known Hoda wasn't happy that Amir was marrying a poor girl from Rod El Farag. That was obvious from the day of the official proposal. But she'd never imagined Hoda was so ashamed that she would invent a story rather than say the truth.

Soufragis—part waiters, part footmen—bussed the guests' tables swiftly, and placed two small tables in front of Laila and Amir, setting them with the dinnerware exactly the way Pierre had. Laila managed impeccably through the first three courses, but the fourth plate had on it something she'd never seen before, a kind of shellfish, and she had no notion of how to eat it.

"Pierre didn't show me that one," Laila said.

"It's a lobster," Amir said, "flown in from France this morning. It was a last-minute change. Mother thought it would be a good addition. Pierre didn't know about it." He picked up his knife and inserted it under the shell, cutting off a piece of the white flesh from the center. Laila copied him.

How were Mama, Naima, and Botros doing? They weren't in the first row closest to the kosha, where Amir's parents sat amid foreigners. She looked out onto the vast hall of white tablecloths and candles, the soufragis, the one pianist now accompanying the jazz band, searching for Mama and Naima, whom she finally saw sitting at a table that edged the outer perimeter of the ballroom.

"Why is my family seated so far away?"

"Mother and I thought they'd be most comfortable there," Amir said.

She stood, saying "Pardon" to Amir, and walked to the table at the edge of the ballroom where Mama and Naima sat with a disgruntled Botros.

"What are you doing here? You shouldn't leave your kosha," Mama said.

"I just wanted to make sure you were all right and talk to you for a bit."

205

Naima smiled and said nothing, the lobster untouched on her plate. In fact, nobody had touched their lobsters, afraid of eating it in the wrong way and embarrassing Laila.

"Ya binty," Mama said, fixing Laila's hair, "we are more than all right. Now go back to your husband."

Laila nodded and returned to her kosha worried about the family she'd left behind.

The reception ended at nearly three in the morning. When the guests had all gone, Amir's parents bid the couple good night and went up to their wing of the palace. Laila kissed Mama, Naima, and Botros good night. When she hugged Naima, she whispered, "Take care of Mama." Amir had the driver take them home. Finally alone, Amir carried Laila up the marble stairs to his bedroom. She committed everything about this moment to her memory: the sound of his footsteps on the marble steps, the heavy ornate bedroom door squeaking open, crossing the threshold into his room. She took it all in, still suspended in his arms, the rich red carpeted floors; the balcony overlooking the swimming pool; the floral patterns of the upholstered chairs; the dense wintery scent of the velvet draperies, just like the ones at Madam Caron's house.

"I missed you," he said as she spotted a radio in the corner of the bedroom. Maybe they could dance again, without strangers watching. This time she wouldn't trip.

He put her down on the bed and sat next to her, removing her veil. "I've waited so long for this day. To be alone with you here, just like this."

He tore off his bow tie and tossed it onto the nightstand. It was a precious charmeuse silk, a fabric she'd come to know in remnants.

"Can we dance first?" she said.

"Darling, we have a lifetime to dance." He put his hand on her cheek and kissed her, not a long, gentle kiss like the ones they'd had in Azbakeya Gardens, but a short and hurried kiss. Then he unbuttoned the top button of her dress, the first in the long string that Mama had sewn down the back. She flinched. He unbuttoned a few more, and air crept along her spine. His warm fingers grazed the nape of her neck.

"Please wait," she said, even as she recalled what Mama had told her about pleasing her husband and saving her virginal blood-stained sheet. "Let's talk and then we can—"

"I don't want to talk." He tugged at the remaining buttons on the back of her dress, tearing the wedding gown, its silk ripping with a jagged sound. The buttons flew off and beads fell onto the plush rug, rolling every which way onto the parquet floor.

"The dress," she said, "it's ruined." Amir would never understand that this gown was the only luxurious dress she'd ever owned, and that Mama had spent so much time stitching the buttons on, checking the embroidery, and altering it so that it fit Laila.

"I'll buy you a million new dresses," he said. "Don't worry about a few simple buttons." He pulled the dress off her shoulders and kissed her all over her décolleté. "I'll buy you Chanel, Lanvin, Dior."

He yanked the torn dress off her shoulders and down her body so fast, she didn't have time to say anything. The gown fell to the floor, and he stepped on it as he stood up to take off his coat, shirt, trousers, and his underwear. She closed her eyes.

"Don't be shy," he said. "You can look." He laughed, but not the kind of laugh they had shared at the reception drinking sharbat. That had been a softer laugh that had accompanied her giggles. This laugh was brazen and mocking.

She didn't find any pleasure in looking at him naked. She kept her eyes shut. "I don't want to see. Put your clothes back on."

She wasn't supposed to say those things. Mama had told her so. This was how God intended for a man and a woman to be, but Amir pushed things too fast. She needed more time, and he wasn't listening.

He covered her body with his. His weight pressed against her. She sank deeper into the satin comforter, and he pushed her legs apart.

207

He kissed her neck. "You smell good." He spoke as though his mouth was full. She felt traces of his saliva on her. "You're beautiful. Relax and you'll enjoy this. I promise."

Pushing her new lace panties to the side, he slid between her legs. Shards of pain spread through her thighs, and the splendid burst of pleasure Naima had told her about didn't come. He squeezed her breasts.

"It hurts." Tears rolled down her cheeks. "Stop. Please stop."

He gripped her hips, moving faster in and out with a steady rhythm. When it was done, he rolled onto his back, a smile returning to his face.

"Next time, loosen up, move a little more," he said, short of breath. "You're too stiff. That's why it hurts."

Amir fell asleep within minutes, his naked body sprawled on the bed, covered with a thin sheet. Laila curled on her side, her eyes adjusting to the soft glow of the nightlight and the vast bedroom that felt too big and too cold. None of what she'd imagined had happened. She got out of bed and wrapped herself in a towel that had been folded on the dresser. Then she picked up her wedding dress and draped it on a chair in the corner of the room. She searched for the missing buttons, feeling for them under the bed. When she'd found a few, she put them on her new dresser. She'd sew them back onto the dress someday.

17

Laila's wedding night was the first night Selma had ever slept alone. The apartment that had once felt small and cramped now seemed vast. She sat on the edge of the bed, took off her shoes, and rubbed her tired feet. Then she picked up a framed photo of Kamal. He was a handsome man, especially when he smiled. "We did it," she said. She'd never spoken to his picture before, not out loud. But now she was alone. "She was the most beautiful bride I'd ever seen, zay el amar." She put the photo back on the nightstand.

Where did God send souls anyway? All she knew was that dead people who'd been good went to heaven, but could they travel between heaven and earth? Maybe God allowed the souls to visit for special occasions. Kamal wouldn't have missed his daughter's wedding.

Selma took off her imported gown and hung it up, then put on her nightgown and slipped under her covers. But sleep would not come. Every sound she'd once slept through now kept her up; a cough from a floor below, the shuffle of footsteps in the stairwell, the meow of a stray cat, a car engine, the sound of the night breeze against her window.

She woke up before the Fajr dawn prayer and got to work on her daughter's sabaheya meal. She made baked chicken, chicken soup with cracked wheat, lamb stew, rice with nuts, kofta patties, yogurt and cucumbers with fresh mint, semolina cake drenched in syrup, and fried sweet balls of zalabya sprinkled with powdered sugar. She packed the dishes in the new portable glassware she'd bought on sale from Cicurel's department store and arranged it all in her large green grocery tote. She put on a clean galabeya, put her hair up, and took a taxi to the pasha's palace in Zamalek. It was almost lunchtime, just in time for the newly-weds to be ravenous.

The butler opened the door for Selma and offered her a seat in the parlor. Then he took the green tote and called for the maid to put the food in the kitchen. "I'll let Madame Laila know you're here," he said, and went up the stairs. The maid returned with a tray of tea and biscuits.

Within a few minutes, Laila and Amir came down to meet her wearing a matching set of white satin robes. They looked like movie stars.

Selma took her daughter in her arms. How had she missed her so much in one day? When Naima had gotten married, Selma still had Laila to look after and Kamal was still alive, so Laila's leaving was harder. She kissed her cheeks, her forehead, not wanting to let her go. "How are you?" she whispered in her ear as she was kissing her cheek. "Are you all right?" Laila didn't respond. Then Selma kissed Amir on both cheeks too, and the three of them sat down.

"Mama will be down shortly," Amir said. "She has a terrible headache."

He was lying, but that didn't bother Selma. Hoda had been against this marriage from the start. In due time, she'd realize that Amir had married a good girl; beautiful, smart, capable.

Selma told Amir to wish his mother a speedy recovery and then went through the list of foods she'd brought them.

"Yeslam eydick, I'm sure it's delicious." Amir took a biscuit from the platter on the coffee table.

Selma searched for a clue on Laila's face. Had she been shocked by the wedding night?

Had Amir been overly aggressive? Or was she just tired? "When do you two leave for Alexandria?"

"As soon as we can get everything packed," Laila said. "You should see the new wardrobe Amir surprised me with. I don't even know what to bring."

"Off to sand and sea." Amir glided his hand through the air.

"For how long?" Selma had never been in a different city from Laila. What if her daughter needed her? What if she got sick?

"Two months or so, depends on how we feel," Amir said. "We'll be at the Cecil if you need to reach us."

"Yes, Mama. And telegraph me there as soon as Naima has the baby," Laila said.

Just then Hoda came down the stairs, joining them in the parlor and greeting Selma with tepid kisses on both cheeks. She wore a blue satin robe, and her hair pulled back in a bun revealed her plump red cheeks.

"They tell me you cooked, Selma. You shouldn't have gone to the trouble. You know we have our beloved chef, Antoine."

"Where I come from the mother of the bride makes the sabaheya meal," Selma said.

"Well, you can rest assured that dear Laila won't ever have to cook again." Hoda picked up her freshly poured cup of tea and a took a sip, the steam rising in her face.

Selma had always been proud of her skills as a cook, and though there was a clear distinction between her place as the cook and Madame Caron's as her boss, she'd always seen cooking as a job to be proud of. At least she was capable, and she'd taught her daughter a useful skill. Now Hoda was speaking as though she were Laila's savior, plucking her out of the hell Selma had put her in. "Hoda, have you ever fed the pasha something you've made with your own two hands?" Selma asked.

Hoda put her teacup down on the coffee table. "Of course not. Why should I?" She let out a small mocking laugh.

"That's a shame," Selma said. "Cooking for someone is an expression of love. I suppose you'll never understand." Selma shook her head. "A real shame. You've really never cooked a thing for your man?"

Amir laughed, and Laila poked him in the shoulder. Hoda's cheeks flushed, but she didn't respond to Selma.

Selma stood up. "I have to go. A few friends are coming over for tea this afternoon and I'm making fresh basboosa, from scratch. Oh, Laila, before I forget, let me get Naima's suitcase from you."

Selma followed Laila up the marble staircase and into her marital bedroom. It was unlike any room Selma had ever seen before, like a small apartment. There was a sitting room and a balcony overlooking the swimming pool; and the bedframe was gold with a brocade canopy that matched the curtains. When Laila closed the door behind them, Selma said, "Tell me quick. Are you all right? Did everything go well last night?"

"I'm fine, Mama." Laila heaved Naima's suitcase up on the unmade bed and unlatched it.

She didn't believe Laila but couldn't ask about the wedding night again. Laila was a married lady now. Bedroom matters were private, and she could see her daughter was uncomfortable. After all, she'd raised her to be discreet.

"I haven't had a chance to unpack yet," Laila said, pulling out the dresses Selma had made her and Kamal's songbook, which Laila placed in her nightstand drawer.

"For God's sake, Laila. I don't care about the suitcase. Naima's not going anywhere. I want the sheet."

Had Laila forgotten? Selma had told her many times about the sheet, the blood, the honor, the tradition.

Laila pushed the suitcase to the other side of the bed and pulled the covers off. She ran her hand along the sheet. "I don't know, Mama. I forgot. I don't know where it is."

"Move." Selma pushed Laila out of the way. She pulled the coverlet completely off the bed and then the top sheet. But she didn't find the stain of blood she was looking for.

Had they not consummated their marriage yet? She didn't know how to pose this question to her daughter. She cleared her throat. "Was Amir too tired last night? I mean, did something happen?"

Laila looked uncomfortable. "It happened all right, Mama. It was just …"

"What?"

"Different than how I thought it would be."

That meant nothing to Selma. What did she mean by different?

"Where's the blood then?"

"I don't know."

"Hoda didn't come by this morning to see it?"

"No, Mama. These people don't think about this stuff. It's not on their minds all the time, and I like it better that way. This is embarrassing, and I don't think anyone needs to see it anyway."

"Listen to me," Selma said. "It's the man's job to be gentle enough to," Selma paused and cleared her throat. "What I mean to say, is that it's just one little droplet, and Amir should have known how to collect it on the sheet or even on a small towel. Didn't Naima explain all of this?"

"She did, but I didn't think about it. Just let it go, Mama. What difference does it make? I'm married now, and his family doesn't even care."

"Hundreds of years of tradition isn't going to change because you married a pasha's son. Now tell me the truth. Did something happen between you two before the wedding?"

"How?" Laila seemed angry. "I couldn't even see my fiancé, remember?"

"Before you two got caught."

"Nothing happened, Mama. Nothing happened before we got caught or after. And I don't know where the blood is. I swear."

"Maybe it's on the dress," Selma said. Without asking for permission, she opened Laila's armoire. It was filled with dresses, shoes, gloves, and purses the likes of which Selma had never seen before. There were more dresses hanging there than Selma, Naima, and Laila had ever owned put together.

And they were scandalous too; strapless, one-shoulder, thin straps. She couldn't believe that Amir approved of all that. "Where's the wedding dress?"

Laila pointed at the chair in the corner of the room where the dress was draped over the back. "What if you find the blood on the dress? What are you going to do with it?" she asked.

"Let's find it first," Selma said. She'd cut a piece of the dress if she had to. "All I wanted was a sheet. I'd do the same thing I did with your sister's sheet, hang it from the balcony. Remember, after your father got better, the ladies came over for to tea to celebrate. You don't remember, do you? You and your baba always lived in another world." Selma picked up the dress and examined it. She turned the dress inside out, combing through the underskirt, the lining, and the tulle.

What was she going to do? The ladies were coming over in a matter of hours, and while it wouldn't be the way they had done it in Asyut where she'd grown up, it was all Selma could do in Cairo. City folk didn't follow traditions the same way. In her village, both sets of parents waited outside the bedroom door on the wedding night for a bloodstained handkerchief. It had been the most embarrassing moment of Selma's life, and Kamal had been against the practice even then, but he did what he was supposed to do. Before the couple could be left alone, they had to provide a blood-stained handkerchief. First, Selma's in-laws inspected the handkerchief, and then her parents displayed it, hanging it on their front door. The whole village celebrated. Now, in Laila's case, it would just be Selma and her friends over tea, a muted and watered-down affair. That is, if she could find some proof of her daughter's honor. But there was no blood and she couldn't explain it to herself. If Laila had been a virgin, where was the blood? She picked the empty suitcase off the bed and pulled the white top sheet out from under the silk comforter. She began to fold it.

"What are you doing?" Laila said.

"I'm taking the sheet anyway."

"Mama, you can't do that. It's part of a set. Hoda will find out. She'll be upset."

"So what? She can't afford a new sheet?"

"It's not that, Mama." Laila looked at the floor.

Selma saw shame on her daughter's face, and the pain of that shame was sharp. She put her finger under Laila's chin and pushed her face up so that she could look her into her eyes. "If you're not proud of who you are, you'll never be proud of who you'll become." Then she bunched the sheet, put it in the suitcase, fastened it quickly, and left the room.

Laila ran behind her and stopped her in the hallway before she was able to get to the stairs. "Wait, Mama. I didn't mean it like that."

"It's all right, Laila," Selma said holding back her tears. "Someday you'll understand."

As they descended one of the spiral staircases, Selma, in a strained voice, told Laila to make sure Amir ate the soup because the cracked wheat was good for young, newly married men. "Eat before you head for Alexandria."

"Hader, ya Mama," Laila said.

Amir was still sitting in the parlor, but Hoda was gone. He was smoking a cigarette and reading the newspaper, but he stood up when Selma approached. "We won't be gone long," he said. Then he asked the driver to take her home.

Selma kissed her new son-in-law good-bye and said, "Take care of my Laila." Then the butler took the suitcase from Selma, put it in the trunk of the car, and the driver drove her back to Gazirat Badran Street.

Once home, Selma put the suitcase on her bed and paced her apartment, practicing how she'd lie to the neighbors. She'd tell them that Hoda had taken the sheet and wouldn't give it to her. No, nobody would believe that. Everyone knew that Selma wouldn't leave without the sheet.

That's it. She would tell them that Amir and Laila hadn't yet consummated their marriage because Laila was too shy. No, they wouldn't believe that either. A worldly man like Amir would consummate his marriage at all costs. Otherwise it would be a shame on him. People would say he wasn't a real man or worse, that he was impotent. Besides, he was young and eager, and Selma had kept the pair apart for a month.

If Nargis or Aisha sensed the lie on Selma, Laila's reputation as a virgin bride would always be in question. It would get to the old crow and this would be devastating for Naima. Selma looked at the clock. The women would be at her door in less than an hour. By now she should have pinned the bloodstained sheet to the clothesline that ran just beyond the balcony railing. She put the tray of basboosa, which she'd prepared earlier, in the oven and then went back to her bedroom. Opening the suitcase, she pulled out the sheet. She examined it again. Maybe Laila hadn't bled much. Maybe Selma would find a faint stain, proof enough of virginity, something to show off. But there was nothing. She threw the sheet on the bed, exacerbated and, for the first time, nervous.

Then she thought of something, and she felt guilty for it. Forgive me, God. She spread the white sheet on her bed, took her sewing box out of the armoire, and pulled a sewing needle out of its red cushion. Holding her hand above the sheet she pricked her finger and squeezed it until three droplets created a bloodstain large enough to elicit any mother's pride. She held a piece of cotton to her pricked finger for a minute and it stopped bleeding. Then, still haunted by the whereabouts of her daughter's virginal blood, she hung the sheet on the clothesline and made a loud zaghrouta to celebrate honor.

18

CAIRO, JUNE 1949

Amir carried Laila across the threshold of the presidential suite at The Cecil Hotel. The room had a corner balcony with a view of the turquoise Mediterranean and high ceilings decorated with scrolls and white plaster moldings. Laila ran her fingers along the satin bedding, the brocade upholstery, and ornate chair rail along the walls. Then she opened the door to the balcony and stepped out, taking in a deep breath of the salty breeze. That scent of the sea reminded her of the happiest summer in her life. She stood still for a moment in the doorway between the room and the balcony. Amir, standing behind her, wrapped his arms around her waist. He kissed her neck and his touch felt different than the previous night, gentler and warmer, like on their secret Sunday dates in Azbakeya gardens. "Like the view?" he said kissing her shoulder.

"It's beautiful," she said, trying to find the exact line that divided the silky sea from the sky.

Amir stopped kissing her and began to pull the pins out of her bun, throwing each pin in a small wastebasket under a writing desk. "Promise me something." He turned her around so that they were facing each other. Her hair was only half free from the bun. "Promise me you'll wear your hair down from now on."

"I promise," she said. She liked the freedom of letting her hair down.

He took the rest of the pins out, and when her long wavy hair spilled against her shoulders, he pulled the curtains closed and picked her up off the floor, setting her down on the edge of the bed. He stood in front of her. He was a tall muscular man with an imposing body that she fully appreciated as she looked at him towering over her.

He took the white linen dress off over her head. "Is this all right?" he asked.

She started to say something but hesitated. What would she tell him, that he'd violated her last night? They were married. He'd been aggressive, but maybe that's how it was supposed to be. All Naima had ever said was that sex was euphoric, "a thrill like no other."

"You're upset, aren't you?" Amir slid her shoes off and threw them into the corner.

"Well, you didn't listen to me."

He kissed her again and undid her bra. "I know last night might have felt too rushed for you. It's just that I'd missed you so much and you looked so beautiful. Give me a chance to make it up to you. Let's start over."

She covered her breasts with her arms. He moved her arms away. "Don't be shy," he said. It was still daylight outside, and the light filtered through the thin seam between the curtains. He slid off her panties, and now she was naked and unbearably embarrassed. She tried to use her long hair to cover her breasts, but Amir pushed her hair back so that she was completely exposed. "Don't cover yourself like that," he said. "It's okay now. You're my wife."

How could it be okay? Her whole life she'd been trained to cover her body, to stay away from men, to pull her hair up in a tight bun. Even an innocent conversation on the street with a man was a terrible violation of social norms. Somehow, Laila was now expected to forget all that, to be comfortable and intimate in a way she hadn't even imagined a day earlier.

Amir covered her body with his and pulled the sheets over them both. He ran his fingers through her hair and over the contours of her body. He kissed her nipples and said "Relax" as he parted her thighs. She felt some pleasure but more shame, so she closed her eyes and thought of the sea to quell it.

When it was over, he lit a cigarette and asked if he'd hurt her.

"No," she said, pulling the sheet over her. It hadn't hurt, but she still felt as though they were doing something wrong. How could she explain that to him if she didn't understand it herself?

"Then what?" He took a puff of his cigarette. "I tried, but ..." He shrugged. "Why are you so cold? Are you upset with me still?"

"I'm just tired," she said. Then she wrapped herself with the top sheet and left the bed to take a shower.

For the next two months, they spent their days on the sand and their evenings in Alexandria's social scene. Each day they went to a different beach along the coast: Chatby, Stanley, Aida, and San Stefano. When they were hungry, they brushed the sand off and had lunch at one of the restaurants that lined the beach road. They ate sandwiches, kabab, fish, and, for dessert, ice cream. Amir didn't look at food prices on menus or count the money in his pocket. He just ordered whatever he wanted. Laila had imagined he lived this way, but experiencing such freedom made her feel sorry for her mother and sister, for herself when she'd been hungry and had to pass ice cream stands and roasted corn kiosks because she didn't have enough coins in her pocket. Indulging herself now was fraught with more guilt than pleasure.

At Stanley Beach, Amir rented a cabana for the day where they could shower and change. Laila wore her new Parisian swimsuits that Amir had bought her. One of them was a polka- dotted ruffled bikini. It was especially difficult for her to bare her midsection, something Mama had taught her was shameful. But slowly, at Amir's insistence, she adapted to the freer life of the upper classes. Almost every day they swam together in the clear blue sea. Sometimes Amir stole a kiss when people weren't around, and she let him, tasting the salt on his tongue. She liked kissing, but sex was still something she had to force herself to endure.

Some nights when they got back to the hotel, she pretended she was too tired for sex, feigning sleep, a stomachache, or a headache. Anything to avoid the loneliness of it. The closer Amir got physically to her, the more alone she felt, retreating into her mind, leaving the bed they were both in. But Amir was relentless until he got what he wanted. He kept nudging and nagging until she gave in. Once he suggested she keep her eyes open. "Maybe you'll like it more that way." Another time he gave her a glass of Scotch to loosen her up, but she vomited instead. He kept asking her while they were making love if it felt good, if she liked it this way or that way, but that made it even worse for her. Admitting to having any desire or pleasure was exactly the opposite of what Mama had taught her. Of course, Mama could have been wrong about this, but what if she wasn't wrong? What if Laila let herself go and let herself feel something? Would he think she was a loose girl, unfit to be a wife? Why was he asking her these things when her job was to simply endure it?

One day, when the shores of Stanley Beach had gotten too crowded, Amir took Laila's hand and said, "Come on. Let's go for a swim. I want to be alone with you."

"Now?" she asked. They had made love that morning despite her attempts to avoid it.

"Yes," he said, and they both jumped into the water.

"Let's swim there." He pointed at three red buoys in the distance.

"No, it's too far," Laila said, still in knee-deep water.

"That's the reason I want to take you there," Amir said. "Come on. It'll be a fun adventure. I promise."

"Let's not." The last time she'd been to Alexandria, Baba had almost drowned. Since then she liked being close to shore where her feet could touch the sea floor.

"Let's go." Amir started to swim. "Come on."

She swam behind him trying to keep up, but he was a fast swimmer and determined to get far away from the crowds. The distance between them grew, and she began to panic. "Wait for me!" she screamed across the water, but he kept swimming. She didn't know what to do. She'd gotten a long distance from the shore. The waters were deep, and the aqua of the shoreline was behind her. She found herself treading water, not swimming in either direction. She screamed for help; but Amir hadn't noticed. He had already swum to the buoys. She saw him waving at her, but he must not have realized she was struggling. Then a man who'd been closer to the shore quickly swam toward her.

When he got to her, he took hold of her arm. "I saw you swimming," he said. His voice was deep and steady. "I know you can swim. Don't let yourself panic."

She couldn't respond to him. She'd begun to hyperventilate, and he looked blurry to her. "Slow your breathing," he said. His voice was calm and deep.

"My husband." She pointed at Amir, unable to say much else.

"You're going to swim with me to the shore a little bit at a time. Your husband will understand. Let the waves push you forward," the man said, calming her. "I'll be right next to you, but you need to swim."

Laila swam next to the man, and when she got to shore, she dropped down, digging her fingers into the warm sand. The man sat next to her, and she thanked him over and over again. "I'm just happy you're all right," he said, and took her pulse. Then he bought her Fresca jam- filled wafers and a Coca-Cola from one of the beach vendors. "I'll stay with you until your husband gets here," he said.

After a few minutes, Amir returned from the deep waters. He stood over her. "I waited for you."

"I almost drowned," Laila said. "I called for you."

"You told me that you could swim." He said this too loudly, and beach-goers turned to watch.

The man sitting next to her stood, brushed the sand off his legs, and said, "I'll leave you two alone."

"Wait," Amir said to the man. "You knew she didn't need your help. You knew she could have met me in the water. But you went to flirt with my wife anyway."

"No," Laila said. "No, Amir." She looked up at him, surprised by his reaction to the man who'd just saved her life.

"Your wife could have drowned out there. I went to rescue her as I would have with anyone." The man took a step back and flashed his palms as if to say he didn't want any trouble, but Amir took a swing at him. The man ducked and then punched Amir in the jaw.

Laila threw her Coke and wafers on the sand and got in between the two men. "Please stop."

Amir tried punching the man again, but Laila hung onto his arm, weighing it down so that he barely grazed the man's shoulder. He stepped back and shook off Laila's hold. She fell to the sand. "You're lucky my wife is here. You're lucky we're on our honeymoon. Otherwise, I'd have destroyed you."

Laila stood up and brushed the sand off of her legs.

"I'm a doctor, you imbecile. I was saving someone. That's all." The man walked away, although he looked strong and could have easily fought Amir.

Amir turned to Laila, his hand on his jaw, his face wet and sandy. "You lied to me. You said you could swim. If I'd have known how pathetic you were, I'd have arranged for lessons. What an embarrassment!"

"I do know how to swim," Laila said gritting her teeth. She knew she didn't know how to swim properly, but still knew how to tread water.

"Of course, you do, just like you know how to do everything else, poorly." He turned and began walking toward their rented umbrella.

"What do you mean by that?" Laila said as she followed him, her feet sinking with each step into the hot sand.

"You know exactly what I mean," he said as he sat back down onto his beach chair.

"I wasn't brought up like you, all right? I can't just—"

"Yes, you can." Amir put on his sunglasses and stared at the Mediterranean. "You can change. You can learn, but you don't want to."

Laila wrapped herself with a towel and sat on her chair next to him.

"What are you talking about? I did everything Pierre told me to do."

"I'm not talking about what Pierre taught you."

Laila wanted to respond to Amir, but she didn't know what to say.

For the rest of the afternoon, they sat on their beach chairs in silence. As the sun set into the sea, Laila wondered if this would have happened if she'd been braver and swum faster? Was she really an embarrassment to Amir? And what had made him think that man was flirting with her? Amir had certainly overreacted. No, he'd acted like a lunatic. It bothered her that while they were fighting, she hadn't said that. What kind of gentleman behaved that way? She wanted to resume the argument, tell him he was at fault. But if Mama were there, she'd tell Laila to apologize to her husband even if she felt she was in the right, especially since it was their honeymoon. But if Baba were there, he might have told her to fight for what was hers and never to acquiesce, that she was as good as any man.

"How long are you going to sit there and sulk?" She reached for Amir's hand. "I tried to follow you out there. I really did. But you swam too fast."

He took her hand and squeezed it. "You know why I wanted to take you out to the buoys?" He took off his sunglasses and turned to her. The green of his eyes looked lighter against his tanned skin, and she was attracted to him. "It's because I wanted to be alone with you and I couldn't wait for another minute. That's what a man does when he loves a woman, but I don't think you really love me."

"Of course, I love you," she said.

"But you don't want me, really want me." He tapped on his chest.

"That's not true. I do want you," she said. "I'm your wife." She wasn't lying about that. There were many times when he made love to her that she almost enjoyed it, but shame always got in the way, like a droplet of water on a candle flame.

"No, you don't. You're a cold woman." He got up from his chair. "Let's go." Laila put on her sunglasses so he wouldn't see her cry.

That night they barely spoke over dinner at the Cecil's Rotunda Café. Maybe Amir was right. Maybe she was a cold woman. She wished she could speak to her sister now, ask her why every time Amir undressed her, it felt wrong, even though she loved him? Nobody told her that honeymoons were this complicated. To her, sex and love were two separate things. Was there something wrong with her? What did he really mean by *want,* anyway?

"I'm sorry," she said over dessert. Amir had ordered her favorite, vanilla ice cream. "I don't know why I'm like this. But I do know that I love you. I wasn't brought up to want things, Amir."

He reached for her hand across the table and held it for a long while. "I know," he said.

That night he took her close to him in bed. She fell asleep on his chest as he played with her long silky hair, and she dreamed that she was the best swimmer in the world, her arms rhythmically moving, propelling her forward through endless seas of blue.

The next day they skipped the beach, and Amir took Laila shopping. They went to one boutique after the other on Rue Fouad, and Amir selected for her cocktail dresses and long evening gowns. He chose the most expensive of everything. "I have enough," she told him, but he insisted that it was their honeymoon and that they should buy what they wanted.

At one of the boutiques, when the saleslady bragged at the cash register that her boutique was the only one that carried the strapless red taffeta gown he was buying for Laila, Amir asked her if she had any more of the same dress in stock. "Two more," she said. "In different sizes." Amir bought the remaining dresses so that nobody in Alexandria could have the same one. Laila begged him not to do it.

"It's a waste of money," she said. "I really don't mind if someone has the same dress. It may never get bought anyway. What will we do with two copies of a dress I already have?"

"We'll burn them," he said.

Laila's throat thickened. She bit the inside of her cheek to keep from crying. Burn them?

"Nothing is a waste when it's for you." Then he kissed her cheek, and they left the store carrying bags filled with dresses, shoes, gloves, and purses.

In the weeks that followed, Amir took Laila from one end of Alexandria to the other. She began to feel comfortable and less guilty when she wore new clothes or let her long hair down. They ate lunch at the seafront Beau Rivage Hotel, sitting in the garden surrounded by mimosa trees and red, pink, and white flowers. At night Amir gambled at the San Stefano Casino, playing bridge in one of the gambling rooms. Laila didn't play, but he asked that she sit next to him, insisting she'd bring him good luck. He only lost once in the two months they spent in Alexandria. Almost once a week they saw an American film, at the Rialto, Lido, Concordia, or the Ferial movie theaters. When they went to the Rialto, Amir took Laila to Fluckiger's Swiss pastry shop during the intermission, where they had chocolate biscuits or clo-clo ice cream.

A few times during their stay they went to the racetrack, and Amir let her choose the horse. One day, toward the end of their honeymoon, as they stood in the bleachers waiting for the races to begin, a woman's voice came from the row behind, calling Amir's name, and Laila turned to see who it was.

"Amir Pasha?" said a tall, slender woman in her twenties. "Is that you in the flesh?"

"Gigi," Amir said, taking her hand to kiss it.

She had red fingernail polish, and her short, shiny light-brown hair bobbed when she talked. She wore a tight low-cut strapless sundress, showing her deep cleavage.

"This is my wife, Laila," Amir said, and took a long look at Gigi's breasts.

"Mabrook," Gigi said, and she straightened so that the dress pulled down slightly and more of her breasts showed. "Laila, you must have some kind of magic. This man is absolutely impossible to catch." Gigi gazed at Amir for a few seconds, and he smiled at her in a way that sparked in Laila a new kind of jealousy, a physical stirring inside her chest.

"There's not a doubt about that, Gigi. Laila is all magic." Amir pulled Laila close to him.

But Laila wasn't magic. She was a cold woman, a bad swimmer, and an embarrassment. Amir had said so, and now there was Gigi who wasn't cold at all. Gigi would have swum to the buoys with Amir. She wouldn't have covered any part of her body in bed. Gigi would have felt something, would have *wanted* him, and from the way she looked at Amir, Laila was certain she probably had. Imagining Gigi and Amir together made Laila feel the same way she felt when she was drowning in the sea, panicked and breathless. This raging jealousy was a fire now burning all of Mama's instructions. She questioned everything she was taught about women, marriage, men, and desire, an order of things crumbling before her at Gigi's feet.

Gigi threw her head back and let out a loud laugh. "Well, I suppose nobody can compete with magic."

Then the races began, ending the conversation. Laila watched the horse they'd bet on through her binoculars, but she couldn't focus and lost the horse altogether. Who was this Gigi? What kind of relationship had she had with Amir? How had she been so bold? That gaze. That laugh.

"Who's Gigi?" Laila asked after the race, as she and Amir walked around the downtown holding hands.

"Just a friend," he said. "Her father and Papa did some work together."

"She seemed to know you pretty well. And the way she laughed. It was so ..."

"I have many friends, Laila, men and women. Please don't make a fuss."

"Well, I don't like this Gigi girl. I don't like her at all. I hope we never see her again."

At the end of the street, a hair salon took up the corner. Laila tugged on Amir's hand, and they stopped for her to look. There were pictures of American actresses taped in the window. She recognized Elizabeth Taylor since they'd just seen *Father of the Bride* at the Rivoli, and she knew Oliva de Havilland, but didn't know the third whose haircut she liked the most. "Who's that?" She pressed her finger against the window.

"That's Lana Turner," Amir said. "She played in *The Postman Always Rings Twice*. Great film. Came out a few years ago."

"They all have short hair." She ran her hand along her long brown hair.

It fell almost to her lower back and it felt heavy. Mama had never wanted her to cut it, but insisted she keep it in a bun when she went out, saying that only loose women wore their hair down. What was the purpose of that anyway? Maybe Mama had been wrong about things. Maybe cold women were the ones who kept their hair in buns.

"Short hair is à la mode," Amir said.

Gigi's hair was short and stylish, just like Lana Turner's but a little longer. "I want to cut my hair. What do you think?"

He laughed. "And you won't cry? Women cry when they cut their hair."

"I won't cry," she said, recalling the last time she'd cut her hair with Naima's sewing scissors and the reprimanding words of Baba's barber. "I promise I won't cry."

"In that case, I think you'll look gorgeous with a cut like that." He pointed at the picture. "Not too long, but not too short," he said, and opened the salon door for her.

The hairdresser was part Italian, part Greek who also spoke French and a little broken Arabic. Laila had learned that this was how things were in Alexandria, even more so than in Cairo. It was rare to hear Arabic spoken in the streets. The European expats were more numerous than the Egyptians. The only conversations that happened in Arabic were common transactions, like buying kazooza or sandwiches from the street vendors, who wore galabeyas. Laila remembered some French from school and a few phrases that Pierre had taught her, but she couldn't converse with the hairdresser, and Amir had to translate much of the time.

"Are you sure you want to cut all that beautiful hair?" the hairdresser asked, scissors in hand.

"I'm sure. I want it short," Laila said.

The hairdresser turned to Amir, who was sitting in the waiting area.

He nodded. "Short enough to be stylish, but long enough for me to run my fingers through."

The hairdresser ran her fingers through her own hair and said, "Like mine?"

"Exactly like yours," Amir said.

Laila followed this conversation by watching the two in the mirror. Was Amir flirting with the hairdresser or was she flirting with him? Or was all of this normal in this new life of bikinis, gambling, and alcohol? Botros and Naima never flirted like that. Not even after marriage.

The hairdresser laughed and said, "D'accord." Then she made the first snip into Laila's thick wavy hair. It fell to the ground, and Laila didn't cry.

After her hair had been cut and styled, the hairdresser held a mirror up behind Laila so she could see the back. "Et voila," she said. "Vous aimez?"

"Oui," Laila said, touching the new ends of her short hair, freeing and light.

When they returned to the Cecil, there was a telegram for them. Naima had had a baby boy, and Laila was so happy for her sister. Two boys. Now the old crow couldn't say a word. That night she wore the new strapless red taffeta gown to the ball at the Cecil. She put on her makeup and dabbed perfume on her décolleté and inside her wrists. She wore a pair of silver high heels and added Vaseline over her red lipstick to make it shine. Then they went down to have dinner at the Cecil's supper club.

On the dance floor, Amir held her close, and she followed his lead as the jazz band played on. She'd gotten used to his frame and to his rhythm, and to the way other women looked at him. It was the first time she'd felt this at ease with her husband, more accustomed to his touch, the sound of his voice, the scent of cedarwood and anise from his cologne. The way she felt about him that night was new to her, and she couldn't explain it, only that she wanted him to kiss her and carry her up to bed. Maybe it was watching Gigi flirt with Amir that day. Flirt in a way that suggested a certain familiarity. Maybe that made Laila want him more. She needed to remind herself that he was hers, that he'd chosen her after all, not Gigi, that he'd defied his mother to have her, that he'd painted a watercolor of her, that he'd kissed her in Azbakeya Garden. Was this what wanting felt like, this strange, silky weakness? And should she tell him? No, it was too embarrassing. Good girls didn't talk about those things. But maybe she was no longer Mama's version of a good girl, and maybe that was alright.

"I want you," she whispered in his ear.

"How about we skip dinner and go upstairs?" he said.

She didn't respond, but she smiled, and Amir signed the check for the drinks they'd had, took her by the hand, and they rushed to the elevator. That night in bed with Amir, Laila finally felt the sweet rush Naima had told her about, and it was the most miraculous thing she'd ever known.

19

Hoda reigned over the family palace, and when Amir and Laila returned from their honeymoon, they fell under her rule. She directed what the servants cleaned and on which days. She dictated the weekly menu to the chef and approved the butler's list of activities. She decided which invitations were accepted or denied; when they'd host a party and the guest list; and what her husband, son, and now Laila wore to those occasions. In the morning after breakfast, Hoda read her books and magazines outside at the swimming pool. When she'd finished her reading, she put on her floral swimming cap and swam for exactly twenty minutes. The butler waited for her, standing in the sun, and would hold open a terry cloth robe as she climbed from the pool. By lunchtime she was showered, dressed, her hair done up in a chignon, and wearing her jewels—rubies, sapphires, and diamonds.

On their first night home after the honeymoon, Amir explained to Laila the fastidious nature of living in the same home with his mother. "It's best not to upset her," he said as they slipped under the sheets. He told her he'd return to managing the textile factory with his father and would have to leave early in the mornings, but that he'd return each day for lunch at two o'clock. "Make sure you're not late to the table. And make sure you're appropriately dressed."

Laila had nothing to do at the palace. In the mornings, after Amir left for work, she took long walks throughout the property, reveling in the trees and greenery of rich people. Growing up, she didn't see that kind of lush greenery except on her walks along the Nile and in the Carons' gardens . It cost too much money to buy and care for plants. But in Amir's garden there were date palm trees and mango trees and a large rose garden that the gardener tended to every day. Sometimes when she was certain nobody was around, she sang freely. She sang Om Kalsoum songs or some of Baba's old songs. Sometimes she only hummed. Apart from when Amir came home, those were the happiest moments of her day because sometimes Baba seemed to be with her out in the lush gardens. When it got too hot to be outside, she returned to the palace, showered, and sat cross-legged on her bed, which had been made for her by the time she returned. Sometimes she messed it up just to make it again. Then she put on her makeup, got dressed, and waited for the two o'clock lunchtime to arrive.

She tried to do everything right at mealtimes, but Hoda always found something to fault. "Next time, make sure you press your dress," she said at the first lunch after the honeymoon.

"Mother, give her a break please," Amir said. Hoda ignored her son and sipped her soup.

A few days later, she noticed that Laila's nail polish had chipped. "Don't you have a manicurist yet?" she asked. "For God's sake, Laila, people will think we're making you do our dishes. Please take care of it."

Laila had done her own nails on the honeymoon. The saleslady at Benzion's department store had demonstrated how when she'd sold Laila her first bottle of nail polish.

Neither Laila nor Amir responded, but Amir took her hand and squeezed it under the table. At dinner a few days after the chipped nail polish incident, Laila's red lipstick had smudged onto her chin, but she hadn't noticed and neither had Amir. "I didn't realize we'd invited a clown to dinner," Hoda said, half laughing as she pointed at Laila's chin. Amir ran his thumb along Laila's chin to wipe off the stain.

"Take it all off, Amir," Makram Yousef Pasha said. Then he turned to Laila. "You don't need lipstick, Laila. You are beautiful without it. Leave the makeup to the women who need it." He scowled at Hoda, but Hoda said nothing.

"I can't do anything right," Laila said later, pacing in front of the bed while Amir changed out of his dinner suit. "She hates me."

"Mother hates everybody. She's a miserable old woman. You have to learn to hear her without listening."

"No." Laila took off her skirt. "She hates me more than she hates any-body else." Baba would have despised Hoda, and he'd have told Laila to fight back like a man, but how? She wasn't a man and this tension was distinctly feminine.

Amir hung up his suit in the armoire. "Someday she'll see in you what I see. Until then"—he plopped onto the bed—"don't upset her."

Makram Yousef Pasha was Laila's consolation. He'd been kind to her ever since the proposal, and because neither he nor she took a midday nap, they spent time together in the late afternoon hours when Amir and his mother were still asleep. He loved to sit outside in the Moorish garden, which had a fountain in its center. The garden was shaded by date palms and a mimosa tree. Every once in a while, a curlew perched on the wrought iron gate that separated the palace from the rest of the world. The first time Makram Yousef Pasha invited her to join him, she'd come downstairs for a glass of water after Amir had fallen asleep. Her father- in-law had been sitting in the reading room, which she passed on her way to the kitchen. "You don't sleep either?" he asked.

"No, ya Pasha," she said, stopping at the doorway.

"I think it's about time you call me Papa. If that's all right with you." He put his book down on the side table, took off his reading glasses, and stood. "Do you like beer?"

She'd never tasted beer and didn't know what to say. Before she could respond, the pasha said, "Come sit with me in the garden."

They sat beside the fountain at a green latticed metal table under a large umbrella. The younger of the maids brought them two glasses of cold beer and a plate filled with cheeses and cold cuts.

"Try this one." He pointed at the salami. "It's from Genoa, Italy." Then he advised her on which cheeses to try and told her which regions of France they had come from. "You see, Laila. This"—he gestured at the garden, the fountain, the platter of food, and the beers—"is what I call mazag." He leaned back in his chair, hands behind his head, reveling in the garden.

She hadn't heard anyone use that word since Baba. "Mazag," he would say when he heard a beautiful song, enjoyed a sunset, or took a long walk along the Nile.

"My baba used to say that."

"I'm sure you miss him," the pasha said. "Very much."

He patted her hand and told her to take a sip of the beer before it got too hot.

"I know nobody can replace your father, but if it's all right with you, you can consider me just like a father. And if Amir ever misbehaves, you know you can tell me. I'll set him straight."

Then he told her about his childhood, the land he'd inherited from his father, the factory he'd built buying one machine at a time, and the day he was given the title of pasha. He told her he had two passions, hunting and film, and that his favorite actress and singer was Ragaa Abdou. "I'll never forgot that day. It was nineteen forty-two, and Hoda and I saw *Forbidden Love* at the Diana Theatre. She was playing opposite Abdel Wahab. From the moment I heard her sing, I was totally in love. I own every one of her records." Ever since that day, he and Laila spent the siesta hours in the Moorish garden eating charcuterie and drinking beer.

Every Sunday, Laila and Naima went to the old apartment on Gazirat Badran to spend the day with Mama. Naima brought the baby with her and left her older boy at home with Botros.

Mama carried the baby around all day, only giving him to Naima to breastfeed. On those days, Laila happily made her own tea in the small kitchen and sifted through rice with Mama on the balcony. Even the creak in Baba's chair made her long for a time before Hoda.

The first time Mama saw Laila's haircut after the honeymoon, she brought her hands to her mouth in a loud gasp and cried. But Naima loved the haircut and asked Laila to turn around so she could see exactly how the layers had been cut, running her fingers through it. Then the three of them talked about everything. Mama told them who in the building had gotten engaged, married, was expecting; or got a job in a new factory; or was arrested for being one of the fedayeen, plotting against the king.

Mama explained that she'd heard from the porter that there was a group of young men gaining strength called the fedayeen. "They don't want the king anymore. They say he's embarrassed the country and that he's stealing the people's money. They say he stands with the foreigners against his own countrymen. If your father were alive, he'd have joined the fedayeen. I'm sure of it."

It was the first time Laila had heard Mama discuss politics with such passion. She'd never cared about these things.

"Suddenly you're interested in politics?" Laila said teasing her mother. Neither she nor her mother have ever really understood politics. After Baba died Laila was far from men's café gatherings where fervent political discussions were had. She only recalled what Baba had told her about the protesters who sporadically gathered in the streets demanding freedom, but as soon as the protests were broken up the reason for their anger faded into the background of Laila's life. Now, with all the talk of the fedayeen she became more curious about what was happening in her country.

"When you see so much unfairness, ya binty, you can't help but look for the culprit."

"Don't worry about unfairness, Mama." Naima explained how her life had changed with a monthly pension from Amir's family. "The old crow," she said to Laila as she suckled the baby, "can't say a word about it. I got a maid, you know."

"I told her not to waste her money," Mama said, coring zucchini for the evening's meal. "But you know your sister." She pointed at Naima with the corer, and a few pieces of zucchini fell onto the balcony floor. "She doesn't listen."

Laila sifted through the rice slowly, and Naima went on. "The maid comes twice a week." She held up two fingers. "And I tell her exactly what to do. The old crow has no say. I do what I want when I want." Naima tapped her stash of cash, which she alternated from one side of her bra to the other, depending on which side the baby suckled.

Laila told Mama and Naima all about Hoda, and soon the three of them were imitating her and laughing. They joked about her floral swimming cap that looked like a garden growing out of her hair, the butler standing in the sun holding the terry cloth robe, the strange jeweled brooches she wore to lunch, and her fat ankles.

"Listen," Naima said, giving the baby to Mama and taking the bowl of zucchini from her. "You have to show her who's boss. Don't let her talk to you like that."

"No," Mama disagreed. She burped the baby boy, who spit up on her galabeya. "Don't make your husband choose between you and his mother. Try to win her over."

One day after returning from her morning walk, Laila smelled okra stew and followed the aroma to the kitchen. There were four people working in there: Chef Antoine and three women helpers. One lady was washing dishes, one was cutting vegetables, and one was frying something in a smaller pan while Chef Antoine tended to the pot. When he noticed Laila, he took off his funny white hat. "Madame, what brings you here?" He spoke in broken Arabic just like Madame Caron.

Laila shrugged. "I smelled bamia."

The chef put his hat back on. "The pasha likes it. But ..." He looked disgusted as he stirred the pot. He closed the lid. "It's not exactly my expertise. Madame Hoda hired me for French cuisine." He beamed proudly as he said these words.

"May I?" Laila took the wooden spoon from the chef and lifted the lid. What was supposed to be a dark, thick stew was soupy and light in color. She dipped the spoon in and took a sip of the steaming liquid. "It's missing garlic and coriander. And you need more tomato sauce."

The ladies stopped chopping, washing, and frying, and Chef Antoine put his hat back on. "You're telling me how to cook? I have a culinary degree from Paris." The chef's hat bobbed as he spoke, and something about that seemed farcical to Laila. She bit her lip so she wouldn't laugh.

"And I learned how to cook from my balady mother, who learned from her balady mother, who learned from her balady mother," Laila said, suppressing her laughter.

"I'm funny to you?" The chef threw the wooden spoon in the sink.

"No, not at all," Laila said, trying to clear her throat. "I just want to help you. After all, it's Egyptian cuisine."

"I appreciate your offer, madame, but I'll do my job as I was hired to do it."

The ladies avoided Laila's gaze. They looked tired, maybe a little afraid, and she felt a strong kinship with them, a quiet misery shared by those in the same trade. She knew the pain in their feet, the annoying sweat running down their necks, the ache in their backs, the burn of chaffing hands. And she remembered how Mama had always made Laila oil her hands when she'd gotten home to keep the skin from cracking and peeling. "At the end of your shift"—she directed her words at the ladies, and especially the youngest one who was washing dishes—"you should rub olive oil all over your hands. It'll stop the burning."

She smiled at the chef. "Good luck, chef," she said, and left the kitchen.

That day the okra stew was awful, and the pasha yelled at Hoda for hiring a chef who couldn't make simple food.

"That's because you long for your simple roots," she said. "I hired a star to make elegant food, not this stew business."

The pasha ignored his wife and asked the servant girl for a plate of pita bread, feta cheese, and olives.

"Feta cheese and olives." Hoda took a sip of her champagne. "I married a man who eats feta cheese and olives although he has the money for caviar and salmon fumé."

Amir shifted in his chair.

"Papa, I can make you all the food you like," Laila said. Hoda glared at her.

"Thank you my dear," the pasha said. "But I couldn't have my young daughter-in-law step into the hot kitchen for me. You're the princess of the palace now. It's the chef's job. That's what we pay him for."

"Give him a day off and I'll make you the best bamia you've ever had." Laila wanted more than anything to do something, to be busy, productive. This idle life felt wrong, almost immoral, and when Amir was at work, she was bored and lonely.

The pasha swallowed hungrily. "I haven't had real balady food since my mother died, Allah yerhamha."

Hoda rolled her eyes and dabbed her lips with the white cloth napkin.

"Let me do it. It would be my honor."

Amir kicked her under the table.

The pasha called the maid back into the dining room. "Go tell Chef Antoine to take the day off tomorrow, but make sure the helpers report to work early." The maid's hands shook as the pasha spoke to her. "Laila is making me a special dinner, but she is to do no cutting or washing." He wagged his finger at the girl.

The next morning, Laila woke up early and insisted that the driver take her to the vegetable market in Rod El Farag where she knew which vendor had the best okra. Then she went to the butcher and asked him for his best cut of lamb. This time, she didn't bargain.

Back at the palace, she showed the girls how to cut the stems off the okra so that it didn't become too slimy in the stew, and to make sure the onions were minced, not just chopped. She ran the fresh tomatoes through

237

a grinder and crushed the garlic herself with the mortar and pestle. Then, as the helpers seared the lamb, she seasoned it with salt, pepper, and allspice. And as the steam rose from the pot, she stood and smelled it, ensuring that it smelled like Mama's

She talked and laughed with Chef Antoine's helpers, and learned that they didn't live far from her old apartment in Rod El Farag, and that the two younger girls were the daughter and niece of the older woman. At first they called her Madame Laila, but she insisted they call her Laila. She had taken off her shoes and stood barefoot in the kitchen with them; the cool floor against the soles of her feet comforted her. Cooking for others was a tough, grueling job, hours of work in a hot kitchen, but it was part of who she was and she'd never been ashamed of it.

Now, working with the three other women, she felt productive and fruitful, unlike her empty and useless daily routine in the palace. After they'd finished cooking, she gave the women extra money as a thank you for their help and told them to come to her if they ever needed anything.

The bamia turned out just like Mama's. The tomato sauce wasn't overpowering, and the mixture of garlic and coriander was just right. She hadn't measured; she'd known by the taste, smell, and consistency. Mama had taught her that the only real way to cook was with the senses, and when it was right "you just know it's right."

"This stew is better than my mother's, Allah yerharmha," said the pasha several times over dinner.

"Papa is right. It's delicious," Amir said after his first bite. He took Laila's hand to kiss it.

"Yes," Hoda said. "It really is very good." She dabbed her mouth with the napkin. "But, Laila, don't you want more?"

Laila put her hand on her stomach. "Thank you. I'm full."

"No, dear, I don't mean more food. I mean more of life. I see you going off for long walks every day by yourself. I know you visit your mother weekly, but aren't you bored? Isn't there anything you want to do? You cooked once, but that's an exception. You know we can't let you cook for us all the time."

What was Hoda getting at? Should Laila be honest, or would that lead to trouble?

In the years after Baba's death, she had lived moment to moment, never thinking about the next day, month, or year. Meeting Amir had been an awakening for her. Being with him was the only thing she'd wanted then, but Hoda was right. Laila was bored. "I suppose I feel a little idle," she admitted. "I'm used to being busy."

"That's what I thought," Hoda said.

Laila waited for Hoda to say anything else, to explain the purpose of her question. What had she really meant to say? But Hoda just filled her bowl with another serving of bamia and said, "You really are a talented cook, Laila. What a loss for Madame Caron."

20

CAIRO, SEPTEMBER 1949

In the months that followed the honeymoon, Amir introduced Laila to his Cairo. They went to friends' parties in villas on Pyramid Road and in Garden City mansions, where she met bankers, factory owners, restaurateurs, and politicians who carried the titles of effendi, bey, and pasha. On Thursday nights they went dancing at the Semiramis rooftop supper club, and Amir taught her the samba, rumba, and tango. He took her to Gezira Sporting Club where King Farouk was a member. Sometimes they watched horse races there. More often, she was a spectator as Amir played water polo, cricket, or went skeet shooting.

She became accustomed to this new life, but there were moments when she felt guilty. Why her? Why was she the one to fall into this life?

One day after Amir's cricket match, the two of them were having lunch at the poolside restaurant when she noticed a swimming instructor coaching a woman. It was obvious the woman knew how to swim, but he was training her for some sort of competition. He looked displeased, shaking his head as he held a pocket watch in his hand. Amir told Laila the trainer was the best in Egypt, and that the woman had won national swimming competitions and was training for another competition. "Somewhere abroad," he said as he spread foie gras on a slice of warm bread.

Laila had been a poor man's swimmer. She understood that now. For her, swimming had become the invisible line that separated the poor from the rich, the unsophisticated from the civilized. If only she could swim like that woman, as if water were air.

"I want to learn," she said.

"Learn what?" Amir asked.

"Swimming," she said, looking down at her plate of smoked salmon. Amir had told her to order the smoked salmon instead of her favorite, pasta Bolognese, because smoked salmon was "more elegant to eat."

"You can't be serious." He took a bite of his bread.

By then, Laila had learned that certain things mattered to Amir. He loved luxury and he reveled in it. More than his love for luxury, though, was his obsession with superlatives. He was the best cricket player and the best at water polo. He had the nicest car in Egypt (apart from King Farouk). He wore the most expensive ties. And as he'd often told her after the honeymoon, particularly before they set out for a party, he had the most beautiful wife in all of Cairo.

"Aren't you the one who said I embarrassed you in Alexandria?" she said, the sting of those words still fresh. "That I didn't actually know how to swim? Well, if I become a good swimmer, I'll never embarrass you in the water again. In fact, people will say, 'Look at Amir Makram Yousef Pasha's wife. She swims like a professional.'"

Amir chewed quietly for a moment and then took a sip of his champagne, watching the woman in the pool training with her coach. "You do have a point," he said. "The mother of my children should know how to swim, and swim better than anyone else."

Did he know she was manipulating him? She should have felt guilty for it, but she didn't.

"Excuse me," Amir said, and then left the table and walked to the swimming pool.

Laila watched him talk to the coach, at times shielding his face from the sun with his hand. He pointed at Laila and back at the swimming pool. Watching his gestures, she tried to guess what they were talking about, recoiling at the idea that Amir was recounting the Stanley Beach incident. As the men continued to converse and the swimmer went back and forth the length of the pool, she regretted asking for lessons. She wanted nothing more at that moment than to take it back, to hide her incompetency and move on, masking it in any way she could. But it was too late.

Amir returned to the table with a triumphant smile. "You start next week," he said as he sat back down. "He only has one time slot, at seven in the morning, and is doing it as a favor to me. The driver will take you in the mornings and pick you up after the lesson. Don't be late." He took her hand in his, kissed it, and said, "My wife will be the very best."

ↄↄ

The coach's name was Magdy Safwan, but everyone called him Battal (champion) because he'd won so many competitions. He told her he was from the south of Egypt and had grown up on the shores of the Nile since his father had been a fisherman. That was how he learned to swim. "If you can swim in the Nile, you can swim anywhere," he said. Before they started their lesson, Battal sat on the top step of the pool with Laila and gave her a black swimming cap and goggles. He showed her how to adjust the goggle straps around her head so that water didn't seep in.

Battal was a tall, slender man with a broad, muscular back. His skin was a deep tan color, and his black curly hair had begun to gray at the temples. In some ways he reminded her of Baba. He had eyes the color of obsidian just like him, but a slightly longer face. He looked like someone in one of those Pharaonic scenes painted onto papyrus and sold to foreigners in the Khan El Khalili market. Battal had a deep, steady, soothing voice that might have made him a good singer, and Laila imagined him singing on the Nile in a small rowboat, pulling in the fishnets at dawn.

She didn't swim on their first lesson. Battal only acquainted her with the pool, going in with her. It was her first time in a swimming pool. She'd only ever been in the sea, and the pool's smooth paved bottom made her nervous because she couldn't dig her feet into the sand to anchor herself. Even though the water only came up to her shoulders, she felt threatened by it as though it might consume her from head to toe.

Battal must have noticed her fear because he put his hand on her arm to steady her. "You can never be a good swimmer until your relationship with water changes. Did you know that your body is mostly made of water and that the earth is mostly water?" He fanned his hand around. "The air we breathe"—he took a deep breath—"has some water in it too. So, if you fear water, you fear the whole world and everything in it. Don't think too much. Courage is here"— he tapped on his chest—"where love is. That's where the courage is."

When he said that, it made sense. The heart was where truth came from, not the mind.

This was something Baba had taught her long ago. The mind lied. It manipulated. It manufactured. But the heart made the music. The heart made the food delectable. And maybe somewhere in her heart there was courage that could make her feel as calm in water as she felt on land.

After his words on courage, Battal showed Laila how to put her face in the water, not just duck under it. He called it "confronting the water." He showed her how to hold onto the side of the pool and kick properly so that the water would carry her and not swallow her. They practiced arm strokes in the air. He adjusted her arms when her form was wrong. He was picky about it, often shaking his head and taking a grip of her arms, adjusting them in the way he saw fit. The hour passed by more quickly than Laila would have wished. She loved Battal's company. He was an extraordinary person who filled a great big space around him with something unseen but keenly felt.

When she got out of the swimming pool and dried herself, she thanked Battal for his patience and said, "I'm going to give you everything I have. I promise." Though she made the promise to Battal, it was really a pact she made with herself. She would prove that she wasn't just a weak, ignorant, poor girl rescued by a pasha. She'd show herself and everyone else that she was strong and capable. Maybe from the outside swimming was just a trivial thing, something people did everyday like sipping on a cup of hot tea in the afternoons, but for Laila it was her act of defiance. Battal smiled and said, "We'll see."

Laila kept her promise. Everything centered on swimming, and although it was just an hour, Battal's lesson occupied her mind all day. She replayed it in her memory to make a list of ways she could improve. She stood in the middle of her room practicing arm strokes. She lay on the bed on her stomach to practice her kicks. In the shower she practiced her breathing rhythm, moving her head from side to side as Battal had taught her. She woke up every morning at dawn, packed her swim bag, had a morning coffee, and went to the club. Sometimes she arrived at the pool before Battal, and once he admitted that, although she wasn't his best student, she had the most discipline. "You can do anything with discipline, but only a few things with talent," he said.

Swimming fortified her in ways she'd never thought possible. When she swam, she was alone in the world, an idea that would have terrified her in the past. Now, the solace of the water comforted her. Thoughts came to her in spurts, in flashing images, and strung themselves together into a depth of perception that seemed to happen best in the water with the rhythm of her body. Sometimes, amidst the motion of her arms and legs, a part of a song emerged from her memory, a maquam, a chorus, or one of Baba's oud improvisations. Sometimes she imagined that Baba hadn't died, that she'd gone to that audition and had become a star like Faten Hamama or Laila Murad. *I'll show everyone*, she thought when she got tired, and her arms and legs begged her to stop. She never stopped until Battal blew the whistle.

She grew stronger. When she stood before the mirror, she saw her arms, back, and legs looking more defined. She'd liked her figure before, but this new powerful body was one to be proud of. She looked forward to being naked in front of Amir. She stopped dimming the lights before they made love. She had a new craving for her husband and an acceptance of her desire for him.

Mama had taught her about boundaries, about suppressing needs, wants, even thoughts. But that was an old Laila. The one who had almost drowned, who'd flailed in the sea. If, as Battal had told her, water was the world and everything in it, and Laila had shed her fear of water, then she'd shed her fear of the world.

"You seem different," Amir said to her about two months after she'd started swimming. He'd been kissing her and had stopped to look at her, holding her face between his hands as if searching for a nuance that might explain what he sensed.

"I'm not different," she said.

"You are," he said. "It's as if you're angry."

"Angry?" She took his hand and put it on her breast. "Does this feel like an angry woman?"

He pinched her nipples and bit her neck hard. It hurt, but Laila didn't pull back. That night when he made love to her, he was the angry one. He was rough with her, gripping her thighs so tightly, she bruised the next day. He pushed and shoved, moving her whichever way he wanted to. Still, she gave herself to him, though this time, their lovemaking felt less like love and more like hate. Through it all he kept his eyes closed as if he didn't want to look at her, to really see her just when she wanted to be seen. When he was done, he turned on his back and fell asleep.

❦

"You're glowing," Naima told Laila the following Sunday at Mama's. The three of them were rolling grape leaves on the small kitchen table.

"Are you pregnant?" Mama said, dipping her hands into the bowl where she'd mixed meat, rice, and spices. She spread a wet grape leaf on the plate. "It's about time. Before you know it, you'll be married a year." She dropped the meat in the middle of the leaf and rolled it so fast, Laila couldn't see her mother's fingers move.

"I'm definitely not pregnant," she said. She hadn't yet told Mama or Naima about the swimming lessons, fearing Mama would reprimand her for wearing a swimsuit and being in a pool with a man. It was all foreign to her mother, and Laila had learned by now that Mama had a way of thinking that was impossible to change. But Laila had changed. She wasn't worried about what Mama or Naima would say anymore. She felt freer since she'd met Battal. "I've been taking swimming lessons at the Sporting Club. I swim every day for an hour." Mama began to say something, but Laila spoke over her. "And I love it!"

Mama shook her head. "I don't understand. Your husband approves?"

"He's the one who arranged it."

"That's why you're not pregnant. You're too busy swimming." Naima laughed mockingly and rolled another grape leaf, slower than Mama but faster than Laila.

"Don't be stupid." Laila pulled a stem from her leaf, the way Mama had taught her. "I swim in the mornings when Amir is at work. There's plenty of time in the rest of the day for baby making. It just hasn't happened yet." Amir had been using condoms, but she'd never share that intimate of a detail with her sister or mother.

"So, your glow is a swimming glow?" Naima centered a row of meat mixture on her leaf.

Laila shrugged. "I guess so."

She could not explain to her sister how she'd changed, why she'd changed, or what part of her had changed. It seemed absurd, now that she thought about it: A girl takes swimming lessons and suddenly she's altered? But it wasn't like that at all. It was a nuance, like one note changed in a song. It was only one note, and yet the song sounded different.

"Don't forget, Laila." Mama took another leaf from the bowl, and a few droplets of water trickled onto the table. "Men are men, and women are women. You keep your proper distance from that swimming teacher. The devil is crafty. You're a beautiful woman and any man would—"

"Mama, please." Laila carefully rolled her grape leaf. "I'm not a child. I know what I'm doing."

Mama lifted a brow at Laila. "Sometimes I wonder about that."

21

CAIRO, SEPTEMBER 1950

One day, after Laila had returned from her swimming lesson, Hoda told her that in the afternoon she needed to be showered, dressed, and ready for teatime with the ladies. "It's about time I introduce you to my friends. You can skip your walk today."

Laila had known that Hoda had monthly teatimes with her friends but hadn't ever imagined being invited. In fact, she hadn't wanted to be invited or meet Hoda's friends. She'd known that social scene from watching many teatimes at Signora Morpurgo's and Madame Caron's. They got dressed up, sipped tea, and gossiped. She preferred to go on her walk and sing among the trees. It had been her daily outlet and had become a ritual, a worship of nature and art. It was her time to think, to contemplate the big questions she'd never gotten answers to.

"I'm really tired today," she said. "How about another time?"

"Nonsense," Hoda said. "I'll send up a cup of ginger tea with the maid. Now, go get ready. We can't disappoint. Which dress will you wear? The pink one maybe?" Hoda nodded as if Laila had responded in agreement.

Laila took a long shower and drank the ginger tea. She rested on the bed. Then when it was time, she put on her pink dress, tied the halter ribbons in a bow behind her neck, and buckled the thin black patent leather belt. She combed her hair and put on pink lipstick, careful not to let it smear, dabbed a little perfume on her wrists, and took one final look in the mirror. Then she checked her fingernails and filed away a small chip on her pinkie.

By the time she entered the parlor, some of Hoda's friends had already arrived. Silver trays of tea, cookies, and small sandwiches were placed on the coffee table and side tables. The new young maid came out every few minutes to refill them.

As Laila entered the room, Hoda stood up and fanned her hand out at her. "Enfin, she's arrived. Everyone, you remember my sweet Laila from the wedding?"

The ladies kissed Laila on the cheek, and she sat down. Soon the maid brought her tea, and as she was stirring in Laila's sugar, Laila asked her how she was doing. Patting the maid on the back, she whispered, "Tell me if you need anything." The new maid had come on after one of the other two had been called home to care for her dying mother. The new girl was young, no older than seventeen. She seemed shy and lonely, and Laila sensed a deep sadness.

Every few minutes someone new came to the door, and Hoda went through the introductions again. She called Laila the daughter she never had, the fresh flower of the house, and her new best friend. When eight women had gathered in the parlor, Hoda said, "Which one of you has read the Widad Sakakini's latest book? I couldn't put it down. Such language and what a feminist story."

Laila didn't know what they were talking about. She hadn't read anything, apart from street signs and menus, since she was in school.

Some of the women nodded. Some said they hadn't read it, and one woman, the youngest of the group, said, "I prefer reading serialized novels in the paper. That's how I know if a writer is really good. Either I'm dying to know what happens, or by the following week I've forgotten about the story completely."

Laila had never known there were serialized novels. Baba had only read the political sections of "Al Ahram", and when he died, she'd lost track of politics. Mama couldn't read, and Naima was only a little better than Laila.

"That's how I read Mahfouz's *Midaq Alley* a few years ago," the woman added. "I fought with my husband over the papers."

The women laughed, the doorbell rang, and Laila resolved to read the newspaper. Hoda put her teacup down. "Brigitte and her daughter are here." She greeted her visitors at the door, and when Laila turned to see who it was, she couldn't control the shake in her hand. She put the teacup down and rested her hands in her lap.

As Madame Caron and Catherine walked into the room, the woman sitting next to Laila leaned over and whispered, "Brace yourself. That woman is wretched."

"I have a feeling," Laila said.

"I'm Moshira, by the way," said the woman. "I figured you should know my name before we start gossiping." Moshira had shoulder-length light-brown hair, eyes the color of honey, freckled cheeks, and a dimpled smile.

Hoda made space for Madame Caron and Catherine on the sofa. "Brigitte, this is my beautiful daughter-in-law, Laila."

"It's a pleasure to finally meet you," Madame Caron said. "So sorry we missed the wedding." She reached for her tea and turned to Hoda. "We were out of town."

What kind of game was this? Laila wondered. Why had Hoda invited Madame Caron?

She knew that Laila had been her cook. And why was everyone talking about authors and books?

"C'est un plaisir de vous recontrer," Laila said, perfectly mimicking Pierre's French pronunciation and tone.

Madame Caron had taught Laila only how to say merci, de rien, and the names of the dishes she had her cook. It was the first time Laila had ever sat across from Madame Caron, sipping tea from the same tea set, stirring sugar with the same silver spoons.

Catherine remained quiet and nibbled on a cookie, looking around the room. The palace was much bigger than the villa she lived in.

"You're just in time," Hoda said to Madame Caron. "We were talking about books. What are you reading these days?"

"*Le Deuxieme Sexe,* to be sure. Simone de Beauvoir excoriates men. She's marvelous." Madame Caron gestured at the maid to fill her cup of tea.

"Ah, yes. Haven't had a chance to read it." Hoda turned to the group. "What's everyone else reading? Have any of you brought something to exchange?"

Exchange? Hoda hadn't said anything to Laila about that.

Some of the ladies took out newspaper clippings from their purses. Someone brought an article from a magazine called *L'Express.* Some brought with them thin paperback books. Only one lady took out a thicker book and put it on the coffee table. "I just finished *Al-Fitna-Al-Kubra* by Dr. Taha Hussain. I just can't get over him. He's amazing."

Hoda smiled. "Of course, he's amazing. He's a graduate of the Sorbonne like me. Who else is better suited to be our minister of education?"

The ladies laughed once again, and more names flowed. There was talk of an outspoken journalist, Salama Mousa; the poetry of Hafez; Rose al-Yusef, a female journalist who had started her own magazine; and a playwright named Tawfiq al-Hakim. Then Madame Caron said, "Laila, whatever are you reading now? You young people always have such good insight."

There was a long pause. What could she say? She couldn't even lie if she'd wanted to. She didn't know any authors, had never read a book, and even if she had come up with a title, she'd make a fool of herself trying to discuss it. Then Moshira said, "Ladies, have you forgotten what it's like to be a newlywed? There's no time for reading and literary salons." Moshira pointed at the coffee table where Hoda had made piles of books and magazines, which Laila had guessed were for the guests to read. "She's in her first year of marriage. My first year we did nothing but …"

The ladies laughed again, and one of the older guests who'd been mostly quiet said, "I never liked those early days of marriage. It's so exhausting."

Then Catherine said, "Tell me, Laila. Does Amir have a favorite food? Do you cook for him? I heard your mother worked as a cook. Is that true?"

"It is true, Catherine. I'm surprised you don't remember. She and I both worked in your kitchen, and if I remember correctly you loved my fasoolya."

The women gasped, shifting their glances between Laila and Catherine, Hoda and Brigitte.

"But I thought ..." the older woman started.

Hoda put her teacup down, and tea spilled over the edge into the saucer. She laughed awkwardly. "Really, now. There's no reason to discuss the past."

Madame Caron scowled at Laila.

"Tell me, ladies," Hoda said. "Who's picked out a dress for the New Year's Eve party?" Beads of sweat had formed on her forehead, and she dabbed them with the back of her hand.

Amir hadn't said anything to Laila about a New Year's Eve party. Besides, it was only September.

Some women said they'd order their dresses from Paris. The eldest lady said she'd buy her dress ready-made from Cicurel's closer to the date of the party, and that she wasn't too concerned about it. She seemed annoyed they were no longer discussing literature.

"I'm having mine made," Moshira said. "I like to feel the fabric in my hands. And I know the perfect atelier on Soliman Pasha Street."

"I just love those parties with all the dancing and music and champagne," Hoda said. "And the Semiramis Hotel is my favorite." She picked up the tray filled with cookies and offered more to her guests. "Please have some."

Nobody took a cookie.

"But you never dance, Hoda," Madame Caron said. "Maybe Laila can sing at the party. You know, for entertainment. Something her awad father might have taught her."

Hoda shook her head at Madame Caron, as if to say *Stop. Abandon plan.* Everyone must have seen what was happening. It was so obvious.

"A musician among us?" Moshira turned to Laila, smiling. "Well, that's new."

Laila nodded. "My father was a composer and played the oud, Allah yerhamoo."

There was a collective soft sigh in the room.

"Sing then," Moshira said.

"Yes, sing," said the lady who'd brought *L'Express.* "We've been doing this every month for years, and nobody has yet brought us music. It's the high art we've been missing."

Madame Caron sat back in the sofa and said nothing. "Laila's tired. She's not up to it," Hoda said.

"Actually," Laila said, "the ginger tea you sent up really worked. I feel much better."

"Sing anything," Moshira said. "Sing a Laila Murad song or something by Om Kalsoum or whatever you want." Her voice rose in excitement.

She looked around the room at the woman in tea dresses wearing white gloves nibbling on macaroons and meringues. She cleared her throat. She'd sing the song Baba had written for her audition at Radio Cairo. Taking a deep breath, she imagined him sitting in his chair holding his oud, the risha between his fingers. She imagined the silver line in the air that moved with her voice the way he'd taught her to see music. And then she began to sing, opening with the maquam improvisations.

"'Ya habeebey.'" Her voice vibrated with the *ya,* and she held that *a,* listening in her memory for the strumming of Baba's oud. She stretched the notes over habeebey, and the room quieted. Her voice came out deep and clear. Nobody sipped tea, nibbled a cookie, or flipped through a book. Every one of Hoda's friends was looking at Laila.

When she stopped singing, the ladies clapped. Then they took their last sips of tea and one by one left the palace. "But we haven't discussed the literature," Hoda said. "I brought out the books." She pointed at the coffee table. The ladies insisted they couldn't stay any longer, and each of them came up with a different reason for her early departure. It was clear to Laila that they'd sensed an uncomfortable awkwardness and wanted to get away from it.

Moshira was the last to leave, and as Laila walked her to the door, she whispered, "You had no idea this was a literary salon, did you?"

Laila shook her head. "Nobody told me. I thought it was just a teatime gathering."

"That's what I thought," she said as she picked up her handbag. "Let's go shopping next week. I'll take you to that atelier I was telling you about."

"I'd love that," Laila said, and returned to her room singing Baba's song over and over.

That afternoon she sat on her bed and sewed the torn buttons back onto her wedding gown. She'd found them on her wedding night and saved them in a small box on her dresser, all except for one. She'd searched under the bed and carpet, behind the puddled curtains, and under the nightstands, but the last button was lost.

22

CAIRO, OCTOBER 1950

Laila's shopping trip on Soliman Pasha Street with Moshira marked the beginning of their easy friendship. The first time they went, Laila bought a gold embroidered cloth from Omar Effendi department store, and Moshira picked up a lavender chiffon from Cicurel's. With new fabrics in hand, Moshira took Laila to Atelier Du Mariam, where she helped her select a dress design for the New Year's Eve gown. They flipped though magazines at the atelier, and Mariam, the seamstress, pointed at various actresses—Rita Hayworth, Ingrid Bergman, Betty Grable, Hedy Lamarr. Laila finally settled on a copy of a strapless gown that Dior had designed for Princess Margaret. "Your body is parfait for Dior," said Mariam, handing her a receipt. "Come back next week for the first fitting."

Laila clutched the receipt in her palm instead of putting it in her purse, and the paper rolled in her grip. The ease with which she could afford expensive fabrics and ateliers still unsettled her, still evoked in her an emotion that was neither sadness nor happiness. As they left, she took note of the plum-colored velvet settee in the center of the atelier, the round wrought iron and glass coffee table with a gilt finish, and the enormous crystal chandelier that hung from the high ceiling. It was all so opulent, so decadent, and unbearably detached from reality. The place was crowded with women in pretty dresses with matching gloves, perusing the magazines and pictures hanging on the walls; or sitting in the waiting area; or walking around the showroom, where Mariam had mannequins dressed in her latest designs. None of them could possibly know the way hunger hurt, the way it burned and twisted the stomach. How could they?

"I'm going back in," Laila said as she and Moshira stepped out onto the street, the glass door to the atelier closing behind them. "I'm cancelling the order." She had plenty of dresses and didn't need another.

"Why? It's gorgeous. Trust me, Mariam is the best."

"It's not that." Laila reached for the door, but Moshira nudged her away.

"Wait. Then what is it?"

"It feels wrong, Moshira. All of this feels wrong. Children go hungry every day, and…"

"And what? Are you going to feed all of them? We do what we can with our money. We give people jobs. We help people out in our circle. But what good will it do if you don't buy that dress?"

"I don't know." Laila folded and unfolded the receipt.

"Listen, Laila." Moshira pointed at the atelier's door. "The money you pay for that dress keeps tens of people's jobs, from the cleaner to the cashier, and they too have children who eat because their parents work at the shop where you just bought a dress." Moshira took Laila by the arm. "Now, come and stop being silly."

What Moshira said quelled Laila's guilt, and it also relieved her. She hadn't truly wanted to cancel the order because she longed for the things she and Baba had looked at in the vitrines of department stores but never been able to buy. But still she wondered, if Baba were still alive would he tell her to accept her new place among the wealthy Cairenes?

❧

Amir, Laila, Moshira, and her husband, Ahmed Effendi, spent much of their time together. It turned out that Ahmed Effendi was Amir's factory manager, and they lived in Heliopolis on the fourth floor of a building that Amir owned. Moshira told Laila that, although she'd wanted to rent the fifth-floor apartment, she was stuck with the fourth floor because, "as you know," the entire fifth floor was reserved for the exclusive use of Makram Yousef Pasha.

Laila pretended she'd known about the building even though Amir had never mentioned it to her. Had he just forgotten to tell her about it? Or was he hiding it from her, and if so, why?

In the beginning of fall as the weather cooled a little, the four of them drove in Amir's convertible on sunny crisp mornings up the Giza plateau to visit the pyramids. Ahmed often brought his new Kodak camera, and once took pictures of Laila and Moshira sitting on the stone block just under the entrance of the Great Pyramid. When they got tired, they went to the gilded King Farouk Rest House, where they drank tea, ate pastries, and took in the view of the Khufu's pyramid through a panoramic window. From there they usually went to the Mena House Hotel, where the men played a round or two of golf, and Moshira always insisted on watching the sun set into the Western Desert before leaving.

When they got together, the men often discussed politics. Ahmed was concerned about the king, who was losing face because his own police were acting against him by protecting the fedayeen at the Suez Canal. Amir disagreed, insisting the king would "crush the opposition." But as they sipped their whiskey and Moshira and Laila drank their champagne, the conversation always turned to other things, like the gossip that came from the Automobile Club or the Snooker Club, about men whose fortunes had been lost in gambling or who were the newest rising stars of the posh Cairene scene.

A few weeks after Laila had met Moshira, Ahmed invited Laila and Amir to see Om Kalsoum in concert in the Azbakeya district. Laila couldn't believe she was going to see Om Kalsoum live. She'd spent her life listening to her songs on the radio. When Om Kalsoum walked onto the stage, the audience roared, clapped and whistled so long that she had to gesture for everyone to sit down. She wore a long glittering gown and clutched her signature silk handkerchief, which rose and fell in her hand with the music. Om Kalsoum opened with her newest song, "Ruba'iyat Omar al-Khayyam." Amir explained to Laila that Omar al-Khayyam was an eleventh-century Persian poet who wrote his poetry in lines of four, and that al-Sonbati had composed Ahmad Rami's Arabic translation of it.

"Four lines at a time?" Laila said. "Is it hard to read?"

Amir nodded. "It's very hard. We studied him in school. I hated those days, but now Om Kalsoum gives it life."

Like most of Om Kalsoum's songs, her "Ruba'iyat Omar al-Khayyam" lasted almost an hour, and the concertgoers sighed with every stanza. "Samat sowtan haatfan fi assahar (I heard a voice calling at dawn.)" As she sang, the oud, the nay, and the qanun carried a slow undulating rhythm of solemnity, interspersed with bursts of celebration. What was al-Khayyam celebrating when he wrote his Ruba'iyat? Laila wondered. Life? Music? "Calling from the unseen," Om Kalsoum sang. "For the unmindful people to get up and fill in the cups of hope before fate fills their cups of life." The music, the lyrics, and the singer's voice moved Laila to tears.

The morning after the concert, she asked their driver to take her to buy the record on their way back from the Gezira Sporting Club. Amir had a small record player in the corner of their bedroom. Laila dusted it off, removed the new record from the sleeve, carefully put it on the turntable, and dropped the needle. "Ruba'iyat Omar al-Khayyam" played. She'd memorize a stanza, then pick up the needle, dropping it back down at the beginning to repeat the one she'd learned and to memorize the next. That day she practiced over and over again until she knew every word, every note, and every rest. By the evening, she was ready to sing it from beginning to end.

When Amir came home that night, he was too tired to hear it. "Tomorrow," he said. "Tomorrow, you can sing to me." But days passed, and Amir never asked to hear her sing. He seemed distracted and completely uninterested in her. At the end of the week, she asked him again if anything was wrong, but he shook his head and said, "It's just mayhem at the factory." Then he turned on his side, his back to her, and fell asleep.

By the end of October, the weather had gotten too cold for swimming, and Battal told Laila they'd resume lessons in the spring. She had become a good swimmer by then. Not as fast or as elegant as Battal wanted —she still splashed too much—but she was comfortable in the water. Though she knew she'd return to swimming in the spring, she'd cried that day all the way home. Swimming was her daily affirmation, a reminder of just what she was capable of when she was alone with her mind and body.

She wasn't merely upset over losing swimming for the winter; her relationship with Amir had fallen into its own cold season. Making love wasn't the same as it had been, rich with tenderness and passion, and she sensed Amir was no longer attracted to her, at least not like before. Laila, on the other hand, desired him in ways she'd never imagined possible, although she didn't fully understand why. There were days when thoughts of him consumed her, and she was unable to do anything but wait up for him. She wore his favorite lace negligee, red lipstick, and the perfume he'd bought her on their honeymoon, but Amir either didn't see her or simply ignored her. She didn't know which was worse.

Their sexual encounters dwindled to once a month by November, yet she didn't understand why. Again, she asked him what was wrong. He gave her the same response he'd given her before; he was just tired. She'd thought that by now he would have wanted to start a family, but that didn't seem to be on his mind. In fact, when she asked if he wanted a baby, he said, "Not particularly."

෴

While Amir was at work, Laila escaped the palace—and Hoda—with Moshira. They went to Atelier De Mariam for their fittings, watched matinees at Cinema Metro, and ate lunch at Groppi, which had become Laila's favorite restaurant. She loved its front façade, its blue, yellow, and red floral mosaics, the chandeliers that dotted the ceiling, and the smell of chocolate, coffee, and vanilla wafting from the bakery. Her guilt of enjoying the finer things faded, though it never entirely disappeared.

After their second fitting at the atelier, Laila and Moshira stopped there for coffee and dessert.

"Your mother-in-law is hosting another literary salon next week," Moshira said.

"I know." Laila cut into her tiramisu. "I tried to read the newspaper, but I don't understand anything."

"Don't worry about all of that. I told you. Just read the first paragraph and the last paragraph and nod a lot. Nobody will ever know."

"But I don't want to pretend. I want to learn. I'm tired of not knowing anything." Because of Battal, she had begun to believe that she could learn things apart from singing, and that all it took was discipline. She just needed some help.

"What do you want to do? Buy a uniform, put your hair in pigtails, and go back to grade school?" Moshira stirred another cube of sugar into her coffee.

"I wish I could." Laila thought of her brief time at the La Deliverande school, how behind she'd been then and how behind she was now.

Moshira leaned across the small table. "Right now you need to focus on the important things." She took a sip of her coffee. "Honeymoons don't last forever, and marriage isn't easy. She pointed at Laila, "Your job is to keep his attention completely on you. And you're not going to do that with *Al Ahram* or *Rose al-Yousef.*"

Did Moshira know something Laila didn't? "What makes you say that?" Laila felt exposed and nervous.

"What do you mean? I've been married for ten years. I know what life is like, and once you have children like me, you have to be twice as vigilant."

Laila was quiet for a long time as she contemplated whether or not to ask Moshira the question she needed to ask. "How long before things slow down?"

"It depends. For me, it was a year. But that's what I mean. You have to keep things going. It's on the woman to do that, not the man."

Laila took her last bite of dessert. She had nothing else to say.

Moshira put her hand on Laila's. "Don't fret. It's normal. Wait until he sees you in that dress. It looked spectacular on you at the fitting. And that's another thing. You'll have to ease up on the sweets or it will be too tight by New Year's Eve."

"Moshira," Laila said, "I need your help. I can't go to the next literary salon without having read something."

"Back to that? I told you. Half the women there don't actually read anything. They just skim through it."

Laila didn't repeat that that wasn't enough for her. But after the taxi dropped off Moshira, she asked the driver to stop at a magazine stand where she bought *Rose al-Yusuf* magazine, written in Arabic. That night she tried reading an article in bed. "I don't understand any of this," she said to Amir. "You've got to help me. You know your mother is having another literary salon soon." Although there had been a distance between them, Laila thought that by asking for Amir's help, she might bring them closer to one another. Besides, he was the only person who could help her now.

"My love, stop worrying. My mother still lives in the Sorbonne. She's in another world."

"I don't want to be made a fool of again. Moshira saved me once but won't be able to again." She flipped through the magazine angrily, looking for something easy to understand. While she was able to read the words, she understood little of the vocabulary.

He sat up in bed. "Who cares what those old women think? They're not important to me. Their opinions carry no weight. And you're already the best. You're the most beautiful, the best dressed, and you have the best husband." He took the magazine from her and threw it on his nightstand. "Reading is for old, ugly women, Laila. And you're not ugly or old." He pulled her close to him as he untied his pajama drawstring.

It had been weeks since he'd shown an interest in her. She thought of pushing him away, demanding that they talk first, insisting that she understand the reason behind his sudden cold shift and his sudden return, but she didn't. She let herself go. She needed to be with him. She wanted him to touch her. She wanted to experience the way her body felt when it was with Amir's. In those moments, nothing mattered. All that weighed on her temporarily lifted. She felt no sadness or anger or fear, just the beautiful ache of desire that he would soon fulfill. Maybe her mother had been right about the dangers of desire. Not because it was wrong, but because it blurred all vision.

⁂

The day before Hoda's literary salon, Moshira invited Laila to her apartment for tea, and Laila sang "Ruba'iyat Omar al-Khayyam" for her. Before she started, Moshira gave her a handkerchief. "So you can get into the spirit," she said. When Laila was done, Moshira cried and said, "I think you just found your poem to discuss at the salon tomorrow."

"You think it'll be all right?"

"Of course. That'll show her to stop being such a snob. Besides, they're going to love you. We're all sick of the same stale conversations."

Laila followed Moshira's advice, and Hoda's next several literary salons slowly centered on Laila's singing. Hoda's friends were more curious about which song Laila had prepared than any book Hoda had planned to discuss.

In early December, before the last salon of the year, which took place once a month, Hoda brought it up over dinner. "I didn't start the salon to have it turned into a cabaret," she said once the food had been served and the young maid had gone into the kitchen.

Amir turned to Laila. "What's Mother talking about?"

Laila hadn't told him that she'd been singing at his mother's gatherings. She didn't answer.

"I'm talking about Laila and her ridiculous coup d'état of my salons," Hoda said.

"Your friends beg me to sing," Laila said.

"They're being polite, but this has to stop. Either you stop the singing or ..."

"I don't come?"

"Yes."

"Then I won't come," Laila said, dabbing her lips with the white cloth napkin.

"I don't see anything wrong with singing. It's an art," Makram Yousef Pasha said.

"I'm not surprised you think that," Hoda said to her husband as the maid came out to refill her glass with water.

Amir looked at Laila disapprovingly. Then he whispered, "Is that why you wanted to sing to me, so you could practice for this circus?"

"No," she whispered back. "You don't understand. I'll explain later."

That night, they fought about it. Laila had never seen Amir so angry. "It's one thing to sing for me in private." He pulled off his tie and threw it on the bed. "But to embarrass me and my mother in front of her friends?"

"How is singing poetry embarrassing? Look at Om Kalsoum. She's worshipped." Laila kicked off her shoes, and they flew across the room, hitting the vanity chair.

"You're not Om Kalsoum, Laila. Stop being delusional." He took off his jacket.

"All I'm saying is—"

"Stop." He put out his hand. "Just stop. No more singing in public. You're a high-society wife now, not the daughter of an awad anymore."

"I will always be the daughter of an awad, and proud of it too."

Amir put his jacket back on and pulled a fresh tie off the rack in his armoire. "All right. You can stay home and be the awad's daughter all by yourself. I'm going out." His car screeched out of the driveway, and Laila sobbed in her pillow.

Amir returned at dawn drunk and he skipped breakfast. Laila went out with Moshira and told her everything during their third and final fitting. "Was he out with Ahmed?" she asked as Mariam let out a few centimeters from the waist and the bust.

"No, Ahmed is traveling for work," Moshira said.

"He didn't tell me where he went, and I was afraid to ask. I hate fighting." Laila stood on the pedestal and looked at herself in the three-way mirror wearing the gold embroidered dress. "It's beautiful," she said to Mariam. "I love it."

Moshira, who was waiting for her turn to be fitted, told Laila to let things calm down with Amir, not to provoke him, and not to bring the subject up again. "If Hoda doesn't want you to sing, then don't go to her stupid salons. You hate them anyway, and so do I. Now we can do something else."

Laila didn't bring up the fight again, but Amir was even more distant and cold than he'd been.

✑

In the middle of December the servants, under the butler's direction, put up the Christmas tree in the parlor, and Makram Yousef Pasha gave strict instructions to play Radio Monte Carlo on the shortwave until after the Coptic Orthodox Christmas on January 7. For nearly a month they heard "White Christmas," "Have Yourself a Merry Little Christmas," "Il Est Né, Le Divin Enfant," and "Le petit reine au nez rouge." Laila memorized the songs, and even when she didn't understand the lyrics, she sang them phonetically. While Amir and Hoda took their naps the pasha asked her to sing for him in the Moorish garden over beer and charcuterie. She loved singing for him, and she'd come to love him as a second father. He was tender and kind to her.

Before Christmas, Laila went shopping for gifts. She bought Amir a silk tie and new cufflinks, a beaded clutch for Hoda, a new cigar box for the pasha, new cloth and sweaters for Mama, Naima, and Botros, and toys for her two nephews. She even prepared envelopes with money for each of the servants. She wrapped the gifts and put them under the tree, just like she'd done growing up.

On New Year's Eve, she wore her strapless gold embroidered dress and a fur coat that Amir had bought her. She styled her short wavy hair and wore red lipstick. The driver took Laila, Amir, and his parents to the Semiramis Hotel, which was on the Nile and adjacent to Kasr al-Nil Bridge. The hotel's entrance was larger than Shepheard's, and its entire foyer was lined with marble. Enormous mirrors and tapestries hung on the walls, and the massive ballroom glittered under crystal chandeliers.

Amir, Laila, Moshira, and Ahmed had a reserved table near the band and the dance floor, while Hoda and Makram Yousef Pasha joined friends at a table farther away from the noise. The tables were set with gold cutlery and silk napkins, just as had been used at Laila's wedding. In the middle of each table was a large silver candelabra, and on each plate was a silver-trimmed menu. Laila counted the courses. "Nine?" she said to Moshira. "It's no wonder my dress had to be taken out. Who eats nine courses in one sitting?"

"The king," Moshira said.

"What's this got to do with the king?"

He's fat and he's here, sitting diagonal to us. Look but don't look." The waiters brought the first course, crème de volaille soup.

Moshira whispered something to her husband, who said, "I know he comes to these things, but I had no idea she'd be here." He sipped his soup, staring at the tall gorgeous blond walking into the ballroom accompanied by a shorter darker man. It was hard for Laila to see her features clearly in the darkened room amidst the flickering candles, but when the woman sat down, Laila was certain she knew that face.

"Is that …" She didn't remember her name. "The American actress?"

"Rita Hayworth," Amir said before he took a swig of his whiskey, not yet having touched his soup. "She played in *Gilda*."

"'Put the Blame on Mame,'" Moshira said. "Yes, she sang it while taking off her gloves."

"God help me," Ahmed said, and Moshira punched him in the shoulder.

"Behave and stop staring," she said. "You look like a fool."

"We're all fools tonight," Amir said trying not to look at the American actress. What did Amir mean by that? Did he believe himself to be a fool? Or did he believe men to be fools for all women, and if so, what did that mean for their relationship? Just then Catherine approached their table. She wore a red beaded fitted gown, and her long golden hair spilled across her slender back.

"Bonsoir, Amir," she said, and then gave a cursory nod to the table.

Amir stood up, took her hand, and kissed it. "Bonsoir." For a second they glanced at each other as though one of them was going to say something more. Catherine left the table as fast as she came. Amir sat back down and dipped his spoon into the soup. Was Catherine just trying to infuriate her, Laila wondered, or was there something more between her and Amir? Laila felt paralyzed. She wanted to say something, but she wouldn't give Catherine the satisfaction of having ruined her night.

Moshira leaned over to Laila. "What was that?"

"I don't know," Laila said, "but I'm going to find out."

Rita Hayworth sat next to her husband, Aly Khan, at the same table with the recently divorced King Farouk and a man who Ahmed told them was the king's cousin, Adel Sabet, who lived in a villa behind the hotel.

The four of them talked about Rita Hayworth and Aly Khan over the paupiettes de filet wrapped in bacon and the selle d'agneau. They talked about Kahn's wives, his horse racing, and his jockeying. They talked about Rita Hayworth, the movies she'd been in, trying to remember them all. There was *Cover Girl, The Lady From Shanghai,* and *You'll Never Get Rich,* which was the only one Laila had seen, with Baba. But Laila only thought of Amir and Catherine. Was that just an innocent hello or was there something else?

"Look at her," Moshira said. "That hair, that body, that skin. She's the benchmark, Laila. She's the standard of true beauty."

"Why?" Laila asked.

"Why what?"

"Why is porcelain white skin and blond hair a standard of beauty?" Laila remembered the blonde dolls she'd always loved to play with at the Carons' villa before Madame Caron banished her to the hot kitchen.

"Because it just is," Moshira said.

Ahmed said he'd read in the paper that the newlyweds were vacationing in Egypt for several months, and that Aly Khan had still been married to his wife when he and Rita Hayworth were dating. "His father is the official imam to the Imām of the Nizari Ismāʿīli Shias, you know. But it doesn't look like he's following in his spiritual footsteps."

"Who's going to think about God when Rita Hayworth is by his side?" Amir said, cutting into his lamb. Was he referring to Catherine or to the movie star? Then he put his napkin down and asked Laila for a dance. Moshira and Ahmed did the same. Amir held Laila close to him, and she felt that maybe she'd been overly jealous. Maybe there was nothing to Catherine at all.

"That Rita Hayworth is a goddess. Isn't she?" Laila said.

"Never mind about Rita Hayworth," he said. "You're the star tonight."

When the four of them returned to their table, they agreed to make an effort not to look at the celebrity table. After all, famous or not, Rita Hayworth and the others had come to enjoy the evening and shouldn't have to deal with juvenile fans on New Year's Eve.

They ate the fond d'artichaut and the cailles traduction as Amir and Ahmed discussed the economy. By the time the waiters brought out the champagne bottles and passed out the party horns and hats, Aly Khan had left the table where Rita Hayworth sat with King Farouk and a few other guests. He had gone two tables over to where four brunettes sat. Maybe they were Italian or Greek, Moshira didn't know, and Aly Khan sat at their table, clinking glasses with the four women. They all laughed, and Aly

Khan leaned over and kissed one of them on the cheek. At the king's table, King Farouk got up and took Aly Khan's seat next to Rita Hayworth. He poured whiskey in her glass and, in an audacious move that made Moshira gasp, he ran his hand over her shiny, wavy blond hair.

"That lucky son of a bitch," Amir said.

"I can't believe her husband just left her like that," Moshira said. "How humiliating."

"Who in God's name leaves Rita Hayworth?" Ahmed said.

"I guess Aly Khan does," Laila said, a sense of dread looming over her.

The more the king tried to console Rita, the more she fidgeted and the more uncomfortable she seemed. And now, the entire ballroom watched shamelessly. Just before the clock struck midnight, Rita Hayworth stood, grabbed her clutch from the table, and strode out of the ballroom.

"That stupid, stupid man," Ahmed said.

"If that were my husband, he'd be sleeping on the street tonight," Moshira said.

"Just because you're royalty doesn't make you a gentleman," Laila said.

By the time Aly Khan noticed that his wife had left, too many minutes had passed, and he left the table of brunettes, running out after the Hollywood star.

The room buzzed. Farouk sat next to two empty chairs.

"If Rita Hayworth can't keep her husband's eyes on her in her first year of marriage," Moshira murmured to Laila, "what hope do any of us have?" She fiddled with a party horn, rolling it on the table.

"I don't know," Laila said, and put on her party hat. "It feels like too much work trying to keep a man like that." Amir had watched the spectacle like everyone else, yet she couldn't help but wonder if he had been looking at Rita Hayworth or at Catherine.

The ballroom dimmed, the countdown began, and confetti was tossed in the air at the stroke of midnight.

"Happy New Year, my love," Amir said, and kissed Laila. Then he asked her for the first dance of 1951.

23

CAIRO, JANUARY 1951

In the first few weeks of the year, Amir's behavior changed even more. It was hard for him to fall asleep. He tossed and turned so much that most of the time he woke Laila up. Some nights Laila awoke to find that he'd left the bed. When he returned, he'd say that he'd been on a walk or that he had gone for a drive. The only times he slept well were on the nights when he'd gone out with his friends, returning at two or three in the morning. Once she got up looking for him and found him in the shower. It was almost four in the morning. She went into the bathroom, afraid he'd fallen and hurt himself. When she saw him standing there she said, "But you took a shower four hours ago."

Amir turned the water off and got out, wrapping a towel around his waist. "Are you counting my showers?"

"No. I'm just worried about you."

One night in the first week of February, Laila was roused by the cold. It was such a frigid night that even the two layers of wool blankets didn't keep her warm. She got up to put on a heavy robe, and noticed that Amir had again left the bed. She decided to go down to the kitchen to make herself a chamomile tea, something to warm her up. When she stepped out of the room, she saw Amir was turning the corner at the end of the long bedroom corridor and was headed for the staircase that led the servants' rooftop quarters. She followed him, tiptoeing up each step. Keeping her distance, Laila watched him go into the young maid's room, closing the door carefully behind him. She pressed her ear against the door.

"No," the maid said. "I don't want to do this anymore."

"I won't hurt you," Amir said. "We'll do it like before."

"No," she said again this time louder than before. "It's haram."

"You liked it before," Amir said. "I know you liked it. Now let your hair down, lie down, and relax."

"No!" She began to scream, but her voice was quickly muffled.

Laila tried to steady her breathing and her shaking hands. How was all of this happening and why? Was he attracted to the maid? Or did he still think Laila was a cold woman? She pushed herself up from the floor and turned the doorknob. Amir hadn't bothered to lock the door, Laila swung open the door and flipped the light switch on. The girl was lying on her back, her thighs parted, Amir's head between her legs.

The maid kicked Amir off, pulled the sheet over her head, and cowered at the corner of the bed.

Amir stood up and pulled his pajamas pants back on. He was still hard. Nobody said anything. Laila couldn't hold back her tears. "You disgust me," she finally said, clenching her fists until her fingernails dug into her palms.

"Laila, she's nothing." Amir picked up his pajama top from the floor. "She's just a nazwa, a passing thing. You're my wife. She's just—"

Laila pulled the sheet off the maid. "Leave now. You don't work here anymore." Then she slapped Amir's face.

He gritted his teeth and grabbed her arm. "I swear…"

Laila pulled her arm out of his grip. "Don't touch me. Don't you ever touch me."

"You don't understand. She's nothing. It's nothing. It's like having a sip of whiskey."

"No, you don't understand," Laila said. She ran down the stairs to their bedroom. Amir followed her. Laila tried to close the door before Amir could get in, but he held the door open and pushed into the room, and then closed the door behind them. Laila flung open the armoire, pulled a simple black dress and knit jacket off their hangers, and threw them on the bed. "I'm not the helpless little girl you plucked out of the Caron's kitchen." She took off her nightgown and changed into her clothes. "This marriage is over." She took Baba's songbook out of her nightstand drawer and put it in her purse.

"Wait." Amir ran after her down the stairs. "I love you. She means nothing to me. You have to believe me."

❣

The knocking roused Selma out of a deep sleep. She'd been dreaming of running through the fields of her happy childhood. She got out bed, rushing to the door. It was almost four in the morning. No knocks at this hour could be good news. A sudden rush of terror weakened her legs.

She opened the door and saw her daughter. Seeing Laila always made her happy, but not at this hour, not with that look on her face. "What in heaven's name are you doing here?" Selma said, taking her baby girl in her arms.

Laila wept and shivered from the bitter cold. Selma guided her to the living room and sat her in Kamal's chair. She wrapped Laila in a wool blanket and, without asking her anything else, went to make her daughter some chamomile tea. When she returned from the kitchen, she pulled a chair up to Laila, put the cup of tea in her hands, and stroked her arm. "Now, tell me what happened."

Selma listened as Laila told her about the past month of Amir's restlessness, his insomnia, his disappearance from bed, his showers before dawn, and his indiscretions with that dirty maid.

"I'm never going back to that pig," Laila said. "I'll find a job cooking for someone again. I can go back to my old life."

Selma put her hand over Laila's. "You have to calm down and think this

JASMIN ATTIA

through." She had hoped this wouldn't happen. She'd prayed that Laila would have a peaceful marriage filled with love and happiness, but women's lives were not so easy. What would she tell her daughter now? Maybe if it had happened a few years into the marriage, it might have been easier to blame it on boredom, but how was the pasha's son already bored?

"There's nothing to think through." Laila's voice was hoarse.

"Men and women are different," Selma said. "For men, sex …" She cleared her throat. "It's just an act. It isn't always connected to love." Selma had never confronted Kamal, but she'd known. He thought he was so smart, so sly, but she'd figured it out. It was in the way he looked at her, the way he touched her—or didn't touch her. Back then, she'd partly blamed herself for it. It was a time when she was busy with Naima and Laila. She'd neglected him, often avoiding him because she was too tired. Men had stronger physical needs than women did. She'd learned that, but it was a harsh lesson. There were women out there, brazen women, who pleased men temporarily in ways God would not approve of. Yet in the end, with patience and a lot of prayer, Kamal came back to her. She was the wife, and these women, well, they were just street women.

"Are you defending him?" Laila said, putting down her tea on the coffee table.

"No," Mama said. "There's never a defense for this. I'm angry with him, but men are weak, and the devil tempts them."

"I don't care about men and their weaknesses or the devil. I'm finished with him and with this marriage."

Selma shook her head and without realizing, she mumbled, "This is bad."

"You're worried about what people will say, aren't you?"

Selma would be lying to herself if she said she wasn't. Words mattered. What people said mattered. "Laila, you haven't even celebrated your one-year anniversary. Of course, people will talk. What will you get out of running away? Nothing. Besides, even if the both of you want a divorce, you know the church has to approve it. It's not an easy thing to do."

272

"I'll get my dignity. I'll get peace of mind. Whether I'm divorced or separated, I don't care. I just don't want to be with him anymore."

"That's what you think. But you'll only be trading one humiliation for another. The best thing for you to do is to go back and keep your eyes on him." Selma picked up the teacup and put it back in Laila's hands, nudging her to take another sip. "You need to keep him in line. Don't let him go out without you. Don't hire young maids. You're the wife now. Take control. Be smart. No matter how innocent a young girl looks, a woman in your house is a threat. That's nature." How could her daughter have been so naïve as to let a young woman into her house? Didn't she understand how tempting that was for a man? And why hadn't Selma warned her before she'd married her off to the pasha's son? Had she expected anything better out of him? Wasn't he the one who'd snuck around with her daughter for months?

"I don't want to go back to a marriage where I'm going to have to police my husband, worrying about every woman he crosses paths with."

Laila threw the glass teacup across the room, and it shattered against the wall. Then she went into her old room and slammed the door. Selma picked up the broken glass and threw it in the trash. She thought of going into Laila's room and sleeping next to her, comforting her, playing with her hair like she had when she was a little girl. But no, she couldn't do that. Laila had to learn to cry alone. She had to learn to console herself. There was a lot of crying in life, a lot of pain, and there was just no way to avoid it. God would help Laila confront her problems.

After making herself a strong tea, Selma sat on the balcony, watching the sun rise and praying. She asked God for wisdom to help her daughter and the patience to do it. She thought about the irony of life. Here was Naima with a loyal husband who was cheap and preferred his own mother over his wife. Here was Laila living the life of a princess in a palace with a man who betrayed her with the maid in the first six months of marriage. Why the maid? Or maybe it wasn't just the maid. Maybe there were more women. No, she'd never plant that seed in Laila's mind. Her daughter had to go on with her life, reestablish herself in that vast house, and firm up her place as the unshakable wife. Temporary sexual encounters for men were just nazwas. It was like craving a piece of chocolate that melts in his mouth. They are consumed easily and quickly forgotten. Good wives like her and her daughters were gold, timeless and valuable. They adorn but are never consumed. They last like the brilliant jewels of the pharaohs.

Just as Selma had expected, Amir came to the apartment looking for Laila. It was around noon and Laila was still asleep. "Don't wake her," Selma told him as she invited him in, careful to be neither too nice nor too harsh.

He looked as though he hadn't slept. His eyes were red and puffy. He sat on the settee, and she sat across from him on Kamal's chair. How she wished Kamal was alive now. This type of reprimanding was a father's job. Then again, would Kamal have been able to truly admonish Amir? And how would she have felt if Kamal were here and shamelessly faulted his son-in-law for the very sins he'd committed?

"Shame on you!" she said to Amir. "With the maid, Amir? In your first year of marriage? If Laila's not enough for you, then why did you marry her?"

"Mama, I love Laila. I was tempted. The girl is a snake, a temptress. It was black magic."

Selma hated that he called her Mama. She wasn't his mother, and if she were, she'd have raised a good man, a loyal man. "Are you going to fall for every snake? I might as well keep Laila here with me." What Selma really wanted to know was, *Why?* Why did men succumb to temptation? Maybe if she understood this, she might be able to help Laila. Was there something she hadn't taught her?

"I don't know why," Amir said. "I really don't."

He wasn't lying. Selma could tell in the way he gazed at her, as if he were looking to her for the answer. What could she tell him? Maybe temptation and sin were not understandable. Maybe the devil confused man so much that even after committing the sin, he didn't know how or why it happened. Still, it was not an excuse. God wouldn't give commandments that were impossible to follow.

"It's as if I was possessed for a while, but I promise it's over. The spell is broken."

"Listen, Amir," Selma said. "You have to understand that love is not always unconditional. Sometimes the greatest love can break, and once it's broken, it can never be put together again." Was that how it had happened for her? Had her love for Kamal been broken? But it felt so whole now, so unbroken, sin and all. "I don't know if Laila will ever want to go back to you. My daughter is stubborn." And Selma wasn't sure she had the heart to force her daughter to return to a man who'd humiliated her so. No matter the consequences, this was Laila's decision.

"I know," Amir said, and cast his eyes down as if unable to look at Selma any longer.

Selma saw in Amir a little boy at that moment. Maybe all men were just little boys forever looking for a toy. Maybe now he was ashamed of what he'd done.

Laila finally stepped out of her bedroom, and Amir stood up. "You're awake. Thank God. Laila, I—"

"Don't bother, Amir. I'm not coming home."

Selma went into the kitchen, leaving Laila and Amir to talk alone, but she listened to the conversation, occasionally peeking at the couple through a crack in the kitchen door.

"I love you, Laila," Amir said.

"You don't know what love is," Laila said. Her voice was cold and unwavering. The words came out like fact and not an opinion. Did Laila herself know what love was? Did Selma know? The only one who understood love was God.

"I'll do anything. Please don't leave me. I made a mistake." Amir got on his knees, kneeling next to Laila, sitting in Kamal's chair.

"But I can't look at you the same way anymore," Laila said. "You broke everything."

Amir cried, "What do you want me to do? I'll do anything." He kissed her bare feet. Selma almost felt sorry for him. His desperation was real.

If Selma had confronted Kamal, he'd have certainly done the same. He'd loved her. She knew that, yet he'd hurt her. She'd never gotten a chance to tell him about the pain she carried for years. Now, she longed for that apology. Just one forgive me from Kamal's lips. Just a minute of contrition on her husband's face. Her daughter's pain had renewed the sting of her unhealed wound. It was like a scorpion that crept out of the desert sands, quiet, sly, unexpected. She asked God to forgive her, for she was angry with a dead man.

For at least an hour, Amir pleaded and sobbed. He kissed Laila's hands and her feet again and again. Laila remained quiet through it all. Too quiet, and Selma worried. Then finally Laila said, "No. I can't do it. I can't."

"Please, Laila." Amir, still kneeling before Laila, put his face in her lap and wept. "I can't go back home without you. You're home now. You're my only home."

Could this all be an act? Selma thought. For what? Amir didn't need Laila. He was in real pain. What a spoiled boy. He'd always gotten what he'd wanted. Right and wrong, good and bad, they'd never meant anything to him, had they? He'd never once dealt with a consequence of his actions. Selma felt a rage rise up in her for Laila, for herself, for every single woman who had to endure, simply endure. And yet she knew, she'd have to quell the anger, subdue her fire. It was too late for her and too early for her daughter to do anything about it.

After a long silence, Laila finally spoke. "No more young maids," she said. Amir agreed. Selma quietly rejoiced. "No more going out without me." Amir nodded. "And this is your last chance. Do this again and not even Mama will know where I am. I'll disappear off the face of the Earth."

Good girl. Good girl. Selma opened the refrigerator in search of something to cook for them. She insisted that Amir and Laila stay for dinner. That night she made the same meal she'd made for their sabaheya. Maybe it would remind them of their wedding night and renew their bonds. Over dinner, she advised them to keep the incident a secret. "People talk. Say nothing about it."

&

For days, Laila barely left her room. Amir served her breakfast in bed, made her sandwiches, and brought her tea and Baton Sale in the afternoon. They took Mama's advice, and neither of them said anything about the incident. They made up a story to tell Hoda. The young maid had disappeared for no reason, and nobody knew where she was; Laila had caught a terrible cold and needed a few days to recover. It was all partly true.

For Laila, the palace was a cold, hostile place where her flowery dreams of love and marriage had died. She still loved Amir, but seeing him with another woman that way had, in an instant, made her doubt everything she'd once believed. Though she'd had fleeting doubts about him and Catherine, she had never thought he'd cheat on her. When she'd gone to Mama's the night she discovered him with the maid, she'd been resolved to leave Amir despite her love for him, despite the jealousy. She'd get over him somehow. But she'd seen Mama peeking at the two of them from the kitchen. Of course, her mother was worried. Why wouldn't she be? Laila's marriage wasn't just about her. Its consequences were far-reaching. There were Mama and Naima to consider. Ending her marriage to Amir would end everything good that had happened to them. Even if Mama had the strength to work in kitchens again, she wouldn't have the strength for the gossip that would ensue.

Women always blamed women. They'd say that Laila wasn't a virgin on her wedding night, or that Laila was the one who'd cheated on her husband, or that she was belligerent.

Nobody would blame Amir, even if they found out about his philandering. They'd say it was normal for a man. How would Mama endure that? And Naima would lose her maid and her emancipation from her mother-in-law. Whatever people said about Laila's honor would be contagious to Naima, and she'd be subjected to the old crow's insults, constantly demeaned.

When Amir had begged for Laila's forgiveness, kissing her hands and feet, she'd wanted to keep saying no. She'd wanted to kick him out. But she was trapped, weighed down by the heavy shackles of responsibility for her own family. She wished she'd never met Amir, never kissed him in the gardens, never danced the afrangi waltz.

Amir pleaded with her to get out of bed. "You need some fresh air. You don't eat. You barely drink," he said, pulling the comforter off her.

"What do you care?" Laila tugged on the bedding, trying to pull it back from Amir, but he wouldn't let go.

"I care a great deal," he said. "You just don't understand men."

"I'm cold," she said, not wanting to hear any further excuses for his behavior.

"Come on now," he said. "Go take a hot shower and get dressed. Go for a walk when it warms up later. I have to go to work, but when I get back tonight, I'll take you out. Do you want to go to the movies?"

Laila had no energy left. No energy to get out of bed and no energy to fight getting out of bed. She got up, took a shower, and took the walk that Amir had suggested. She walked the path she always had, but in silence this time. She didn't feel like singing. She was trapped in the marriage of any girl's dreams.

Laila lost track of time. Day became night, and the weeks that went by soon became months. It was even worse than after Baba's death. At least then, she'd had Mama. She'd had work to do, something to occupy her. Laila never thought she'd look back fondly on her days in Madame Caron's kitchen, but now she did. She wanted something to cut and chop, something to boil and bake, the numbing monotony of it. No matter how bad things had gotten in those days, she'd kept a glimmer of hope inside. But now, she lived in a black room, inside four walls through which light never seeped.

Moshira called her every day, inviting her over for tea, to the movies, or out for a cup of coffee, but Laila declined. One day Moshira came over and coaxed Laila out of bed. "Amir told me you weren't yourself lately, but I had no idea it was like this. You look so thin and pale, and your hair, don't you own a brush? That's it. We're going out." Moshira wouldn't leave until Laila agreed to go out with her, until she got out of bed and dressed. Over coffee, Moshira asked what was wrong, but Laila didn't tell her. She couldn't. She was embarrassed and humiliated. She didn't want Moshira to know that Amir had lost interest in her so fast.

Amir kept his promise. He didn't go out with his friends alone. Once Laila had agreed to leave the palace and started going out with Moshira, Amir took her to dinners and parties again where Laila faked smiles and polite laughter. He stopped roaming the palace in the middle of the night. After two months of pushing Amir away, she finally let him make love to her again, but she felt nothing. It was like those early days of her marriage when she suppressed her desire. Except this time, she had no desire. She simply endured him like she was enduring her whole life.

Her return to swimming in April helped, but even Battal noticed the change in her. "Where's the passion? Where's the hunger?" he said, shaking his head. "You're not listening to me. What happened to your strokes?"

Sometimes she slept in and missed her swimming lessons. When Battal threatened to stop coaching her, she promised to be more diligent. Laila learned to perform her daily life in the darkness that surrounded her. Light, sound, and color had all diminished around her. Sometimes old memories of Baba came to her and brightness flickered, but it left as fast as it came. Most of the time she was alone in her mind. Even when she went to visit with Mama and Naima, she felt removed from them. She told them that things with Amir were better than they'd ever been. She said she was happy and found a way to forge a false smile.

One day after her morning swim and a long walk around the palace grounds, she went up to the rooftop, to the maids' quarters. It was a quiet, peaceful place with a gorgeous view of the Nile. She leaned over the concrete railing and watched the birds swoop down and snatch their food from the surface of the water. For a long while she thought about her life. How long would it take for it to pass? She wanted it to pass, to be done with it all. She wanted to get old now, so old that she'd sleep in her bed and never wake up. But life was going by too slowly, too painfully.

She fantasized about falling off the roof. Over and over she envisioned it until she was straddling the concrete railing. There she was, one leg dangling on the side of death and the other on the side of life. It would be easy if she could just muster the courage to push herself off. It would happen quickly. Then she wouldn't be trapped anymore. It wasn't that Amir had cheated on her that made life so unbearable. It was that she had no real options. Where would she go if she left him? With death, she'd be free. But what would happen to Mama and Naima? They'd have to keep living. They would remain in their lives, trapped in their bodies, struggling even more after Laila's death. How would they survive? The shame of a suicidal daughter or sister would loom over them. And Laila doubted Amir would continue supporting them.

She couldn't even die, Laila thought as she swung her leg back in. That day she went to bed at noon and woke up the next morning. Markram Youseff Pasha said something to her over their afternoon charcuterie and beer. "You seem different, ya binty. You're like a light that's been dimmed. Is it Amir or Hoda? You can tell me." He put his hand over hers and patted it the way Baba had.

"It's nothing. I think maybe I just miss my family." She didn't like lying to him, but what else could she say?

Her father-in-law took a deep breath and said, "Whatever it is, I'm here when you're ready to talk."

☙❧

For their one-year anniversary in June, Amir took Laila for a weekend getaway at the Mena House hotel. They stayed in a suite overlooking the Great Pyramid. In the morning, Laila waited for Amir to play a round of golf, and then they ate lunch at the poolside, where they talked. But she didn't hear the conversation they were having. To her, he was a mime whom she had stopped trying to decipher. She wasn't sure whether she was still angry or jealous or whether she still loved him. The only thing she knew for certain was that she felt alone, in an unbearable void she couldn't escape. The second and final night at the hotel, he arranged for a candle-light dinner on their suite's veranda. Over dinner he told her stories about his friends, his travels around the world, and how he'd felt the first day he saw her.

Amir kissed her hand. "Please cheer up. I know these last few months have been tough, but things will be alright. You have to believe that. Maybe we should try to have a baby," he said. "A baby will change our lives for the better."

Laila didn't want to have a baby. She didn't want anything at all. "Sounds perfect," she lied and didn't understand why she was lying.

Then Amir reached in his pocket and gave her a red velvet box. Inside were a pair of diamond earrings. Laila thanked him and put them on.

For the next few months he made love to her like he did when they'd first got married. He was passionate and seemed to crave her with the same intensity. Their lovemaking for her was like a beautiful dream and a night-mare all at once. Laila enjoyed the intimacy, but every time she fell into the bliss of his touch, the image of her man with another woman flashed before her, sending her into torturous jealousy. Still, being with him was a small triumph over the other women she imagined (the Gigis of the world), a way of reclaiming something that was hers. Somehow the emo-tional torment of sex with him was less painful than being completely alone in her thoughts.

By late summer, Amir started going out again at night, returning at dawn. He slept past noon, went to the factory late, and sometimes didn't go in to work at all. Even his father got angry with him for not taking the business seriously. Amir stopped having sex with Laila. She missed the physicality, but this time when he stopped sleeping with her, she hardened herself, deciding never to ask him why. Even though she didn't ask, Amir offered up excuses for his behavior. He told her he was tired and over-whelmed with business meetings, prospective clients in cotton textile. He said he had to show them a good time in Cairo and soften them up before signing the contract. "Did you know our cotton has made it all the way to America?" But she'd learned that when Amir lied to her, he never looked her in the eyes, that he repeated his lies to make them sound like truth. Almost every night he brought back with him traces of another woman— the scent of perfume, lipstick stains, a long blond hair stuck to his suit jacket.

She could have fought with him, interrogated him, threatened to leave him again, but what would be the end result? She would never leave. She couldn't do that to Mama and Naima. At first, the jealousy and loneliness were intolerable. She imagined the women he'd been with, the color of their hair, the sounds of their voices, the texture of their skin. But in time the jealousy faded and turned to anger, the anger to disgust, and then there was no feeling at all. By December, when the pasha turned on Radio Monaco and Christmas music played in the palace again, Laila felt neither love nor hate for Amir. It was the first time in her life that she felt nothing for someone.

Laila found a way to keep going, living but only half alive, breathing but taking the shallowest breaths. She felt like one of those worms that Baba had told her about, living in constant darkness, the earth packed in all around her, buried but not dead.

24

CAIRO, JANUARY 26, 1952

The fabric department of Cicurel's was crowded with loud, pushy women in search of cloth for their spring wardrobes. Laila, Amir, Moshira, and Ahmed had been invited to a Sham El Nessim party at the villa of Taalat Harb Pasha, one of the most prominent bankers in the country. And although the spring celebration of Sham El Nessim wasn't until the Monday after Coptic Easter, such an event, according to Moshira, required meticulous preparations. Laila had no interest in going to the party, of buying cloth and returning to the atelier for yet another design. But Moshira nagged and Laila acquiesced.

As usual, Moshira started perusing cloth on one end of the department and Laila on the other, picking up anything that looked pretty. "Pick up what you like. I trust your taste," Moshira said before they parted.

Every time Laila reached for a bolt of fabric to take to the cutting station, another woman grabbed it faster. Finally, Laila found a lustrous pink silk that piqued her interest. It was bright but elegant. She picked up the bolt and put it under her arm. Then a woman started pulling it from her. "I saw it first!" she yelled.

"No, you didn't." Laila hung on to the silk fabric with all her strength until the lady walked away, calling Laila a low-class nouveau riche. She didn't even know why she didn't let go of the fabric, but it was one of the first things she'd wanted in a long time.

As she rushed to the cutting station to meet Moshira, the chatter of shoppers became louder and more chaotic. A scream came from a level below, and then the sound of breaking glass. "What's wrong with people these days?" said the saleslady who'd just measured out seven meters of Moshira's lavender linen. "They lose their minds during sales."

"I smell smoke," Laila said. When she looked behind her, women were screaming and crowding the staircase that led down. Fabrics were strewn on the floor in their wake.

The saleslady dropped the scissors. "Fire!" she screamed. Moshira and Laila ran toward the stairs, and Moshira yelled at the women to form lines and stop pushing. Nobody listened.

Moshira took Laila's hand, and they squeezed through the panicked crowds, edging their way down.

On the first floor, men in galabeyas were gathered outside, shattering the tall plate-glass windows with metal sticks. The demonstrators chant-ed, "Our blood for freedom." Pieces of glass flew into the store. The hordes of men grabbed piles of merchandise and threw them into the street where a bonfire had been started. Some people looted, taking satin ties, socks, wool sports coats, and bottles of perfume. But others threw the Cicurel's fineries into the growing fire.

Just as Laila and Moshira were about to step out of the store, Laila slipped and slid across the floor. She hit her head against the hosiery wall. Her first instinct was to get up and run, to push through the crowds and get out. She heard Moshira screaming her name and saw her trying to get back inside through a broken windowpane, but she couldn't. The crowds were stampeding in every direction. Laila wasn't hurt, but she didn't push herself off the floor. It was too hard to run out, to return to her existence. The fire grew, its heat crawling over her.

She lay still and coughed. If she died now, it would be an accident. There would be no whispers of shame in it for Mama and Naima. They'd mourn Laila. They'd have her arb'aeen ceremony forty days after her funeral. Mama would be devastated, but she'd survive. She'd take comfort in God. And Amir would take care of them. He had to. It would look bad if he didn't, and Amir didn't like looking bad. He'd be the best widower son-in-law. The best.

Yes, Mama would be all right, Laila convinced herself. Here was her chance to end the pain whose root she'd forgotten. But where had it come from? It didn't matter now. All she wanted was relief, and this death would be easy. Laila coughed and closed her eyes. A gorgeous rosy haze draped over her. She heard Baba's oud music and the sound of her own voice singing in the distance, as if there were two of her; one on the floor dying and another singing a song somewhere nearby. But she wasn't singing, was she?

ﻋﻭ

Selma hated the scent of the hospital, that mixture of medicine and rubbing alcohol. She hated the white floors and walls, and the doctors with stern faces and white coats. When Amir sent the driver with the news, she'd already known something was wrong. She'd been pacing around the apartment, a shiver at the nape of her neck that wouldn't go away. She'd even gone into the kitchen to make herself tea with honey. But nothing can quell a mother's sense, not even herself. She didn't remember what the driver had said to her when she'd opened the door, something about a fire and Laila and a hospital. She'd put on her sandals and run out wearing her house galabeya. Binty, binty, binty. My daughter. Had she said it out loud or just thought it? The entire car ride was a blur.

When she'd got to the hospital, Laila was already in what the doctor called a ghaybooba, a deep sleep from which, the doctor said, Laila may not wake. But she was breathing through the oxygen mask and her heart was beating. For four days she sat at Laila's bedside holding her hand.

"Take me," Selma pleaded with God. "Take me instead." Selma had done everything she needed to on Earth. She'd gotten married, become a mother, raised her two daughters, and she'd even seen two grandchildren. What was left for her to do?

"Take me instead. Take me."

Amir too hadn't left Laila for a minute. He'd sat at the other side of the bed, only leaving to talk to the doctors. Sometimes he raised his voice when speaking to them, but he was always calm when he explained things to Selma. If Laila hadn't been able to afford nice things, she would have never been shopping at Cicurel's and wouldn't have gotten caught in a fire. But could Selma really blame Amir? It was the protestors' fault.

During the day, the hospital room filled with visitors. People Selma didn't know nodded at her sympathetically and placed one flower bouquet after the other on the hospital side table and armoire. Hoda and the Makram Youseff Pasha sat in the room all day too, along with Naima and Botros. The old crow stayed home with the boys, but she had come to visit once when Naima and Botros went home. She'd leaned down and whispered in Selma's ear, "I know it hasn't been the best between us, but I want you to know that I went to Alexandria and prayed for Laila at the shrine of Saint Mina. And every day I've been lighting candles at our church."

Selma took the old crow's hand and squeezed it. It was the most touching thing anyone had done for Laila. Her throat constricted, and she was barely able to get the words out, but she thanked the old crow and said, "You went all the way to Alexandria?"

Samia looked down at Selma, her eyes filled with a mother's tears. "And I took the boys with me. You know the purity of a child's prayer."

"Yes," Selma said, patting her hand. "I know." The Romans had tortured and killed Saint Mina. Then they tried to set him on fire for three days and three nights, but his body didn't burn. "Can I ask you for one more favor?"

"Anything," said Samia.

"Would you light candles for the girl who saved Laila? Her name is Moshira."

"Moshira," she repeated as she left the room.

Selma hadn't met Moshira yet. She was home recovering. They said she had burns on her hands and a deep cut on her leg from the broken glass. But that same night, she'd gone home to her children. Thanks be to the Lord. Amir said that had it not been for Moshira, who somehow made it back through a broken window into the store, and a kind man whom nobody knew, Laila would have surely died. The man and Moshira carried Laila to safety, but she was unconscious by then. Selma wanted so badly to take Moshira into her arms now and to find that man who'd driven her daughter to the hospital. He'd left before anyone could get his name. Amir said that if he ever found him, he'd give him an enormous cash reward. "He'd be set for life," Amir said.

"He's a good man," Selma said. "He probably went back to save more people. God protect him and his family."

What kind of person burns buildings with people in them? Did the protestors think that ransacking foreign stores would chase the colonizers out of Egypt? Kamal would have never approved. And what did they gain? Ashes and destruction. Nothing more. Selma overheard the pasha and Botros talking about it. The fedayeen, who'd been volunteer fighters, had stormed canal cities and attacked the British, whom they considered occupiers, striking their camps. The British demanded they retreat, but soon realized the fedayeen were secretly being protected by the police, so they turned their canons on the police barracks in the canal zone, killing fifty. At the same time downtown was being set on fire, demonstrators had surrounded Abdeen Palace, where the king was hosting a lavish buffet lunch to celebrate the birth of the royal heir to his second wife, Nariman. By four o'clock, he had sent tanks into the city to quash the protests. Many were arrested, and the king returned to his posh life. It seemed to Selma that he had lost his grip on the government the way a man can lose his grip on his family.

"But it started as a demonstration. The fringe groups hijacked it," Botros said, and Selma wasn't sure if he was defending the protestors.

"The Muslim Brotherhood has been trying to get rid of Western influence for decades," the pasha said. "They want King Farouk out. Those bastards." He shook his fists, and Hoda tapped him on the shoulder as if to remind him that it was not a time for politics. "Anyway," he said. "Our main focus now is our princess, Laila."

When Laila opened her eyes, four days after the fire, Selma had been telling her the story of how she fell in love with Kamal. Laila loved stories about her father, and Selma thought that if she told her stories she'd once liked, maybe she'd wake up. Besides, now more than ever, Selma needed to remember Kamal. The first thing she'd noticed about Kamal were his eyes. Any woman would have envied those eyes, big almond-shaped eyes and lashes so thick, it looked like he had lined them with kohl. It wasn't just how his eyes looked that had attracted her to him, but how they looked at her. Nobody looked at anybody like that, taking the time to study the person in front of him as though he were trying to understand not just observe the shape of a face or the curves of a body. Understanding and seeing were two different things and Kamal had an unabashed glimmer that betrayed him. It was the musician in him, the artist that didn't know how to—or wouldn't—hide what he was feeling. Laila had gotten those eyes, and when she opened them and looked at Selma, it was as if she'd seen Kamal. What she felt at that moment couldn't be described as just happiness or relief. It felt like a resurrection for a dead part of Selma that she hadn't known had died; her soul, her daughter, returning to her, a surge of warm blood coursing through her veins once again.

It happened early in the morning. Selma kissed her daughter's hands and arms and forehead, afraid to move the oxygen mask. Amir was there too, and when Laila opened her eyes, he wept, then ran to get the doctors.

At first, Laila was confused. She kept asking where she was and why Selma and Amir were crying. As the doctors came in to check her, she began to remember. She mumbled something about a pink silk she'd found at Cicurel's, Moshira screaming for her, and fire. "Where's Moshira?" she asked groggily.

"She's fine." Amir rubbed Laila's arm. "She's at home with the kids."

"She saved your life," Selma said. "God's written you a new life."

⌘

Laila heard Mama's voice as she woke up. Her head hurt, and for a while (she couldn't tell how long) she wasn't able to string together what she was saying, or what her mother was saying; something about God and a new life and Moshira. Yes, Moshira. Laila remembered she'd been shopping with her and remembered running with crowds of people. "I slipped," she told her mother. "I hit my head," she said as the events of the day came back to her.

"Moshira said you fainted when you hit your head," Amir said.

"Thank God for that girl," Mama said. "I have to meet her and thank her."

"Yes, I must have fainted right then," Laila lied. She remembered what she'd done, and was ashamed.

How could she have thought that Mama would be all right? How selfish and weak of her to attempt such a cowardly escape. "Mama, you need to go home and rest. You look tired." Mama's face was yellow. Her eyes were red and swollen, her lips chapped and dry. How long had Mama sat vigil at her bedside?

"Your mother has barely eaten," Amir said.

But Mama shushed him. "I'm fine. As long as Laila is awake, I'm fine."

The room was filled with flowers. There were vases on the windowsills, on the side table and armoire, on the floor in the corners of the room. Mama told her she'd been in a coma for four days, that everyone had come to visit, and that the old crow—"God forgive me for calling her that," Mama said—had gone to Alexandria with Naima's boys to pray for Laila at the shrine of Saint Mina. "And you know the power of Saint Mina."

"The old crow did that?" Laila pushed herself up on the hospital bed, and Amir propped her with a few pillows.

"We really should stop calling her that," Mama said. "I feel bad."

The doctors wanted to keep Laila under observation for a few more days. Laila insisted on sending Mama home, and Amir finally convinced her to go with the driver. "I'll stay with her, Mama," he said. And he did. He did everything and anything for Laila. When she said she was craving something sweet, he went and got her a box of every pastry she'd ever tried and liked. He rubbed her feet and brushed her hair when she was too weak to do it.

He told her that when he thought he'd lost her, he felt his life had ended. He said he regretted hurting her. "I was stupid and arrogant, and you didn't deserve that. Laila, I love you. I've never loved anyone else. I want you to know that."

It would have been easy to blame Amir. It would have been simple to convince herself that it was his cheating that had darkened her life, made her lose her way. But it was more complicated. It was a gradual slide she'd experienced, she'd forgotten what had broken inside her, when it happened or how. She could have blamed Mama and Naima too, not directly, but wasn't it because of them that she couldn't leave Amir? Was that the truth?

Could she have left Amir without affecting her mother and sister? No. She couldn't have, but why? It was because she didn't have any power. Money was power. Even the small amount of money she'd made from Madame Caron was power. Now she had none. Besides, Amir had taken her away from the only life she'd known how to navigate. Sure, she'd learned etiquette from Pierre and swimming from Battal, and had found a way to survive the awful literary salons, but who was she?

She was no longer the carefree Laila who happily sang at cafes with Baba, no longer the Laila that cooked coq au vin just because Madame Caron asked for it. And yet she hadn't really fit in to Amir's life. And it wasn't because she didn't know how. It was because after all the glamour had faded, she'd found his life tasteless. Being loved by him was a façade, a figment of his own imagination. Amir didn't understand love. To him, love was an affliction that drove him every which way, a personal need he tended to. It was all about him, for him. Understanding this about Amir freed her. Deep within, she must have understood this about him from the day she met him, but had never confronted herself with it. She hadn't wanted to. She knew that now.

"I don't want you to worry about anything," he said. "I'm going to order you the best dress from Paris for Sham El Nessim. You'll be the most gorgeous woman at that party. You won't need to go anywhere for the dress. The dress will come to you."

"I don't want a new dress and I'm not going to that party," Laila said. "I want Mama to make me a dress like she used to. I want to sit with her and Naima in our small kitchen and dye eggs for Sham El Nessim, prepare the fish and salads, put them in our old picnic basket, and go to the park. I want to sit on the grass and watch the sun set with my family." She wanted Moshira and Ahmed to join them, but she knew Moshira had been looking forward to the big party and she wouldn't want her to miss it.

"If that's what you want," Amir said, "that's what we'll do."

"Yes, that's what I want," Laila said, and sat up on the bed.

25

CAIRO, FEBRUARY 1952

Laila's first day back from the hospital, Moshira came to visit her at the palace. Laila opened the front door, threw herself into Moshira's arms, and for a long time they stood embracing and crying together in the doorway.

"If it weren't for you," Laila said, taking Moshira by the arm, leading her into the parlor.

"Don't say it." Moshira slowly lowered herself in the chair, still recovering from the deep gash in her leg.

The maid brought tea and cookies. Laila stirred two cubes of sugar into Moshira's tea. "It doesn't seem real to me."

"I know, but when you drive by it, it's so real. All gone. Everything we loved: the Shepheards Hotel, Diana Cinema, the Rivoli Theatre, Groppi's, Benzion's, Omar Effendi. And of course, as you know, Cicurel's."

They said nothing for a few minutes as they sipped their teas.

"Listen," Moshira said, "we can't dwell on this. We have to return to our normal lives as soon as possible, or we'll—"

"I can't," Laila said. "I need a break from the parties and clubs and concerts. I need to spend time with my mother and sister, figure things out for myself. Too much has happened. I can't explain it all, Moshira."

"But you have to go to the party at Taalat Harb's place. It will be good for you."

"I'm not going." Laila shook her head. "I already told Amir that I want to spend Sham El Nessim with my family."

Moshira said she understood, and that if Laila changed her mind, she'd heard of a small boutique called Haroun's in the Jewish district of El Daher. "The fabrics there are gems," she said. "And they say his prices are so reasonable. Just in case you want to have a new dress made."

It took three nights for Amir to return to his old habits of staying out all night, returning at dawn. Laila wasn't surprised. Amir was never really in control of himself. She understood that now. Maybe he'd been so spoiled he'd never had to deprive himself of anything. Or maybe he was forever in search of something that wasn't there. In a sense, she pitied him. Perhaps he was in his own darkness, an abyss from which he saw no way out, much like the darkness that had oppressed her for a year. No more, she thought. She'd never let anything take her down again, not even her own emotions.

A week after returning from the hospital, Laila asked the family chauffeur to drive her through the downtown so she could see the damage. He was reluctant, citing her nerves after the fire.

"My nerves are fine. Just take me."

She refused to cry in the car, and her throat thickened as she held back the tears. As they drove down the streets, the driver pointed at gutted buildings, solemnly announcing their names: the Opera House, Sala Badia Nightclub, Barclay's Bank, the Turf Club, Thomas Cook's travel agency, the Shell service station, the Automobile Club, the Chrysler showroom, and the one that broke Laila the most— the Shepheard's Hotel with its big glass-domed ceiling and its wide terrace. A few weeks later, the newspapers reported that the fires consumed ninety-two bars, seventy-three restaurants and dance halls, sixteen clubs, and forty cinemas.

Over the next months, Laila visited Mama and Naima more often. She spent time with them talking and catching up on their lives. Mama had begun to volunteer at the church to keep herself busy. She cooked for the poor and mended clothes. She even helped clean the church and planted fruit trees on the church grounds. "I'm happy to do it for God. He's blessed me so," she said. Laila had always envied her faith. If only she could have had a faith like Mama's.

Naima had taken on more of Mama's sewing and had built her own clientele, women came to her house with pictures cut from fashion magazines of dresses they wanted. These were the women who couldn't afford department store prices, but had just enough money for nice fabrics. Naima showed Laila her latest work. It was even better than the fancy atelier Laila had gone to.

"I studied the magazines, you know," Naima said. "I looked at the seams and the stitching on the mannequins in the vitrines on Soliman Pasha. Then I kept trying and trying, until I finally got it right." Laila examined the precision of her sister's work. "I love doing it," Naima said, "I love imagining something and then making it with my own two hands." It was the first time Laila had seen passion for something on her sister's face.

"Then you're making our dresses for Sham El Nessim. I'll get the fabrics," she said.

Naima smiled, and Laila realized that her sister had gone from a beautiful girl to a stunning woman. Not even the models on magazines covers could compete with her sister's perfect nose, full lips, and flawless skin.

Once when she was a little girl, Baba had taken Laila for a walk along the pyramids just before sunrise. It had been two days before Sham El Nessim, and she was upset that he'd woken her so early. It was one of the few times he'd taken her in a taxi. When they got to the Giza plateau, it was still dark, and they found a spot to sit on the ground. The gravel hurt her legs, and she pulled her galabeya underneath her. As the sun rose, Baba pointed at the first rays of light.

"Look," he said. "See how the sunlight aligns with the tip of the Great Pyramid? That's how the ancient Egyptians knew that spring had come."

He explained to Laila that this celebration used to be called the Feast of Shmo—the revival of life—in ancient Egyptian. "Then the Arabs came and renamed it Shem El-Nessim—inhalation of breeze—and scheduled it for the Monday after Coptic Easter."

For Laila, that particular spring was a true personal revival. She'd come so close to death that life had new meaning. Her marriage, her social life, all of it seemed insignificant. The only thing that mattered was loving living again; and in order to love her life, she'd do things on her terms. Mama had told her in the hospital that God had written her a new life. Maybe Mama was right, and Laila wouldn't ever squander it again.

With Sham El Nessim coming up in April and the stores in Soliman Pasha still under reconstruction, Laila decided to visit the fabric shop Moshira had told her about. "It's down the alley from the Ets Hayim synagogue. You can't miss it. If you get lost," she'd added, "just ask for Monsieur Zacharias. He's the owner, a nice man."

The entrance to the fabric shop had a double door with wood-framed glass and a softly ringing bell that signaled the arrival of patrons. It was a small place compared to the burned-down stores on Soliman Pasha Street. Bolts of fabric were stacked atop one another in cabinets that rose to the ceiling. A long counter spread along the back of the store, and on one side of the counter was a glass case filled with buttons, ribbons, patterns, and sewing needles. Haroun's was busy but not overly crowded, and she stood in the middle of the store surveying the fabrics. A few silks in one of the upper cabinets caught her interest. She stared at them, trying to imagine the kind of dress Mama and Naima might make and which colors would best suit their skin tones.

A young man approached her. He was tall, tanned, and had dark brown eyes. "Can I help you?" he asked.

Laila pointed at the bolts of silks and asked to see them. The man got a ladder and pulled them down, then carried them over to the counter where she could inspect the fabric. He apologized for the small space as he walked behind the counter, telling her she'd chosen the best silks in the shop.

"You have good taste. We just got them in from France."

She ran her hand along the fabrics and asked to speak to the owner, who Moshira had told her was Monsieur Zacharias.

The man reached his hand over the counter. "Just call me Zacharias."

She had imagined the owner to be a white-haired older man. "I'm Laila," she said as she shook his hand.

After a few minutes, she decided to buy Mama and Naima six meters of each. That way they could make two dresses. But before she paid, she asked Zacharias what else he could show her.

He took her around the store, pulling down rolls of fabric, allowing her to touch them, run her hands over the beads, the silks, the velvets. He explained things like durability and the risks of tearing during the sewing process, the origin of the fabrics, how many seas they'd traveled, the methods with which they were milled. In the end, she decided on three more fabrics. As Zacharias was cutting and neatly folding, she noticed a few books piled on a small shelf behind him. One of them was *Ruba'iyat Omar al-Khayyam*. "You like poetry?" She pointed at the book.

He smiled. "Something like that. You?"

"Something like that," she said.

He put the cut fabrics to the side, took the pile of books from the shelf, and set it on the counter. "Which one caught your eye?"

Laila pointed at *Ruba'iyat Omar al-Khayyam*.

"It's yours then." He gave her the book. She hesitated.

"I insist," he said.

"Thank you." She put the book under her arm, then opened her purse and took out the money to pay for the fabrics.

He shook his head. "How about you pay next time … when you come back to pick up the next book." He held up a collection of poetry by Nizar Qabbani, *Tufulat Nahd (Young Breast)*. "Besides, I want to know what you think of the *Ruba'iyat*. It's not every day I meet someone who likes to read."

She'd never be able to read anything of worth, and if she came back to Haroun's, she'd have to pretend, just as she had at Hoda's salons. Laila was tired of pretending. "The truth is ..." She gazed at her wedding ring. "I love the poetry, but I'm a terrible reader. The only part I know of the Ruba'iyat is the one that Om Kalsoum sings. I'm sorry." Somewhat relieved, she gave him back the book.

He refused to take it. "If you can read one word, then you can read a whole book." He put the fabrics in a bag imprinted with the name Haroun's and came around the counter to give it to her. "And if you need help, I'm here every morning at seven. The store doesn't open until ten. Reading with you would be a welcome reprieve from the mundane tasks of running the store."

"Please let me pay for this," Laila said. "I don't know when and if I'll be able to come back." She studied his face. He was a very attractive man with olive skin, dark eyes, and thick brown hair that looked soft to the touch. He was tall too, taller than Amir.

"Then that's a chance I'm going to have to take," Zacharias said.

Laila left the store resolved to send him the money with the butler and never to return. The man was too presumptuous. What made him think she'd come back? Was it because he knew he was attractive? Had he sensed her curiosity—or was it loneliness? No, it wasn't just curiosity or loneliness she'd felt. It was indeed attraction, but not the physical kind she'd felt when she'd met Amir, just a naïve girl then. This was a sudden inexplicable gravity. And that was even more reason why she shouldn't go back. She was still a married woman, no matter what Amir had done. But what she should do and what she wanted to do were two different things.

She needed to go back to Haroun's. She wanted more than anything to read like those women at Hoda's salons. She wanted to read poetry, novels, political magazines, and the newspaper, but not to prove anything to anyone. She just wanted to understand the world, really understand the world. Besides, she had to know who Zacharias was. Why had he piqued her interest? He was confident but not pretentious, attentive but not flirtatious. She put *Ruba'iyat Omar al-Khayyam* into the bag with the fabrics she'd bought and thought about Zacharias all the way home.

That night, Amir stayed out all night. When he came back home, the sun had already come up. He smelled like cigarettes and alcohol, and he was so drunk that when Laila asked him the name of the woman he'd been with, he actually told her. "Sonya," he said. Then he passed out on the bed without taking off his clothes. She should have been jealous, but she'd used up all the jealousy she'd had in her. The only thing she felt was pity for Sonya. It was nearly six in the morning, and Laila didn't go back to sleep. She showered, put on a beige suit, and slipped *Ruba'iyat Omar al-Khayyam* into her handbag. Then she took a taxi to El Daher district and knocked on the glass doors of Haroun's. Zacharias opened the door.

"I need your help," she said, and took the book from her bag. She wanted to pay him for the fabrics, but she knew he'd be insulted if she tried.

"I was hoping you'd come."

Zacharias led her into a dimly lit storage room that smelled of dyes, fabrics, and the nutty aroma of steeping tea. A square wooden table stood in the middle of the room, a crowded bookcase leaned against a wall, and off in the corner, an oud sat on top of a few empty boxes.

"Welcome to my library," Zacharias said. "Or at least, I like to call it that." They sat at the table across from each other.

"You play?" Laila pointed at the oud.

"I used to, but I haven't practiced in a while," he said.

"My father used to play. He had the most beautiful oud. It was a gift from his music teacher in Asyut. It had gold and silver scrollwork on the front, and on the back there was an inscription that said 'Small deeds are great in the eyes of the small, and great deeds are small in the eyes of the great.' My baba said it was a line from Al-Mutanabbi."

"I'd love to see it someday," Zacharias said. "This oud was handed down to me from my grandfather. He was the one who'd really played. It's over a hundred years old."

For a second, she'd had a delusional thought that Zacharias might have been the Jewish man who'd bought Baba's oud, but that was stupid and naïve. Now, disappointed, she had to catch her breath.

Laila told him her mama had sold the oud and how she had learned it was then resold to a Jewish musician. "Every once in a while, I go to instrument shops around the city looking for it. Sometimes I get excited. I keep saying to myself 'This is it. Today you'll find it', but it hasn't happened yet."

"I'm sorry," Zacharias said. "It's hard to lose something so precious."

He was easy to talk to. His voice was low and soothing. When he smiled, a dimple appeared on the right side of his mouth. And when Laila talked, he listened. She told him a little about Baba, Mama, Naima, the old nun at her school, how she'd met Amir. They laughed together about Pierre, the etiquette trainer. Then she told him about Hoda's literary salons and her embarrassment at her lack of education. But she didn't tell him that she was trapped in a failed marriage or that part of the reason she'd returned to his shop was to see him again.

He nodded, and his eyes met hers. She looked down at the book.

Zacharias told her about his family too. He had two sisters. His father started the business by selling fabrics in a small cart at the souk. It grew into Haroun's. But Zacharias had never wanted to run the shop. He had studied literature and philosophy at Cairo University.

"I wanted to be a professor. But then my father got too sick, and when he died, the burden fell on me. Now, I'm a frustrated professor with no students."

He told her he'd grown up attending services at the Ets Hayim Synagogue, but over time, none of it made sense. "I questioned God. I questioned life and death. I questioned the difference between reality and my thoughts. That's why I studied literature and philosophy."

Laila laughed. "Well, my mother slapped me on the church steps because I asked her why God never helped martyrs. That was my lesson in philosophy."

They laughed and talked about life in a way that strangers rarely do, and then he looked at his watch and stood up.

"Yalla, let's start." He searched the books on his shelf, running his finger along their spines. After a few minutes, he made a selection and sat back down at the table. "This is perfect. *Ana Hurra* (*I'm Free*)." He put the book down and tapped the cover. "It came out earlier this month. The writer, Ihsan Abd al-Quddus, is very progressive, and he writes in colloquial Arabic. It's a good place to start, and I think you'll like it." Zacharias flipped to the first page. "Go ahead. Read. I need to see where you are."

"What about the poetry?" Laila didn't want to read in front of him. She was nervous and embarrassed.

"We'll get to the poetry, but let's start with this."

Laila looked at the first line and tried to read it in her head, but every time she opened her mouth to read out loud, she hesitated. Once she started reading, she'd be exposed. He'd know her in a way no one else did.

"Laila," he said, "I'm not judging you. You have to trust me."

She looked at his hand holding the book open and tried to read. She stumbled on her words, confusing the letter ayn for ghayn and the ha for kha. He made her go back and circled the mistakes she'd made with a pencil. "Read again," he said.

If she didn't know the meaning of a word, he stopped her, wrote the word and its definition on a sheet of paper, and asked her to memorize the list for next time.

By the end of the lesson, it was already ten o'clock and time for him to open the store.

But she'd read five pages of *Ana Hurra*. It was about a girl named Amina whose mother was pushing her to quit school and get married. But Amina didn't want to follow any conventions. Laila was curious to know what would become of her.

"If you come every day," Zacharias said, "and practice your reading at night, you'll be reading anything you want in a year."

"How do I repay you?" Laila asked as she was leaving.

"Read," he said.

26

CAIRO, MARCH 1952

Laila saw Zacharias every morning. She'd come to love the soulful sound of the Fajr prayer because it meant a new day had come and she'd see him again. As soon as she heard the muezzin's voice, she stepped out onto her bedroom balcony to watch the sky, her gaze set far beyond the palace gardens at the striations of red and pink that would soon melt into daylight blue. It was at this time that Amir returned from his nights of drinking, gambling, and whoring.

As he threw himself onto the bed and passed out, she got dressed and went on what everyone believed were her long daily walks. This had been her routine from the start—a long walk, and when it finally warmed up in the spring, a swim at the Gezira Sporting Club. She'd gotten good enough to swim without instruction. Amir was too drunk to notice, and neither Hoda nor the pasha questioned it. After all, spending a long part of the day at the sporting club was what society women did. But the three hours she spent every morning with Zacharias were her guarded secret. Those three hours that started with the Fajr prayer, those three hours that gave her just enough happiness and reprieve from being Amir Makram Youseff Pasha's wife.

Laila went to church on Easter with Mama and Naima. She still hated church, but she loved being with her family especially on Easter because Sham El Nessim was the next day. After Christmas it was her favorite holiday because it was celebrated by every Egyptian of every religion, a reverence to spring, to life, to nature. That night, nearly a month after having met Zacharias, Laila, Naima, and her two boys stayed at Mama's so they could wake with the first rays of sun and dye the eggs around the small kitchen table. Naima brought with her the dresses she'd made Mama and Laila. After the boys fell asleep, she made final adjustments to Mama's blue sundress and Laila's pink floral A-line. Laila and Naima slept next to each other in their old bed and chatted into the night about their childhood, Baba, and the early days of Naima's courtship with Botros. "Remember the stupid poem?" Laila teased her sister. They laughed, and Laila couldn't help but think of Zacharias. If Naima knew about him, she wouldn't approve.

In the morning, Mama packed the old picnic basket with cucumber salad, long green spring onions, and the feseekh fish that she'd dried and preserved in brine for weeks. Because Naima hated the pungent feseekh, Mama made her renga, a milder herring that Naima could stomach.

Botros and his mother waited for them in front of the building on the corner of Gazirat Badran Street for their traditional walk to the grassy area on the banks of the Nile, where Naima and Laila had spent every Sham El Nessim of their lives. They spread blankets under a large acacia tree that provided shade all day, and a light breeze carried the scent of silt and the blooming greenery growing all around them.

Amir met them there as promised. He was sober and looked rested, but it made sense. The night prior was Easter. He too had certain obligations to his family. He still looked out of place wearing his shiny shoes and his white pressed shirt, but he took Laila's hand in his, and together they watched Naima's boys play ball, running with unbridled innocence. She remembered the days she used to walk along the banks of the Nile with Baba, climbing rocks and jumping off them with no notion that she might fall and scrape a knee. Baba had never told her to stop as Mama would have.

"I want a boy," Amir whispered to Laila, inching closer to her on the blanket. "What do you think?"

Amir, she had come to realize, lived in a world of delusion, a realm in which his actions had no consequences, in which they could be erased from existence so long as he pretended they hadn't happened. And now he looked at her as if he truly believed he'd been sleeping next to her all night long, every night, that he'd been an exemplary husband.

"I'd love that," she lied, but this time she knew why she was lying. She didn't want to ruin this beautiful day, and she knew that Amir would forget about having a boy as soon as the sun went down.

Mama and Botros's mother talked a lot that day. Laila watched them. She was close enough to hear their voices but too far to listen to their words. Botros and Naima too sat next to each other, and they seemed to be in happy equilibrium, putting food on the other's plate or feeding one another a bit of this or that. It looked like comfort more than romance, but nonetheless it looked like love to Laila. Love. How simple she'd thought its meaning and how complex it had become. She imagined that Zacharias was sitting next to her and holding her hand instead of Amir. She thought about what fidelity might have felt like in a marriage. Zacharias weaved in and out of her consciousness from sunrise to sundown every day, and in her sleep, she dreamed about him.

They had a routine. Every morning, in the shop's backroom with the radio tuned to Radio Cairo, he boiled the water for tea on a small burner next to the bookcase. Before they sat at the square wooden table in the middle of the room, he put two sugar cubes in her tea and stirred it.

Then he set the steaming cups next to the pile of books and newspaper clippings he'd set up, always in the order in which they'd read them, from top to bottom. Zacharias never had to shuffle for something in the pile. He never lost his train of thought, never forgot to review a concept he'd planned to cover. A lamp stood on the table, and he turned it on and the radio off before he began the lesson. First, they read a few pages of the novel he was teaching her, then he made her read a newspaper clipping from *Al Ahram*, and finally, they read poetry.

The smell of newsprint ink reminded Laila of Baba. She'd watched him read on the balcony, lines of consternation on his face, deepening under the rising sun. Often Baba would slam the paper on the small end table he kept next to her balcony chair, muttering inaudibly. In those days Laila never asked Baba why he'd been so upset, and after Baba died newspapers disappeared with him. After all, there was nobody in the apartment who could read them. But now there was Zacharias pointing at a front-page story for Laila to read aloud. She was not a fluid reader, but he was a patient man.

She began understanding politics in a way she'd never thought possible. What once was blurred became clearer like when the morning haze lifts off a cityscape and all the building tops are visible. One morning Zacharias decided to spend the whole three hours making sure Laila understood how things had come about. "These aren't just topics that men discuss at cafes," he said, pushing the novel and books of poetry to the side. He looked grave and had an urgency about his voice. "History and politics are woven into all of our lives. To some extent what we eat, do for a living, and study are all impacted by the British occupation." He shook his head. "Not just here, but everywhere. And it's still ongoing."

Zacharias was a born storyteller, and when he began to tell Laila the story of their country, he captivated her with the same interest that Baba had when he'd told her fantastical tales of Arabian princes and battles at sea. Zacharias explained that in the early 1500s the Ottomans conquered the Egyptian Mamluk army, who were a special class of military slaves. "You see, at that time, Egypt was under Ottoman rule, but the Mamluks were very powerful and so the Ottomans couldn't fully control them. That's why they gave us a little autonomy. It stayed that way for centuries, until a short angry Frenchman named Napoleon invaded." Zacharias made a funny face mimicking Napoleon and Laila laughed. "Now, we were under French occupation but that lasted for just three years because a powerful Albanian military officer of the Ottoman empire defeated Napoleon. His name was Muhhamed Ali." Zacharias's voice rose. "And that's the bloodline of King Farouk." Laila had walked past Muhhamed Ali's palace in Shubra hundreds of times, admiring the rolling gardens and vast colonnades, but she'd never known the story of its builder. "For a while things were peaceful. He ruled a virtually independent Egypt, until the British declared Egypt a protectorate in nineteen-fourteen"

"So, the British just took the country?" Laila remembered the protests she'd watched as a child and how Baba had once explained to her that the men were angry because something had been taken from them, likening Egypt to his own beloved oud.

"Well, it's a little more complicated. First, the British didn't like the Turks joining to fight with the enemy in World War One. So, they didn't want them to have control over Egypt. Second, the British needed control of the Suez Canal, so, yes, as you said, they just took Egypt. They simply needed it. And ever since then the British have been using this country, its people, its land, its oil to enrich themselves. They haven't invested in education so that the people wouldn't ever really understand what the British were doing. Of the jobs that are available, preference is given to British citizens and other foreigners. That's why so many Egyptians are poor and uneducated. That's how imperialism works, you see. And now here we are." He pointed at the newspaper article that Laila had been reading about the nationalists and the sympathizers. "You understand now? The nationalists opposed the king for his extravagance and his allegiance to the British imperialists, his lack of concern for the common Egyptian, and more recently his failure to protect Palestine in the failed nineteen forty-eight war." Laila remembered that war, how confused she'd been about the establishment of a new country and a British promise.

Now it was making sense. The nationalists felt the King was unprepared for war due to his decadence and ineptitude. The sympathizers, like Amir and his family, supported King Farouk for a system that enriched them. Losing the war to Israel in 1948 didn't affect their loyalty to the King.

"What do you think about Israel?" Laila asked Zacharias. For years after Baba's death, she hadn't contemplated these things. She and Mama were busy surviving and hadn't paid attention to protests about wars or skirmishes with the British.

"I believe that imperialism is wrong. Occupation is wrong. In my opinion, that applies to everything and everywhere. But what's wrong and right never really factor into political decisions. It's just what's right for the powerful. What's wrong for the weak doesn't matter."

Laila remembered Baba saying something like that. A new anger and frustration rose within her as she began to see her poverty, her family's struggles, their lack of education, Baba's joblessness, and Laila's perpetual sense of inferiority as a result of powerful entities making decisions that didn't consider her because she was part of a group of people who were "the weak." She felt the same way she'd felt the first day of school when she realized that the big, beautiful school building was not where she'd attend, that she'd have to go to school in a small makeshift building designated for those receiving charity. She'd felt like a beggar then and though she was no longer poor, she now felt like a beggar again.

Before Laila left that day, Zacharias gave her a poem and a short story to read. "This is how the writers resist an occupation. They write." He gave her a thin magazine called *al-Katib al Masry*. "Luckily, I kept the periodical because a few years ago all the stories were published as a book, and then the King banned it."

"Banned? Why?"

Zacharias smiled. "You'll see when you read it." Then he gave her a small book entitled *Poet of the Nile, Hafiz Ibrahim*. "Read this poem first," he said, putting a bookmark in the book.

That day Laila was too upset to go to the sporting club, so she took a long walk home, roaming the city, thinking about her life. She missed Baba and wished she could speak to him. She remembered the day he'd pained over playing oud at the Suez Canal Club, a place in which Egyptians were not even allowed. She understood now why he'd asked for her forgiveness. And she wished she could ask him to forgive her for marrying Amir.

Before she fell asleep, she read the poem under her breath:

O you, who manage our affairs, have you forgotten
our loyalty and affection?
Reduce your armies, sleep soundly, search for your game
in every corner of the land.
Should the ringdoves be lacking on the hill,
surely there are men enough for you to shoot.
We and the woodpigeons are one, for the rings
have not parted from our necks.

They all had rings around their necks, Laila thought, bringing her hand to her throat. Then she picked up the magazine and began to read *Saleh*, the banned story by Taha Hussein. She wept for Saleh who suffered from poverty and hunger as his classmates looked on, oblivious to his plight. She thought of all the nights she'd heard Mama cry alone in her bedroom and recalled the excruciating pinch of a starving stomach. When she'd finished the poem and story, she understood what Zacharias was trying to explain to her. She just wished she hadn't.

Within a span of three months, Laila and Zacharias had gotten through two novels. It wasn't easy. Laila spent hours practicing every day after their lessons. The first, *Ana Hurra*, had riveted Laila, and she loved Amina's character, a feisty woman who insisted on going to college and marrying the man of her choice. They also read Tawfik Al Hakim's play *Scheherazade*. But it wasn't what Laila had thought it would be, the old tale of Scheherazade that both Mama and Baba had told her. It was a play that picked up after Scheherazade had finished telling all her stories. Laila loved reading plays because she and Zacharias switched between different characters' lines.

When Laila first started meeting with Zacharias, she had tried to think of him as her friend and teacher. But that was the lie she told herself to quell her guilt. The truth was that she was a married woman who'd fallen into love with another man. She wasn't confused about this. Zacharias had become to her a man who saw her naked mind, who understood her deepest curiosities, vulnerabilities, and dreams. It had just happened that way and it was clear to her what she was feeling. This love was natural, silky, shameless. She took him in like a melody of a favorite song, a song that could not be teased out into disparate notes.

She fantasized about having him. It wasn't just teenage lust like when she'd first met Amir. This was the depth of how a woman loved a man and wanted him; all of him. He'd revived her intellectually and physically all at once. She imagined his hands on her body, the way his lips might feel on her breasts, and how he might move inside her. But Laila had to hide all of this from him, from Amir, and even from herself. There was no possibility of her actually being with Zacharias. When they were together, though, she didn't think about possibilities and realities. Her time with Zacharias was, to her, a separate world in which she could experience the happiness of being with him even if it was short lived.

Over time the favorite part of their lessons had become the poetry reading. Zacharias had dozens of poetry books. Every lesson, after they read the newspaper, and a bit of a novel, he took a book off a shelf, gave it to her, and said, "Open to whatever page you want." Then they'd read whichever poem she'd opened to. He read her the poetry of Ibn Al Rumi, Al Khansa, Al Mutanabbi, Hafez, Rumi, and Gibran. He read with rhythm and melody, stopping at the end of stanzas to explain and discuss the craft of each poet.

She thrilled when his hand brushed against her as he took her purse from her to hang it behind the door, or when he leaned over her, tapping the page she was reading, moving his finger along the words. She waited for those moments. Sometimes, he leaned close to emphasize symbolism, imagery, or use of language. Those were the times she could smell his cologne and hear the sound of his breathing. Other times, she'd make a mistake and he'd want her to read the lines again. Arabic grammar was complex, and the entire meaning of a word changed if she neglected to read a consonant with a vowel, like the damma, the fatha, or the kasra. The vowels were small marks and easy to miss, but these types of mistakes irritated Zacharias, and he always said the same thing to her: "The details, Laila. The details." Those were the times when his elbow hit hers or his arms brushed against hers as he leaned in and pointed at the pages; and although she didn't want to make mistakes, she longed to be close to him like that.

One day in early July when it came time to read poetry, Zacharias pulled out Qalat li al- Samra' by Nizar Qabbani. The Syrian poet, he said, was young and new on the poetry scene. "This one," he said, giving the book to Laila, "was published two years ago. The clergy and religious leaders have started a war against him for his free language, but nobody could stop his poetry. Every schoolboy recites Qabbani's poems by heart."

She riffled through the pages of the poetry collection and then stopped at a page randomly as she always had. Zacharias took the book from her, careful not to lose the page she'd landed on.

He cleared his throat. "This poem is called Your Breast. In it, Qabbani is talking to his beloved brunette." And then he read, his voice deep and clear. "'Unlock the treasury! Lay bare your burning breasts. Don't smother your imprisoned fire. Your breasts are the two most beautiful paintings.'" He gave her the book. "You read now," he said, pointing at the line where he left off.

"'Two balls of silk spun by the generous morning. So come close to me my little cat. Let yourself free. Come close. Think of the fate of your breasts. With the turn of the season. Don't panic. Foolish is she who hides her breasts. And lets her youth pass without being kissed. I pulled her body to me. She neither resisted nor spoke. Intoxicated she swayed against me. And offered her quivering breast. Saying in drunken passion, 'I cannot resist touching fire.'"

She looked at Zacharias for a long time after she'd read that last line, after the book had closed on her hand because she'd forgotten to move it off Qabbani's words. Those words meant so many things to her:

surrendering to love, the physicality of it, touching fire. What was it about touching fire that felt so natural with Zacharias? That's all he'd been since the moment she met him, a fire she wanted to touch. But he knew nothing about her. To him, she was a married woman just there to take reading lessons. Though the way he looked at her now made her think otherwise. He took the book from her, setting it aside, and held her hand in his.

When she didn't move it, he said, "There's more to your story, isn't there?"

"Yes," she said so softly she barely heard herself.

He took her face between his warm hands. "Your husband?"

"In name only. It's been that way for a long time," she said. "And now, I've fallen in love with someone else."

Zacharias came closer. His lips brushed against hers, and they took a breath together. Then he kissed her. Time and space lost their meaning in those moments. She knew only his touch, his taste. The fire they couldn't resist touching.

After they parted that day, Laila spent hours at the Sporting Club, swimming and wading and swimming again. When she swam she tried to sort her life out under the water as she listened to the sound of her body moving through the pool. She'd fallen in love with Zacharias, and she was sure it started on the day they met. He'd had an inexplicable pull on her. It was different from with Amir. With Amir, it had been a young love, a curious love. This was unexpected and uncontrollable. What difference did it make though? She'd fallen in love, but things weren't different for her. She still had no choices. Even if by some miracle she could leave Amir, how would she be with Zacharias, a Jewish man whose family would be deathly opposed to a Christian divorcée? Impossible. It was all so impossible. Still, she recalled again and again the Qabbani poem addressed to *his brunette* and the kiss that followed. It was both bliss and agony, more than she'd ever known.

27

CAIRO, JULY 23, 1952

Laila stayed up all night reading *The Call of the Curlew* by Taha Hussein, which Zacharias had given her the day before. But memories of their kiss in his backroom amidst his novels and poems kept interrupting. She thought about his hands on her face, the feel of his lips on hers. She could hardly wait to see him again, and she stopped trying to understand their new affair, to make sense of it or plan for it. Her new love for him, for literature, and for herself were all intertwined and indistinguishable from one another.

She knocked a few minutes early on the backdoor of Haroun's fabric shop, the book tucked in her purse, a bookmark between its pages. She wanted to impress Zacharias more than ever now. She didn't want him to think that because a nascent romance had sprouted between them that she'd set the reading aside, or that it hadn't mattered to her from the start. She had prepared more than usual for this lesson, practicing pronunciation and underlining new words she'd looked up in the dictionary. She'd written their meanings in the margins and had summarized the first scene of the book.

She was intrigued by the story and eager to learn what had led the main character, Amna, to work as a maid for the lascivious engineer. Hussein's language was extremely difficult for her, and it took her a long time to read just a few pages. But she and Zacharias had read many books together, and she had improved. She didn't have to stop as much as before, grammar made sense, and her vocabulary had expanded.

Zacharias opened the door. As he greeted her, his gaze lingered on her a moment longer than usual. When she stepped inside, he locked the door behind her. "I couldn't sleep last night, thinking about you and us," he said, and he took her in his arms and kissed her again.

"Neither could I," she said, resting her head on his chest.

"Laila, what are we going to do?"

"I don't know," she said, and they kissed again for a long while.

He took her purse from her as he always did and hung it on the hook behind the door. Then he went to make the tea. She sat at the table and ran her finger along the spines of the books stacked on the table. Which poem would he read to her today? What articles had he clipped from the newspaper? How would they focus and where would all of this lead them?

He returned, setting the cup of steaming tea in front of her. She took out her book and opened it to the first pages. The radio played softly in the background and she, once again, practiced the opening lines of the novel, mouthing the words, preparing to read them out loud, her mind half on the lesson and half on her desire.

Zacharias set his teacup on the table, sat next to her, and turned on the lamp. He took her hand in his. "I can't think. You know how hard it is," he said.

"We have to try," she said, and started to read, but couldn't concentrate any longer. Hussein's words were just sounds to her now. The opening lines of *Call of the Curlew* were nothing but phonetics, and the meanings of words she'd begun to understand faded. She was aware only of Zacharias's presence next to her, the way his cologne smelled of pepper and lavender. She closed the book. "I don't even know what I just read."

As he was about to reply, several strident beeps blared from the radio, cutting off the song that had been playing. A serious bellowing voice followed. Zacharias turned up the radio and stood still in front of it.

"Nation," the man began.

"What's going on?" Laila said.

Zacharias raised his fingers to his lips, and she quieted.

The voice continued. Zacharias didn't move. Laila sat still in her chair and stared into her cup of dark tea as ominous words poured from the radio.

"Egypt has passed through a critical period in her recent history characterized by bribery, mischief, and the absence of governmental stability. All of these were factors that had a large influence on the army. Those who accepted bribes and were thus influenced caused our defeat in the Palestine War. As for the period following the war, the mischief-making elements have been assisting one another, and traitors have been commanding the army. They appointed a commander who is either ignorant or corrupt. Egypt has reached the point, therefore, of having no army to defend it. Accordingly, we have undertaken to clean ourselves up and have appointed to command us men from within the army whom we trust in their ability, their character, and their patriotism. It is certain that all Egypt will meet this news with enthusiasm and will welcome it. As for those whose arrest we saw fit from among men formerly associated with the army, we will not deal harshly with them, but will release them at the appropriate time. I assure the Egyptian people that the entire army today has become capable of operating in the national interest and under the rule of the constitution apart from any interests of its own. I take this opportunity to request that the people never permit any traitors to take refuge in deeds of destruction or violence because these are not in the interest of Egypt. Should anyone behave in such ways, he will be dealt with forcefully in a manner such as has not been seen before and his deeds will meet immediately the reward for treason. The army will take charge with the assistance of the police. I assure our foreign brothers that their interests, their personal safety, and their property are safe, and that the army considers itself responsible for them. May God grant us success."

"God help us," Zacharias said. "God help us all." He shook his head.

"I don't understand," Laila said.

"A revolution," he said. "The military, they've taken over. They want to oust the king." He reached behind the door and took her purse off the hook.

"But isn't this a good thing? Isn't this what we've wanted all along, to get rid of British influence? Weren't we just talking about this?" If Baba were alive, he would have been happy. He'd always said that the king had given Egypt away to the occupying British. Were things finally changing for the better?

"Yes, of course, but I don't know how it's going to look with a military takeover," Zacharias said. "This isn't how I'd imagined ridding ourselves of the British. I don't know. I don't know anything." He gave her the purse. "You've got to get home. There's no telling what the streets will be like. Your husband will be looking for you, and I don't want you to get hurt because of me."

"But what about—"

"It will have to wait," Zacharias said as he put Taha Hussein's novel in her purse, which now hung over her shoulder. "I'll find you a taxi."

Outside, crowds were dispersing from the kiosks where they'd gathered to listen to the radio. Men in galabeyas danced and cheered. Women trilled zaghroutas in the streets as if they were on their way to a wedding. "The traitors are gone!" a man shouted from a balcony above Daher Street.

Zacharias hailed a taxi and paid the driver extra to return with the news of Laila's safe arrival home. "Come back," he told the driver. "Meet me here." He pointed at Haroun's storefront.

"I don't know if I can," the driver said, giving Zacharias back his money. "The tanks are in the streets."

"Try." Zacharias pushed the money into the driver's hand. "And when you get here, I'll pay again." He opened the taxi door for Laila and took her hand in his. "I love you," he said.

Laila tightened her grip around his hand. At that moment, the whole world could have toppled down. The streets could have burned once again. The only thing she wanted to do now was to be near him. But he let go of her hand, helped her into the taxi, and closed the car door. "I love you too," she said just before the taxi drove off.

Cars and buses crammed the streets. That morning was just like any other, except for the military planes circling over the city, the tanks that people cheered for as they rolled by, and the new love consuming Laila's life.

✿

Laila stood in the foyer, afraid to go in and unable to leave again. Quietness had fallen over the palace. The sounds of morning work were muted. The maids treaded softly as they mopped. The driver sat on a stool beside the car, but didn't have his morning cigarette, and the gardener didn't come at all. Hoda sat on the velvet brocade sofa, her morning tea cooling, her petit fours untouched. Makram Yousef Pasha paced back and forth between the foyer where Laila stood in the parlor, his hands crossed behind his back, the soles of his shiny shoes tapping an angry rhythm on the marble floor.

"We're finished," he said every time he passed under the crystal chandelier. "We're finished, finished, finished."

Laila caught up with her father-in-law and patted his arm. He was the only person in that palace she loved. He'd always been kind to her, and over the years he'd been like a father to her. She often thought he sympathized with her loneliness. "Insha Allah, things will be all right, Papa," she said.

He stopped and turned to face her, his hands still behind his back like a soldier. "It's not going to be all right, ya binty," he said. His eyes were red, and his face was drained of its tan color. Now it was yellow. "This is the end." He looked around at the palace and fanned his hands out as if showing off its beauty. "All of this is finished. Everything I've worked for all my life is finished."

"Sit down, Papa." She guided him to his favorite wing backed chair where he took his morning coffee and read the paper. "All of this could be over by tomorrow. El sabah rabah." Baba had always said that to her when she'd worried about something. "Tomorrow is a day of wins."

She knelt next to the chair, her hand over his, and she missed Baba. As miserable as the pasha was, Baba would have been delighted with what had happened. To finally have the British gone, the British who for so long had humiliated the Egyptians, who'd once beaten him so badly, he never recovered from his limp. Still, seeing the pasha so distraught pained her.

"No." He shook his head as he lowered himself into his chair and took a sip of cold tea. "These Free Officers," he said with disgust. "They're young, determined, and they have support. I've spoken to my sources inside the government. These military boys want socialism! Do you know what that means?" He shouted this last sentence with the sort of madness Laila had never seen. Then he slammed down the cup of tea. The saucer cracked in half, and tea spilled all over the imported oriental carpet.

Laila was still kneeling next to her father-in-law, and she reached for the broken glass on the side table, but Hoda put out her hand in between Laila and cup. "I'll take care of that," she said. "Go wake Amir. Makram needs his son."

Laila, Amir, Hoda, and the pasha spent the next few days in the parlor, sitting around the radio waiting for any further communications. Breakfast, lunch, and dinner were served on the parlor's coffee table and consisted of charcuterie and light sandwiches. Nobody ate. While some announcements were made on the radio, most of the news came to the pasha over the phone from his connections inside the king's government, which would be fully dissolved in a matter of days. The culprits of this "calamity," the pasha said, were three young officers who, according to him, should be arrested and swiftly executed. Their names were Mohamad Naguib, Gamal Abd El Nasser, and "this stooge named Anwar Sadat who made the announcement on the radio." But the only person Laila could think of was Zacharias.

At first there had been hope that the Americans would step in and stop the coup in support of King Farouk. Amir had cheered at this news. "The Americans, of course," he said, lighting a cigarette, "will destroy those nobodies." But the young, unknown Anwar Sadat, who'd been put in charge of all revolutionary communications, preempted the king. He'd already notified the United States and Great Britain of the change in power, a change to which both countries had agreed. The Americans didn't assist the king, and within three days King Farouk was forced to sign abdication papers after Officer Sadat, a second lieutenant, informed him of his two choices: either Farouk leave Egypt peacefully by six o'clock on the evening of July 26 or he would be charged as a rebel and suffer the consequences.

That evening, after it had been announced that the king had set sail to Cypress, Amir got dressed and left the palace. He didn't tell anyone where he was going, and neither the pasha nor Hoda seemed to notice their only son had left. Amir stayed out all night, and Laila stayed up and read. She read about Amna deep into the night, how her sister was tricked into sleeping with the engineer she'd worked for, and how their mother had forced them to move out of that village running away from the sisters' tarnished reputation. Then Laila closed the book, put her clothes on, and left the palace. If Egypt had officially become a republic and the mighty king had been forced to leave, then nothing would stop her from seeing Zacharias.

When Laila arrived at Haroun's four days after the revolution, Zacharias took her in his arms and said, "I was afraid I wouldn't see you again. I was afraid he'd take you and flee the country."

She looked up at him. "I wouldn't have gone," she said. When he let her go, she put her purse on the table where, for the first time, there was no neat pile of books and magazines, and the lamp had not been lit.

He said nothing. Then he lit the lamp and put the day's newspaper down on the table.

"Did you hear me?" she said. "I wouldn't have gone with my husband. I would have stayed here with you."

"That's impossible," he said as they sat down.

"A lot of things are impossible." She took his hand. "But they happen."

He looked glum, and Laila didn't push any further.

They read the morning's *Al-Ahram* newspaper, skipping the novel reading. "Read," Zacharias said to Laila as he pointed to the headline.

She read the title, "The King Leaves Egypt for Cyprus with His Family Aboard His Yacht *Al Mahrousa*." Zacharias nodded, and she continued reading the article. "King Farouk abdicated his throne and sailed away last night ..."

Above the article was a picture of the *Mahrousa*, Farouk's large white yacht, sailing away from the shores of Alexandria. Laila looked intently at the picture, and for a moment she was afraid of the revolution, not because the king had left but because the only order of things she'd known was gone.

⁊

The king was replaced by Prime Minister Mohamed Naguib within two months of the revolution, but according to what Laila had learned from Zacharias, Nasser was the one making all the decisions. Farouk's pictures were taken off walls in public buildings, and nationalist songs played on the radio, but for two months after the revolution nothing changed in daily life. Soon, the happenings at the palace fell into their old routine. Hoda continued her morning swims and readings. The driver took the pasha to the factory. Laila went to see Zacharias. And Amir returned drunk at dawn to sleep all day. But on September 11, the new government led by the Free Officers passed law 178, and those three numbers—1, 7, 8—created new upheaval.

Law 178 redistributed land, taking it from its owners and giving it away piece by piece to the fellaheen who'd farmed it. The maximum number of feddans a person could keep was two hundred. When the pasha read this in the paper, he fainted and fell to the floor, hitting his head against the side table. Laila screamed for the butler to get a doctor and for the maid to tell Hoda, who was taking her morning swim. Laila put cold compresses of rose water and orange blossom on the pasha's face until he woke up.

When the doctor examined the Pasha's head, he pronounced it was nothing serious and prescribed sedatives. "He's in shock. Give him these pills twice a day for the next few days to calm him down." He opened his bag and gave Hoda an envelope filled with pills. Then he patted Laila's hand and said, "Your papa will be fine."

"Makram Yousef Pasha doesn't take sedatives," the pasha said an hour later when the color had returned to his face and the dizziness wore off. He stood up. "I'm going to the factory. I have a business to run, and nobody"— he wagged his finger—"is taking my land."

But there was nothing the pasha could do. The government redistributed all the land he owned in Aswan, and it happened within a matter of days. No bribe worked to dissuade them. The pasha's two thousand feddans shrank to two hundred, and he became just like everyone else. When the official government papers arrived confirming the redistribution, Makram Yousef Pasha wept, head in hands. Hoda cried too, dabbing her eyes with a silk handkerchief. Amir stood beside his father patting his back. "Papa, please, don't do this to yourself. We'll get it back somehow."

"It's over, ya ibney," he said. "There's no way out."

The pasha was right. There was no way out. The cotton harvest that came from the lands he'd once owned was the raw material for the textiles he made in his factory and then exported. What the family earned from the remaining two hundred feddans barely paid the factory's utility bill. Within a few months, the textiles in inventory were all sold, and the rest of the contracts with foreign buyers had to be broken. Then the lenders came demanding their payments on the new machines the pasha had bought for the factory. When he couldn't pay, the machines were repossessed and the factory closed.

The pasha tried to find a job managing a factory or even in textile sales. He called friends and business acquaintances, but everyone he knew were landowners who'd also lost their fortunes, just as he had. Now everyone was equally poor.

"That's it," he said one day after getting off the phone with Nahas Pasha, the deposed king's former prime minister. "There's nothing left to do." So, he went to bed early and slept in late. He stopped reading the newspaper and turned off the radio. He stopped writing letters in his den, stopped listening to Ragaa Abdou records, stopped drinking beer in the Moorish garden, and when he ate, he only took a few bites and left the rest of the food on his plate.

At first, the family decided to stay in the palace. After all, it had been paid for, but living in it was costly. One day, soon after the factory closed, Hoda suggested they try to cut expenses, and the stipends they were sending to Mama and Naima stopped first. Laila couldn't say or do anything about it, but she worried for her mother and sister. Next Amir, Hoda, and the pasha agreed that letting the butler go was the least painful.

If someone came to the door, any one of them could greet a visitor, and Hoda said that she didn't actually need the butler to hold her bathrobe at the poolside. She could get out of the pool and endure being wet for a few seconds while she put the robe on by herself. But the butler's salary was a small fraction of the family's expenses; and a few weeks later they let go of Chef Antoine, who stormed out of the palace angrily after throwing his chef's hat on the foyer floor. He was upset because Hoda renegotiated the salary of Chef Antoine's youngest helper and had her stay on. "We at least need someone to prepare the sandwiches and such," Hoda said.

After Chef Antoine left, Laila did most of the cooking, and whenever she put a pot of stew on the table, the Pasha smiled and said, "Just like my mother's, Allah yerhamha."

The driver's job was eliminated next, and the gardener's days were cut down to once a week. Then the maids were all fired except for the youngest, who agreed to work for free as long as she had a place to sleep and food to eat. Still, their expenses were higher than the money that came in from the two hundred feddans they had left. So, they began to sell their jewelry at auctions, and Hoda cried every time her jewels sold.

The pasha sold his watch collection. Hoda sold her semiprecious jewels first and then she sold the diamonds. Laila gave them everything she had in her jewelry box. One day over dinner, Hoda and the pasha asked Amir for his watches and cufflinks to sell too, but he admitted he'd gambled them away. At hearing that, the pasha got up from the dinner table, his food untouched, and slapped Amir across the face. Then he spat at him. "You're not my son," he said. "You're a sayaa, loser. I should have beaten you when I had the chance."

When the jewelry had all been sold, they started selling their artwork, and every day the walls became barer. They sold watercolor paintings from France, tapestries from Spain, original music sheets the pasha had received as a gift from a Swiss banker, and two Carrara marble sculptures from Florence. Then they sold the crystal chandeliers, the Persian rugs, and the Louis XVI settee that Hoda had loved to sit on.

It took a year to empty the palace of its riches, and by the fall of 1953, it had become sparsely furnished and dimly lit. The pasha finally decided it was time to leave it. "It's no longer a palace," he said somberly as he looked around. "All that's left is the marble floor, and I would have sold it too if I could have." He suggested that the four of them move into the empty apartment on the top floor of their building in the new city of Heliopolis. Laila loved the idea of living one floor above her friend Moshira.

Because law 178 fixed rent prices too, the building didn't make the pasha much money, but between the cotton land that was left and the small earnings from the building, the four of them could afford to live in the apartment. "If we take with us what we haven't sold and hang some framed photos on the walls, it can look decent," the pasha said. The young maid was sent to the new apartment to clean it up, and the moving date was set for a month later so that they would be settled in the new place before Christmas.

As Laila had suspected, Mama and Naima had saved some money, and though it would be hard, for now they had enough to eat and pay rent. Mama came to the palace almost every day to help with the cooking and packing. She felt sorry for the pasha and advised Laila to do what she could to make her father-in-law comfortable. "After all, he's like your father now."

But despite the situation at the palace, Laila's swimming and her morning with Zacharias remained constant. When she was in his arms, kissing him or listening to his voice, sitting amidst books and papers in the backroom of his fabric shop, nothing else was important.

There were two things the pasha refused to sell: his dining room table and the set of fine china he'd received as a gift from the late King Fouad. It had been sent to him in wrapped boxes tied with red bows and a note of congratulations on his new, now obsolete, pasha title. Etched in gold on the rims of each plate were the words Makram Yousef Pasha. Laila had seen the dinnerware once, on her wedding day. Only the most honored guests had their places set with it.

One day, a few weeks before they were scheduled to move to the apartment in Heliopolis, the pasha came home ecstatic after an interview he hadn't told anyone about. "I didn't want to tell you until I knew for sure. It's a miracle," he said. "I never thought it would happen. They offered me the job on the spot. I start tomorrow." He announced that he'd gotten an executive position with a multinational corporation. "I'll have to travel," he said. "They needed someone with my experience, my know-how, and they loved me. It's not like owning your own factory, but it's very good money."

Laila hugged and kissed the pasha. Amir looked relieved, and Hoda said, "I knew you could do it."

"I want you to buy it all back," he said to Amir, pointing at the ceiling and the walls. "I want new chandeliers and paintings. Call the auction house. See what they have. Get your mother her jewels back. Put it on credit. Tell them I'll pay in a few weeks as soon as I get my first paycheck. They know me. They trust me."

Laila didn't know how auction houses worked or how to buy paintings, but that was Amir's responsibility. She was just thrilled the pasha was happy.

That night the pasha asked her to make her bamia for dinner to celebrate his new job. Okra stew had always been his favorite meal. He also asked Hoda to take out the fine gold- etched china "from King Fouad," he said proudly. For the first time in over a year, since the revolution, he held his head up and straightened his shoulders as he entered the dining room, just as he had before. The table was set with the dinner plates he'd wanted, as well as the gold tableware, silk dinner napkins, and crystal water goblets. Laila got up to serve her father-in-law a heaping spoon of okra stew over rice. "I want more sauce this time," he said. She ladled more of the garlicy tomato sauce on his plate so that it soaked the rice.

"Bil hana wil shifa," she said, wishing him a good meal.

Amir ate quickly and sat back in the chair. "I was really worried about you, Papa," he said. "I'd never seen you like that before." He seemed anxious to leave the table, and Laila suspected that he'd had a rendezvous he didn't want to miss.

"And you'll never see me upset like that again." The pasha smiled. "That's a promise."

They chatted about plans to repurchase what they'd auctioned off. "I want to have the rings remade," Hoda said. "And that ruby necklace we sold. Quelle dommage." She shook her head.

"Of course, my dear," the pasha said. "Anything you want. Call the jeweler tomorrow."

After the pasha finished his meal, he had a glass of whiskey that he'd poured himself from the crystal decanter on the mahogany buffet table. Then he stood up and said, "I'm going to sleep now." Before he headed up the circular staircase, he kissed Hoda on the lips, took Laila's hand and kissed it, and kissed the top of Amir's head. He'd never done any of those things before, and Laila felt optimistic about this new beginning.

She had started to clear the table when the loud boom of the revolver came from upstairs.

At first, she didn't realize what had happened until Amir ran up the stairs and his wail echoed through the empty palace.

28

CAIRO, JANUARY 1954

Amir washed Makram Yousef Pasha's body the way a good son should. His father lay on the morgue bed, his fatal wound patched, his body cold and shrunken. He'd planned it all. He'd even ironed his uniform and had set it out neatly on the bed; the white pants and long tailed suit jacket, the red sash that was worn across his chest decorated with the medals he'd earned, a red felt tarbush, and the long standard which would be fastened to his gold belt. The pasha had had many years left to live, good health left unused, but he'd rejected them, like the shipments of raw materials he'd returned to manufacturers, writing on notepaper, "Incorrect order." He'd toiled all his life, accumulated wealth, and then the revolution took his possessions and life. Amir sponged his father's chest. Had he ever really known his father? There had always been a wall of formality between them, as though the pasha weren't his father but a distant relative, a strict guardian. He wept. He wept because his father was gone, and he wept because he had always been gone.

Nothing mattered in life, Amir thought. His father would be buried before sundown, but Amir had nothing to say about him other than that he had worked hard and amply provided for his family. When he finished sponging his father's arms and legs, he looked at him for a long while. Was it worth it, all the worry and effort? It was for naught in the end, wasn't it? If his father could speak right now, what would he tell Amir? And would his words matter? If this was the fate of a man who'd given everything to succeed, maybe Amir's carefree life of seeking only pleasure had been the right path all along.

Amir dressed his father in his military uniform, covered the pasha with a white sheet and said, "Allah yerhamack, ya Baba." His quivering voice dissipated into the small room of the dead, and he closed the door behind him.

⁊;

It had all been a lie. There was no multinational company, and the pasha had never been offered a job. The day he'd announced his fake new executive position, he'd made the rounds of visiting all his old friends. Laila and Amir learned this in the days that followed the pasha's death.

Amir delayed the move to the apartment until after the forty days of mourning had passed. During that time, Laila and Hoda wore black and stayed inside the quiet, empty palace. Amir went to Aswan to see to his father's land, what was left of it. When he returned to Cairo, he slept all day and went out all night, just as he had done for the last three years. Laila took on the responsibility of preparing meals and caring for Hoda, making sure she'd eat and take the medicine the doctor had prescribed for her nerves. She mourned her father-in-law. He was the only one who'd ever understood her in that big cold palace. His death brought back the same tragic anguish of Baba's. But Baba had fought for his life. The Pasha just ended his. Why? She understood more than she cared to admit to herself. Hadn't she too almost done the same? That darkness. It consumes. She questioned herself, whether she could have done something to help him. No, his wealth was his identity, and that identity had died. The new government had even done away with titles. There were no more pashas, beys, or effendis. Just people, and the Makram Youseff Pasha could never be just a regular person. For him, she concluded there were some fates worse than death. Still, she cried for him for days until, just like after Baba, she had no more tears to cry, just a quiet desperation.

After their only maid quit and went to work at a villa on Pyramid Road, Mama and Naima started coming to the palace twice a week to help. They cooked with Laila, helped her change the sheets, wash the clothes, and pack up the crystals she'd take with her to the apartment. Mama noticed that Amir was always in bed when she came over, but she told Laila that grief made people sleep.

"Don't fret," she said. "Be patient with him. Men are like that." Laila nodded. "Maybe having a baby would help lift his spirits, give him a new beginning. It's been three years. It's about time," Mama said.

As was the tradition, on the fortieth day of Makram Yousef Pasha's arba'een, visitors came to offer condolences once again. Shortly after that Hoda took off her black dress, stopped her medication, and left Egypt for Paris to live with her sister. Laila and Amir moved to the penthouse apartment in their Heliopolis building. Laila started to see Zacharias again. Without a driver or a lot of money at her disposal, she walked an hour each way from Heliopolis to El Daher.

Heliopolis was a new district, a small city edged by the desert. Its tree-lined streets were wider than those in Rod El Farag, and the new buildings gleamed white against the cloudless blue sky. Laila loved her new cozy apartment. It opened directly into a small family room that led into a dining room. The door to the kitchen was in the short corridor shared with the main bedroom. The kitchen only comfortably fit one person, but she liked being alone with the refrigerator, stove, and oven, chopping and frying her own way and at her own pace. She thought about life in that small kitchen and mentally honored Baba and Makram Youseff Pasha, often muttering Allah Yerhamhom, hom for them. From the balcony off the living room she had a view of the ornate Heliopolis Hotel, the Heliopolis Sporting Club, and her favorite, the Heliopolis Basilica with its double colonnade and semicircular apse. There she read and had tea after the heat of the day dissipated, and it was on that balcony that, after several months, she continued reading *The Call of the Curlew*. When Amna's sister was killed by her uncle in the name of honor Laila cried and closed the book, roamed the apartment and returned to read of Amna's plan of revenge.

Since Moshira now lived only one floor below Laila, she saw her every day, and every day it was a struggle for Laila not to tell Moshira about Zacharias. But she couldn't bring herself to do it. She had never told her about Amir's cheating either. They had morning coffee and lunches together, and sometimes Moshira came over for afternoon tea and forced Laila to put her book down.

One day as they watched the sunset from Laila's balcony, Moshira told Laila about their financial struggles.

"Since the factory closed, we've been living on our savings, but I don't know what we'll do when the money is gone."

"He'll find another job," Laila said. "You'll see." She patted her friend's hand.

But Laila was wrong. President Mohamed Naguib had just been a façade for the free officers, and by that February of 1954 Nasser had become the prime minister of Egypt, his socialist leanings pushing the country into further economic decline. Still, people loved him. They saw Nasser as a kind of savior. Ahmed didn't find another job. Because of his old ties to the deposed king, nobody would hire him for the scarcely available positions. One day, Moshira ran up to Laila's apartment weeping. Her hands shook, and she could barely catch her breath to tell Laila what had happened.

"Damn the revolution. Damn the Free Officers. They've ruined our lives." She took a handkerchief from her purse. "We're leaving. Ahmed got an offer to run a factory in Canada."

Laila cried with Moshira all morning, until Moshira dried her swollen eyes and went back to her apartment to cook dinner for her husband and children.

The night before Moshira and her family left for Canada, Laila cooked an elaborate dinner for which she recruited Mama's help. There was lamb and potatoes and baked chicken and a large pan of negresko pasta. It was one of the few times she and Amir ate together, and he surprised her. He was a gracious host, offering Ahmed a glass of whiskey before dinner and bringing out nuts and appetizers to the coffee table before the dinner table was set. Moshira cried throughout the dinner, and Ahmed rubbed her back. At one point he turned to Amir and said, "I told you the king was losing control. I told you this would happen." Amir said nothing to his friend and kept eating. At the end of the night, Laila took Moshira aside and gave her a fur coat. It was the only thing she owned that hadn't been sold at an auction, and she wanted her friend to have it.

"I can't take it," Moshira said.

"Take it." Laila pushed it into her hands until Moshira took hold of the coat. "You'll need it there. And when you're warm, think of me."

Laila's throat thickened. Moshira had been her only friend, had saved her life from a literal and figurative fire. She'd leave an unfathomable void in Laila's life. The women wept and held each other for a long time. Then Moshira gave Laila the key to her apartment.

"Take care of it," she said. "I left the furniture in place, and when I can convince Ahmed to leave Canada and come back home, we'll have coffee together on your balcony, just like old times."

"Of course," Laila said, and put the key in her skirt pocket. "I'll make sure it's dusted and ready for you, and I'll run the faucets and polish the wood."

Then Moshira gave her a framed photograph of the two of them sitting together on one of the stones at the foot of pyramid, the background tan with desert, their eyes squinting from the sun. "Don't forget us, how we were then." Laila gripped the frame in her hand and threw herself into Moshira's embrace. For a long while they wept in eachother's arms for everything they'd lost.

The next morning Amir and Laila drove Moshira, Ahmed, and their two children to the airport. They barely fit the suitcases in the trunk, and

Ahmed wanted to get a taxi instead, but Laila insisted they be the ones to drive them. She sat next to Moshira in the back seat, one child on each lap.

"It'll be all right," Laila said. "Send me a telegraph when you get there. You'll be back. I'm sure." But Laila had never heard of anyone returning from the West. People left Egypt and never came back. Zacharias had shown her a world atlas. Canada was far, and its winters were harsh. How was it that in the span of a day, the women would be separated by a deep, dark ocean? This parting felt like death to Laila, and she was certain Moshira felt the same.

Laila and Amir watched their friends climb the stairs that led up to the silver plane. Every few seconds Moshira turned around and waved, and with each wave she got smaller in Laila's view, her features blurred. Then Moshira walked through the airplane door and onto the other side of the earth. Laila reached in her pocket and wrapped her hand around Moshira's cold, jagged metal key.

When Laila got home that day, she tried to read out on the balcony and got up to the part where Amna starts to work for the engineer who slept with her sister and vows to avenge her dead sister. But Laila couldn't concentrate any further, so she busied herself with laundry and cooking. A few times during the day, she automatically opened the front door to go see Moshira, remembering only as she turned the doorknob that her friend was in the sky somewhere over the Atlantic. Still, she stepped out onto the landing and looked one floor down over the railing at the door to Moshira's empty apartment. She missed the sounds of life that had come from there; children running, a mother yelling, a father turning the radio up.

That night, Amir didn't go out. Instead he waited for Laila in bed, and when she'd slipped under the covers to go to sleep, he reached for her. She pulled away. "What are you doing?" she said.

"I want a boy," he said. "I'm tired of this aimless, meaningless life."

She sat up. "We don't do that anymore, remember?" She pulled away from him. "You've been with a different woman every night. You don't think I know? I know. And now you want to have a baby?"

"People change," he said. His breath smelled of alcohol.

"You're right," she said. "And I don't want you anymore."

Amir got on top of her. He pulled up her nightgown and yanked down her panties. "You're my wife," he said. "You do what I want, when I want."

She kicked and screamed, but it was no use. He was strong, and she couldn't push him off her. He held her down and parted her legs. He kept rubbing against her, but he was soft. The more he futilely tried to penetrate her, the more furious he became.

"Look what you've done to me. Cold woman!" Still straddling her, he hit her face. But as he was hitting her, he let go of her hands and she scrambled away from him. He ran after her and hit her again, this time against her back. She fell to the floor. "You're not worth it," he said as she lay on the floor. He stalked into the sitting room and poured himself a glass of whiskey.

She'd never seen him this drunk, this angry.

Laila got up, the pain radiating from her back to her legs, and dressed quickly. If he decided to lock her inside the apartment there was nothing she could do, no law to protect her. She had to get out of that apartment, and fast.

She put Baba's green leather-bound songbook in her purse, and ran to the front door hoping Amir wouldn't notice her fast enough, but he grabbed her by the arm as soon as she'd reached for the door handle. "Where do you think you're going?"

"Let me go!" She tried to pull away from him, but his grip was tight and now she felt the same panic she'd felt that day in Alexandria when she was drowning, the water swallowing her down into darkness. Then she remembered how Battal had taught her to swim, how she'd vowed never to drown again. And she remembered something else, something Baba had taught her when she was just a child playing soccer with the boys, when they were playing rough, pushing and tripping her. "Tighten your stomach," he'd said. "That way you won't fall. Kick them back. Kick them hard and use your voice. Roar like a lion if you have to."

Laila opened her mouth, but she didn't scream. She growled. All her anger, all her pain. all her fear released in a deep guttural sound that came from her chest. Amir loosened his grip for a second, and though she tried to pull away from him, he tightened it again.

"Are you possessed?" he yelled.

"Yes! I am possessed." Then she kicked Amir, not once, but as many times as her legs would let her. Still growling, she kicked him like she'd wanted to kick all the boys in the alley. When he let go of her arm to protect his abdomen, she reached once again for the front door, managing to open it. But Amir caught a handful of her dress and pulled her down. She fell to the floor but pushed herself up quickly and ran out of the apartment. She kept running down the stairs, floor after floor.

Amir followed her and yelled, his voice traveling down the stairwell. "Go ahead. Leave me, but I'll never divorce you. You'll be my wife until you die, until you rot of old age. My wife!"

He shouted the last two words so loudly that the neighbors opened their doors to see what had happened.

Laila didn't care whose wife she was on paper. That was an old Laila, a Laila who'd believed in the façade of tradition and custom. She'd never let herself be shackled again.

෴

Laila sat in Baba's chair, and Mama put oil on her swollen eye and the bruise on her cheek. "I got it from the priest," Mama said, holding the clear glass bottle of oil. "It's blessed. It has the power to heal."

"I'm sorry, Mama," Laila said, wincing as her mother's finger grazed over the bruise. "I know people will talk, but I'm not going back to him. This time he hit me, but what about next time, and—"

Mama shushed her as she dabbed more oil on her eyelid. "You've endured enough. Let the people talk. God knows the truth. Tomorrow we'll go to church and light a candle."

Her mother looked tired. The blue under her eyes was particularly dark in the lamplight that evening, and when she walked to the kitchen to make Laila a cup of tea, her slippers shuffled against the floor under her heavy gait. When she sat, she had to ease herself down into the chair; and one time, she wrapped her arm around her stomach as if from a sudden and sharp pain.

"What's wrong, Mama?" Laila said. "Does something hurt?"

"No." Mama shook her head. "It's just indigestion. You see, Nargis invited me to dinner tonight, and you know how horrible of a cook she is. That poor husband of hers."

They laughed, and the side of Laila's face ached.

That night, Laila slept in the bed of her girlhood and had peaceful dreams of Baba and music and walks along the Nile. When she woke in the morning, she felt refreshed and hopeful. She looked at her face in the oval mirror above her old vanity. The swelling had gone down a little, and she was able to open her eye. Then she went into the kitchen and made two cups of coffee just as she used to when she and Mama still worked for Madame Caron, but when she went into Mama's room, she heard her moaning.

Laila put the tray of coffee on the nightstand and sat on the bed next her mother. "What's wrong, Mama?"

"It's just a stomachache," Mama said. "Don't worry. I'll be all right."

Mama could hardly push herself out of bed, and Laila insisted on taking her to the doctor. She helped Mama down the stairs, and they took a taxi to the downtown to see the most famous doctor in Cairo, Dr. Aly Ibrahim. He owned his own hospital, and people came from all over the country to see him. Laila and Mama waited for three hours before the assistant called them into an examination room, and by then Mama's pain had worsened.

Dr. Ibrahim examined Mama's abdomen, asked her about her diet and the frequency and intensity of her pain. When he finished his examination, he told Laila he'd ruled out appendicitis. "I think it might be a stomach ulcer. Stay away from coffee, tea, and spicy food." He prescribed some medication and told Laila to bring Mama back if she didn't improve.

When they got home, Laila made sure Mama took her pill. She'd spent all the money she had left on the taxi, doctor's visit, and the medicine. Aside from the few piasters Mama had saved in the old beet jar, they were destitute. Laila paced her small bedroom, thinking. She could go back to cooking, but since the revolution, people weren't hiring that much anymore. She could clean, but cleaning paid less than cooking, and she might have to be a live-in maid. That wouldn't work. She needed to be with Mama. She could ask Naima for money, but her sister barely had enough to take care of her own family. She could ask Zacharias, but he had his mother and sisters to take care of.

If only Baba hadn't gotten sick. If only she'd made it to the Abd El Wahab's movie audition and Kareem Al-Asyuty had cast her. She might have been a star by now, and stars didn't fret over money. Then she had an idea and ran downstairs to ask Haaga Saffeya to stay with Mama. "I need to get money for Mama's medicine. I don't know when I'll be back. Please just take care of her until I come home."

"Anything for you, Laila." Haaga Saffeya said a prayer for Mama as she shuffled up the stairs.

29

CAIRO, MARCH 1954

The Studio of Egypt was located on Emad Al Din Street, and because Laila had run out of money, she walked there from Gazirat Badran. It was a very cold February day, and when the frigid gusts of wind swept through the city from the desert, her fingers and face numbed. It took her almost an hour to get there, and when she'd finally arrived, the studio porter wouldn't let her in.

"Who are you?" he asked. "You're not in a film."

"I'm Laila Abdel Malek. I'm here to see Kareem Al-Asyuty."

The porter shook his head. "He usually tells me when he's expecting someone new."

"When he sees me, he'll remember me."

"That's what everyone says."

"Please." Laila wanted to tip him, but she had nothing. "I had a date to audition here years ago, but my father died, and instead of auditioning I went to his funeral. Have some mercy and just see if he'll talk to me."

The porter looked at Laila for a long time, scanning her from head to toe. "Stay here. You better not be lying to me."

The porter was gone for a long time, and when he returned, he said,

"He says he doesn't remember anyone named Laila Abdel Malek. But said to let you in anyway."

Kareem Al-Asyuty's office was smoke-filled and messy. Papers were strewn all over his desk and on the floor. As soon as she walked in, Kareem nodded. "I remember you now," he said.

Laila breathed.

"Sit down." He pointed at a chair. "What happened to you back then?" He leaned on the edge of his desk facing her and lit a cigarette. "I had a stellar role for you. You were going to be my star." He shook his head.

"My baba died just days before the audition."

Kareem paused and then said, "Allah yerhamoo. He was the most talented oud player I'd ever heard."

"I need a job," Laila said. "I thought maybe you'd have something for me. I'll take anything."

Kareem took another puff of his cigarette and then left it in the ashtray without putting it out, a string of smoke snaking through the small office. "I'm sorry. I have nothing. But listen." He reached in his pocket and pulled out a business card. "Call me in a few months. I may have another film coming up."

She thanked him, took the card, and left.

It was stupid of her to think she could just show up at a studio and get a movie role. It was a childish hope. But now how would she pay for her mother's medication and their living expenses? There was only one person left who could possibly help her, and she didn't know if she'd ever find him. She went to the Rod El Farag music district anyway and waited for Ahmed the qanun player to arrive for practice.

When he saw her, he laughed out loud and kissed her on the forehead. She told him she was desperate, that Mama was sick and she needed a job. She told him about Amir and the pasha's suicide. "Everything is gone," she said. "And my husband, the pasha's son, is out gambling and drinking, losing what he has left." Then she pointed at her bruised eye as if it didn't need any explanation.

"We can't change what Allah has planned, ya binty. These things are quadar. Come tomorrow for practice. I'll give you a spot in the show. It doesn't pay much. The café owner gives us all a percentage. Lately people haven't been spending money."

❦

The next morning as Mama slept, Laila went to see Zacharias. "Where were you yesterday?" he asked. "What's wrong with your eye? What happened?"

"It's over. I left him," she said. "He's lost his mind and suddenly wants a baby. When I said no, he got violent. I was afraid he'd lock me up in the apartment. He said he's never going to divorce me."

Zacharias took her in his arms. "We'll figure a way out of this. Don't worry."

They held onto each other for a long while that morning, and then they finished the last few pages of *Call of the Curlew*, and he gave her a new book to read, *Palace Walk* by Naguib Mahfouz. "Just published," he said. "You're going to love it." They then talked about Laila's plans to sing again, and about Zacharias's plans to expand and open a new store in Heliopolis.

He tried to convince her not to sing. "A nightclub, Laila? That's not a place for a woman like you. I'll give you money. My new store will take off. I'm sure it will."

"If there ever was a place for me, it was always there among musicians. I know it's not an ideal place to sing, but I also know that I have to sing. I won't take money from you. I have to take care of myself."

Zacharias didn't say anything more about it, never brought up her singing. Reading together became their way to assuage the pain of their uncertain future. Zacharias was right. Laila loved *Palace Walk*. She loved the intrigue of Al-Sayyid-Ahmad Abd Al Jawad's double life, the love triangle between him, his son, and the sultry belly dancer, Zubayda. What would become of the poor oppressed wife?

Laila performed with the ensemble every weeknight, but Ahmed gave her the earlier time slots so she could get home at a decent hour and take care of her mother. At the intermission, he accompanied her home. "I won't allow you to walk home alone. You're Kamal's daughter, and I'm like your father now."

Word of a new girl with a mesmerizing voice traveled throughout the district, and the café began to fill up. Within two months, the tables for the early show were occupied every night, and when Laila finished her number, the people stayed to watch the belly dancer and ordered more food, drinks, and shisha. At the end of each week, Ahmed divided up the pay among the ensemble. "You're good luck to us, Laila," he said. "Wishick helew." With that money she was able to buy Mama her medicine and groceries.

One night after she'd finished her performance at the café, two men stopped her as she was about to get into the taxi with Ahmed. One of them was dark-haired and tall, the other short and slight. "Please wait," the tall one said, and Laila signaled for the taxi to wait.

"You're the one," he said. "You're the star of my show."

"I think you have me confused with someone else." Laila took a step away from the stranger and covered her shoulders with a shawl.

"I'm sorry," the man said. Beads of perspiration formed on his forehead despite the cool breeze. "I've gotten ahead of myself. Let me explain." He spoke in broken Arabic. "I'm Silvestro Marino, and this is my dear friend Lorenzo." He motioned at the man next to him, who was much shorter and wore a yellow shirt and white ascot. His eyebrows were groomed, his skin taut and shiny.

Lorenzo shook Laila's hand. "Piaceri di conoscerti."

"You see," Silvestro said, "we're opening a nightclub in the downtown. It'll be called Sempre Notte. It's going to be the biggest and most expensive club in Cairo. We've done it before in Rome, and we're replicating it here."

"Si," Lorenzo said. "A Roma."

"Your face," Silvestro said, "your voice, your mannerisms." His eyes gleamed. "You have no idea how many clubs, weddings, and hotels lobbies we've been to. We almost gave up."

"When do you open?" Laila asked. If these two men weren't lying to her and she could be the star of their show, she'd be able to make more money, take better care of Mama and Naima, and even repay Ahmed for his kindness.

Silvestro said something to Lorenzo in Italian, and then explained to Laila that Lorenzo spoke very little Arabic. Lorenzo responded, counting something on his hand.

"He says one week for rehearsal and another week for costumes." Silvestro smiled. "What do you say? Just come audition. You see if you like the place and we see if we like you. And if it all works out, there's money in it for you, a lot of money. No club pays what we plan to pay."

"I thought I was your star, your muse?" Laila said. "What am I auditioning for? You've already seen me sing."

"Yes, but I haven't seen you sing in Italian or French or English," Silvestro said.

"Silvana Mangano," Lorenzo said.

"She's prettier than Silvana Mangano," Silvestro said to him.

Laila didn't know anyone named Silvana Mangano, and she had never sung in any language other than Arabic, regretting not having paid attention in French class. She was trained to sing accompanied by oud, qanun, and nay. It would be impossible to learn anything that new within a week. What made them think she spoke other languages? But the idea of an elegant nightclub and foreign patrons, of being the star of a show and making money to take care of her family, made the offer hard to turn down. If Baba were alive he'd have told her to take it.

"What songs do you want me to rehearse?" she asked. If she knew the names of the songs, then she could buy the records, listen to the songs, and learn them phonetically. After all, she'd learned "Ruba'iyat Omar al-Khayyam" that way. She hadn't known the meaning of so many of the classical Arabic words.

"Which songs?" Silvestro said. He turned to Lorenzo. "Quale canzoni?"

"Cosi tanti," Lorenzo said, and stopped to think, tapping his white leather shoes on the sidewalk "Si si. 'C'est Si Bon,' Eartha Kitt. 'Non Dimenticar,' Silvana Mangano." He stopped to think some more, and Silvestro took out a pen and small pad from his jacket's breast pocket and jotted down what Lorenzo was saying, as if Silvestro was the student and Lorenzo the professor. "Si, si. 'Kiss of Fire,' Georgia Gibbs. 'You Belong to Me,' Jo Stafford."

Silvestro tore off the piece of paper. "Here," he said folding the paper before giving it to Laila. "I've written the four songs and the address. Come next week around seven o'clock."

She didn't sleep that night. She thought about those four songs and the foreign women who sang them, about Mama, Amir, and the impossible affair she'd been having with Zacharias.

The next morning, Laila made Mama breakfast and took it to her in bed. She propped her up on pillows and made sure that she ate. But Mama only took a few bites of her fava beans and a few sips of her tea at Laila's insistence. "Don't worry about me. I'm feeling better," she said.

Laila went down to Haaga Saffeya's apartment again and asked for her help with Mama. "I have to go see about some work. Can you stay with Mama?" Haaga Saffeya put her hand on Laila's cheek. "I'd give my eyes to your mother if I could." Then she put on her slippers and headed up the stairs. Haaga Saffeya was the only one who knew the truth, that Laila was separated from her husband, that she sang at the café at night to earn money, and she promised to keep it a secret. She had told all the other women who lived in the building that Laila had come to live with her mother on account of Selma's health and that she went to care for her husband every evening, returning again to spend the nights with her mother.

Laila took a taxi to El Daher Street, and as soon as she walked into Haroun's backroom, she said to Zacharias, "We can't read today. I need to learn these four songs by next week." She took the small piece of paper out of her purse and gave it to him. "Do you have these records?" She told him everything that Silvestro and Lorenzo had said, how the club would be called Sempre Notte, how they'd seen her sing at the café, and how much she needed the money.

"I'll give you the money," Zacharias said again. "Don't go work at a club. I don't trust these people. Let's focus on a way to get Amir to divorce you. Then we can get married, even if it means a civil marriage. Who cares?"

"I promise you," Laila said, "once I get my life under control, we'll sit together and figure out a way to get him to divorce me, but for now I need to learn these songs. And please, don't say you're going to give me money. You have enough responsibilities between your sisters and your mother. I'm not taking money from you." Laila said this in a way that left no room for discussion, no opening for Zacharias to push. Besides, he probably didn't have enough money to spare. Haroun's was a busy shop, but it wasn't big and she knew it was already difficult for him to keep up with rising prices food and goods. "Please, just see if you have the records."

He searched through his small collection, which he kept on the bottom of the bookcase. Small clouds of dust formed as he riffled through the records. "I have one," he said, taking out a small vinyl record. "'Kiss of Fire.' It's a tango." He put the record on the player, and Laila thought of Pierre, his portable record player, and the Swan Lake Waltz she'd danced to awkwardly across the marble floors of the palace. It had been only three years ago, but those memories felt as though they were of someone else, not her.

Zacharias turned on the record player and dropped the needle. Then he sat next to her, and they both listened to the crackly sound imported from America. The words jumbled into one another, and Laila strained to decipher the *f* sounds from the *v* sounds. "I can't make out what she's saying," she said.

Zacharias picked up the needle and wrote down the words in Arabic phonetics. "Here," he said, and put the paper down on the wooden table. "I know you know the French letters, but you've been reading a lot of Arabic lately, so I think you'll learn faster this way." He tapped his finger on the paper. "I will say the words and you repeat them. 'I touch your lips and all at once the sparks go flying. Those devil lips that know so well the art of lying.'"

Each time she learned how to say a line, Zacharias explained to her what it meant, and then he played that segment of the song over and over again until she'd learned how to sing it. "Kiss of Fire" reminded her of Qabbani's poems. Laila listened to the song about lips, kisses, and desire. She'd have to find herself in those words, believe in them so that she could sing them. Baba had always said that the power of performance came from sensing the meaning of a song, not just understanding it. Within an hour and a half, she'd learned to sing the whole song, and she performed it, singing between the bookcase and the table where Zacharias sat and watched. She liked the power in her voice, how it filled the room, how she was able to control it, taking it high and low.

"May I have this dance?" he asked, standing up and taking her hand.

Dancing with him felt effortless and uncomplicated, like breathing. He pulled her close to him, gripped the small of her back, and she followed his lead to the slow, slow, quick, quick, slow tempo of the tango. He told her that she had a "mesmerizing voice", and that she was just as talented in singing as Qabbani was in poetry.

By the next morning, Zacharias had gotten her the other records. Within a week, she'd learned the three other songs: "Non Dimenticar," "C'est Si Bon," and "You Belong to Me." She was especially happy about "You Belong to Me" because an afrangi had written about her pyramids in the first line. Baba would have loved it despite his disdain for what he called the elementary nature of Western music. "Our music doesn't rush," he'd always said. He also would have loved the idea of her being the star of the show, but he'd have hated Silvestro and Lorenzo, especially Lorenzo's flamboyance. Laila found it endearing, and she was looking forward to the audition.

She arrived at Sempre Notte at a quarter to seven wearing a black crepe dress, cinched at the waist and with a sweetheart neckline. Naima had made her the dress in a week, staying up late into the night to finish it after the final fitting. Before Laila had left the house, Mama groggily said it was "too revealing," but then let her head fall back to the pillow. She'd been sleeping a lot more than usual, and Laila assumed it was the medicine.

Sempre Notte had been built on the recently renamed Soliman Pasha Street. It was now called Talaat Harb Street after the founder of the Bank of Egypt, and all the street signs had been changed. Laila remembered the shoe, jewelry, and dress boutiques that used to be there before the Cairo fires. Silvestro and Lorenzo had taken over their spaces and opened them up into one big nightclub.

The nightclub reminded her of the elegant movie theaters she'd been in. It was a red-carpeted two-story hall. The first level was filled with round candlelit tables surrounded by velvet chairs. The second level had a curved bar with bartenders in white tuxedos. The stage too was multilevel, and a short staircase with a black lacquered railing connected the levels.

Silvestro was yelling at one of the waiters for not wearing his bowtie during rehearsal. Laila hadn't realized the waiters were rehearsing too. But there were dozens of round tables, and they were all occupied. People were ordering drinks and food, smoking and drinking. There was a girl still auditioning on stage, singing "C'est Si Bon." She was tall and blond, wore a sparkling low-cut ivory gown, and she'd prepared a routine to go with her song. She sauntered down the stage's stair, smiled at the audience, and at the refrain she shimmied her breasts so that they jiggled.

"Bellissimo," Lorenzo said at the end of her number, standing up and clapping. But Silvestro didn't clap, and as the woman in the ivory dress walked off stage, the two of them quarreled. Lorenzo pouted and crossed his arms over his chest as Silvestro yelled, pointing at the stage and then at the waiters. They hadn't noticed that Laila was there until she walked up on the stage and stood in the center, hands crossed in front of her. When they both saw her, they stopped arguing.

"Which song do you want me to sing first?" she asked.

"'C'est Si Bon,'" Silvestro said.

"No!" Lorenzo shook his head. "'Non Dimenticar.'"

"All right," Silvestro acquiesced.

Laila sang "Non Dimenticar." She sang just as she'd practiced with Zacharias, articulating every word, singing to the notes of the crackly records whose music she'd memorized.

When she finished, Silvestro stood up and clapped. "Brava. Brava." The audience clapped too, and she heard one of the men in the front row of tables say, "What a voice!" But Lorenzo didn't budge. He sat still in his chair. He and Silvestro quarreled some more, and finally Silvestro said, "Laila, you did great, but we need you to dance a little. Move a little on the stage. Be dalooa, like Shadia, you know, the way she flirts with the camera. Try that in your next song."

"How?" Laila said. She'd come to sing. Nobody had said anything about dancing.

"Lorenzo will show you," Silvestro said, and Lorenzo joined Laila on stage.

"Come questo," he said, which she guessed meant *like this*. Lorenzo wore a button-down floral shirt and light blue pants, and he shimmied his shoulders and shook his hips on the stage. Then he fanned his hands out like Rita Hayworth in *Gilda*, pranced up the stairs to the second level of the stage, and slunk down each step seductively. "Come questo," he said again. "Cantare 'Kiss of Fire.'"

Laila didn't know how to do those things. She'd never shimmied her shoulder or shaken her hips. She was a singer and she'd focused on her voice. Om Kalsoum never shimmied. She stood on a stage waving a handkerchief for hours, just singing, and the whole world fell at her feet. Now Laila had to shimmy, and down a flight of stairs at that? But she didn't have much of a choice. She needed the money and the independence and security it would bring, and she really wanted to be the star of the show. Maybe it was vanity. Maybe it was a competitive spirit that the lady in the sparkling ivory dress had brought out in her. She wanted to win the spot and be the star of Sempre Notte. But if she tried the shimmying and hip shaking, she'd look like a fool, so she decided to tango instead. She knew how to tango well, and she remembered every step she'd taken with Zacharias.

So, she'd pretend he was dancing with her on stage. She'd sing to him even though he wasn't there. He'd be her muse and come what may. She held her hand out in the air and took an invisible hand, positioned one leg in front of the other as though Zacharias were leading. Eyeing the stage, she judged there was enough room for her to move. Then she cleared her throat and began singing, deciding at the last second to start an octave lower, a range she felt comfortable in. The spotlight shone on her, and she began.

"'I touch your lips and all at once the sparks go flying. Those devil lips that know so well the art of lying.'"

The audience roared, but she stayed focused on the thought of Zacharias. "'And though it burns me and it turns me into ashes'"—she turned at this point, picking up her feet—"'my whole world crashes without your kiss of fire.'"

When she finished, the audience gave her a standing ovation. Lorenzo, standing on his chair, put his fingers in his mouth and whistled. Silvestro met her on stage, took her hand, and congratulated her on her new job. "I knew it," he said. "I knew you were my star the moment I saw you."

Over the next week, Laila went to rehearsal every night. One day Lorenzo took her into a room behind the stage where a film reel and screen were set up next to a sewing machine. On the floor was a pile of fabrics Mama would have loved. He signaled for Laila to sit down, and Silvestro rolled footage of foreign films and musical numbers from Italy, Spain, France, Brazil, and the United States. She saw Rita Hayworth sing "I've Been Kissed Before" and Eartha Kitt sing "C'est Si Bon." Lorenzo took her measurements and sketched the dress. It was strange having a man measure her, but Lorenzo was so occupied with the dress, he didn't seem to notice she was a woman.

But then he consulted the calendar on the door and went into a tirade she couldn't understand. "No abasstanza tempo." He crumpled up a club flyer with the opening dates and threw it across the room. Then he kicked at the bunch of material on the ground.

When he picked up his scissors to launch them across the room, Silvestro intervened. He caressed Lorenzo's shoulder, and Laila took a step back, afraid of what Lorenzo might do next.

"Did I do something to upset him?" she asked Silvestro.

"No. He's upset because he can't find a good seamstress, and we don't have enough time to sew all the dresses he wants." Silvestro took Lorenzo's hand and guided him to the chair. "Calmati," he said.

"My sister is a talented seamstress," Laila said. "She might be able to help."

Silvestro translated, and Lorenzo looked skeptical. Then Silvestro said, "Bring her with you tomorrow to rehearsal. If she's any good, we'll keep her."

The next day, Lorenzo showed Naima the film reels he'd shown Laila. Naima cut one of the patterns out of the tracing paper Lorenzo gave her. She asked him to go back to the scene of Rita Hayworth so she could see the side of the dress. Then she organized the fabrics by texture and color, folding them and putting them into bins. Lorenzo would sew two costumes, and Naima would make the other two. "I can have the dresses done in a week," she said.

Every morning, Laila spent the first three hours of the day with Zacharias practicing a piece of music or reading again. Then she returned home to take care of Mama, whose stomach pains were not improving, until about 6:30 in the evening, when she had to leave for the rehearsals. That was usually when somebody from the building or Naima came to stay with Mama until she fell asleep for the night.

Sempre Notte had a spectacular opening night. All the big names of Cairo came to the show—the actresses Faten Hamama and Ragaa Abdou; Samia Gamal, the famous belly dancer; and Ismail Yasin, the biggest comedian in the country. *Al-Ahram* wrote about the unlikely Egyptian star of the Sempre Notte who'd sung in four languages and "wowed" audiences.

30

CAIRO, JANUARY 1955

Mama's stomach pains did not improve, and Laila decided to take her back to see the doctor.

"I don't know why they insist on bringing me here. I'm fine," Mama said as the doctor examined her, asking her if it hurt here or there. Mama winced a lot but said nothing.

"I need to know where you feel the pain," Dr. Ibrahim said, reexamining Mama.

Then he turned to Naima and Laila. "I don't like what I'm seeing." He said that the best thing for Mama was an exploratory surgery.

"No," Mama said. "Nobody is cutting me open."

"Mama, you can't go on this way," Laila said.

The doctor told them that the surgery would cost two hundred pounds, but that he could give them a discount of fifty pounds. "Try not to delay. In the meantime, until she gets the surgery done, give her this." He gave Laila a bottle filled with a brown liquid. "Give her three drops under her tongue. It will ease the pain, but it will make her drowsy, so don't let her walk unaided."

Between Laila's earnings from the percentage of tickets sold and Naima's pay for sewing the costumes, they were able to pay the doctor for

Mama's surgery. But it was all the money they had. A week later, the day of the surgery, Naima and Laila held hands as they waited for Dr. Aly Ibrahim to come out of the operating room. Naima prayed for Mama under her breath, asking Christ to heal her and deliver his "faithful servant Selma from illness." The surgery took all morning, and when the doctor came out of the operating room, he pulled down his mask and asked Laila and Naima to follow him into his office.

"It's cancer," he said. "I wish I'd seen her earlier ..." He paused. "But I got what I could, and there's a chance that I got it all. Now, we monitor her."

"What do you mean, doctor?" Naima said, looking at him incredulously and then beginning to cry.

"It's up to God now. You'll take her home in a few days. Insha Allah she'll get better." Laila and Naima decided not to tell Mama that she'd even had cancer.

"Mama," Laila said to their mother when the anesthesia wore off and Mama opened her eyes. "You'll need to stay here a few days longer and then you'll come home to heal. The doctor fixed everything."

Mama smiled weakly at her daughters and said in a hoarse voice, "I hate the hospital."

It was hard for Laila to focus on her singing with Mama sick, but she tried to separate the two. Still, Lorenzo yelled at her at rehearsals because he said she wasn't paying attention and they had a whole set of new songs to practice.

"I'm sorry. My mother is sick. I'm worried about her." Her voice quivered. After Silvestro had translated, Lorenzo nodded and said, "*La* Mama."

Then he gave her the dress that Naima had finished sewing that morning. It was a copy of the dress Rita Hayworth had worn in the movie *Affair in Trinidad.* Lorenzo had gotten a film reel, and they'd all studied the "I've Been Kissed Before" number. He'd played it over and over again as Naima had sketched the sequined halter dress on a small pad of paper. Then she'd cut the pattern and remade the dress exactly as Lorenzo wanted. At the same time, Laila had memorized the lines of the song and then, with Lorenzo's help, learned the choreography. She'd gotten better at dancing over the last six months. He showed her how to take her shawl off at the beginning of the number, how to snap her fingers and bring her arms up above her head seductively while shaking her hips and shimmying her shoulders when she reached center stage.

"Come quello," he'd said.

Now, as she put on the dress, she tried to calm down, to imagine Mama getting better, not worse. After all, the doctor said he thought he'd gotten all the cancer. She was comforted that her sister had made the dress she was slipping on, that her sister's hands had sewn on the sequins, adjusted the fringes on the slit, and she took that scant comfort with her on stage.

"'I've been kissed before,'" she sang. "'Arms have held me fast.'"

Her voice had a different power that night, and the crowd whistled and clapped. It was the kind of power that came from the gut, not necessarily the voice. Baba had said there was power in pain, and maybe that's what the audience felt that night, that the singer understood the pain.

"'You can tell by my kiss you weren't the first and you won't be the last.'"

When she was on stage, she could act. She could be Rita Hayworth or Silvana Mangano or Georgia Gibbs. When she was on stage, she ran from her pain. The deeper her pain, the further she escaped. The better her performance, the more poignant her vibrato. Laila didn't sing as softly as Rita Hayworth. She started the song with her chest voice, deep and low, and it came out velvety. When she varied her style, hitting the high notes, the audience clapped, and she held the notes longer than usual.

That night, she decided to end the show her way, with "a song that birthed every song I've sung," she told the audience. "You see," she said into the microphone, "my father was an oud player from the old part of Cairo, but since he's not here, I'm going to ask you to listen for his oud in my voice."

She didn't care if Silvestro and Lorenzo were angry. That audience was hers now. She had missed the Arabic music she'd always sung, its soulful-ness, the improvisation of the maquam, the expression of love in it. There were no lyrics about kisses and fire, but when she stretched out ya habeeby over the notes like Om Kalsoum, it encompassed everything there was to say about love, about desire, and about pain. She sang Baba's song sitting on a stool, a cappella, the audience hushed. After she finished, she heard the clapping for a long time as she slipped behind the curtain to change and go home.

After the night Laila sang Baba's song, the club attracted more patrons, and Silvestro and Lorenzo insisted she finish every show with Baba's song. How had they not thought of that before, Silvestro said to Laila. "You're a musical genius."

"I'm not the genius," she said. "My father was the genius. I'm just sing-ing his song."

෨෮

"I got you the best divorce lawyer there is," Zacharias said one day after their lesson. "She's a woman. Her name is Mufidah Abdul Rahman." He took her hand. "I can't bear the thought that you're still another man's wife. I can't."

It was the first time she'd seen Zacharias upset and angry. "I can't think about that right now," she said. "I'm sorry."

"I want to be with you." He raised his voice. "I want to legitimately be with you. I'm tired of hiding. I'm tired of pretending."

"And what would you do if I got a divorce, marry me? Do you really think your family would even consider it?"

"My family has no say over me. I do what I want to do." He calmed down a little, but still seemed agitated.

"Everyone's family has a say. Whether we like it or not. I wouldn't make a good wife, not anymore. My life is complicated right now. I'm a star in a nightclub. I'm taking care of my sick mother. I know what they'll say."

"I don't care about any of that." He pulled her into his arms. "I'm in love with you. Whatever happens, I'm going to find a way to be with you. And not like this in a dingy backroom. I mean, like normal people with normal lives."

"We're not normal people," Laila said.

By mid-1956, Laila had become a local celebrity. *Al-Ahram* did a write-up about her, and she was on the cover of *Al Kawakib,* an entertainment magazine. They wrote that she was a would-be film star that had found the stage instead; that her father, an oud player from old Cairo, had taught her music; that his talent coursed through her veins; and that her international appeal was a feather in Cairo's cap.

When Laila's neighbors finally learned of her separation from her husband and local fame as a singer, they didn't shun her as she'd expected. They basked in the fame too. They enjoyed their neighborhood being written about and printed in the papers, and they liked the importance the journalists from entertainment magazines brought. They each took turns telling journalists how they'd heard Laila sing as a child, how they'd always known she was talented and destined for stardom. And Laila came and went as she pleased, finally free from Mama's fear of gossip.

Sempre Notte expanded, adding a floor that served as a loge for spectators. Silvestro imported more stage lighting and microphones from the United States, and they rented out the stage during the day to film studios. Laila and Naima both got raises, and Naima was hired to sew costumes for a new film starring a young actor named Abdel Halim Hafez.

Mama had gotten better after her surgery. Her pain had decreased, and she slept less. Her walk improved, and as soon as she could, she returned to volunteering at church. But one night in July the pain came back. Mama screamed, "It's intolerable," between panting breaths.

Laila rushed her to the hospital and sent for Naima.

When Dr. Ibrahim saw her, he took her into emergency surgery immediately.

For hours the sisters waited again, praying, pacing, sleeping, and waiting some more. When the doctor came out of surgery, he again took Laila and Naima into his private office.

Mama's cancer had come back, just as he'd feared. "It's spread, but I still took out what I could." He shook his head. "Now, we just need to keep her out of pain. That's all we can do." He pulled a prescription pad out of his white coat pocket, wrote on it, and tore off the square sheet of paper. "These are powerful drugs," he said, and tried to give Laila the prescription.

She pushed his hand away. "No." She shook her head. "This can't be. She can't be."

Naima said nothing. She stood still, staring at the doctor. Then she reached for the prescription that Laila had refused to take, folded it, and put it in her purse.

Laila began to cry. "That's it? You can't leave us like this. You didn't fix it. You have to fix it. That's my mother."

The doctor took Laila's hand in his, as if to say, there's nothing I can do. "I'm no god, ya binty. I'm just a human like everyone else."

The doctor told Laila the only thing that could work for Mama's pain was imported from the United States. "Percodan," he said as he scribbled on his prescription pad. "But it's expensive. I don't even have a supply in the office."

Laila spent most of her money buying Percodan, and with each passing week, Mama needed larger doses.

☙❧

Selma thanked God every night in her prayers, and when she was strong enough, she kneeled before the painting of Mary that had hung on the wall across from her bed since the day she'd moved into the apartment with Kamal. It was endearing how Laila and Naima tried to keep the truth from her, but the process of death couldn't be kept a secret. It was something she felt, something she knew to be true, that slow slipping away feeling that happened mostly at night.

But this was what she'd asked for, the bargain she'd made with God when she'd asked him to take her instead of Laila. How merciful and kind the Lord was. And Selma was a blessed woman. She would never have to bury a child. She'd seen women bury children, especially in the village where she grew up. Women lost many a toddler to sickness back then. Oh, the wails. They shredded the air around them. She hadn't ever asked God for much, only that she never have to bury a child. What was the pain of the body compared to the anguish of a mother's heart? Nothing. She would gladly endure that.

She was proud of her girls. Naima was a talented seamstress, a good wife, and a great mother. And Laila, well, Laila was everything a mother didn't expect to love—obstinate, unafraid, and combative. Kamal, Allah yerhamoo, had seen the strength in Laila long before Selma understood what it meant. She would have loved to leave her daughter as a happily married woman, but now she understood how much more important it was to leave a daughter as a resilient, unflappable woman. Kamal had always wanted to raise her the way he would have raised a boy, but he'd never fully explained to Selma why. Perhaps he didn't have the words to explain it, but that it was something he felt she was capable of. It must have been. He'd been wrong about one thing, though. Laila didn't have the fortitude of a man. She had the muster of a hundred men. It wasn't in what she said, really. It was in how she walked, how she carried herself, the tone of her voice, that determined look in her eyes. Yes, she was proud of her daughters and thankful to God.

31

JULY 26, 1956

Laila got her own dressing room at Sempre Notte, and at her request, Lorenzo ensured there was a radio in it. She kept the radio tuned to 621 AM, Voice of the Arabs, which had started as a segment on Radio Cairo but then became its own station. She loved listening to it mostly because they played Om Kalsoum and Abdel Wahab songs, but also because it kept her informed of the news with its political shows and broadcasting of major events. Baba would have loved its tagline: "Sawt al-Arab, calling to the Arab nation from the heart of Cairo."

On Thursday nights, the show at Sempre Notte started at 10:30, and Laila would sit in her dressing room after rehearsal to do her hair, makeup, and relax before the performance. Usually they played Om Kalsoum at 9, but on this night, Voice of the Arabs aired President Nasser's speech, which he was giving in Alexandria to celebrate the third anniversary of the revolution.

Laila was ambivalent about Nasser and the revolution. On the one hand, it had destroyed people like her father-in-law, but on the other hand, a new national pride was energizing the country.

Nasser gave the average Egyptian a feeling that he mattered. He'd often say in his speeches, "Lift up your head, my brother." Laila had struggled to lift up her head her whole life. The days she'd spent in the beginners' class at the Deliverande school; the way Madame Caron had looked at her, keeping her away from Catherine as if Laila had a contagious disease; the times she had to borrow money for Baba's medicine or when she wore Catherine's hand-me-down clothes; being told by everyone that a foreign language was better, foreign instruments were better, lighter foreign skin was better, foreign food was better. But here was Nasser refuting all that, and it soothed a wound she'd never known was there.

She listened intently to Nasser's speech and, despite her fears of an uncertain future, a sense of hope filled her. Nasser talked about the centuries of humiliation the Egyptians had suffered at the hands of the Western powers. Laila's eyes filled with tears as she recalled the story Baba had told her about how a British soldier had beaten him. She could never bear the image of Baba being beaten, yet it was an incident that lived with him every day of his life, his slight limp with every step he took. She hated it now more than ever because she understood what it had meant.

"Today we're going to get rid of what happened in the past," Nasser said, his voice unwavering. "Some of your fellow citizens have just taken over the canal." The audience got loud. "Now," he said, and then repeated, "Now." Then, as if it wasn't clear, he said, "The Suez Canal Company shall be nationalized."

The crowds got louder on the radio and outside Sempre Notte.

Laila dashed out of her dressing room. She ran down the hall and opened the back door to to the nightclub, which opened out onto the street. People were dancing and screaming in joy.

"Long live Egypt!" they shouted. "Long live Nasser!" Across the street, someone lit fireworks from his balcony and yelled, "We'll build our own dam." The canal had finally been returned to its rightful owners, and now Nasser had a source of funding for the much-needed Aswan Dam. Laila returned to her dressing room filled with pride. *If only you lived to see this day, Kamal Abdel Malek.*

That night when she sang on stage, she felt as though she'd just won something, and when she sang the line, "See the pyramids along the Nile," she stretched the word pyramids and Nile. Her audience stood, clapping and whistling.

After the show, Laila went home to relieve Naima of Mama's care.

"Nasser did it," Mama said after Naima had left. "He did what none of them could do before." Mama's voice was hoarse, and it was hard for her to get her words out. She took a shallow breath. "Your father would have been dancing in the streets today. Allah yerhamoo."

"Allah yerhamoo," Laila said. "Now get some rest, Mama." She stroked her mother's head until she fell asleep. Mama's face was bony, her skin ashen, and her white hair had thinned so much, revealing her scalp.

Sometimes, despite the pain, Mama refused the medication, which made her drowsy, so that she could sit on the balcony in the morning and take her coffee. It was too much for her to drink it, but she liked to inhale the aroma as she held the warm demitasse in her hand. One day, Laila offered to move Mama to a bigger apartment with a view of the Nile, but Selma refused to leave the place that had been her home for so many years.

Three months later, on October 29, Israel attacked Egypt in retaliation for the nationalization of the Suez Canal. Two days after that, Britain and France followed. Suddenly, Egypt was at war with three major powers, and there were bombs falling from the sky.

Everything in Cairo closed: cinemas, bars, and nightclubs, including Sempre Notte. Car headlights were painted black. Everyone taped dark blue paper on their windows. Brick walls were erected in front of buildings, and people were instructed to hide behind them in case of an explosion. Before sunset men ran around the city calling "Turn off all lights," and Laila's beloved city turned dark. People were only allowed to leave their homes in the mornings to buy food and necessities. And nobody knew how long the bombings would last.

At the same time, Mama's condition worsened. She began to hallucinate because of the medication, and Laila didn't tell her what was really happening. She unplugged the radio and told Mama that it was broken.

She asked the neighbors not to mention anything to Mama, explaining that she was too frail to worry about war. The reason they had to turn off the lights, Laila lied to Mama, was because Nasser had asked the citizens to conserve energy. Mama believed it and happily agreed to comply with Nasser. "He's a good man," she said before drifting off to sleep.

Every day, Laila would step out onto the landing to listen to the neighbors' radios for news of the continued fighting in the Suez Canal zone. And every morning she went to see Zacharias. She had planned to meet with the lawyer, but everything came to a halt because of the war. So, she remained the wife of Amir Makram Yousef Pasha. She hadn't heard from Amir since the day she left him.

Together, Laila and Zacharias read the newspapers. Russia, which supported Egypt, threatened nuclear war. Zacharias explained to her that a nuclear bomb could obliterate a whole city. "In a second, everything turns to dust," he said, his hands motioning in the air ominously.

Al-Ahram reported that the American president, Dwight Eisenhower, was opposed to the military action and had threatened sanctions against Britain, France, and Israel. When Zacharias read that part, he smiled and let out a sigh. "I think they'll pull out soon." And he was right. Britain and France withdrew in December, but Israel stayed.

One morning in late February of 1957, Laila went to see Zacharias, but Haroun's was locked up and the windows were boarded. Frantic, she asked workers from the neighboring shops about him, but nobody had seen him. She kept knocking on the backdoors of every store on Daher Street until the owner of the silver shop told her he'd heard Zacharias Haroun had been arrested.

"Taken from his home in the middle of the night." The jeweler shook his head. "It's a shame what's happening. The secret police just come and they take whoever they want now. No reason. No crime. No trial. Nothing."

Laila walked up and down Daher Street until she couldn't walk anymore. She wanted to contact his mother or sister, but she didn't know where they lived. Besides, they didn't know who she was. She barely slept at night, and every morning she got out of bed at Fajr prayer to go see if Zacharias had returned or if anyone had heard anything about him. She then spent the rest of the day with Mama, who'd gone from hallucinating some of the time to most of the time. The pain had gotten too intense for her, and she took Percodan at twice the highest dose.

One morning, two weeks after Zacharias had supposedly been arrested, she found the backroom door at Haroun's unlocked. When she walked in, he was standing in the middle of the room. Everything was destroyed. The table they used to sit at was turned over. The bookcases were on their sides, books and papers strewn everywhere. The cash box was broken. Reams of fabric were unrolled into piles of silks over taffetas, cottons over lace. Their teacups and saucers were shattered, and worst of all, the books they'd read were torn, their spines twisted, the pages of different novels scattered all over the room. And Zacharias had been beaten. One eye was completely closed shut and his lip was cut. When he saw her, he limped toward her. She ran to him, and he wept in her arms. "Dogs!" he said. "Dogs!"

As they stood in the rubble of Haroun's backroom, Zacharias told her everything. The Egyptian secret police arrested him on false charges, accused him of spying and of colluding with an uncle in Israel. Ever since Israel had attacked Egypt, Jews were under scrutiny for possible espionage. "They accuse and charge anyone and everyone. My uncle lives in Brazil. He never even so much as visited Israel, but they still beat me and threatened to have me executed for treason. Finally, they must have figured they had the wrong person. Otherwise, they'd have killed me. I thought I was going to die. And then an officer came, took me out of my cell, and said—" His voice cracked. "Said I had six days to leave the country, that I was no longer welcome in Egypt. Do you understand what this means? This is the only home I've ever known." His bruised lips quivered.

"Why?" Laila said. "They know you're innocent. Why?"

"Because they can," Zacharias said. "They're getting rid of foreigners one by one, some peacefully and others like me, but I'm not a foreigner." He explained that there had been an internal campaign to rid the country of foreigners because Nasser had moved in a nationalistic direction and wanted loyal citizens. So, he gave all foreigners a choice to either relinquish their other passports and nationalities or leave the country for good. "That's in the case you don't get arrested. For those of us who get falsely accused and beaten, we don't even get a choice. We get threats and ultimatums. I can't take more than one suitcase with me, hardly any money. My sisters and mother leave for New York tonight, and I follow them in four days." He ran his hands through his hair and looked around the room incredulously. "The irony of it is that my family came here in the fifteen hundreds to escape the Spanish Inquisition. More than four hundred years. Do you know how many generations that is? I don't have other citizenships like those who came from Europe in the forties. I'm Egyptian." He tapped his chest, weeping. "This is home."

Laila kissed his bruised eye. Then she stroked his cheek and kissed his lips, tasting the blood on them.

"Come with me." He pulled her closer to him. "We can start over. Away from your husband and that dog Nasser. Away from everything."

She looked at him, at his beaten face, his swollen lips. "My mother's dying, Zacharias. And my sister shouldn't have to bury her alone."

"They'll kill me if I stay."

"Death on both sides of us," she said, unbuttoning his shirt.

She kissed his neck and let him kiss her back. He picked her up and made love to her for the first time against the wall where the bookcase had once stood. For her it might as well have been the first time she'd made love with anyone. Being with Zacharias made all her times with Amir feel like one of the rehearsals she did before the real show.

When it was over, they sat on the floor on the loose book pages and torn-up newspapers. They talked until the afternoon, and before she left that day, they made love once more, this time atop the papers as though they were silk sheets. After Zacharias's mother and sisters left for New York, he took Laila to his apartment. She helped him pack one suitcase with family pictures, birth certificates, a family tree, an old Torah, and his mother's kiddush cups. She stood by his side as he cleaned his father's grave one last time, and she wept with him.

The night before Zacharias left, Laila spent the night with him. They made love in his bed and wiped tears from each other's eyes. He held her all night long. Before she left him that morning, he gave her a piece of paper with his cousin's address in New York. "We'll be staying there for a while until I can get on my feet. Write me." Then he told her that if she ever needed to get out of the country, to go to an accessories store called Dalal at the bottom of Daher Street. "Ask for Rachel. Tell her this exact sentence: 'I bought some buttons from you, but they keep breaking.'" He made Laila repeat the sentence just as he had with so many other lines before. "If you need anything, go there. Promise me."

"I promise," she said as she stood by his door. She took the piece of paper, folded it, and put it in her wallet. Then she kissed him. "I'll never love anyone else," she said before she left.

Mama died at dawn on March 19, the same day Israel withdrew from the Suez. Zacharias had been gone a month. Naima and Laila washed their mother's body and buried her at the Coptic cemetery. Naima insisted that Laila stay with her for a few days before returning alone to their small apartment on Gazirat Badran Street. Laila grieved over Mama differently than over Baba. Mama had been in so much pain, and every time Laila wept over her mother, she reminded herself that Selma was finally in peace. Yet, Selma had left the greatest, widest void in Laila's life, and for the first time she felt that she'd lost her bearings.

When Mama was still alive, Laila had wanted to move her to a nice apartment, a better neighborhood. Mama had said no, and now Laila didn't want to move either. All she wanted to do was go back to the home Baba had chosen for them nearly three decades ago, where on the big chair in the corner he'd named her Laila and taught her to sing, and where near the balcony doors he'd pretended to sword fight with her, where Mama had taught her to sew and cook, and where she'd returned after her failed marriage. Maybe in the comfort of familiarity she could learn to live again.

After a few days with Naima, Laila went back to her apartment. It was ransacked just like Haroun's. Mama's old clothes and sewing supplies were on the floor. The sewing machine in the corner was turned upside down, its motor broken. The kitchen cabinets were open, pots and pans lying atop one another in the middle of the floor.

"Sorry about your mother," someone said. That's when she noticed a man in a black suit sitting in Baba's chair. She gasped. Another man sat across from him on the settee, wearing the same exact suit. They'd even made themselves two cups of coffee and were sipping them, as if this were their apartment and Laila had come unexpectedly. "And sorry about the apartment."

The man in Baba's chair put his feet up on the copper coffee table. He still had his worn, scuffed shoes on.

"Just doing our jobs," the man on the settee said, throwing his hands up in the air. "I hope you're not too upset about your boyfriend. He needed a little beating the way he talked to us, you know. No respect."

"Who are you?" Laila said, still standing within view of the kitchen, even though she knew exactly who they were. "What do you want from me?" She tried to hide the fear but couldn't still the tremor in her hands.

"What did you see in that dirty Jew anyway?" asked the man on the settee.

"Is that what you're here to ask?" She didn't want to provoke them, but they'd made her angry. If they knew about Zacharias, if they'd gotten into her apartment, if they were sitting calmly having destroyed her home with no fear of the law, then they were above the law, and there was nothing to protect her from them.

"You know he's innocent. You wouldn't have let him go if you thought otherwise, so what do you want with me? I'm just a nobody." She heard desperation in her voice.

The man in Baba's chair turned to the man on the settee and said, "Do you think she's a nobody?"

"No," said the other man. "I think she's a somebody, and I think if she's willing to fuck a lowly fabric shopkeeper, she'd be willing to fuck for her government. It would be patriotic, really." Then he addressed Laila directly. "What other Jews have you been fucking and what information do you have?" He took a sip of his coffee, Mama's coffee. "If you love your country, you'll tell us what you know."

"You know everything about me," Laila said. "You already have the answer to that. I have nothing of what you're looking for." They had to know she wasn't involved in anything So, what did they want?

"You're too good for him, you know. Kamal Abd El Malek wouldn't have liked his daughter whoring around, would he?" said the man on the settee. "You don't understand, do you? We're not here to charge you. We're here to recruit you. Women like you don't come along every day, a singer, connected, beautiful, seductive. Do you know the secrets men spill when they're horny?"

The man in Baba's chair laughed. "And your father actually prepared you all along, taking you to the cabarets and such. I must say, your performances at Sempre Notte were …" He threw a kiss into the air.

"Don't talk about Kamal Abd El Malek," Laila said. "Kamal Abd El Malek was a good, honest, hardworking man. He loved music and he loved his country, which is more than I can say for you, arresting your countrymen, torturing them and killing them. Recruiting women for prostitution." She spat at the men.

"We love our country too." The man sitting on Baba's chair stood up and walked toward her. "That's why we're clearing out the traitors. Sometimes you need a lesson to change your ways. Maybe we can change your mind."

He lunged at Laila. She screamed. He put his hand over her mouth and dragged her down to the floor.

"Don't bother screaming. Nobody can rescue you from us." He flipped Laila on her stomach, ripped off her clothes, and raped her in the middle of her childhood family room. When he was done, he said, "That Jew didn't deserve you." The other man went next. Unlike his friend, he took his time.

By then Laila had stopped kicking and biting. He was right. Nobody could rescue her. They were an ugly extension of the Nasser regime and, for the moment, it was all-powerful. She understood that as her cheek rubbed against the old rug she'd once pretended to be a magic carpet. Her mind felt rage, but her body went cold and limp. These men wanted nothing more than to humiliate her, just like the British soldiers had beaten Baba and humiliated him, marking him with a limp all his life. Baba was wrong. It wasn't just the foreign occupiers who oppressed. An oppressor could be anyone so long as they had the power. Wasn't her husband an oppressor too? Hadn't he done to her the very same thing on their wedding night. Yes, she'd been raped before, her white gown torn, buttons scattered under her marital bed. These men were giving her an ultimatum, either she work for them as a prostitute and spy, or they'd make rape look like a light punishment.

"That's a good girl," said the second rapist. "A very good girl." He squeezed the nape of her neck and finished with a long moan. "When we come back," he said, zipping up his pants, "we expect even better cooperation. We have special work for you, government work. Then you can show us how patriotic you really are. And if you don't, well, use your imagination."

She didn't move. The men got dressed and left the apartment. When she heard the door close, she pushed herself off the floor and vomited in the bathroom. Then she showered, scrubbing between her legs with soap until she felt an acidic burn running down her legs to her toes. But she didn't cry. She wouldn't cry anymore. She gathered her hair into a wet bun and put on a black dress. When the porter saw her, he offered his condolences for Mama and said that her mother had been a fine lady; and just before she took the last steps out of her building, he said there'd been two men snooping around the building, but that when he'd looked around, they were gone.

"I don't like strangers in our building," the porter said. "If you see any-one you don't recognize, let me know. I'll call the police."

"I will," Laila said. "But I haven't seen anyone." What was the point of telling anyone?

Laila walked along the street and looked around nervously, afraid she might be followed. There was no one behind her, across the street, or in a parked car at the corner. They'd gotten what they wanted from her, and for now they were done. But she was certain they'd keep their promise and come back, and she would rather die than do their dirty work.

The shop named Dalal was exactly as Zacharias had described it. It was even smaller than Haroun's, and its shelves and rounders were crowded with accessories. Laila looked around the shop and picked out a few packs of bows, buttons, and hair clips. Then she stood in line. Fear surged through her so full she felt her knees almost buckle. As she neared the counter, she thought of the abrupt ending this line would bring her, an end to living in a city she knew. She remembered the picture in the news-papers of King Farouk's yacht, the *Mahrousa*, sailing away from Alexandria and Moshira's silhouette disappearing onto the airplane. She thought of her sister and father and mother. She couldn't tease out the difference between emigration and death. They were both cold, harsh separations. When she'd gotten up to the counter, she asked for Rachel.

"I'm Rachel," the woman said, and took the items from Laila. She opened a pad of receipts and began to tally the items with a blue ink pen. She was a short plump woman about fifty years old. She had light brown hair and small intelligent eyes that seemed focused on everything at once.

"I bought buttons from you, and they keep breaking," Laila said.

Rachel put the pen down and pushed the items to the side. Then she directed the line of customers to the other cashier. "In that case," she said to Laila, "let me see if I have something in the back for you."

Stepping from behind the counter, she signaled Laila to follow her. They walked down a long dark corridor, through a storage room filled with boxes, and then into another small room. Rachel locked the door behind her. The room had a desk, one light that turned on with a string that dangled from the ceiling, and a safe.

"What's your name?" Rachel asked suspiciously.

"Laila Abdel Malek."

"Name the books you read with Zacharias in order."

Laila answered Rachel carefully so that she didn't make a mistake.

"Wonderful," Rachel said. "Zacharias told me you'd come. I just didn't know when."

"Can you get me out of the country?" Laila asked. Rachel didn't say anything. "I'm separated from my husband. I would need his permission to travel and that would be impossible."

"My job is to deal with the impossible," she finally said. "But you'll have a Jewish identity, so you won't be able to take much out of the country. Will you need me to make you gold buttons?"

Laila didn't respond. Was it another password that Zacharias had forgotten to give her? She was terrified she'd lose her only way of getting out. There was no future left for her in Egypt. The government would always find, harass, and terrorize her. Images of her rapists rose before her. She shuddered. They could hurt Naima or her children. Everyone was better off with Laila gone.

Rachel laughed. "I suppose Zacharias didn't explain. You see, because Jews can't take their assets, I exchange cash and property for gold." She pulled open the desk drawer. It was full of gold buttons. "Pure gold," she said. "I sew them onto your jacket. It's amazing how many ounces of gold can fit on a long jacket. An international currency sewn to your clothes. It's really very simple." She laughed again.

"I don't have much money to take with me," Laila said. Sempre Notte was still closed, and she had spent almost all her savings.

"Very well. Let me get your picture." She took a camera out of the desk drawer and snapped a shot of Laila. The flash hurt her eyes. "Come back in three days. I'll have everything ready for you, and don't worry about the ticket. Zacharias left the money for that. In the meantime, don't give any indication that you're leaving. Nobody should suspect a thing."

That day, Laila didn't want to go back home. There was nothing but destruction there, and she wasn't ready to tell Naima what had happened. She walked from Daher Street all the way to the base of Kasr El Nil bridge. There, she bought roasted nuts and corn on the cob. Then she crossed the bridge, stopping to look at the Semiramis Hotel with its opulent rooftop supper club. She walked her old path to Madame Caron's villa. In her memory it had looked much bigger, and as she got closer, she realized the house had been abandoned. Weeds had grown over the flagstone path to the front door, and the tall grasses scratched her legs as she waded through them to get to the back of the house where the swimming pool and gardens were.

The swimming pool was only half full now, its water a mucky green color. The kitchen window that overlooked the back had a crack in it, and the sunflowers that Baba had died for had died too. There was nothing left of them but desert sand. Laila sat on the ground where Baba had watered those unnatural sunflowers, and wept.

During those three long days, Lorenzo sent word that the club was opening back up now that the war had ended, and he wanted her to come for practice. She arrived on time and ready to work.

She went back to Dalal's at the end of the week, just as Rachel had instructed. This time Rachel took her to a different room in a basement behind two locked doors. The small brick-walled room was completely empty.

"I have everything for you," Rachel said. She pulled a loose tile up from the floor and took out a thin stack of paper held together by a paper clip. Then she gave her a passport. "From now on your name is Rebecca Cohen."

Laila riffled through its pages. Her picture was on the first page.

"You have a visitor's visa. When you get to New York, you'll contact Zacharias and he will take care of the rest." Rachel gave her more papers. "This is your certificate of birth, your college degree in music"—Rachel winked at her—"and your plane ticket. You leave tonight via Zurich. Well, not really tonight. Your plane leaves at two-fifteen a.m., but you need to get to the airport tonight." She smiled and put her hands on her hips. "I told you my job is to make the impossible happen."

"I can't leave tonight," Laila said without thinking.

"Why?"

"I don't know." She shifted her glance between Rachel and the papers in her hand.

Rachel grabbed her by the shoulders and pulled her so close that Laila saw the speckles of green in Rachel's brown eyes. "You have to leave tonight. Rebecca Cohen is leaving on that plane tonight. Do you understand me? If you don't show up, the authorities will look for her, and they'll trace her to me. I can't explain any further."

Laila nodded. "I understand."

"Wait," Rachel said. "There's one last thing I have to tell you. Zacharias left me with strict instructions. He said that before you leave, you should go to the Jewish antique instrument dealer in the Azbakeya district. His name is Moussa. Ask about him and someone will direct you."

Laila put the documents in her purse, followed Rachel up one flight of steps through dark cave-like tunnels, and back into the store. Before Laila left, Rachel tallied up a few items Laila had never chosen and put them in a bag. As Laila was leaving, she whispered, "It's better if you don't come back here."

In the taxi on her way to Azbakeya, Laila held her purse close. She was afraid to hope for what might be at the antique shop. Maybe Zacharias had left her a letter with further instructions, or maybe a book he didn't want to leave with Rachel. Whatever it was, Laila had about twelve hours left in her country, and if she didn't go to the antique shop now, she'd never go.

At an instrument shop in Azbakeya, she asked for Moussa's store and a young boy pointed in the direction of the Ibn Tulun mosque. "Follow the minaret, and when you pass the bread maker, take a right."

The shop smelled of old wood and incense. Inside, a white-bearded man sat on a stool playing an oud. It was hijaz maqam, and the man was a good player, but not as good as Baba. He stopped when Laila came in.

Even though he wore thick glasses, he squinted. "Who's there?" he said, a risha held between his fingers.

"I'm Laila Abdel Malek," she said. "Are you the owner of this store?"

He smiled and nodded. "Yes." Then he stood and put the oud on the counter. The store's shelves were crowded mostly with ouds. There were some guitars, a few tablas, and one qanun. "I'm Moussa. I've been here for forty years, same place," he said with pride. "How can I help you?"

"Zacharias Haroun sent me here. He says you might have something for me." Her hands shook, and she tried to calm the sudden surge of hope she felt inside, afraid of disappointment.

"Oh, yes," he said. "My sight might be poor, but my memory is sharp. Give me a moment." Moussa opened a cabinet behind his counter and took out what looked like an oud wrapped in a cotton quilt like the ones Mama used to put on her bed. He lay it on the counter. "I bought it without its case," he said as he unwrapped it.

Laila swallowed against her tightening throat. It looked like Baba's oud, and there was an old risha tucked between the strings, but she couldn't be sure until she saw the inscription, an inscription she hadn't been able to read when Baba died.

"Would you turn it around for me please?" she asked. "There should be an inscription on the back."

Moussa turned the oud around, and Laila ran her finger along the gold inscription etched on the curved back of Baba's oud. She read Al-Mutanabbi's words out loud. "'Small deeds are great in the eyes of the small, and great deeds are small in the eyes of the great.'"

She looked up at Moussa. "This belonged to my father," she said, her voice weak. "How much do you want for it?" Her hands shaking, she reached in her purse, prepared to pay him everything she had.

"It's paid for, ya binty," he said. "Zacharias bought it for you a month ago. He said you'd pick it up, and I've waited for you ever since. He even bought a case. It's right there. He said you'd be traveling with it." Moussa put Baba's oud in the new black leather case and gave it to Laila. She tried to tip him, but he refused to take money from her. He said that reuniting a girl with her father was enough payment for him.

ↄ৲

Laila knocked on Naima's door, oud in hand and purse on her shoulder. "You need to come on a walk with me," she said when her disheveled sister opened the door.

"Laila, I'm in the middle of making dinner, and the kids need help with their homework. Is that a oud you're carrying?"

"Put your hair up, put some shoes on, and come with me," Laila said. "I'll wait outside."

"You're scaring me," Naima said. "Can't you come in?"

Laila shook her head. "No."

Naima got dressed in minutes, and when she closed the door behind her, she demanded that Laila tell her exactly what was going on. Laila refused to say a word until they got to the old section of Azbakeya gardens where Amir had once kissed her. There, behind the waterfall in that empty spot, she told Naima everything. She told her about Zacharias, the secret police, the rapes, and the ransacked apartment they'd grown up in. "I'm leaving tonight. You can't tell a soul."

"How can you leave me alone?" Naima's lips quivered.

"You're not alone. You have your husband and your children. Besides, I have no choice. It's safer for you if I'm not here. I'm leaving you some money under the floorboard in Mama's room. You have the key. I'll send you word as soon as I'm settled."

"You can't go." She wrapped her hand around Laila's wrist until her nails dug in. "You can't leave me."

Laila held her sister, and together they cried in the garden, the curlews hovering over them, the sun shining, the water rushing over stone.

Laila packed her mother's Bible, Baba's songbook, a few sweaters, Mama's wool coat. Then she put *Palace Walk* in her purse. It was the last book Zacharias had given her just before he'd been arrested. She'd find out on the plane what happened to Ahmed Abd Al Jawad's family. Just before midnight, she took her last trip down the narrow stairs of her father's first apartment and exited from the back of the building so that nobody would see her. She'd miss her apartment on Gazirat Badran, the small balcony overlooking the narrow alleyway, the kitchen where Mama cooked, cheating poverty with bones and meat scraps, the bed she'd shared with Naima, fighting over a cotton quilt. How happy they'd been back then. How little they'd known. She hailed a taxi and refused to let the driver put Baba's oud in the trunk. Instead, she held it on her lap, hugging it against her so that it wouldn't shift at turns.

When the taxi driver dropped her off at the airport, he said, "May you return to us safely."

"Insha Allah," Laila said, as she paid him.

When she reached the front of the line to board the plane, the man behind the counter checked her passport and ticket once again, looking at her picture and then at her. "Rebecca Cohen?" he said.

She nodded and thought about the real Rebecca Cohen. Was she dead or alive, and if she was alive, where was she?

He made a small tear in the boarding pass and gave it back to her. Laila picked up Baba's oud, followed the passengers up the long set of metal steps into the airplane, and took her seat where the stewardess indicated, beside a window. She'd never flown before, but she didn't fear the sky. It was always blue up there, and maybe up there she'd be closer to Mama and Baba and Makram Youseff Pasha. She was in a way, touching death by leaving everything behind, holding documents with a new name. On paper Laila Abd El Malek will have never left Egypt. This thought gave her comfort. If Baba were alive, he'd have said, "Be a man, Laila. Fight for what's yours and tell me how it is in America." Baba had said once after watching a film that someday he'd go to this place called America. Perhaps, through her, in some way he was going. Uncertainty was not a pleasant feeling, but uncertainty could also be a grand adventure. This is how she chose to see her forced emigration, an adventure that began a long time ago when a oud player from old Cairo wrote a song he named Laila.

It was still dark out when the plane took off, and she watched herself lift away from her Cairo, leaving behind its ancient people, the scent of its spice markets, the rhythm of coppersmiths' hammers, and the only streets she'd known how to navigate. Soon the cafés, hotels, and monuments faded into a cluster of lights, and from above, Cairo was a jewel, shining from every facet.

ACKNOWLEDGMENTS

First and foremost, I would like to thank Timothy Schaffner of Schaffner Press for creating a space for literature of global concern, and for making the investment in this debut work. Thank you to my very patient editor, Sean Murphy, whose commitment to language was equal to his commitment to staying true to the author's voice. I'm forever grateful to the calm and brilliant Elizabeth Barrett, my independent editor, who was my anchor as I wrote and rewrote this novel. Special thanks to Lauren Crerand for taking a chance on a little-known author and guiding me through the maze of publicity.

This novel would never have matured without my professors at Bennington Writing Seminars: David Gates, Dr. Alice Mattison, Lynne Sharon Schwartz, and Dr. Douglas Bauer. Immense gratitude to my professor in Arabic language and culture at the University of Florida, Dr. Aida Bamia, without whom I would not be equipped with the language I needed to write this story.

Love and gratitude to my aunt, Angela Wassily, who gifted me with my first Naguib Mahfouz novel. Special appreciation to my early readers Lisa Lauer, Judy Adelson, Natalie Mitchell, Anna Morgan, Lisa Wheeler, Patty Kilgallon, Joanne Gordon, Margi Greenfield, Jennifer Ligeti, Susan Dubbin, Cindy Sperling, Luz Chandeck, and Andrea Doyle.